# SUCK IT, SISTER!

## Twice Bitten: Book Three

CRYSTAL-RAIN LOVE

# ACKNOWLEDGMENTS

Thank you to Christle Gray for reading chapter by chapter and telling me I don't suck. Thanks to Greg Bennett for the editing help, and, of course, I must thank "Big Rome" Kimbrough for letting me turn him into a character and beat up on him.

A very special thank you to Manuela Serra for creating such wonderful cover art for this series! I can't wait to see what you create for the rest!

# ONE

I sat in a chair in a small room in the basement level of Midnight Rider next to the bed Shana rested in, waiting for her to open her eyes. My vampire sire-slash-boyfriend, Rider, leaned back against the wall on the opposite side of the room, staring down at the floor, his hands deep in his pockets. Both of us were still covered in Shana's blood and neither of us were talking.

"Are the restraints necessary?" I finally asked, looking at the steel cuffs holding Shana's wrists to the bedrails.

"Yes," he said softly. "She could wake up bloodthirsty and kill you."

"She wouldn't kill me."

"You don't know what she'll do," Rider said, looking me in the eye for the first time since he'd turned her. Since I'd pretty much forced him to turn her. "Not everyone is meant to be turned. I know she's your sister, but she's selfish and conceited. These are not good traits for a vampire."

He wasn't lying. She was the ultimate snob, but she hadn't always been that way. "You barely know her," I told him. "You've only seen one side of her. Being stuck-up doesn't mean she's going to wake up a monster. She's my sister, Rider. Despite her flaws, she's my blood. She won't hurt me."

"Ryan was my blood," he reminded me.

"Shana is nothing like Ryan."

He looked at Shana and shook his head before returning his gaze to me, deep worry in his eyes. "For your sake, I really hope that's true."

Selander Ryan was Rider's half-brother. He was also the incubus who attacked me in the alley behind Midnight Rider a little over two months ago, determined to turn me into a succubus and use me to make Rider's life a living hell. Rider had fought him off and bit me too. His plan had been to redirect the change, turn me into a vampire instead of a succubus. I'd turned into a hybrid instead, which means I am half succubus, half vampire. Rider literally ripped Selander's heart out of his chest and crushed it in his hand about two weeks after I was turned, but the evil bastard planned ahead, and with the help of dark magic, he's still around. He likes to come to me in my dreams, and not that long ago, thanks to something called the Bloom and a symbol he'd carved into my breastbone with magic, Selander possessed my body and almost made me kill Rider.

"You really should get cleaned up," Rider said, his watchful gaze returning to Shana's supine form. "She might not even wake tonight."

"She might, and I have to be here when she does," I said. I was still wearing my bridesmaid dress, the soft pink ruined by large blotches of dried blood. Rider still wore the suit he'd had on when he'd surprised me at the reception, before the men hunting us arrived and all hell had broken loose. It was black, so the blood wasn't as visually obvious, but I could smell it. "You could take your own advice."

"I'm not leaving you alone with her."

"What do you think I'll do, kidnap her?"

"No, I'm afraid of what she might do to you," he said, looking at me. "I can't leave you alone with her. You're

2

emotionally compromised right now."

"Emotionally compromised?" I barked out a laugh. "Is that what you call it? Emotionally compromised? Let's see, my sister got married today and before she could even make it through her reception, she was gunned down because I led a team of assassins to her. Hell yes, I'm emotionally compromised."

"That team was there for me." Rider looked down at the floor. "I shouldn't have gone to the reception."

But he had, because of me. He'd tried to explain the danger of showing his feelings for me. Rider was the master of the city. I was still learning what that fully meant, but from what I'd learned so far, he was the top dog in the paranormal community. He ruled over a nest that included vampires, shifters, trusted humans, and he had powerful witches who helped him when the need arose. I was the first vampire he'd ever sired. The rest of the vampires in his nest served him because he'd freed them from cruel sires. He'd made many enemies in his centuries as a vampire by doing that, and he'd been making more since I'd entered his life. He'd kill anyone who tried to hurt me, and in addition to his own half-brother, he'd killed Barnaby Quimby, a hunter from a long line of hunters he'd had a pact with. Quimby broke the pact by going after me, but his brothers didn't care. Rider killed Barnaby, so they went after Rider, which meant they went after me too.

He'd tried to tell me that his enemies would use me to get to him, but I'd been upset that he wouldn't go to the wedding with me. He'd surprised me at the reception to make me happy, and it was just what the men hunting him had been waiting for. They'd ambushed us outside the reception hall and my sister had gotten caught in the crossfire, all because my self-esteem was in the toilet and I just had to have my hot boyfriend there to prove to my family that I could get and keep a good-looking, successful man. Now Shana was cuffed to a bed underneath his bar and he was pissed because he hadn't wanted to turn her.

"Did you give her enough blood?"

"Yes."

"You only gave her some in the SUV. That was hours ago. I remember you giving me more throughout the change. I woke up several times, and you gave me more blood each time."

"Ryan bit you first. Your turning was nowhere near a normal turn. Our marks fought each other through the whole process." He looked at me, his blue eyes darkened by anger. "I did what you wanted, despite knowing in my gut it's probably going to end up biting us all in the ass. Don't accuse me of lying to you, Danni. I don't deserve that."

"You didn't want to turn her."

"I sure as hell didn't."

"Why should I believe you'd give her enough blood if you didn't want to turn her in the first place?"

His eyes went from dark and fiery to ice cold. "If you really have to ask that question, you don't know me at all."

A heavy knock sounded on the door and Rome, a tall, dark and very muscular human member of Rider's security staff, stepped into the room wearing his regular attire of black T-shirt and pants. Daniel, my newly acquired personal bodyguard and friend, stepped in beside him. He was also tall and powerfully strong, but that was mostly due to the fact he was an Imortian dragon shifter. He definitely had muscle, but next to Rome he looked like an average guy, except, of course, for the shaggy rainbow colored hair which was actually natural and the silver hoop in his nostril. He'd served as my date to the wedding, much to my mother and grandmother's dismay, but had since cleaned up and changed clothes, now donning a black AC/DC T-shirt and distressed jeans.

"The cops have been crawling all over Danni's apartment," Rome said. "They've both been reported missing. We could try to swing this as a new bride running off with her sister after realizing she didn't want to be married after all, but not with all the carnage left in that alley behind the reception hall. They all heard the gunshots. No eyewitnesses except for some homeless dude that saw everything, but the cops didn't consider him a reliable source of information once he started talking about seeing a dragon roasting people."

This was something Daniel would usually at least grin about, but his mouth had been set in a sympathetic frown from the moment he'd stepped into the room, his gaze locking onto mine before shifting over to the bed.

"What about our people inside the police department?" Rider asked.

"They're doing what they can," Rome answered. "It's a missing persons case so their hands are tied, but once you figure out what cover story you want to go with, they're ready to spin it. They'd appreciate getting instruction as soon as possible. The mother and grandmother are driving them nuts and they've just recently told the police Danni was last seen with you and, I quote, a tutti-frutti-haired freak." Rome grinned. "The new husband is talking about reward money for any information on Shana. It's going to be hard hiding her from the public if that's the route you were planning to take."

Rider's eyes narrowed. "He's only offering a reward for Shana?"

Rome cut a pitying look my way before answering. "Yeah. He's offering a pretty good chunk of change, but only for Shana."

"These people disgust me," Rider muttered before looking down at himself. "I need to get cleaned up before the cops show up here asking questions. Danni, so do you."

"I'm not leaving Shana," I said, folding my arms over my chest.

"You need to get cleaned up and get out of those clothes, Danni. She's most likely not going to rise in the few hours left before dawn, not after all the damage she

5

took before I gave her my blood, and the minute she does rise I'll feel it and tell you anyway."

"Danni." Daniel stepped over to the chair I sat in and crouched beside me. "Sweetheart, you are covered in your sister's blood. I know you love her and want to be here when she wakes up, to help her understand what's happened, but come on. You don't want to sit there with her blood all over you."

I looked at Daniel, saw the concern in his eyes, and shook my head. "I have to be here. I can't leave her."

"She'll be safe here."

"I don't know that." I glared at Rider for just a second, just long enough for Daniel to understand why I didn't want to leave her alone.

"I'll stay with her," Daniel offered. "You two can get cleaned up and if by some chance she wakes up, I'll be a familiar face. Imagine what will go through her mind if she wakes up to see you covered in her blood. You're still wearing the bridesmaid dress from her wedding. That's not an image you really want her to wake up to, is it?"

I shook my head as I imagined what it would be like for her once she woke up. I'd been given a choice in my turning. Well, Rider had given me the choice after I'd already been attacked by Selander, but I was conscious during both bites. Shana had been out of it when Rider had finally agreed to turn her. Her last memory was probably of stepping out of the reception hall to ask me why I was leaving. That was as far as she'd gotten before she'd been shot. She'd bled out so quickly after that, I doubted she even remembered us moving her into the SUV. Maybe she didn't need to see me covered in blood when she woke up in a strange room strapped to a bed, a strange hunger gnawing at her. But as much as I loved him, I feared Rider being the only person with her when she woke.

"Rome, handle the police if and when they show up here," Rider ordered as he strolled forward and grabbed my arm before yanking me out of the chair. "Daniel, guard this door while Danni and I go upstairs to clean up."

"I'm not leaving!" I yelled as I tried and failed to pull out of Rider's grasp.

He tightened his hand around my arm until I felt the barest threat of pain and pulled me against his chest. "Do not make me angry," he growled, his dark gaze boring into mine with a stern warning before it shifted to Daniel, who'd risen from his crouching position and now stood to my side, his jaw and hands clenched. Alarm slammed into my stomach. Daniel and I had gotten close, and he was protective of me, and not just because it was his job to be.

"Remember your place, dragon. I appreciate you being a friend to Danni, but you work for *me*. I can end that in a heartbeat."

He could end *him* in a heartbeat. I shook my head as slightly as I could as Daniel glanced over at me, silently asking him to stand down. I'd nearly lost my sister. I couldn't lose my friend.

"Yes, sir," Daniel said, visually relaxing, but his eyes still held contempt. Although he'd replied using the correct verbiage, his tone was all wrong, and I prayed he didn't pay the price for it. Rider was kind to me, normally extremely gentle, but he hadn't become master of the city by being gentle with everyone else.

I held my breath as Rider and Daniel stared each other down, time seeming to stop. Finally, Rider's eyes softened a bit and he turned, pulling me along with him to the door. He released my arm as we stepped through, and ushered me up the stairs to the first sublevel of Midnight Rider, past the gym, through the control room he called the Bat Cave, and up another set of stairs. I didn't fight him, not daring to fuel the anger I felt seeping out of his pores. Judging by the carefully averted gazes of all we passed along the way, I wasn't the only one who felt it. We continued on in silence, not stopping until we were inside his small apartment above the bar.

His apartment was just a bedroom with an attached bathroom. A wonderful bathroom with a rain shower and large clawfoot tub, but still, just a bed and a bath. A television rose out of the bar on the side of the bedroom with the touch of a button, but other than it and the activity that went down in Rider's bed, there wasn't much else to do in the room. He'd told me he'd only used the room for sleeping before meeting me. Busy with his business and protecting the city from supernatural threats, he hadn't seen much point in having a full house or a normal apartment with an actual living or dining area. Also, the small area was easier to defend. He'd had it spelled so no one could enter unless he wanted them to. The entire building, including the apartment, the bar below, and the sub levels underground, were warded against fire.

"You didn't have to be so rough," I snapped, rubbing my arm.

"I wasn't rough. I was assertive." He stepped forward until there was barely space to breathe between us and glared down at me. "I wouldn't have to be if you would just do as I ask without always giving me a fight. Do you even listen to the things I tell you? I don't know how many times I've told you the way things work and still you fight me. I cannot have you defying me in front of my nest. They will not serve a weak master. My enemies will not fear a man who can't even con—" He clamped his jaw and closed his eyes, breathing in deeply to calm himself.

"Say it, Rider. Control. You want to control me."

"You know that isn't true!" he snapped, opening his eyes. "And you know if it was, I would do it. I can do it. I can make you do whatever I want, but I don't use my power over you like that. I don't want to force your will, but damn it, Danni, can't you just do as I ask?"

"Why?" I asked, not bothering to point out he had, in fact, used his power over me occasionally in the past. I let it slide because other than once forcing me to sleep rather than continuing an argument, he'd only used it over me during times it was necessary. Like when he'd held me back from killing a werewolf I'd already beaten in a fight. "Why can't I disagree with you or speak my mind?"

"You can, and you know you can, but not in front of my nest. That act of defiance that just happened down there? If you had any other vampire for a sire, you would have been disciplined for that. Hell, if any of my nest openly defied me, I would have made an example of them, but I can't do that with you. I can't bear to hurt you and I've told you what a dangerous secret that is. I trust Rome and I know you and Daniel have developed a friendship, but if that had happened in front of any other members of my nest, I couldn't have let it slide."

A cold chill snaked up my spine. "What are you saying?"

"I'm saying you're going to get people hurt. I can't allow members of my nest to think I'm weak. I can't allow them to even entertain the thought of usurping my power for themselves or reveal my weakness to my enemies. What happened today was because of my enemies knowing my weakness. They came for me when I was with you. They tried to get you first. I have never had an enemy use a woman against me because I've never loved a woman like I love you. Every time you defy me and I don't make you pay for it, my nest knows you're special. Secrets leak out. Shit like today happens. Damn it, Danni. I turned your sister for you. You have no idea the shitstorm that's going to cause, the whispers already swirling." He ran a hand through his hair as he turned away and opened the dresser drawer he'd filled with clothes for me, pulling out one of his shirts I'd pretty much claimed as my nightshirt and a pair of skimpy underwear. "The next time you think of defying me in front of a lower level member of my nest, I want you to consider the fact I might have to kill that poor bastard to keep my control over this city and protect its people. Also, I will be having a serious conversation with the dragon."

"Daniel hasn't done anything wrong," I said as he turned around. "He saved me when the Quimbys and those hunters tried to shoot me on the street. He torched a lot of the people who attacked us earlier today."

"I know. That's why I didn't give in to my impulse to kill him on the spot for daring to call my woman *sweetheart* right in front of me."

My mouth dropped open, and I blinked a few times before I gathered my wits enough to speak. "Are you serious? You're jealous?"

"It's not about jealousy. It's about respect. You're my woman and my entire nest knows it. None of them would dare flirt with you. What he did has to be dealt with."

"He didn't flirt with me. We're just friends. He wouldn't even be crazy enough to flirt with me in front of you."

"Love and desire make men do stupid, crazy things every day, Danni. I can't have my men getting that friendly with you. Furthermore, he stepped in to persuade you to leave after you openly defied me. As if I needed the help. As if I were weak."

"He's my friend, Rider. He was just acting like a friend."

"He acted like a man who thought he had more leverage with you than I have. I love you, Danni, and I try to make you happy as much as I possibly can, but I can't let you have your way with everything, not if it means I could lose my position of power and my ability to protect those who need it. That includes you. If I have to piss you off to keep you safe, I will. If I have to descale that fucking dragon, I will."

"Daniel's my friend. Killing him would more than hurt me."

"I never said I was going to kill him." Rider's eyes narrowed. "I've asked you before and now I'll ask one more time. Do I need to be worried about you and this guy?"

"No!" I heaved out a frustrated sigh. "I'm with you. I can care about a guy friend without being in love with him. I can't even believe you're asking me this now while my sister is downstairs cuffed to a bed and I don't even know if she's going to wake up. You're so worried about your nest and your position in the paranormal community, but have you even stopped to think about me and what I'm going through? I've been reported as a missing person. Cops are looking for me. My voicemail is probably overflowing with messages from my mother and grandmother, and what the hell am I going to tell them anyway? Have you thought about me at all during all of this?"

Rider's eyes darkened. "Really? None of this would have happened if I hadn't been thinking of you! I knew better than to go to that wedding but I couldn't get your sad, pouting face out of my head so I went to the reception just to make you happy, and that's why we were ambushed and that's why your sister got shot! I did not want to turn her, but once again I couldn't take your crying and pleading so I did it despite everything in my gut telling me not to and that's why she's cuffed to a bed under my bar, that's why I have to worry about cops investigating me as the last person you were seen with, and why I have to figure out what the hell to do with her if she survives the turn. I could have created a monster today, and I knew that was a risk, but I did it anyway because of you! Everything I've been doing for the past two months, every move I've made, every single decision has been made with the thought of you filling my head and my heart so don't stand there and accuse me of not thinking of you, of not caring about you. If it weren't for you, I'd have let the spoiled bitch die and wouldn't have to deal with all this shit!"

My open palm hit Rider's jaw before I'd even realized I'd thrown the slap. Pain ricocheted up my arm and burst in my chest as he backed up a step and looked at me, mouth parted, eyes wide in surprise. Stunned. Angry. Hurt. Because of me.

I grabbed the clothes out of his hand and ran for the bathroom as tears sprang free from my eyes. I slammed the door, turned the lock, and slid down it to the floor as deep sobs wracked my body. I wasn't sure what upset me the most; the fact my sister hadn't woken up yet, the fact I'd hit the man I loved more than anything, or that as awful as everything he said was… it was all true.

I showered quickly, knowing Rider still needed to get cleaned up, and stepped outside of the bathroom with my heart in my throat. He'd discarded his jacket, dress shirt, and shoes, and stood staring at the bed, his mind a million miles away. He could read my mind when he really wanted to unless I was actively blocking him, but I had yet to learn how to purposely break into his thoughts. Maybe it wasn't possible for a fledgling to break into the vault of her sire's mind. I'd accidentally taken a deep dive in there when he'd killed Selander Ryan and dropped his guard completely, and I'd relived the most horrible moments of his life with him. Judging by the look on his face, maybe it was best I couldn't dive in there like that again. I might not like what I saw.

"I'm sorry I slapped you," I apologized. "That was wrong. I'd never—" He quickly moved past me and entered the bathroom, closing the door behind him before I heard the water start running in the shower. "— purposely hurt you," I whispered to myself as I unwrapped the towel on my head and started drying my hair with it.

It didn't take him long to step out of the bathroom donning only a towel around his waist, his long black hair damp but slicked back into a ponytail at the nape of his neck like he always wore it. Rider Knight was a gorgeous man, with piercing blue eyes, chiseled features, and golden skin. He was lean but muscular, every inch of his tall frame powerfully strong. The sight of him usually made me warm inside, but I felt cold and unsure as he looked at me with an expression I'd never seen in his eyes before. I couldn't place it, but I knew slapping him was something I'd regret for a long time. I was pretty sure I felt worse than he did and he was clearly hurt.

"She hasn't risen. She won't tonight. The sun is almost up. I can sleep on the floor if you want the bed to yourself. We both know I don't fit well on the chaise," he said, reminding me of a previous spat when he'd tried to sleep on the chaise so I could have the bed, refusing to allow me to sleep anywhere but the most comfortable place in the room. He was always considerate like that, even when I frustrated the hell out of him.

"You take the bed," I told him. "I was going to grab some pants and go back downstairs with Shana."

"She's dead to the world and you will be too when you go to sleep," he said. "I have her room guarded. She's safe. You're not going down there until after you sleep."

"I can sleep down there."

"No." He walked over to the bed and pulled back the cover. "I'm not asking you. I am telling you as your sire to sleep up here, where you are safe. You will be able to go downstairs with her after you wake. Please don't make me say it again."

"But—"

I opened my eyes to see the ceiling. I was in Rider's bed, alone, and my internal clock told me the sun had risen long ago and was now in the process of falling once more. He'd used his power to make me sleep in his bed through the whole day. I wasn't sure if I had the right to be angry after I'd hit him, but that didn't stop me from growling out a string of curse words as I tossed aside the covers and sat up, ready to find Shana and make sure she was all right.

# TWO

Considering the police were searching for us and we had yet to come up with a cover story, I figured I wouldn't be leaving the building for the night so I pulled on black leggings, socks, and shoes, ran my fingers through my hair and brushed my teeth. I made time for a quick swipe of tinted lip balm and down the stairs I went to check on my sister. Night had just fallen, so as far as I knew, she could have awakened already. Rider had said he'd tell me the minute she did, but that was before I slapped him. If he was upset enough to use his power over me, knowing I hated it, I figured he was upset enough to not tell me anything. Hell hath no pettiness like a pissed off vampire sire.

Eager to check on Shana, I used a bit of my vampiric speed to practically glide down the stairs to the Bat Cave. The techy members of Rider's staff tapped away at keyboards, not bothering to look up as I swiftly moved past them and down the hall, past the gym and training rooms. I looked through the glass, searching for Daniel, but didn't see him working out or training with anyone. I recalled Rider's warning about having a conversation with him and shuddered, hoping it hadn't happened yet.

Rider was old enough to stay awake as much as he wanted during the day, although he didn't like to. If business or security needs dictated it, though, he did what he had to do. Thanks to my hybridness, I'd gained the ability to be awake during the day much faster than most freshly turned vamps, but since I'd claimed Rider as my true sire, it was more difficult to do. I weakened in the day much faster. If not for trying to hold on to my normal life and relationships with my family, I'd probably willingly sleep through the day. As I descended the last staircase to the second sublevel, I wondered how long Rider had been awake and what damage had been done during that time I'd been dead to the world.

Two men whose names I didn't know stood guard outside Shana's room. I could sense they were shifters, but couldn't sense what kind of shifters. I hadn't gotten that good at the whole paranormal identification thing and there were so many out there, I was still learning. They nodded at me as I approached, their bodies relaxed. Clearly, they knew who I was, and I wasn't going to have any issue getting in. I sensed Rider beyond the door, so figured as much.

I pushed through to see Shana still unconscious in the bed, her wrists still cuffed. Rider stood at her left side, next to a side table, which held a jug of blood and two glasses. He was dressed in black pants and a dark gray button-down shirt, the sleeves rolled up to just beneath his elbows. Without even looking at me, he poured a glass of blood and held it out toward me.

"Drink," he ordered.

I sighed. When it came to blood, fresh straight from the vein was definitely the way to go. Unfortunately, after I'd been turned, I secreted a venom from my fangs that filled men with lust. Rider was powerful enough not to fall completely under my spell so I'd been feeding straight from him. Then I claimed him as my true sire and we'd thought the succubus stuff was all out of my system. I fed from Daniel once without issue and continued feeding from Rider as well. Unfortunately, we'd learned I was still my screwed up hybrid self, and my succubus traits came back during a cycle called the Bloom, venom and all. Also, Rider thought my temper was getting out of control, so even while not going through the Bloom, he'd taken me off blood fresh from the tap. It sucked drinking blood from bags and jugs, but it was a necessity.

I walked over to his side and took the offered glass. My lip curled involuntarily as I looked at it, but I knew I needed it, so I guzzled it down as quickly as I could, surprised by how warm and fresh it was. "This is high quality. You've been holding out on me."

"Unexpected recent donor," he said. "I hate to be wasteful."

I swallowed. Hard. "Who did this blood come from?"

"Not Daniel," he answered, tone a bit snide. "You know how we handle certain people here. Don't look so alarmed."

I set the now empty but blood-stained glass on the table and looked at Shana. Rider was a vampire, not a cop. He protected the city from monsters, and some of those monsters fell under the category of rapists, murderers, and pedophiles. When his security staff apprehended such people, they didn't bother turning them over to the police or giving them a day in court. They made sure those particular monsters never had the chance to hurt anyone ever again, and maybe it was the bit of monster I had in me, but I didn't much care.

"Why is she still sleeping?" I asked, changing the subject. "Night fell. Shouldn't she have popped right up?"

"It doesn't always happen that way. I told you I'd tell you the moment she woke. You didn't believe me?"

"Well, let's see. You're pissed at me, so I figured you being petty wasn't such a crazy idea."

"I'm never petty. Brooding, maybe, but never petty. And I'm not pissed at you."

"You used your power to make me sleep through the whole day and now you won't even look at me."

He looked at me, but said nothing.

"I tried to apologize last night. I really am sorry."

"I know, and I am too. I shouldn't have said what I said. I think she's deplorable, but Shana is your sister. It took me centuries before I could kill my brother, and he's pretty much pure evil. I can't expect you to cut your family loose so quickly."

I stood there, blinking, as I tried to figure out where to even begin with processing what he'd just said. As far as apologies went, it sucked, and not in the good way.

"What?" Rider asked, frowning down at me.

I shook my head, not wanting to start an argument about my family. If Shana was about to wake up, I didn't want him in a foul mood because of her. Yes, she was spoiled rotten and about as vain as one came, but she was my sister and she deserved a chance. However, I couldn't continue to stand there and not know anything about other issues going on. "You've been awake a while?"

"Yes. With everything going on, I had to wake early."

"Care to clue me in on things? I mean, I'm a missing person. Last night, you were concerned about the police. Did they come?"

"Yes, but thankfully a pair I have on payroll managed to get the duty of coming by the bar to interview me. One's a shifter, the other is human but has abilities. They know what actually happened and that both of you are here. They're helping to cover for us until Shana wakes and we figure things out. I think we'll go with a runaway bride scenario if we're able to convince her to sell the story. Yes, there was obviously a shoot-out that went down yesterday, but we're going to say Shana freaked out about getting married and she ran away right before. You went along and convinced her to come back."

I looked at Shana's pale skin and worried my lip with my teeth. "But she went through with the ceremony. Who runs off after the ceremony? That'll be a hard story to sell."

"Can you think of one better that doesn't involve any type of scenario where the police will be out looking for culprits?"

"We can say we witnessed the shoot-out and got snatched but can't identify the men who took us. If they have no description, they can't arrest anyone."

Rider groaned and pinched the bridge of his nose as he shook his head. "You're so ridiculously innocent sometimes. That's how innocent people get arrested every day. Besides, we left a lot of damage in that alley. They'll never believe you didn't see *anyone* in that mess, not with all that gunfire and fire damage."

"But they'll believe my sister went through with the whole wedding ceremony and then just ran off from the man she loves?"

"Didn't she screw a bunch of guys in the bathroom at her bachelorette party?"

"I see your security reports *everything* back to you," I muttered, crossing my arms defensively. "And it wasn't a bunch of guys. I think it was just one of the strippers, two or three guys tops, maybe, and my mother and grandmother don't know that. Her husband certainly doesn't know that. Trust me, by now they've told the police all about how deeply in love Shana and Kevin supposedly are."

"Her running scared is still a more believable story than the two of you being abducted and managing to somehow get free yet not being able to recall who took you or where you were held. Did you even think of that part?"

"No," I answered, my shoulders sagging.

Rider looped an arm around my shoulders and kissed my right temple. "It'll be all right. No matter what happens. Worst-case scenario, we move to another country."

"Geez." I frowned at Shana. "Shana too?"

"If she comes with us, it really would be a worst-case scenario."

I elbowed Rider in his side. "Give her a chance!"

"Babe, I turned her for you. I gave her a second chance at life."

"Yeah, but you're acting like it's the worst thing you've ever done."

"That's because I'm afraid it might actually *be* the worst thing I've ever done."

"You're impossible!" I moved across the room, putting space between us before I gave in to the urge to smack him.

The door opened and Rome walked through, again dressed in all black. To my relief, Daniel appeared behind him, dressed in similar attire. I'd never seen Daniel dressed in the all black outfit Rider's security staff wore. From the moment he'd started working for Rider he'd been assigned to guard me whenever I was away from Rider and he'd always dressed however he wanted so he would blend in, not that he really blended in with his rainbow-colored hair, nose ring and if I was being honest, a hefty dose of hotness.

Both men walked toward Rider, stopping at the foot of the bed. Daniel didn't even glance my way, which was highly unusual. My gut twisted as I watched him purposely keep his gaze on Rider.

*Daniel?* I spoke to him telepathically.

*Not now, Danni. I'm all right.* I felt Daniel close his mind to me good and tight after that. I didn't even think he knew how to do that, being even newer to the telepathy thing than I was.

"Shana's husband wanted to go on air to offer a reward for her return," Rome advised. "Our people on the inside planted a seed of doubt in his mind and are trying to keep that from happening."

"They told him Shana could have run off on her own free will?" Rider asked Rome, but his gaze stayed locked on me. I realized he'd been watching me watch Daniel, so I turned to watch Shana instead, not trusting myself to look at him without glaring.

"Yeah, and it's working for now, but if she doesn't turn up soon enough, he might still go to the news. It's been over twenty-four hours and the dude is freaked the hell out. Their mother and grandmother are a hot mess. If Shana doesn't wake soon, Danni might need to call them and tell them something so they chill out."

Rider leaned over the bed and peered down at Shana with narrowed eyes. Before I could ask what was happening, he reached for the jug of blood and started pouring a fresh glass. "She's about to rise. Keep me posted."

"You got it, Boss." Rome turned for the door and Daniel followed suit, neither of them acknowledging me as they exited the room.

I walked over to the bed as Shana's eyelids fluttered, my concern about Daniel put on the back-burner as I chewed my lip, waiting for Shana to awaken. Rider had told me the change slightly altered physical appearance, and I already noted the golden glow to Shana's skin and the silkier texture of her blonde hair. A bitter voice in my head grumbled at the unfairness of how my bombshell sister's appearance got an unnecessary helping hand while I'd gone through the turn without noticing any change at all. Rider claimed I'd gained muscle tone, brighter eyes, better skin and fullness to my breasts, but I didn't notice any of those things and was still a 34A so I wasn't a fully satisfied customer of the vampire transformation program, especially since I'd had to cancel my breast augmentation after turning. No surgeries for vampires. Our blood is thin and we can't afford the risk of losing too much.

Shana's eyes opened and after getting past the initial shock of how much bluer they were, I grabbed her hand. "It's all right, Shana. I'm here. You're going to be fine."

She looked over at me and frowned. "What? Where…

Ugh, I'm so thirsty."

Rider pushed a button on the side of the bed and Shana was raised into a sitting position.

"The hell?" Shana exclaimed, noticing the metal cuffs binding her wrists to the bedrails. She pulled at them, growling, while looking around the room wide-eyed. "What's going on? Where am I?"

"Drink," Rider ordered, practically shoving the glass of blood into her mouth. The second the coppery liquid touched her tongue, she gulped heartily, quickly draining the glass.

"More," she said, her voice raspy, and licked her lips.

Rider looked at me with raised eyebrows before pouring another glass and holding it to her mouth. She drained that one just as quickly as the first and turned her head toward the jug on the side table. "More."

"Pace yourself," Rider said, his tone indicating his displeasure.

"I want more!" Shana yelled defiantly, and instantly tensed, gritting her teeth.

"Rider!" I leaned over the bed as if covering Shana could stop whatever Rider was doing to her.

*Defy me in front of her and I will ban you from this room*, Rider warned me through our telepathic link. *You get away with a lot because I can't bear to see you hurt. I have no such problem with your sister. Is that understood?*

I gasped at the clear threat and shrank away, not daring to do anything that might cause Rider to take his frustration out on Shana. He wasn't a cruel man, and I knew he wouldn't hurt her for his amusement like so many other vampires did to their fledglings, but he would establish dominance and, as he'd told me before, he wouldn't tolerate anyone trying him. He already didn't like Shana. She clearly wasn't going to receive the same leniency he'd always given me.

"You were shot at your reception," Rider told her as she relaxed, no longer affected by whatever he'd done to

22

her. "You bled out and would have died, but I drank what little blood you had left and gave you some of mine. I turned you into a vampire like myself. Like your sister. Do you understand?"

Shana blinked at him a few times, looked between the two of us, blinked some more, and looked at me again. "Oh my gawd, Danni. Of course you'd hook up with a psycho. Vampires? You actually believe this crazy stuff too? You think you're a vampire?"

"I know I'm a vampire," I said, not bothering to explain the hybrid thing to her. It wasn't important at the moment and would only sound more unbelievable to her. "You are too. Do you remember being shot?"

Shana rolled her eyes. "No, because that didn't happen. I knew something had to be wrong with this guy when he didn't come on to me. You're in a freaking cult and you kidnapped me." She frowned and looked down at herself, noticing the long cotton shirt she wore. "Where the hell is my wedding dress? Do you know how much that thing cost? I swear, if you got one wrinkle, loosened one thread or lost a single bead—"

I felt Rider's power fill the room, and Shana abruptly stopped talking. Her eyes widened and her mouth dropped open as a myriad of emotions passed over her face. I knew Rider was showing her something, but he wasn't sharing with me, so I could only assume he was showing her what had happened when we'd left the reception hall and she'd unfortunately followed us out and nearly died.

"Whoaaaaa," Shana said, her eyes rounded as I felt Rider draw his power back in. Her mouth spread into a wide smile. "I don't know what y'all gave me, but it's better than that stuff I had at Coachella."

I groaned and shook my head.

"You were just as bad," Rider told me. "Seriously, there must be something in your family's damn DNA that makes you reject reality or something."

"Well, in our defense, being a vampire isn't something

any normal person expects to be a possibility."

"Yes, but most catch on pretty quick when they start craving blood." He picked up the jug and held it in front of Shana. "Want more of this?"

She licked her lips and leaned forward. "Yes, and I want out of these restraints and… Where am I? Where's my party? There are very important people at my reception. I need to get back there."

"Shana, that was yesterday," I told her, "which I'm sure Rider showed you. You were shot, and he had to turn you. You've been here ever since."

"Let me out of here, Danni, or I swear I'm telling Mom."

Rider unfastened one restraint and handed Shana the jug. She immediately grabbed it and guzzled down the blood.

"You're drinking blood," Rider told her after she downed the majority of it.

Shana lowered the jug and looked at it. It looked like paint. Thick, red paint. With a shrug, she brought it back to her mouth and downed the rest of it before tossing it aside. "I don't know what it is, but it's good and I'm still thirsty. Whatever you've been doing to me, you clearly haven't given me anything to drink for a long time. I'm dehydrated. This is insane, Danni. I know you've always been jealous of me, but getting your psycho boyfriend to play this game with you is ridiculous. I'm married to a rich, successful man and you're still sad and alone. Get over it, get my fucking wedding dress and let me out of here before I start screaming for the cops!"

She lunged for me, but Rider effortlessly grabbed her arm and shackled her free wrist back to the bed. "And that is why I used restraints," he said in an I-told-you-so voice.

Shana fought against the cuffs, letting loose a string of obscenities as her bright blue glare seemed to cut right through me, the promise of murder in the crystal depths.

*Are you all right?* Rider asked me telepathically.

I realized I'd recoiled and crossed my arms defensively after Shana yelled at me and told me I was jealous. I relaxed them, forcing my hands to hang loose at my sides to appear unbothered. *Yes, she's just confused and scared. She doesn't understand what's happening and she's just reacting. She doesn't mean what she's saying.*

*She's my fledgling, Danni. I feel what she feels. She's confused, yes, but she's not scared. She's pissed off, she's ravenous, and she meant exactly what she said.*

I shook my head and forced the tears I felt burning behind my eyes to stay where they were. I had actually been aware of being bitten, and I still hadn't believed the whole vampire thing after I'd awakened and Rider had tried to explain it to me. I'd been horribly mean to Rider and adamantly refused to believe anything he told me, even when the sun burned my skin and I clearly recalled drinking something that did look and smell like blood. Of course Shana wouldn't believe us. No sane human being would believe they'd been turned into a vampire, especially since we didn't just walk around with our fangs hanging out all the time. Accusing me of kidnapping her and mistreating her in some kind of jealous fit hurt, but I guess that was easier for her mind to accept than the crazy truth.

"Help!" Shana screamed after finishing another string of obscenities. "Help! I've been kidnapped!"

"Silence!" Rider roared, his voice bouncing off the walls as his power once again filled the room, hanging over us like a thick blanket. He leaned over Shana. "Eventually you will come to realize that you are what we say you are, but know this now; you were almost dead and this woman you dare disrespect saved your life. I would have let you die. I gave you a second life at her request, but I can and will take that life away if I choose. Respect me, respect my people, or I will drain you of every drop of blood I gave you."

Shana's eyes watered but she sniffed and clamped her jaw tight before resting against the pillows, the fight gone from her, for the moment at least. I was sure the storm still brewed inside her. "My new husband has money," she said, her voice softer, but the anger still there simmering underneath. "He'll stop at no expense to find me and you'll be sorry you ever met me."

"I already am," Rider told her. He reached across the bed, took my hand, and led me to the door.

While I'd waited for Shana to awaken, I'd vowed I wouldn't leave her, but as Rider opened the door, I felt no desire to stay in the room. He released my hand and placed his on the small of my back to guide me through the doorway. Stepping through was like coming up out of quicksand, and as the door closed behind us, I realized Rider had done something to the room while we'd been inside with Shana.

"No one enters that room, no matter what you hear coming out of it," Rider ordered the two shifters standing guard. "She is to be given no blood by anyone except me, even if she begs for it."

"Understood," one of the shifters said as the other nodded.

Rider guided me down the hall and up the stairs to the first sublevel of the bar. I again looked for Daniel as we passed the gym and training rooms, but he was not among the members of Rider's staff I saw working out through the windows.

The techs looked up at us as we passed through the Bat Cave, but went back to their work after Rider passed them with barely a glance. He grabbed a jug of blood off a cart near their station and we continued up the stairs in silence, passing the door leading to the bar, and went straight to Rider's room.

He twisted the cap off of the jug once we entered his room and took a long draw before passing it to me. It was the first time I'd seen him drink from anything other than an actual person, so I stared at him for a moment, temporarily stupefied, before I took the jug and sipped the warm liquid.

Rider grinned. "We're vampires, Danni. Bloodthirsty killers, remember? You don't have to be so delicate."

"Just because I'm a creature of the night doesn't mean I can't still be a lady," I said, but thirst won out and I took a big swig. Hell, I'd been an emotional eater before I'd been turned. It made sense I'd want to gulp down the whole jug after what I'd been through the past few days, since blood was almost the only thing my newly turned vampire tummy could handle without upset.

"I've never known you to not drink fresh from the actual source," I said, licking my lips to make sure I didn't leave anything behind.

"Missed a spot." Rider pulled me to him and kissed me long and deep, licking all traces of blood from my lips as he withdrew. The kiss wasn't full of the normal fiery passion Rider's kisses held, but there was a lot of emotion. I got the impression he was being careful with me. "The blood's pretty fresh and I didn't want to leave you alone to feed. I know you don't like to watch."

I felt myself blush as he took the jug and drank more before setting it on the bar. Rider's personal blood supply was a group of former hookers he paid to drink from. He swore he never used them for sex and that feeding from them wasn't intimate, but it seemed intimate enough to me, especially since when I drank from him, it usually ended up with both of us naked.

"Very considerate of you. Trying to butter me up since you threatened to kill my sister?"

"It wasn't a threat." He took my hand and led me to the bed, pulling me down to sit beside him at the foot before he leaned forward, clasping his hands together. "You understand why I had to do that?"

I nodded. "You had to establish your power. I understand, but I don't like it."

"You don't have to like it. You just have to trust me and not openly challenge me. It's very important you don't challenge me in front of her, and don't tell her you're a hybrid."

"Why?"

"She'll use it against you."

I shook my head adamantly. "She wouldn't do that."

"She would. Damn it, I know you love her, but don't let that love blind you to what she is."

"A scared person who has no idea what's going on and actually thinks she's been betrayed by her own sister?"

Rider muttered a curse and sat up, taking both my hands in his. He held my gaze with a look in his eyes that told me whatever he was about to say, I so didn't want to hear it. "I tried to explain to you before about how the turning elevates everything inside you. If there is even a drop of evil inside a person, turning them into a vampire is pretty much guaranteed to create a supervillain. Even characteristics that aren't necessarily evil can be twisted into those that are."

"You're really sitting here trying to tell me my sister is evil?" I tried to pull my hands away, but Rider held on tighter, not tight enough to hurt me, but tight enough to force me to stay where I was and listen.

"I'm not saying she's evil, exactly, but she is very susceptible to it. She was already incredibly selfish and vain before she was turned. She lacked strong morals. She lived in a world centered around herself. These are all incredibly horrible traits in a person that can warp into something extremely volatile in a new vampire."

"Shana isn't going to be a monster," I told him, sensing that was where he was going. "She can't even fight. I used to have to defend her from jealous girls who wanted to hurt her when we were still in school. She's all bark but no bite."

"That idiom clearly doesn't work now that she's a vampire," Rider said, no amusement in his tone. "You know yourself that strength and ferocity come with the change. Remember what you did to that werewolf you fought when we were in Pigeon Forge?"

I thought back to how I'd grabbed the wolf by her tail and slammed her around, breaking a few trees with her body, and winced.

"No matter what fights you may have gotten into in school or how many bullies you protected your sister from I'm sure you never did anything close to that, and knowing you as I do, I'm sure you never fought unless it was absolutely necessary."

"That's true," I conceded, "but I still don't understand why you think vanity is going to turn Shana into such a nightmare."

"Remember why I put you back on bagged blood?"

My lip curled involuntarily, still perturbed I couldn't get my blood straight from Rider's throat. It was so much more desirable than the yucky stuff in bags, stuff that sometimes had clots and who knew what floating around. "You said my temper was getting out of control. I slammed one werewolf around, Rider. She started the whole thing."

"What you did to her was overkill, and if you'd seen how you drank that gangbanger to death down in interrogation, you'd understand. The way you looked at Rihanna for just talking to me in the bar... You didn't really have any necessarily bad traits when I changed you, but even your insecurity has proven it can develop into something very problematic. However, you're a good person and the good in you outweighs the issues that turning has caused. We can contain your rage and maybe, hopefully, work it out of your system with time. Shana's vanity and selfishness have been in her a long time. Those traits are deeply embedded in her and will affect every thought she has, every action she takes."

"What are you afraid she will do?"

He sighed as he released my hands to tuck a strand of hair behind my ear. "I'm afraid she's going to want to be the queen bee in my nest. She's used to being doted on, and she craves it like oxygen. She's not going to like it that you are clearly more special to me than anyone else in this world. She's going to be jealous of you and she's going to handle that very poorly."

For a moment, the concept of Shana being jealous of me caused a little flutter of excitement in my belly, but that lasted all of two seconds before I had to laugh. "Not possible. Shana has always been the beauty queen, the most popular, the woman every man desires."

"Not every man," Rider said. "I am the most powerful man in this area. She's going to want to be my favorite and when that doesn't happen, she's probably going to want to challenge me, or she's going to want to hurt my favorite. You know I can't allow either of those things to happen."

My entire body froze as I recalled the moment I'd discovered just how ruthless Rider could be to those who conspired against him. I'd seen him effortlessly remove a man's head. Not long after that, I'd seen him reach inside his own brother's chest and remove his heart. "You know what killing my sister would do to me."

His eyes filled with the same emotional pain I'd seen there when I'd accidentally slipped into his mind after Ryan had been killed and relived the memory of him having to kill his own mother with him. "That's why I didn't want to turn her, but if I didn't I could lose your love. I'm afraid it doesn't even matter now because I've felt what's inside her, and I'm afraid I'm going to have to do something that will make me lose your love anyway, but even if you end up hating me, I cannot lose you."

# THREE

My heart ached with the need to reassure Rider that no matter what happened between us, no matter how many centuries we would live, he would never lose my love, but I couldn't ignore the unspoken promise that he would kill my sister. I loved Rider, but family was family. I couldn't just throw my sister under the bus for a man, not even if that man was my soulmate, which, according to a psychic we'd spoken to, Rider was.

"You know I don't *want* to hurt her, right?" he asked, saving me from having to somehow formulate a response.

I nodded. "But you're afraid you might have to. Is there any chance you might just be overthinking this and assuming the worst because you don't like her? You're very protective of me and always want the best for me, which I love about you, but isn't it possible that your disdain for my family is coloring your thoughts about Shana?"

"You heard her outburst."

"She was angry and scared. Sisters say horrible stuff like that to each other all the time. It doesn't mean things will get bloody."

"You're thinking of her as your human sister. Whatever

quarrels you've had in your past will be nothing compared to what you'll have as vampires. Both of you have fangs now. You've proven yourself to be very violent when outraged. I expect even worse from her."

"So, what do you plan to do with her? Keep her locked up?"

"That wouldn't be such a bad idea, except it would probably drive her mad and the only thing worse than a reckless, gluttonous, bloodthirsty vampire is an insane one."

"Gluttonous? You're assuming a lot. She just woke up."

"Did you not see the way she consumed that jug of blood? Could you not feel the insatiable hunger practically spilling out of her pores?"

"She's a vampire now. You fed me blood throughout the whole change, but she only got the blood you gave her when she turned. She just woke up. Of course she's thirsty. I don't see the difference."

"Again, your turning was not a normal one and you can't compare the two. She was hungrier than you, yet you had two very powerful beasts fighting inside you for dominance. She shouldn't be anywhere near as hungry as she is right now."

"It can't be that bad."

Rider touched his fingertips to my temples and closed his eyes. I was immediately hit with an intense hunger so strong it seemed to be gnawing my flesh from the inside, threatening to devour me whole. I remembered feeling thirsty while I'd undergone the change, painfully so at times, but nowhere near what Rider was sharing with me. I writhed as I gritted my teeth against the sheer torture of it. Soon it became unbearable, and I cried out in agony, clenching my stomach with my hand.

Rider immediately withdrew his power and grabbed my arms, bracing me. "Are you all right?"

"That was awful," I said between panting for breath.

"That's what she's feeling right now?"

He nodded.

"You can feel her feeling that? How are you even able to function?"

"Thankfully, I can seal it away, like locking it in a vault."

"But she can't and you ordered your guards not to let her have any blood. You have to feed her. She's suffering!"

"She has to learn to pace herself. I won't let her starve and while feeling that thirst was painful for you, it's just a really strong inconvenience for her. Her selfishness and the way she was so spoiled in life has made her ravenous now. She must be taught to control her desire for blood if there's any chance of her being released from that room. I can't let a vampire that bloodthirsty out into the world. You weren't even close to that, and you remember what happened when you allowed yourself to get too hungry."

I looked away, full of shame.

"You didn't mean to kill that man, Danni, and if it helps, he wasn't that great of a guy."

"That doesn't change the fact I murdered him."

Rider gripped the back of my neck and pulled me close. He brushed a gentle kiss on my forehead before standing to move over to the bar. "No, but at least you feel guilty about what happened. I don't think your sister would," he said as he picked up the jug of blood and downed what remained.

"You're using a lot of your power on her, aren't you? I felt it in the room, and I've never seen you drink from a jug. You must really need to refuel."

"I used a lot of power to soundproof the room while you were in it, in case you fought me. I didn't want the guards to hear if you did. You actually did very well down there. I know I can seem harsh at times and I'm sorry for that, but you understand why I can't broadcast the hold you have over me if I am to remain in control of my territory and protect the people in it. Thank you for trusting me enough not to argue with me down there. I know it goes against your nature, and I do love the fire in you, but it will only make it that much harder for her if you don't control it."

I nearly rolled my eyes. "You make it sound as if I'm the one with all the power."

"When it comes to me, you are. We wouldn't be having this conversation right now otherwise."

I opened my mouth to respond, but closed it, unable to think of what to say. He'd turned Shana for me, and he wasn't going to ever let me forget that. Fortunately, the only other people in the vehicle with us had been Daniel, Rome, and Tony. Rome and Tony were two of his most trusted people, and despite the issues between them, Rider trusted Daniel enough to protect me, or at least, he did. I remembered his threat of having a conversation with him and the way Daniel avoided looking at me in Shana's room earlier. I wanted to ask about that but saw no point opening another can of worms when the one already opened was still overflowing. "You said something about there being a shit storm because you turned her? Rumors? I know Rome and Daniel wouldn't say anything, and you've always seemed to trust Tony. The man doesn't talk much anyway."

"I do trust Tony. I trust all three of them... to an extent." He folded his arms and leaned back against the bar. "You were the first vampire I ever created and now, just a few months later, I've turned your sister. They didn't need to say a thing for the rumors and unease to start. It's odd enough I would just start making fledglings after living as a vampire so long without ever doing it before, but a pair of sisters? It just seems..." He shrugged.

"It seems what?"

"It seems kind of kinky."

"Ew, like a sister fetish or something?" I wrinkled my nose and started laughing, but sobered as I recalled the instant attraction Rider and I had shared. "Wait. The bond you and I have? You're bonded to her too?"

"She's my fledgling, so we have the normal bond every sire and fledgling has," he said, his brow creasing as he studied me. "You know what I have with you is more than that."

Did I? Did he? I was his only fledgling before Shana, so how would he know for sure how much of his love for me was actual love and how much was a byproduct of having turned me? Yes, Auntie Mo had told us we were soulmates, had even been together before in a previous life, and Selander Ryan had confirmed as much when he'd confessed to locating and killing me in several of my previous lives just to keep Rider from reuniting with his truest love again, but did all that matter now? Did he truly love me now in this life, or was it all just because of the sire-fledgling bond and the power of persuasion? What did the whole soulmate thing really mean, anyway?

"Whatever is going on in that head of yours right now, I don't think I like it," Rider said, his brow furrowed. "Talk to me."

I shook my head, thankful I'd gotten better at blocking him out of my mind. I didn't want to voice my fears. I knew I wasn't the most confident person in the world, my self-esteem had been practically nonexistent for most of my life thanks to living in the shadow of the most gorgeous sister anyone could have and suffering through constant criticism from my mother and grandmother, which was why Rider loathed them so much. The only supportive person I'd had in my life had been my father, and he'd been taken far too soon by cancer. I liked to think I'd been improving since I'd been turned. Rider adored me, and I'd made a much needed friend in Daniel. I felt secure in those relationships, but the moment I thought about Rider and Shana sharing a special bond, the old green-eyed monster was back with a vengeance. There was no point telling Rider I had doubts because, if experience had taught me anything, men had a tendency to tell us what they thought we wanted to hear. I didn't want to discuss this with him, but there was someone else who might be able to offer some sage advice.

"I want to talk to Auntie Mo."

Rider raised his eyebrows. "About?"

"Girl stuff," I said, hoping that prevented any more questioning. "Well?"

He studied me for a moment, a deep frown etched into his face, before straightening. "I'll arrange transport."

Auntie Mo was a psychic who lived in Louisville's West End, an area of the city known for crime and generally not a place you wanted to be at night, especially the block where she took visitors. As a vampire and badass in general, Rider didn't have any qualms about the area. Neither did Rome. Auntie Mo was his actual great-aunt. The only thing he feared in the area was the woman herself. She had a tendency to pinch his ears and make threats I didn't believe to be idle. As for the others in our little convoy, they all had fangs or claws and had faced off against far worse threats than the local thugs.

Rider and I were alone in his SUV, Rome and Daniel ahead of us in another, and Tony drove the one behind us, a vampire I didn't know riding shotgun. We didn't expect a lot of trouble, but I'd learned early on that when you were a paranormal, shit tended to happen.

We parked in an alley and exited the vehicles. Rider scanned the area before directing Daniel and the vampire I didn't know to watch the SUVs. Rome led the way down the alley toward the small house where Auntie Mo awaited us while Tony trailed behind us, just in case a threat came from behind. I would have argued that Daniel was the better protector since he had the ability to shift shape and fly away with us if something happened, something he'd actually done with me before, but I sensed a thick tension between him and Rider. Tony was no slouch, though. I'd seen the guy shift into a tiger and *eat* a man before.

We reached the small house and saw two dark-skinned men standing on either side of the back door, guns in hand. Rome walked ahead of us to speak with them. We waited as he exchanged words, did a complicated handshake thing with one and bro-hugged the other, then waved us over. Tony stayed behind, turning his back to the building to keep a watchful eye on the alley.

We stepped through the backdoor and opened the other door, revealing the staircase leading down to the basement where Auntie Mo saw guests. Like the previous time we'd visited, it smelled of mold and laundry detergent. The paint was still chipped, and no carpeting had been installed over the poured concrete floor. Décor wasn't of much importance to Auntie Mo. The only furniture in the room other than a washer and dryer I saw in the far corner being a small round table covered in a white tablecloth. A single candle burned in the center. Auntie Mo sat in one of the four chairs surrounding it, waiting for us.

Auntie Mo was a dark-skinned woman a few shades lighter than Rome's rich chocolate, small and thin, yet she exuded strength and wisdom. Her dark eyes were soulful, all-knowing, and it was mostly the gray and white cornrowed hair that gave away her age.

"I did not see you at church this morning," she said to Rome as we approached, narrowing her eyes on him.

"Something came up," Rome said, struggling to hold her gaze as his shoulders sagged and his head dipped down, a puppy sensing it was about to get smacked with a rolled up newspaper.

Auntie Mo crooked her bony finger, motioning him over to her. "You had something more important to do than praise the Lord?"

"Nothing more important than the Lord, ma'am, but I

did have something important to do."

"It's my fault," Rider jumped in to rescue his employee. "We had an emergency, and I'm afraid I needed everyone on duty."

"Do you think you are more important than the Lord?"

"Not even close, ma'am," Rider answered.

She narrowed her eyes. "I never see you at our church, although I have invited you several times."

"I don't get out much during the day," Rider joked.

"You move about it enough," she said. "Vampires need Jesus as much as the rest of us, maybe even more."

"Yes, ma'am."

She held Rider's gaze for a long tense moment, seeming to read him, before her arm shot out in a snake-like motion, grabbed the collar of Rome's T-shirt and yanked him down to her eye level. "Be at church Sunday," she ordered, before smacking the side of his head and pushing him away. "I will speak to your friend now."

"Yes, ma'am." Rome rubbed his ear as he walked past us, grumbling under his breath, "I hate it when I have to bring you here."

"I'm old, but I'm not deaf," Auntie Mo snapped. "I can still paddle that ass!"

"Yes, ma'am," Rome grumbled as he reached the staircase and quickly jogged up it.

"Sit," Auntie Mo instructed. "Talk."

I grabbed Rider's arm as he reached to pull a chair out for me. "I'd like to speak with Auntie Mo alone."

He frowned as he looked between us.

"She will be safe with me, vampire. You have your own guards outside and you know I am no danger."

Rider seemed to think about it, then slowly nodded his head and turned away. I watched him ascend the stairs and waited until I could sense he'd left the house before I sat down across from Auntie Mo.

"My child, you have a great deal on your mind."

I nodded as I focused on the candle in the center of the

table, watching the flame dance atop the wick. "So, have you seen anything interesting lately?"

"I see many interesting things. What exactly are you curious about?"

I sighed as I lifted my gaze from the candle to her wise eyes and struggled to find the words. I didn't even know what I wanted to know; I just wanted to know… something.

"You appear very troubled, child. Lost. Afraid."

I nodded.

"You seek reassurance?"

I nodded again. "Rider turned my sister into one of us. She was shot and about to bleed out. It was all my fault and I couldn't let her die, so I made him do it."

"*You* made *him* do something he otherwise would not have done?"

"Yes," I said, remembering how crazed and desperate I'd gotten as I realized Shana was dying, how angry I'd been with Rider when he'd refused to turn her. I'd attacked him with my fists and swore I'd never forgive him if he let her die. I'd never forget the look in his eyes as he listened and knew I meant every word. I felt a pang of guilt, but what else could I have done? She was my sister. It was my job to protect her. "He didn't think she was a good fit for a turning, but I refused to accept that."

"But the reassurance you need isn't about your sister," she said, her dark eyes narrowing as they studied me, her gaze seeming to go through my skin to study my very thoughts. "Your entire life, you have sought for one thing. Love."

I slowly nodded as my eyes grew wet. I wiped them with the backs of my hands and forced a small laugh. "I sound so pathetic, I know."

"Not pathetic," she said, shaking her head as a gentle smile curved her lips. "Hungry. You had love as a child, but it was taken from you when your father died. You were left behind with family that was not so kind. The people who were supposed to shower you with love never did and as a result, you steadily grew starved for the love you'd once known and feared never finding again."

"You know a lot about me, about my childhood," I said, fighting back tears. Every word she'd said hit home. "When I last visited, you told Rider you didn't know anything about me until ten minutes before we'd arrived."

"I see what I see and in whatever way it chooses to be shown," she said, repeating what she'd told us during our last visit. "None of this was as important then as it clearly is now. During your last visit, you were being hunted by very bad people. That took precedence over everything else, so that is what I saw."

"I'm safe from that threat now?" I questioned.

Her brow furrowed, and she shook her head, her mouth pursed in a thin line. "No. There are still demons after you, child."

"Selander Ryan?"

"Yes." She nodded. "He is one. He has been wounded, but not destroyed. He is a determined one and will not give up so easily on getting his revenge on Rider. You are the portal through which he will get that revenge. If he succeeds," she quickly added.

"Will he succeed?"

She laughed. "The future is not so cut and dry. Whether he wins or loses is up to too many variables for me to say what will come to pass. I can tell you this: He is not the only demon you must worry about. There are other demons seeking to destroy you, some that have been with you since you were very young, and some that are a very part of you. Do not be so focused on the demon you can see that you allow yourself to be destroyed by the demons you cannot see."

I groaned as I sat back in the chair. "Why do you always talk in riddles? What's inside me, and how do I kill it?"

"Some things you cannot kill, but you can tame."

"Another riddle. Great." I sighed heavily.

Auntie Mo grinned. "I promise I am not purposely difficult. I can only give you what comes to me in whatever way it comes to me. The universe will not allow me all the answers at once. Life would be too easy then, and life was never meant to be easy, not for anyone."

"Yeah, well, I think I got someone else's helpings of the hard stuff piled on with mine. I just can't win. Ever. I mean... my whole life I've longed to be loved just as you said and according to you, Rider is my soulmate. We're together. We should be happy, but every time I turn around, there's some major issue hanging over our heads, ruining everything. His brother wants to kill me and make him suffer. He killed, or tried to kill, him to protect me, yet he's still out there somewhere terrorizing us from the great beyond. I have this horrible Bloom thing, which, by the way, I went through the first cycle and nearly killed Rider. I have another round of that coming up sometime. I suppose you don't know when that's scheduled?"

Auntie Mo shook her head and patted my hand. "I'm sorry, honey. I don't see things that exact, but over time I think it will become easier."

"Over time," I muttered. "How much time? How many times do I have to go through this period of being a turbo ho? I almost sexually assaulted your nephew!" I slapped a hand over my mouth, realizing what I'd let slip. "Oh geez, Auntie Mo. I'm sorry. Nothing happened. I was stopped before I could do anything. Thankfully."

Auntie Mo gave me a small, reassuring smile and patted my hand again. "You cannot blame yourself for what is out of your control. You must focus on what you can control."

"Nothing is in my control," I whined.

"Everything is in your control," she countered. "Danni, you have more power than you realize, and everything you've ever wanted has always been with you. You have to stop looking in the wrong places and realize you possess

41

what you need already."

I stared at her, processing her words. All I'd ever wanted was to be loved, to have someone genuinely care for me, someone who would never leave me. She'd told me Rider was my soulmate, and he told me over and over he loved me. He'd torn his brother's heart out for me. He'd turned my sister. Yet, I didn't feel the security I should feel if I truly had him.

"You said Rider and I were soulmates."

"I said you are soulmates," she corrected me. "You always were, and you always will be."

"Soulmates are pretty special, right?"

She smiled. "I should think so. People spend their lives searching for soulmates, and not all are lucky enough to find theirs. To find yours in more than one life is a true gift."

"So Rider and I will be together, no matter what? Nothing can tear us apart?"

"That depends on the two of you," she said. "Soulmates are extremely special, yes. Two halves of the same soul is a way generally used to describe them, but being one's soulmate is not a guarantee that once united you will never part. Some soulmates aren't even romantic pairings, but friends."

The bottom of my stomach hollowed out, and I imagined my heart dropping into the pit of darkness left in its place. "Rider could leave me? He could want to be with someone else?"

"Yes, and you could leave him and want to be with someone else as well," Auntie Mo said, cocking her head to the side as she studied me with what I imagined to be disappointment in her eyes.

"So everything he's said about loving me could be a lie."

"No." Auntie Mo reached across the table and gripped my hands tight in hers. "I am a woman of God and I would not associate or allow my nephew to associate with a creature like Rider Knight unless he had high moral character. I will not sing Rider Knight's praises. He is no angel, far from it to be honest, but he is a good man at heart. He is no liar. He loves you. Of that, you can be sure."

"But he could leave me?"

"And you could leave him." She released my hands and sighed. "Quit looking in the wrong places to find what you seek."

"I don't know what that means," I snapped, standing from the chair to pace the room. Was Rider the wrong place? He was my soulmate. How could he be the wrong place? We shared a freaking bond. What good was a bond if it could be broken? What was the point of being someone's soulmate if they could leave you? Why would he leave me if he loved me?

"Why are you so upset, Danni?"

"Because everything's a lie!" I yelled. "Soulmates are supposed to be an unbreakable bond. That's what all the romance novels say. I thought I finally had someone, but I guess I never did. I knew it. I knew it was too good to be true."

"Danni."

"I knew it! I actually thought I'd finally found someone who loved me more than anyone, someone I didn't have to compete with the Shanas of the world for, someone… Shana." My stomach curdled with nausea as I thought of Shana lying in the bed beneath Rider's bar, of how he could feel her hunger. He was connected to her. "How much of what Rider feels for me is because of us being soulmates, and how much is because he sired me?"

"I'm afraid I don't know enough about vampire bonds to answer that for you." Auntie Mo eyed me warily. "Why do you ask?"

"The vampire-fledgling bond is very powerful, like the bond between soulmates. It can cause feelings, right?"

She shook her head. "I'm not sure about the vampire-fledgling bond. I sense the bonds you and Rider have are strong, all of them. Danni, I never said Rider would leave you. I said it was possible that he could. I also said it's possible you could leave him."

"Something really bad would have to happen for me to do that though."

"Yes, I imagine so. Maybe."

"Something unforgivable." I felt the rage bubble up inside me as my skin flushed with heat. My heart raced, fury growing stronger as my fears clawed their ways from the depths of my heart to overcrowd my mind.

"Danni, you need to take a moment and breathe."

"No." I turned on my heel and quickly made my way up the stairs and through the back door. I heard Rome release a curse and jump back as I passed him. Rider looked over from where he stood talking with Tony and frowned.

"Danni!" he called out as I passed him, my fists clenched and my head down. I didn't stop, but instead continued down the alley toward where we'd left the vehicles, a thousand racing thoughts arguing inside my head. One tiny voice cried for me to slow down, think, but much stronger voices told it to shut up and stop being so stupid.

"Danni, stop!"

My body came to an abrupt stop, forced to a halt by Rider's power over me, the same power he had over Shana. I fought against it, growling from deep in my throat, but couldn't break free.

Rider's eyes were wary and concerned as he rounded in front of me, cutting off my view of the vehicles we'd left and the men guarding them. "Danni, what the hell is wrong? You look kind of crazy right now."

"Oh, does that make me less desirable to you?" I managed to ask the question from between clenched teeth.

Rider glanced back at the men guarding the cars before grabbing my arm and guiding me to a narrow space between two garages along the edge of the alley. "What's wrong with you? What did that old woman tell you?"

"She told me the truth. Soulmates doesn't mean a damn thing."

He frowned. "I don't understand."

"You can leave me and be with someone else."

"I'm not leaving you and I don't want to be with anyone else." He studied me. "I know a lot is going on, but I've given you no reason to think I'd leave you. Unblock your mind, Danni. Let me see what's going on in your head."

"Oh, you'd like that, wouldn't you? Then you could just control me even more, maybe fill my head with lies so I'm not smart enough to see what's happening."

"What the hell are you ranting on about? I don't lie to you."

"Really? You act like you're not attracted to Shana, but everyone's attracted to Shana. She's perfect."

"Shit." Rider huffed out a breath. "I don't know what the hell happened down in that basement with Auntie Mo, but I have no attraction whatsoever to your sister."

"You turned her!"

"You made me!" Rider yelled, then snapped his mouth shut. He closed his eyes and took a calming breath before continuing. "You said you'd never forgive me if I didn't and you were pretty damn convincing. I couldn't risk losing you. You forced my hand."

"Oh, so it's my fault. I'm sure you'll spin it to be my fault when you fuck her too!"

Rider's mouth hung open.

"What, no denial? You're going to do it, aren't you? You're going to fuck her and cast me aside for—"

"You've lost your damn mind," he cut me off. "I wouldn't fuck that bitch with someone else's dick. You know I wouldn't hurt you in that way. Where is this coming from?"

The small voice in my head pleaded with me to stop,

telling me Rider loved me. A darker, louder voice screamed that he was a liar, like every other man in the world. They warred with each other, more voices chiming in until it felt like an entire army of screeching demons were arguing in my skull. I grabbed the sides of my head and groaned against the pain throbbing at my temples.

"Danni?" Rider grabbed one of my wrists and jumped back as I looked at him. "Danni, you need to calm down right now."

"Why?" I growled. "Am I getting to the truth?"

"Nowhere close to it, babe." He shook his head as he stared at me, eyes full of worry. "But your eyes are bright fucking red."

# FOUR

"Just calm down, Danni. Something's wrong, but we'll get it figured out." Rider continued to talk, but his words were drowned out by the voices in my head telling me he was mine, but I'd lose him if I didn't do something.

"You're mine," I growled.

Rider stopped talking and looked at me a moment, blinking. "Yeah, I'm yours."

"Not hers."

"No." He shook his head, his brow furrowed. "I'm yours. You're mine. Everything's going to be all right. We're just going to go see—"

"You're mine!" I screeched as I lunged for him, sinking my fangs into his throat before he could block me. I heard him gasp as his back hit the garage wall and he pushed at me, but his hands relaxed as I drank from him, his warm blood gliding over my tongue, soothing aches in my body I hadn't been aware of having before I'd opened his skin. There was one ache his blood wasn't going to cure though. I unfastened his pants.

"You don't want to do this here," he said, his voice strained as his hands gripped my arms tighter.

"You're mine," I growled as I shoved him against the

47

wall and stepped back just enough to step out of my shoes and leggings.

"Shit," he muttered, but didn't put up a fight as I shed my underwear and jumped on him, moving up and down the length of him in a fevered frenzy as I again sank my fangs into his throat and gulped the sweet nectar I found there. The more I drank, the harder I rode him, and the louder the voices in my head told me it wasn't enough. I had to possess him body and soul, suck him dry of every ounce of power inside him, then leave him hollow. He was mine, damn it, and I wasn't sharing, even if I had to kill him to keep him from desiring another.

"You... are... MINE!" I roared and sank my teeth into the other side of his throat, mauling him.

"No!" he yelled, then his hands were in my hair, pulling my head away. "Control it, Danni!"

"You're mine! You want me! Only me!"

"I do," he said, agreeing with me as he used one hand twisted in my hair to keep my fangs out of his flesh and the other cupped my bottom to hold me as he pressed my back against the opposite garage wall and overpowered me, thrusting inside me until I lost my groove and allowed him to remain in control. The ride became more pleasurable, less about domination and more about sensation. "I love you so much, Danni. Feel that, not anger. You love me too. You don't want to hurt me. That's not you."

His fangs sank into my throat and images filled my head of the first time we'd made love the night he'd taken me to Pigeon Forge, my favorite place in the world. He'd been so gentle with me, aware I'd only been with one man before and the experience hadn't been great. He'd made up for that and then some. I saw him watching over me after I'd been turned, protecting me from danger even though it meant putting himself in direct sunlight for extended periods of time, I saw him asking me to dance when my family had taken me out to eat only to ridicule me. I saw him watching over me as I slept, pure unconditional love in his eyes. The more he filled my mind with images I knew to be true, the weaker the voices in my head grew, the more the hunger for his blood ebbed, until I could only feel him inside me. I cried out as he gasped and fell against me, one arm bracing us against the wall as he withdrew his fangs. "Are you all right?"

I opened my mouth to speak and started crying, realizing what I'd just done. I'd just attacked him on the freaking street. I'd been crazed, indecent. And there'd been a moment I'd wanted to hurt him.

"Don't cry, honey. It's all going to be all right. Let's get ourselves put back together, okay?" He carefully lowered me to the ground and held me until my Jell-O-like legs strengthened enough to support my weight. He pulled his pants up and fastened them in a flash of movement before quickly gathering my discarded clothes and helping me into them. All as I cried, mortified. Once I was clothed, he made a movement with his hand and what looked like sheets of blackness floated away from us.

"You wrapped us in shadows."

"Yeah," he said, moving my hair out of my face to look into my eyes. "It's pretty dark out and we're in-between these two garages, but I took the extra precaution. I know how modest you are. Please stop crying."

"I attacked you." I looked at the side of his neck I'd bitten so roughly. Part of it wasn't healed and still bled. "You're still bleeding. I mauled you."

"Yeah, I know." He moved his hand to my jaw and ran his thumb over my bottom lip. "Drop those fangs for me."

I opened my mouth and allowed my fangs to drop down from my gum. Rider pressed the pad of his thumb against the tip of one and looked at the blood welling from it before placing it inside his mouth, healing the puncture. "I had venom?"

"Oh yeah, you had venom, but you don't now." He angled his head to the side, allowing better access to the wound I'd left on his neck. "Heal me up?"

I drew my fangs back in and tip-toed up to run my tongue over Rider's skin, my saliva healing the damage I'd done to him. Normally he would have automatically healed from my saliva almost immediately after I withdrew, but he'd pulled my head back so quickly my saliva hadn't touched him. "I'm sorry."

"It's not your fault," he said, studying me with deep worry lines creasing his forehead as I backed away as far as I could, which was only about two steps in the narrow space. "That was too short to be the Bloom, but that was definitely something succubus-related or you wouldn't have had the venom, and your eyes were red. I've never seen you do that before. I've never seen anyone do that except shifters."

"Your eyes turn gold when you draw on a lot of your power," I told him.

"Gold, not red. That was scary," he said, running his thumbs over my cheeks, wiping away tears. "All of this was scary and out of nowhere. You accused me of wanting to sleep with your sister, Danni. Your *sister*. Do you realize how completely fucked up that is? Where did that come from?"

I shook my head as tears fell harder. I'd been so mad, so sure my sister was going to take him away from me, so sure he'd fall in lust with her just like every guy I'd ever liked before him.

"All right, you don't have to answer that now." He gathered me against his chest and rested his chin on my head. "We'll get this all straightened out. Let's get you over to the hospital. I'd like Nannette to look you over, see if she can find anything strange going on inside you that might explain whatever this was."

I looked at the alley beyond the garages we were hidden between and groaned, realizing what lay beyond waiting to greet us. "I can't go out there. Rome, Tony, and Daniel are out there, and that vampire guy I don't even know. They know what we were doing back here. They might have even seen. I wasn't caring to pay attention to my surroundings."

"They didn't see anything and they don't know anything. I wrapped us in shadow, remember? Besides, what happened falls under my personal business and they've all been given pretty powerful incentive not to pay any attention to my personal business."

"What? The promise of death?"

"Or worse."

There was a time I wouldn't have thought there could be anything worse than death, but then I'd been turned into a vampire-succubus and had seen some things. A lot of those things were things Rider had done himself. I no longer questioned the concept. "You can make sure they don't comment on what happened, but no threat can stop them from knowing."

"They didn't see anything."

"Was I loud?" I asked, fresh tears welling behind my eyes. Rider looked away, not wanting to lie, but not wanting to tell me the truth, either. "I'm a skank!"

"What?"

"I'm a skank, a slut, total trash. I just had sex on the street. You know who does that? Whores do that!"

Rider started to grin, but quickly wiped the expression from his face as he looked at me. "Lots of people have sex in public places, and we weren't on the street. We're in-between these garages. This is kind of private."

"I'm a whore!"

Rider closed his eyes and pinched the bridge of his nose. "You're not a whore. You never would have even done this here if something wasn't wonky with you. We need to get you checked out, and we need blood. I assure you that even if the guys know what we did, they don't care. No one is judging you."

"Easy for you to say," I muttered, wiping the wetness from my face as I sniffed, gathering myself. "You're the stud in this situation."

"I'm the stud in every situation." Rider winked at me, laughing as I swatted him in the chest. "Come on, babe. We're wasting night and we don't know what the hell caused this or if it's going to happen again, so I'd like to get you to a better location as soon as possible."

"You think it could happen again?" I asked, as he led me back to the alley. "Soon?"

"No idea," he said as we stepped out of the space between the garages. Daniel and the vampire still stood guard outside of the SUVs. Tony and Rome had joined them and I tried not to think of the fact they'd had to walk past the two garages to get to the vehicles. "You want to tell me what you and Auntie Mo were talking about before you stomped out of there? Something pissed you off and triggered this."

"I'd rather not have this type of discussion with an audience," I said softly as we approached the others.

Rider nodded as we reached the SUVs. "Change of plans, guys. We're dropping by the hospital."

Nannette wasn't my most favorite person in the world, mostly because I knew I wasn't anywhere close to being hers. In fact, I was pretty sure she hated me and wouldn't shed a tear if some sort of awful tragedy befell me. If it weren't for her devotion to Rider, she might volunteer to be the awful tragedy.

She was tall for a woman, slender, but curvy, with the smoothest skin I'd ever seen. It was like whipped chocolate pudding, absolutely flawless. Her eyes were dark, her eyebrows perfectly arched, and I got the impression she didn't even have to tweeze them. She had full pouty lips women would pay for but never be able to perfect, wore her nearly black hair shaved very low, and walked with a swagger that warned she wasn't someone you wanted to try. She worked as a nurse in the underworld ward of the hospital when she wasn't fighting at Rider's side or doing whatever she did in her off time, like, I don't know, peeling the wings off flies, kicking puppies or throwing darts at pictures of my face.

Needless to say, I wasn't overcome with joy when Rider pulled into the hospital parking garage, guided me to the elevator, and pushed the down button three times, our secret way of accessing the hospital's sublevel known as the underworld ward. He'd called ahead, telepathically, to let Nannette know we'd be arriving, giving her time to think of ways to abuse me.

"What's wrong?" Rider asked as the elevator descended. "No one said anything. I told you they wouldn't."

I shook my head, sighing. "Why do I always have to see Nannette? She's a nurse. Why haven't I seen an actual doctor?"

"Honestly, there's not that much difference between nurses and doctors. I'd argue that sometimes nurses actually know more, like in this situation. She is very intelligent, and very dedicated to her work. Nannette's medical studies have allowed her the ability to help all members of the paranormal community, but her focus has been on vampire physiology because most paranormals gravitate toward what they relate to the most. And I've known her a long time. I trust her with your care more than any of the doctors here."

"I'm not just a vampire," I said as the elevator doors opened and we stepped out into the dimly lit corridor.

"She's amped up her succubus studies since you were turned. She's been putting in a lot of hours studying up on, and discreetly conferring with other experts, on your unique physiology. She's been trying to figure out the Bloom ever since we first learned of it. She may not have the friendliest demeanor, but she's doing all she can to help you, Danni."

I rolled my eyes. The woman would dissect me and sell my organs to science the first chance she got if not for the fear of what Rider would do to her.

The young girl at the admissions desk quickly straightened as we approached, instantly recognizing Rider, and motioned for another young woman in scrubs to take us back immediately. Rider was on the board of directors for the ward, although he had no medical expertise. From the way he'd explained it, he was a huge financial backer of the ward and his company, MidKnight Enterprises, provided the security. When he arrived, the staff treated him like visiting royalty, not daring to make him wait. The various vampires, shifters, and who knew what else waiting their turn in the waiting area didn't even grumble as we were walked right past them and through the doors leading to the exam rooms. They all knew who he was and understood he would be considered far more important than any of them.

"You shouldn't need to remove any clothing," the young woman said as she opened the door to an examination room and stepped aside for us to enter. "Nannette will be right with you."

I crossed the room and perched on the exam table as Rider remained standing, leaning with his back against the wall, arms folded in front of him. The room was small and filled with the normal things you'd find in any hospital examination room, but I expected there were locked rooms full of things you'd never find in a normal hospital somewhere within the ward.

"She's going to need to know everything," Rider told me as we waited. "I trust Nannette not to share my secrets, which includes anything you tell her, so you need to be open and honest with her so she knows exactly what she's dealing with. We have to figure out why this happened."

"I understand."

"So you're going to tell her what you and Auntie Mo discussed? You still haven't told me."

The door opened before I could respond and Nannette glided in, a small Asian woman behind her, both carrying trays. The Asian woman's tray held two small jugs of blood and two glasses. She set the tray on the counter and poured a glass of blood from one before handing the rest of that jug to Rider.

"I know you said you both needed blood, but I would like to do a test on Danni," Nannette said as she set her tray of syringes next to me on the exam table. "She has been on bagged blood exclusively since the incident, correct?"

"Right," Rider answered, before tipping the jug back and draining it. He wrinkled his nose and appeared to force himself to swallow down the last gulp. I felt sorry for him, knowing he'd been using a lot of power taking care of me, and doing what he had to do to block out Shana's hunger. I felt so bad for him I barely cared that Nannette had apparently been told about how Rider had taken me off fresh blood because he felt I'd enjoyed draining the gangbanger who'd wanted to kill me a little too much while we'd had him in interrogation.

Nannette grabbed my arm and proceeded to stick me with needles, drawing multiple small vials of blood. She had yet to make eye contact, and I was pretty sure she'd be jabbing me much harder with the needles if not for Rider standing in the room, watching her work.

"Hi, how are you today?" I asked, pasting a fake cheery smile on my face as I batted my lashes. "Oh, me? I'm just peachy. Thanks for asking."

She looked at me then, dark eyes hard, but the corners of her mouth twitched. She finished taking my blood, labeled each vial, and handed the tray to the Asian woman, who I was pretty sure was a shifter. Judging by her graceful feline movement, I was guessing some sort of cat.

"Run these, please," she said as the tray exchanged hands, "and send in the witch on duty."

"Yes, ma'am," the Asian woman said, leaving with the

vials.

"Were her eyes glowing when they turned red?" Nannette asked as she grabbed an instrument from a drawer and used it to shine light into my eyes.

"It was exactly what happens when a shifter's eyes turn red."

"Interesting," she murmured as she finished checking my eyes and put the instrument away. "Danni doesn't have any shifter in her physiology, which makes that very unusual. Succubi are of the demonic family, but their eyes tend to flood to black, not red. Did your vision change at all during this occurrence?"

I blinked. "Who, me? Am I in the room? I wasn't sure since there was all this talking about me, but not to me."

"Danni," Rider said my name like a mother speaking the name of a child she was two seconds away from snatching up. His mouth was soft and slightly curved with amusement, but he shook his head, gesturing for me to behave.

"My vision wasn't affected," I told Nannette as she stood before me, waiting for an answer, no trace of amusement on her face. "I wouldn't have even known my eyes turned red if Rider didn't say something. Were my eyes red when Ryan possessed me during the Bloom?" I asked him. "I remember everything being tinted red then, like I was looking through a red lens."

He frowned. "No, they were dark, but they weren't red."

Nannette made a sound in her throat and wrote something on a clipboard. "Before this happened tonight, did you feel similar to the way you felt before the Bloom was brought on roughly three weeks ago?"

I thought about it. "No. When that happened, it came out of nowhere and I was overcome with the need to…" I looked at both of them as heat filled my face.

"It's all right," Nannette said, completely emotionless. "I'm a medical professional for the paranormal. I've seen and heard almost everything. You were overcome with the need to what?"

"To screw every man within reach," I muttered, avoiding Rider's gaze. "I didn't care who. My body just craved men, any men. Tonight wasn't like that."

"What was different?"

"I just wanted Rider," I said, gaze still averted. "But I didn't just want the sex. I was angry, consumed with it, and fear."

"Fear?" She angled her head to the side. "What did you fear?"

"Losing him?" I shook my head. "I don't know. There were voices in my head. One was trying to calm me, telling me I needed to stop, but the others were pushing me. They were so loud and overbearing. They told me I wasn't good enough, that I was nothing. They told me Rider would throw me away, and I needed to make him pay. I needed to … take his power."

The room grew deathly silent. I looked up to see Nannette staring at me with raised eyebrows, her mouth tightly pressed shut. She jotted something on her clipboard and looked at Rider. "That was definitely a succubus thing … and very dangerous."

I forced myself to look at Rider and was hit hard with the weight of his worried gaze on me. He nodded. "Danni, did any of those voices sound like Ryan?"

I shook my head.

"Did any of the voices sound like your own?" Nannette asked.

"The small one," I answered. "The one voice telling me I needed to stop."

"How many voices there?" She awaited my answer, pen poised over the clipboard.

"I don't know." I shook my head. "They were all female, I think, even though some voices were deep. Some didn't even sound human. They were loud, screeching … they hurt my head and then I just kind of snapped and that's when I attacked Rider. The voices kept egging me on until…" I looked at Rider again. "Until you overtook me. You pulled my head away so I couldn't secrete any more venom into you and you took control. How did you know to do that?"

"Instinct," he said, shrugging his shoulders. "It became clear there was a power play and I couldn't let you have it. I had to take back control."

"You put images of us together in my head when you bit me. Nice images that broke through. You did that intentionally."

He nodded. "I tried the same when you were going through the Bloom, but it didn't work then. Ryan had too much control over you."

"This wasn't the Bloom," Nannette said, scribbling furiously on her clipboard. "That's a good thing because the Bloom works in cycles and not much time has passed since the last. It would be a disaster if she cycled this fast. This was still caused by the succubus part of her physiology, though, which tells me that even when she's not in Bloom, that part of her is still very much active."

"I thought it was dormant now when she's not going through the Bloom," Rider said, weariness in his voice. "She claimed me as her master and her vampire traits intensified. The venom went away except for the Bloom cycle, which made sense. Why would it have come back tonight just for her to attack me, then just go away again?"

"Something forced it to the surface." She looked at me. "You asked to see Auntie Mo. You spoke to her alone, then came out of there angry, and your succubus traits took over. I need to know why you wanted to see her and what you spoke to her about."

I looked between the two of them. "It was personal."

"You could have killed Rider," Nannette snapped. "That would be instant death for anyone else."

"Nannette," Rider growled her name, a clear warning.

"It would be," she said, refusing to back down under

his murderous glare. "What do you think would happen to her if you weren't here to protect her? We need to know what happened with Auntie Mo if we're going to understand this and actually help her."

"Could I have really killed you?" I asked him. "I know I definitely could have when Ryan possessed me, but you survived that. I didn't think I was powerful enough to kill you without him possessing me."

"I survived that because Seta showed up in time to help," he said. "I don't know, Danni. You might have killed me otherwise. And, yes, you have the capability to kill me when your succubus traits take over. I'm powerful enough not to become a completely useless humping dog when you secrete the venom into me, but there's only so much of it I can take at once, especially if I'm not expecting it."

"For your safety, and for his, I need to know what brought this on," Nannette said, her tone a bit gentler than before. "Clearly, something happened with Auntie Mo that set you off."

The door opened and an extremely thin woman with gray hair and bright green eyes entered, smiling softly at us. She appeared to be in her fifties and despite her tiny frame, emitted enough power I recognized her to be a witch. "Sorry. I was held up a bit, but I'm ready now."

"It's all right, Marigold." Nannette smiled at her before turning to Rider. "I'd like to use Rome for this. She's already drunk from Daniel and has that connection to him as well as the more recent one," she said, I assumed referring to the soul stitch attachment that had been created after Selander Ryan had possessed me. He'd used the mark to connect me to him in the afterlife. Rider's friend, Seta, had tried to reattach the mark to Rider, but Ryan had worked in a failsafe, altering the mark so it couldn't be attached to a vampire. If she stopped in the middle of the transfer, Ryan could have completely possessed me permanently. If she tried to destroy the mark, I would have most likely died. Rider had made the decision to attach the soul stitch to Daniel and to ensure Daniel couldn't possess me, he'd had her create another attachment, this one to him. Now I was attached to both of them, eternally linked to them even if they were to die, but neither could possess me, and more importantly, neither could Selander Ryan.

"You're going to have her drink from Rome?"

"We'll do a venom check right before, but yes."

Rider smiled as he turned for the door, his back shaking with silent laughter. "Oh, he'll love this. Be right back."

# FIVE

Rome and the others had stayed in the SUVs, in the parking spaces right next to the elevator, which were reserved just for Rider and his men. Rider could have telepathically requested his presence, and as I remained behind in the room with the witch I didn't know and the vampire I knew hated my guts, I wished he had.

*Would you feel more comfortable speaking to me without Rider in the room?* Nannette asked inside my head as she pulled a wheeled cart over to the table and started setting up for whatever she was about to do to me.

*You and I aren't exactly best buds,* I replied mentally. *I feel like everything I say is just more information you can use to hate me.*

*I don't hate you. I just don't like you very much.*

*Oh gee, thanks. That's a big difference.*

Her lips twitched. *I won't use anything you tell me against you. I need you to trust me so I can help you.*

*You expect me to believe you genuinely want to help me after you just admitted you don't like me?*

*You don't like me either,* she pointed out, *and I'm doing this for Rider. No matter how I feel about you, I care about Rider, and I owe him a debt that can never be repaid. He cares very strongly for you, so I will do everything in my power to help you.*

*I don't like you because you don't like me,* I shot back. *I've never done anything to you to make you not like me. I know I've made Rider's life more difficult, but it's not like I'm trying to.*

*You're not trying not to either,* she responded. *You're annoying, self-absorbed, and he spoils you no matter what the cost is to him. You didn't ask to be attacked by Ryan and survive only to be turned into a hybrid, I'll give you that, but Rider has bent over backwards trying to keep you safe and you keep causing more problems for him.*

*I can't help what the succubus shit inside me makes me do!*

*Did the succubus shit make you force him to turn your sister?* She glared at me as she picked up the glass the Asian nurse had poured earlier, before she'd given the rest of the jug to Rider. *You have no idea the trouble you've brought on him because of that.*

"Drink," she ordered, causing me to jump a little after having gotten absorbed into the mental conversation. Hearing her actual voice again in the small room was a little jarring.

I took the glass from her hand and gulped it down as I watched the witch. She'd poured my extracted blood into a small wooden bowl and chanted over it. Now she raised her hands and my blood separated into two separate blobs, undulating in the air beneath her palms.

Nannette looked down at her clipboard resting on the cart and I noticed words and numbers flow across the paper before the page flipped on its own and two columns rose on a bar graph that hadn't been there a moment before.

"What in the Harry Potter is going on?" I asked.

Nannette took the glass from my hand, poured blood from the other jug into a fresh glass and handed me that one. "Drink this now."

I looked at the door, hoping Rider would hurry back, and drank the blood. I didn't notice any difference in taste between it and the previous glass, but the blobs of my blood changed shape and more magical documentation occurred on the clipboard.

The door opened and Rider stepped in, nearly dragging Rome along with him. The large and normally very intimidating man's shoulders were hunched and his meaty hands were shoved deep in his pockets. Rider fought back a smile as he resumed his spot leaning against the wall and prodded Rome forward.

"Right on time," Nannette said, reading the clipboard. "Give Danni your wrist please."

Rome held his wrist to his chest as if it had just been slapped and looked back at Rider. "I thought this was gonna be like a blood draw thing."

"It is," Rider said, a smile spreading across his face as his eyes sparkled with amusement. "Fangs are kind of like needles."

"Not her fangs. Her fangs are like a date rape drug. If she bites me and I start hunching on her that's on y'all, man. You can't kill me for that. She isn't even my type. I mean, she's fine, Boss. You got a hot woman, no disrespect, but I like my own women. I gotta have that melanin." Rome looked around, seeming to realize he was rambling nervously, and locked on to Nannette. "How you doin,' girl?" he asked, winking.

"Don't even think about it, little boy," Nannette said, nostrils flaring as she looked him up and down and made a clucking noise with her tongue. "I'd break you."

Rider laughed and stepped forward. "Bite me, Danni."

I lowered my fangs and bit his wrist, drew a tiny amount of blood, and sealed up the punctures. Rider showed Rome. "We were going to do a venom test first. She's all clear. You'll be just fine."

"Oh. I knew that." Rome squared up and stepped forward. He held his arm out, offering me his wrist. "Get some."

I looked at the offering and, despite still being pretty thirsty, didn't want to take it, not after what he'd said. I knew I secreted venom that filled men with uncontrollable lust when my succubus side took over, but hearing someone I actually cared about refer to it as a date rape drug made my stomach queasy.

"Is there a problem?" Nannette asked, watching me.

I shook my head and took Rome's arm, felt his pulse all but jump out of his skin. The overgrown, muscle-bound lug was scared, which normally would have amused me, but all I felt as I sank my fangs into his meaty flesh was shame, even when he bit back a tiny squeal. I drank until Nannette told me to stop, sealed up the punctures, and released him.

"I get a bonus for that, right?" Rome asked as he stepped away, eying his wrist.

"Yeah," Rider said. "As a bonus, I won't tell Daniel you nearly pissed your pants."

"The dragon didn't volunteer to do this," Rome said, trying to save face.

"You didn't actually volunteer," Rider told him, grinning. "Daniel did volunteer to feed her before, right after meeting us, and he went through with it."

Rome looked between the two of us. "How'd he do?"

Rider shrugged, his grin growing into a full smile. "Go back and wait with the guys. Nobody has to know about that little whimpering sound you made."

Rome's shoulders slumped as he left the room, Rider's deep chuckle trailing after him.

"Last one," Nannette said, pushing back her sleeve to expose her wrist, which she offered to me.

"You want me to drink from you?"

She nodded. "I have a theory. Drink."

I took her arm and looked at it for a moment. I had no appetite whatsoever. I'd never fed from a woman and I knew the succubus part of me didn't care for females. It craved the testosterone found in males.

"I know the succubus part of you rejects females, so force yourself if you need to. This is important."

I looked up at her and nodded, figuring it must be if

she was offering her own blood up to me, seeing as how she hated me and all. I closed my eyes, took a deep breath, and plunged my fangs into her, pretending her arm was a chicken leg and I could actually still eat chicken. Her blood was fresh and packed more power than Rome's, but nowhere near as strong of a hit as I got from Rider or Daniel. Despite the power, it was bland. More desirable than the bagged stuff, but it wasn't exactly a treat.

"That's enough," she said.

I withdrew my fangs and let what saliva I'd naturally secreted during the process heal the puncture marks I'd left. The witch did her thing with the blood blobs and the chart magically updated. Marigold sighed heavily, sounding a little tuckered as she lowered her hands and the blood blobs fell back into the wooden bowl.

"I appreciate your help, Marigold," Nannette thanked her as she took the bowl to the sink. "That will be all."

Marigold smiled and bowed her head to the three of us before leaving. Rider pushed off the wall and stepped over to me as Nannette cleaned out the bowl. "You seem upset."

I shook my head, not wanting to go into it. "I'm tired. How much more poking and prodding do I have left?"

"Physically, none," Nannette said as she finished with the bowl and walked back over to us. She scooped up the chart and looked through the information on the pages. "I had you drink bottled blood from a man, bottled blood from a woman, fresh blood from a man, and fresh blood from a woman. While you were doing that, Marigold was studying the reaction to your own blood. She drew blood and separated it so she could study how your vampire side and your succubus side reacted."

"But the blood she used wasn't actually in me while she was doing that. How could what she did mean anything?"

"Magic," she said, as if that explained everything. "Rider, you were right that the blood she drinks affects her, but sticking her on strictly bagged blood may not have been the best idea. I have a good idea what caused her attack tonight, but to solidify my theory, I really need her to reveal what happened with Auntie Mo."

They both looked at me expectantly. I averted my gaze and might have squirmed a little. I'd already accused Rider of wanting to sleep with my sister earlier, and I didn't want to go through that again, not in front of Nannette.

"Rider, can Danni and I have a moment alone?"

I jerked my head up and watched as Rider silently conferred with Nannette before looking over at me. He slowly nodded and backed toward the door. "I'll be close," he said, and left us.

"Do you truly love him?" Nannette asked as the door clicked shut. She stood in front of me, arms folded, eyes filled to capacity with steely determination.

"Yes," I answered, not having to give the question much thought.

"*Truly* love him," she said. "As in, you would do anything to help him, to keep him safe?"

"Yes," I repeated, my tone sharper than before.

"Then you need to show it. You might not mean for these incidents to occur and I know you hate the Bloom. I know you don't do a lot of the things you do with the intention of screwing his life up, but everything you do affects him. You could have killed him tonight. At the very least, knowledge that he has a woman he would allow to nearly kill him could leak and make him look like prey, so cut the bullshit and tell me what happened at Auntie Mo's so we can work together to protect him."

"You love him too," I said, surprising myself by not feeling the jealousy I would normally feel thinking of another woman loving Rider. "Not romantically, but … you love him."

"I have great respect for him," Nannette said, her tone clipped. "As I said before, I owe him a great debt."

I nodded my understanding and took a deep breath as I squared my shoulders and smoothed nonexistent wrinkles from my leggings, fumbling for a beginning. "I honestly don't really know where to begin."

"Rider told me you had asked to see Auntie Mo, and you chose to speak with her alone. Why did you request to see her, and why privately?"

I thought back to the moment I'd thought of Auntie Mo, which led me to thinking about what had led up to that moment, and the moment itself. "I think it started with Shana's wedding. I really wanted Rider to go with me. My family has never thought much of me when it comes to beauty and success." I dropped my gaze back down to my lap, not wanting to look into the beautiful, flawless face of the nurse, who I knew also happened to be a freaking warrior princess when it came to fighting. I'd had enough of the women in my family looking down on me. I didn't need the amazing Nannette's judging eyes devouring me too. "I wanted to show them I was capable, worthy of an intelligent, attractive, successful man like Rider. When he actually showed up at the reception, I was so excited. It felt like I finally had something I'd always wanted, but then the hunters came and my sister got caught in the crossfire. She was shot because of me and I know we haven't really been close in many years, but we were once before, you know? We're barely a year apart in age. We were like best friends before school started and slowly, with each year that passed, she got prettier and more popular, and, well, I didn't. Then my father died and we just... unraveled completely, but as she bled out, I saw the little girl who was once my best friend and there was so much guilt. She'd been shot because of me, because of what I'd become."

"You made Rider turn her."

I nodded. "I begged him, and he did, but he didn't like it. We took her to Midnight Rider and waited for her to wake up. He was angry with me."

"And that made you angry?"

"Yes, but not just at him, if I'm being honest." I fiddled

with my fingers and tried to unwind the twisted thoughts in my brain, trying to figure out what I'd felt. "Have you ever had a bunch of different thoughts and emotions all jumbled up inside you like a twine ball? Everything overlaps and twists and you can't really figure out where it starts?"

Nannette didn't answer, but instead she rolled a stool over and sat on it, studying me. "What thoughts and emotions were you feeling?"

"Anger. I was angry that Rider was upset with me, and angry that Shana had followed me out of the reception. I was angry I had been so pathetically me that Rider had taken pity and showed up at the reception knowing the hunters were after him, after me, after both of us. I felt guilty because Shana got caught in the crossfire, guilty that I'd had Rider turn her, knowing he didn't like her, but I was angry that he seemed so set on her being awful, that he wasn't giving her a chance. I was afraid. I was afraid she wasn't going to wake up and not only would my sister be dead, but Rider would be mad at me for nothing. And, I was afraid…"

"Afraid of what, Danni?"

"I was afraid she would wake up and take everything away from me."

Nannette stared at me, eyes rounded in surprise as silence hung between us, thick and heavy. She made a notation on her clipboard and cleared her throat. "Part of you didn't really want your sister to survive."

I wiped my eyes with the backs of my hands, wicking away wetness before tears could fall. My chest ached as guilt formed a ball of nausea in my stomach. "I know. It's awful. I begged him to save her, then as I sat there watching her… it's like I was split in two. I kept focusing on the thoughts and feelings a good sister should have. I defended her to Rider. I thought of all the good times with her. I prayed for her… but this fear curdled inside me the whole time, this nagging worry that once she woke, my life would be over. Then she did wake, and I behaved like I thought I should, like the dutiful, protective sister."

"But the fear was still there?"

I nodded. "Did Rider ever tell you that Auntie Mo told us we were soulmates?"

Nannette nodded. "Ever since you were turned I've been tasked with finding out as much as I can about your unique physiology, and once it became clear Selander Ryan had plans to use you to hurt Rider I've been looking into that as well, along with Eliza. He tells us only what we need to know to help us do that. The soulmate thing was something he thought we'd need to know."

I nodded. "So you know we're supposed to have this special bond. I'm sure you also are very aware that I was the first person Rider ever turned, and I was the only one he ever turned until Shana. After she woke she was afraid and angry, and I gave her a pass on it, on the horrible things she said to me. I remembered saying horrible things to Rider after I woke up like this. I didn't believe him. I mean, who believes in vampires for real? But then we were talking and it kind of dawned on me that I wasn't so special anymore. Rider has a bond with Shana now. *Shana.* She's my sister and I do love her, but I've lived in the shadow of her beauty for so long. I've lost count of how many guys I liked who were so enthralled with her they didn't pay me a moment's attention, or worse, they used me to get access to her. I know she can't help the effect she has on men, so I try not to hold it against her, but it's hard to live with. Rider was the first man who seemed to genuinely adore me and I had the special bond of being his only fledgling. I was connected to him in a way no one else was, but now Shana has that connection and I practically gave her that by begging Rider to turn her."

"You think he feels the same way about Shana as he does about you?"

"Yes. No." I heaved out a frustrated sigh as I struggled to find words to explain. "It's these damn voices I told you about. I have one voice telling me everything is fine, that Rider wouldn't hurt me, but all these other voices are so much louder. It sounds crazy, and maybe I am crazy, but when Rider shared that he could feel Shana's hunger, it solidified my worry that they now shared a bond as well. My special fledgling-sire bond with him isn't that special anymore. I remembered the soulmate thing Auntie Mo told us about and that's why I wanted to speak with her, to learn more about that bond."

"So you went to see her." Nannette jotted something on her clipboard, then tapped it with her pen. "What did you discover that made you react the way you did?"

"In a nutshell, I wanted to know if the bond between soulmates was unbreakable. According to Auntie Mo, being a soulmate isn't a guarantee a couple will remain together forever. Rider and I do share a special bond, but he could leave me. He could love another. It's possible."

"And that set you off and made you attack him?" She looked at me with something between anger and incredulity in her eyes.

I shook my head. "I didn't set out to attack him when I left Auntie Mo's. I was full of this rage that had been brewing, or more like simmering inside me. It's almost always there. It's jealousy, and insecurity, and fear, and everything bad in me and it just simmers and feeds these voices until it all boils over." I choked back a sob and clamped a hand over my mouth, then slowly breathed until I gathered myself, not wanting to fall apart in front of the strong warrior nurse, who I was sure never cried. "All I could think was that being a soulmate gave me no guarantee. The voices seized on that and my head just filled with all these terrible thoughts, and the fear of Shana taking everything away from me grew and grew until it just burst and I had to get out of there. I was so angry, and then Rider stopped me and it's like all the bad stuff inside me latched on to him and this need to claim him rose inside me. I had to have him, to consume him."

"You had to have him so no one else could."

"Yes."

"You'd rather he be dead than with someone else."

I met Nannette's hard gaze and burst into tears. Hearing the horrible thought I'd had verbalized sent a pain straight into my chest and the nausea inside me rose. I closed my eyes and breathed in deep through my nose to combat it. My eyes flew open in surprise as I felt a tissue dabbing away my tears.

"It's not your fault," Nannette said, shocking me even more, as she wiped the wetness from my face and then, to my ultimate surprise, gave me a quick hug before seeming to realize she was showing affection to someone she loathed. "I think I can fix this," she said, tossing the soggy tissues into the trash can and straightening her jacket. "Pull yourself together."

I nodded and wiped the remaining wetness on the bottom hem of my shirt before taking a deep breath and slowly releasing it through my mouth. "It really sucked hearing you say that. I got a little nauseated."

"I can imagine." She looked toward the door, and a moment later, Rider stepped through, clearly being summoned telepathically. He stopped just inside, looking quizzically between the two of us.

"Danni cannot be restricted to bagged blood only," Nannette said, speaking with an air of authority. "Although her vampiric traits are more dominant outside of the Bloom, she is still very much part succubus, just as she is still very much still vampire during the Bloom when the succubus traits are in full effect. The succubus part of her needs fresh blood every once in a while, as does the vampire part. Alternating between bagged blood, fresh blood from males, and fresh blood from females will help balance out her traits. I believe your brother is still screwing with her mentally. Even without the soul stitch attachment he has a connection to her and I'm afraid that putting her on the restrictive diet starved the succubus part of her enough to make it reach out to its creator. Those voices she hears drowning out her own are the work of dark magic. Incubus magic."

"I don't understand," Rider said, hands on hips as he studied me, as I just sat there, blinking. If he didn't understand, I definitely didn't have a clue, because it all sounded like a bucket of crazy to me.

"Succubi feed off blood and sex, as you know. However, succubi feed off multiple partners, but you and Danni have this ... relationship," Nannette said slowly, as if testing her words, trying to tread carefully so as not to overstep her bounds. "Succubi don't tend to get into committed relationships because they need sex with multiple men frequently. Since she is a hybrid and fortunately her devotion to you causes her vampire side to be dominant most of the time, Danni doesn't need sex as much as a full-blooded succubus, but she still needs it. If she's not going to feed her succubus side through sex with multiple partners, then she needs to at least offer it a hearty supply of fresh blood from men other than just you."

"She's definitely not going to feed off sex with multiple partners," Rider said, folding his arms over his chest.

"Definitely not," I agreed. I felt chafed just thinking about it.

"I didn't think either of you would want that," Nannette said. "Alternate her blood sources. She can drink from bagged, and should continue, but it can't be all she has. She can continue drinking from you, it may actually do some good strengthening her vampiric side drinking directly from her sire, but she needs to drink straight from other men as well, to get that mix of testosterone her body needs, and she should drink straight from a woman now and then to curb the strong emotions she gets from drinking from men. Think of female blood as a mild sedative."

Rider mulled over this new information and nodded.

"That's what caused what happened tonight? Me sticking her on bagged blood?"

"That's what gave her succubus side enough strength to come out like that outside of the Bloom," Nannette told him. "Part of the issue comes from inside Danni's mind, which Selander Ryan has tapped into with magic. I don't mean that he's in there reading her thoughts, but as an incubus, he preys on fears and insecurities. He's still messing with her. A hybrid is like two beasts battling inside one body. Fresh blood will help sate both, make it easier for them to coexist. Bagged blood thrown into the mix helps with the rage that drinking fresh intensifies, as does the female blood, but with Ryan working on her mentally, she needs more than a special diet to combat his influence. She needs an outlet. She needs to be trained to fight."

"I've already had her work with Daniel and Rome," Rider said, "learning the basics. I can increase their workouts."

"I'm not talking about working out with someone, learning to defend herself," Nannette said, setting the clipboard on the counter before turning toward us and eying me, seeming to size me up. "She needs to be trained to *fight*, and she needs to be allowed to fight."

I choked down a hard swallow as I looked at Rider, seeing the hell no in his eyes. "Like my security? You expect me to put her directly in danger?"

"I want you to allow her an outlet for her rage so it doesn't build up, and she doesn't kill innocent people or continue attacking you, which we all know is a greater danger if your enemies find out you have a fledgling you can't control. With the right training, she'll be fine," Nannette assured him, narrowing her eyes on me thoughtfully. "I'd like to work with her."

# SIX

"She's going to kill me."

"She's not going to kill you," Rider assured me as he pulled into the garage attached to the back of his building and killed the engine. He turned to look at me, a hint of amusement playing about his mouth, before he pulled me closer and brushed a light kiss over my mouth. "For the umpteenth time."

I sighed as he climbed out, moved around the front of the SUV and opened my door for me, wishing I had his confidence in the matter. "She hates me."

"She wants to help you."

"She wants to help *you*."

"Well, then she won't kill you, will she?" Rider helped me out, ever the gentleman, and closed the door before guiding me out of the garage and into the hallway. I could hear music from beyond the door leading into the bar. Someone was playing the jukebox and having a good time.

"I'm headed down to take care of your sister," Rider said, watching me for a reaction. "You going with me, or do you want to hang out in the bar? Sounds lively tonight."

"You're not going to demand I stay locked in your room?"

"Geez, babe, you make me sound like such an ass," he said, hand over his heart as if wounded, "and no. The Quimbys are dead, Daniel torched Torch, and I have no knowledge of any contracts out on you so for the time-being you're pretty safe to hang out in the bar, although you're still a missing person, but I'm hoping after Shana gets some more blood in her and chills out a bit we can remedy that before your pictures are released to the news stations."

"Then maybe I should go downstairs with you, stay out of the bar just in case the police come by again."

Rider narrowed his eyes as his brow creased in thought. "Is that really why you want to come along?"

"Is there a reason you don't want me to come along?" I asked, carefully keeping my tone playful to avoid a fight. I felt rotten enough about the previous events of the night without adding more drama.

"It hurts that you don't trust me," he said on a sigh as he turned for the door leading to the staircase that would take us down to the sublevels.

"I trust you," I said as I followed along. "She's my sister. I want to see her and help her through this if I can, and it's not like you have the utmost trust in me. You practically keep me under constant surveillance."

"That's not because I don't trust you. That's because people keep trying to kill you… or worse."

"Po-tay-to, po-tah-to."

"Cute," he said, grinning as we reached the door leading to the floor with Shana's room and opened it. "I'm just trying to keep my potato from getting mashed."

"I'm your potato?" I pouted. "That's not cute. You think I'm like a dumpy old potato?"

"No, I think you're a sweet, delicious … nut bar."

I smacked his arm and feigned offense, earning a hearty chuckle for my effort. "I'm not nutty."

"You've had your moments," he said, but his tone was light, joking. The tone and the slight curve of the mouth that went with it vacated the premises as we approached Shana's door. The same men who'd been stationed there when we'd left were still on guard just outside, standing with their backs ramrod straight, hands clasped together. "Any issues?"

"No, sir," one of the guards answered. "There was some screaming, a lot of threatening and cussing, but I think she's tired herself out."

"No blood?"

"No one has been past these doors," the man assured him.

"Very good. Bring two gallons," he said as he moved through the door, holding it open for me.

Shana rested, sitting up in the bed as we'd left her. Not that she had much choice of position with her wrists still shackled to the bedrails. She rolled her gaze across the two of us as we neared the bed, and if looks could incinerate, we'd both have gone up in flames. "It's about damn time you came back," she snarled.

"Have you had time to think about things and adopt a nicer disposition?" Rider asked, looking down at her, not a single flicker of concern in his dark gaze.

"I've had time to fantasize about hearing your cell door slam shut after I have you arrested for kidnapping," she replied, "and my bladder has had time to build up enough to burst. Get me out of these damn cuffs."

"Are you going to be nicer to your sister?"

"Shana, we're really not trying to hurt you," I said. "Do you honestly think I would be part of kidnapping and torturing you?"

She glared at me for a moment, but the evil eye eventually softened and her bottom lip pooched out in a pout. "No, but what the hell, Danni? I'm chained up!"

"You're not chained up," Rider corrected her. "You're cuffed, and you know why. You lunged for your own sister earlier. No one has laid a hand on you since you've been under my care. I will take the cuffs off if you control yourself."

"I want to leave. People are looking for me."

"Yes, they are," Rider said, "because you've been missing since your reception yesterday. I don't intend on keeping you locked away here, but you have to understand what has happened to you before I let you go, and you need to accept the change your body has undergone and learn how to control your hunger so you don't hurt anyone."

Shana stared back at him, blinking. I could almost see a hamster running on a wheel inside her head as she processed this information, clearly still struggling with it. I'd struggled with acceptance myself, not willing to admit what I was until I'd felt the painful burn of the sun on my skin, lost a chunk of flesh and miraculously healed, and caught myself pouring blood off of a steak into my coffee.

"It's easy to believe the blood she's been drinking out of a jug is something else," I told Rider. "She's going to have to see something harder to explain."

Rider looked over at me and nodded before I felt his power fill the room. He growled, revealing elongated fangs as a golden glow took over his eyes. He stared at Shana, holding this pose for a moment before he drew his power back in, his fangs going back into his gum as the golden color faded from his eyes. He raised an eyebrow. "Well?"

"I have to make tinkles," she said, her hands wrapped tight around the bedrails, her eyes wide as saucers.

Rider blinked at her for a moment before placing his hand over one of the cuffs. He effortlessly unlocked it and freed Shana's other hand from the other one. "The bathroom is over there. Don't try anything stupid, and maybe we can keep these off for good."

Shana swung her legs over the edge of the bed as she rubbed her wrists, looked between the two of us, then quickly shuffled off to the bathroom. I heard the door lock after she closed it.

"Make tinkles?" Rider looked at me, eyebrows raised,

expression pained.

"Ladies don't say they have to take a piss," I explained, shrugging.

He held my gaze a moment more and shook his head. The door opened and one of the guards stepped in with two gallon jugs of blood. Rider took the jugs from him and sent him back to his post.

"Is that all for her?" I asked as he set the jugs on the bedside table.

"Hopefully not," he said. "She needs to learn to control her thirst before I can let her leave this building."

"I'm guessing that won't be tonight."

"No, not tonight." He ran his hand over his face. "You need to call your mother and tell her you and Shana are together. Stick to the scenario we discussed earlier. She's freaked about being married, wondering if she made a mistake. She just needs time to get a grip and you'll have her home as soon as possible. If they ask about the shooting behind the reception hall, you and Shana heard gunfire as you left. Already on the road, you didn't actually see anything. Just stick to that."

"She's going to want to speak to Shana."

"If you put Shana on the phone now, the first words out her mouth will be that she was kidnapped by me."

"Yeah," I agreed.

"Tell your mother she's passed out drunk. Shana can't have any access to the outside world until we know she won't implicate me in a felony."

"I really got you in a mess, didn't I?"

"Sweetheart, you keep me in a mess, but so far, I can't complain about the perks." His gaze did a slow roll down my body, and up again, ending with a wink. "You owe me."

"If I call her from my cellphone, she'll have the number and I'll never get her to stop calling me directly," I said, ignoring his comment. I knew I owed him and we both knew it would be no problem collecting. "Screening her calls through my voicemail on my landline is the only thing that keeps me from going banana balls."

"Well, we wouldn't want you going banana balls. You're trouble enough as it is." He grinned. "And we don't want the call traced back to here, so use a burner phone. I keep a stash."

The toilet flushed, and the water started running in the sink. We both stood watching the door, waiting expectedly. The water continued running for much longer than required to simply wash hands.

"She's not trying to escape, is she?" I asked.

"We're two sublevels underground and there's no way out of that bathroom except for the door anyway. No sharp objects. Nothing removable." He closed his eyes and stilled for a moment, shaking his head before he reopened his eyes to look at me. "She's trying to quench her thirst with tap water."

He walked back over to the bedside table and removed the lid from one of the jugs, allowing the smell of warmed blood to fill the air. A moment later, the water shut off and Shana opened the bathroom door. Her head poked out, nostrils twitching, and she crossed the floor in quick strides to scoop up the jug and turn it back, her normally flawless etiquette forgotten.

"Pace yourself or you will make yourself sick," Rider warned her, walking back toward me. I noticed he placed himself in front of me, angled so that he didn't block me, but Shana would have to get through him to even try to harm me. He made a disgusted noise in his throat as Shana continued to gulp greedily. "Control your thirst, Shana."

She turned a bright blue eye toward Rider and glared at him before downing the last drops of blood from the jug and slammed it down on the table. She licked her lips, making sure she wasted nothing, and reached for the second jug.

"You're going to regret that," Rider warned her. "Control your thirst, or you're going to overdo it and throw everything back up."

"Less calories to burn off later then," she said, removing the cap to the second jug.

"Shana, please listen to Rider. The sooner you learn to control your thirst, the sooner you can get out of here, and not knowing how to control your thirst is dangerous, not just for us vampires, but everyone around us."

"Oh, for crying out loud." She rolled her eyes. "We are not vampires. I don't know what Hot Stuff over here has done to you, but it's going to take more than parlor tricks to get me under this delusion."

"Come on, Shana, you *felt* Rider's power, and you just downed a whole gallon of blood that drew you from another room."

"I also just pooed!" she snapped.

I stood silent for a moment, blinking at her. "Um... I'm not sure what that has to do with anything..."

"I pooed, Danni. I pooed!"

I looked over at Rider to see him watching Shana, looking as baffled as I felt.

"Ugh." Shana rolled her eyes. "I *pooed.*"

"Okay, you're going to have to explain the significance of that to me," I finally said.

"Who *doesn't* poo?" she asked.

"Incredibly cranky people in bad need of fiber?" I asked, shrugging, completely clueless to her point.

"Vampires!" she snapped. "I can't be a vampire if I just had to poo because vampires don't poo!"

A small strangled sound escaped Rider's throat, and I looked over to see him struggling not to break out laughing as he shot me a *you're on your own* look and turned away.

"Um..." I found myself struggling as well, looking for where to even begin. I had never been as delicate as Shana when it came to these matters, but discussing the big number two in front of my boyfriend wasn't anything I'd ever planned on either. It was a universal girl thing that we just didn't do that. We didn't belch, we denied ever farting, and defecating was simply not mentioned ever. "All living things have to use the bathroom," I explained. Suddenly my head was filled with images of shifters squatting in their animal forms and I had so many questions I wanted to ask Daniel, but I remembered the grief he'd given me before just because I asked about dragon genitals so I pushed the thoughts away.

Shana stared at me for a moment, her eyes steadily hardening. "It's not in any of the books!" she finally said, stomping her foot. "They never mention pooing in any of the vampire books or movies!"

"Well, they don't mention it in *The Hunger Games* either, but I'm pretty sure Katniss and Peeta took a few dumps in the arena."

Rider made a choking noise, and I looked over at him to see his head down as he focused on a tile in the floor, his jaw clenched tight, his entire body tense with the urge to release the silent laughter he struggled to contain.

"You mean this is really blood?" Shana's eyes widened, glossed over with horror as she stepped away from the second jug she'd been ready to devour a second ago. Her lip curled in disgust as she looked at the one she'd drained, a thin layer of red still coating the inside. "I've been drinking real, actual blood." Her hand slapped over her mouth. She made a gagging sound, and flew into the bathroom, the door barely slamming closed behind her before I heard the sound of blood coming back up.

"Was that because she drank too much of it or because she's finally realized it's blood and is that disgusted?"

"Hard to say," Rider answered, sniffing. He discreetly wiped unshed tears from his eyes and took a deep breath.

"You're having fun."

He grinned. "Is her logic the same reason why it was so hard for you to accept you'd been turned?"

"No!"

His grin grew wider. "You got all the brains."

"Yep," I said. "Shana got all the boobs, and I got all the brains."

"You lucked out."

I wasn't sure how to respond to that, not used to men not going all goggle-eyed and drooly-mouthed over Shana's boobs, so I said nothing as we waited for her to rejoin us. Based on the sounds coming from the bathroom, it was going to be a little while. I looked over at the bed, my gaze resting on the opened cuffs. "How did you get her cuffs off? You didn't use a key."

"I don't need keys."

I looked at his hands, recalling how he'd simply placed them over the cuffs and poof! Unlocked. "Magic?"

"Power. Not all vampires can do it, but it's something some of us develop over time."

I pondered that and wondered what other neat tricks he knew. Before I had time to really think about it, I heard the toilet flush and water run in the sink. Shana emerged shortly after, her new vampire-enhanced golden complexion replaced by a clammy white pallor. She stumbled to the bed and rested with her hand over her flat belly.

"I was really shot?"

"Do you remember it now?" I asked, hopeful.

She nodded, then shook her head. "I don't remember getting shot, but I remember seeing you leave my reception and following you outside. I stepped out the door, called out to you, and there was this pain, like hot fire zipping through me, and then I woke up here, completely fine other than being really thirsty."

"We pulled you into our car and were going to take you to the hospital, but you bled out too fast. We never would have made it," I explained. "Rider had to turn you, or you would have died. I couldn't sit there and watch you die."

She looked down at herself and when she looked back up, her eyes were wide with fear. "Please tell me my dress survived."

Rider made a disgusted noise and shook his head as I stood there staring at my sister, dumbfounded.

"Where is it?"

"I don't know." We'd brought Shana to Midnight Rider after she'd been turned, no longer seeing the need for the hospital, and a trio of Rider's female employees had cleaned her up and put her in the clean shirt as I watched over her, making sure she wasn't harmed. A lot of his female employees gave me the evil eye when I walked past, and I didn't know how they'd react to Shana being his newest fledgling. They'd never liked me. "The dress was cut off of you and—"

"CUT OFF OF ME?" Her voice seemed to ricochet off the walls as she stared at me, incredulous. "You let someone cut my dress?"

"Shana, it was covered in blood and had a great big bullet hole in it," I explained. "Your body started healing as soon as you were turned, but you were a bloody mess and so was your wedding gown. There was no salvaging it."

Her mouth fell open and then the flood came. Her chest heaved as a deafening wail bellowed out of her throat and a steady stream of water gushed down her cheeks. Her shoulders shook with the onslaught of emotion.

"That's a lot of blubbering for a dress," Rider commented, grimacing, looking as if he'd rather be anywhere but near the sobbing mess that was my sister.

"It was a really nice dress," I said, raising my voice to be heard over Shana's fit.

He looked at me and shook his head, bemused. "Make it stop."

"You're her sire. You're the one with the power to control her."

"I can freeze her in place, toss her across a room or squeeze her organs," he said, "but I can't stop whatever the hell that is."

I stared at him for a moment, sure all color had drained

83

from me, as I thought over that squeezing organs comment.

"What?"

I shook my head and turned my attention back to Shana, finding her crying fit easier to deal with than the fact my boyfriend, who was also my sire, could apparently squeeze my organs with his mind if he chose to. "Shana. Shana!"

I clapped my hands, trying to break through her crying spell and gain her attention. "Shana, it was just a dress. The important thing is you're alive."

"It was a Vera Wang!" she screeched and started crying even harder.

"I give up," I yelled over to Rider. "Can you put her to sleep?"

He gave me a look. "You get pissy when I do that to you."

"Just do it!"

He looked at Shana, his expression hard, eyes focused, and she fell back against the pillow, knocked out. The sudden silence after the deafening wails of a spoiled rotten young woman mourning the loss of her ridiculously expensive wedding gown was jarring.

"Shit," I said. "I was really hoping she'd be cool about everything and we could just resume normal life."

"Danni, there is no normal life with you," Rider muttered, his subtle grin taking the sting out of the comment. "Suck it up, babe. You're going to have to call your mother."

Oh joy.

It's not that I hate my mother. I love my mother. She's my mother, after all. She gave me life and all that stuff, but she's a pain and I'm pretty sure being turned into a vampire spared me from the inevitable ulcer I would have developed just by being her daughter.

"You've been staring at that phone for twenty minutes. You have to call her."

I blew out a sigh as I looked at Rider sitting at his desk, looking up at me, amused. "You call her."

"I'd rather set fire to my pubic hair."

"Same." And I meant it, but I knew I had to dial the damn number and face the shrill voice of the woman who'd given me life and seemed to regret it since the time she'd realized I was never going to be the beauty queen she'd wanted. I couldn't let my family or Shana's new husband release our pictures to the news stations and have the whole city looking for us, thinking we'd been abducted by Rider. I dialed the number and turned my back to Rider as I settled atop his desk. With Shana unconscious, we'd moved to his office where he'd given me a burner phone to do what I had to do.

"Hello?" My mother's voice was frantic. "Who is this?"

"Hi, Mom."

"Danni?" I heard her gasp. "Where's your sister? Is Shana all right? Let me talk to her!"

"She's asleep," I said, managing to talk around the lump of disappointment in my throat. Of course, I shouldn't have been surprised my mother would instantly want to speak to Shana. Shana was the beauty queen, the child who'd managed to snag a rich, successful husband, the ultimate goal we'd both been groomed for.

"Well, wake her up! Where are you?"

"Mom, calm down." I took a deep breath as I tried to remember the scenario I was supposed to be selling. "Shana and I are fine. We're safe. She, uh, got a little freaked out about being married and she split, but I stayed with her. I'm making sure she doesn't get into any trouble. We should be home soon, so just don't worry. Tell Kevin there's no need for alarm. I'll make sure she gets home safe."

"That doesn't sound like Shana. Shana wouldn't run off

on her husband."

Shana screwed some random guys in a bathroom at her bachelorette party, I wanted to say, but didn't. "Maybe the wedding was rushed. She felt too much pressure."

"Pressure? She couldn't wait to marry Kevin. He was a good catch. Let me speak to her. Wake her up."

"Mom, she's not sleeping. She's passed out. She had a lot to drink."

There was nothing but the sound of my mother angry-breathing through her nose for a full beat. "How could you let this happen? We expect this type of embarrassment from you, but not Shana. Whatever ideas you've been putting in her head, you stop it right now. Don't drag her down just because you can't manage to land a husb—"

Rider reached over and snatched the phone out of my hand, thumbing the End button before he tossed it on top of his desk. "If she wasn't your mother, I swear I'd set her out in the break room as a snack for my employees. Are you all right?"

I nodded my head, although my back was still to him, and sniffed. It was a reflex. There were no tears. I'd gotten used to the general *why can't you be beautiful and perfect like your sister* mentality of my mother. My grandmother was just as bad, maybe even worse. "You heard her?"

He didn't answer and didn't need to. Vampire hearing, and my mother wasn't exactly a quiet woman. Of course he heard her. The leather rustled as he moved from his chair and rounded the desk to stand over me. He tipped my chin up, held my gaze for a moment, and brushed a light kiss over my mouth. "Nannette said you should be able to work your emotions out through fighting. She's not going to start working with you until tomorrow. Why don't you go down to the training room and I'll send you a sparring partner?"

"You don't want to spar with me?"

"After what you did to Rome when you sparred with him?" He grinned. "I think one of his nuts is still lodged somewhere in his stomach. I have plans with you that require the use of that region."

"Something to look forward to," I said as I slid off his desk and left the office. Since I'd dressed in leggings and one of Rider's T-shirts, appropriate attire for a sparring session, I went straight down to the training room. It was on the first sublevel, past the Bat Cave area the techies did their thing in, and past the gym where Rider's employees ran on treadmills or lifted weights.

I stepped into the training room and looked around. It was a basic gym room with basic off-white walls and hard maple wood floor. One wall was lined with mirror, mats were stacked on one side, a couple of chairs rested in the corner, and a couple of training dummies were placed near the back. I noticed a new one had been purchased, replacing the one I'd busted after I'd gotten angry and pretty much tossed it across the room despite its heavy weight. Gotta love that vampire strength that kicks in when pissed.

I was contemplating throwing a few jabs at one of the sand-filled dummies when the door opened and Daniel stepped inside, dressed in the same black security clothes he'd been wearing when I'd last seen him.

"I'm supposed to let you beat the hell out of me until you perk up," he said before stopping in the middle of the room and raising a finger, "but stay away from my balls unless your intention is to perk *me* up."

# SEVEN

"You sure you want to joke like that?" I looked around the room, even though I knew it was just the two of us there. "What happened? Rider had a talk with you, didn't he?"

"Yep." Daniel crossed the room to set his large water bottle down in front of the mirrored wall and walked back over to me.

"Just a talk?" I narrowed my eyes, searching for evidence of physical punishment, despite knowing I'd probably never find it. Daniel was a shifter. He could simply shift shape to heal almost all damage. "What happened? You wouldn't talk to me earlier."

"Your boyfriend has concerns," he said as his gaze slowly rolled over me, seeming to focus on my mouth for a while before he raised it to meet mine again. "Genuine concerns. I'm fine. I'm too valuable to be killed and tossed aside easily, but I appreciate your worry." The hint of a smile softly curved his mouth, but the usual sparkle in his eyes was missing.

"Tell me. What did he say?"

"It's not that big of a deal, Danni. We just had a discussion about our roles, and where we all fit into each other's lives. I'm your personal bodyguard, and I'd like to think your friend, but I work for Rider. He calls the shots. As much as we all know I struggle with authority, I have to remember that. He doesn't just sign my paycheck, he decides what I do for that paycheck, and I'd much rather earn my keep by protecting you than by doing other stuff while worrying my ass off about where you are and what danger you might be in."

"You worry about me?" I grinned as my belly filled with warm and fuzzies.

"Sweetheart, I wouldn't have done this shit for just anybody," he said, tapping his fingers over his breastbone where Seta had burned the soul stitch. I reached out and touched the spot without thinking and felt Daniel go completely still. Our eyes met. His were hazel fire as they drew me in, held me there for a moment before his gaze shifted, once again locking on to my mouth. He licked his lips, then shook his head as if shaking himself awake and stepped away, disconnecting himself from my touch. "I've been told you're supposed to be training to fight for real alongside us. We're going to spar today, which means if you don't block me, I will hit you. Understand?"

I nodded. "Like when we worked with the dummy?"

"More than that. There's not going to be a dummy between us this time. Think of me as one of Selander Ryan's goons and don't let me knock you out."

"Okay. I got it."

"Good," he said, and then his fist flew toward my face.

It became evident pretty quickly that despite his warning, Daniel was pulling his punches. He still managed to get in a few jabs to my sides and some open-handed hits to the side of my head. He never put his full force behind a punch and avoided connecting directly with my face or kidneys. Unlike the last time we'd worked out together, I didn't lose myself to rage and flip him over my head to send him sprawling to the floor, nor did I ram his balls into his stomach like I'd done with Rome. He threw, I blocked. I threw, he blocked. Sometimes we connected, but neither of us inflicted any real harm on the other.

"You're babying me."

His eyebrows rose as he ducked my fist and threw a half-assed punch toward my head. "Oh, you wanna go hard? You think you can take me?"

Now it was my turn to raise my eyebrows. I wiped sweat from my brow and smiled. "I remember slamming you on your ass in here once before."

"Yeah, you're a firecracker when you're pissed," he said, ducking another punch, "but don't get cocky." He dove for me, grabbed me around the waist and we both went down to the floor in a frenzy of tangled arms and legs as we rolled around, both of us wrestling for dominance.

I ended up flat on my back, chest to chest, face to face with Daniel, his large hands engulfing both of mine as he pinned them to the floor above my head. My legs were parted, and he was nestled in-between them, his most personal bits pressing against mine.

"I have moves you haven't seen," he said, his gaze doing that heated roving thing again, slowly easing down to lock onto my mouth. I had no clue what it was, but something there seemed to keep catching his interest.

I felt his heartbeat thumping against my chest, racing from the exertion he'd spent sparring and wrestling on the floor. Sweat beaded on his skin. My gaze shifted, following the sound of his heartbeat, steadily growing louder. I locked on to a pulse point in his throat and felt pressure in my gums. I felt pressure building elsewhere, but felt it safest for all to ignore it. "I'm about a second away from sinking my fangs into you."

He released my hands and rolled off me. We rested there side by side, slowly breathing in and out until our hearts resumed a normal beat. "I think that's enough for tonight," he said several minutes later, as he stood from the floor and offered me a hand up.

We walked over to the mirrored wall and sat on the floor with our backs to it, knees raised, elbows resting on them. He uncapped his water bottle and drank half before offering it to me. I took a couple of sips, more to cool myself than to quench any thirst, and handed it back.

"Are you all right?"

"Yeah." I released a big breath and nodded. "I had a decent amount of blood earlier when we visited the hospital. I was never out of control."

"I wasn't worried about you losing control." He took another swig from the bottle and rested the back of his head against the mirror, his eyes closed.

I took the opportunity to study him, taking in the hard angles of his face, the lightly colored eyelashes, straight nose, and thin lips that promised the softness of velvet. His shirt fit tight against his chest, and I knew for a fact it hid pecs and abs hard as rock, along with a trail of fine honey-hued hair starting from his naval and spreading to...

"You're staring at me."

I wrenched my gaze back up to his face, pushing aside the memory of the view I'd been given when he'd changed shirts in front of me the first day he'd worked as my personal guard. "Your eyes are closed."

"I can feel it." The corners of his mouth lifted. "You're not going to start asking me about dragon balls again, are you?"

I rolled my eyes and shot him in the shoulder with a playful jab, earning a chuckle as he opened his eyes and looked at me. He smiled and this time it reached his eyes. "You act like I'm the only person in the world who would think to wonder about dragon anatomy. A lot of people would be curious."

"Hmmm." He laughed a little and took another drink from his water bottle. "Usually, when women are curious about that particular part of my anatomy, they let their fingers find the answers."

"Ugh." I jabbed him in the shoulder again. "I was curious about dragon balls, not *your* balls."

"How many dragons do you know, hon?"

"Oh, shut up." I felt my face flush with the heat of embarrassment as he continued laughing and finished his water.

"How's your sister doing?" he asked as he set the bottle aside, and his laugh lines smoothed out, his face a mask of seriousness.

"I think she's accepting she's been turned now. She didn't believe us at first. It's a hard concept to grasp."

"You didn't accept it right away?"

I shook my head. "Even though I was conscious for both bites, I thought I'd been drugged. Selander Ryan told me Rider spiked my coffee before he took me into the alley and attacked me. He said I was seeing hallucinations, so I believed it, even when I felt the pain. I woke up several times during my turning because I'd been bitten by two different types of … creatures," I said, wrinkling my nose, not thrilled with calling Rider a creature, but the description definitely fit his monster of a half-brother. "Despite that, I thought it was all hallucinations, or a really messed up fever dream. I had no reason to believe Rider when he told me. For all I knew, he was a psychopath with a vampire fetish."

"I guess it's easier for shifters. Once you take on the form of another animal there's no convincing yourself it's all in your head." He moved a little, his shoulder touching mine, spreading heat from his body to mine. He always seemed warm, full of contained energy. "So she's dealing with it well?"

"I wouldn't go that far," I said. "She accused me and Rider of kidnapping her, said some pretty awful things to me. She was afraid though. Now, she's grasping we're not crazy, and this isn't a cult thing. She was actually more upset about her wedding dress being ruined than anything."

Daniel made a disgusted sound in his throat and shook his head. "Well, she has her priorities, I guess. What about you? How are you dealing with all of this?"

"I had to call my mother and spin her a story."

"Aw, man, I missed the call. I love listening to calls with your family. You try that titty-zapper yet?"

I growled at him, earning a hearty laugh. Daniel had been with me once while I'd listened to my voicemail and received a message from my grandmother that she'd ordered some contraption that was supposed to electro-shock my meager excuse for breasts into something much more buoyant. "I think it's called the Jug-Jolter 2000 and last I heard, it's been delivered. A vampire Rider had stationed outside my apartment put the package inside for me."

"Very thoughtful."

"Yeah."

"You know you don't need that crap, right?" He looked at me. "You're a beautiful woman with no need for any changes. Your family is ridiculous."

"They're family," I said, keeping my gaze on the floor, my face flushed. I'd never been good with compliments. "Do you think it was a bad idea to have Rider turn Shana?" I asked, changing the subject. "He's not happy about it."

"I know he really didn't want to do it, but I was there and understand why he did. You really forced his hand. I think everyone in the vehicle stopped breathing when you went off on him."

"I didn't go off on him."

"Danni, you were hitting him with everything you had in you, and you sucker-punched him with the mother of all guilt trips. I still have a lot to learn about vampires, but from what I've gathered, what you did would have gotten any other fledgling killed or seriously hurt. You dominated him. Fortunately, it was just me, Rome, and Tony there to witness it. I don't want to even think about what he would have done to save face if there had been anyone there he doesn't trust."

"Great. You sound like Rider."

"Gee, thanks."

I gave him side-eye. "You find that insulting?"

He shrugged. "Rider's a pretty decent guy. He just needs to unpucker his ass and chill a little."

"I'll be sure to tell him that."

Daniel smiled with full wattage. "Yeah, just make sure you get a picture of his face when you do," he said, knowing I had no intention of telling Rider and risking causing problems between the two of them. "I'm just saying, the man has a lot of money, a freaking army of vampires and shifters to do his bidding, and he wakes up next to you. He has too much going for him to be walking around looking all constipated all the time. Granted, there are grumblings about Shana being turned. Apparently, it's usually not a good thing when vampires suddenly start creating multiple fledglings, especially when they seem to have a particular type."

"Rider's not turning a bunch of women," I said. "I was turned like two months ago, his first fledgling ever, and turning Shana wasn't planned. It was done to save her life, and at my request. Besides, we are nothing alike, so there's no type."

"You're sisters."

"And?"

He shrugged. "It's kind of kinky."

"What is kinky about turning sisters? It's not like he's sleeping with both of us."

"They don't know that, and from the things I've heard, a lot of sires do sleep with their fledglings. After they get their fill of the goods, they loan the fledglings out to the highest bidders. A lot of the vampires in Rider's nest came from those types of sires."

"Yes, I've been told." I flexed my hand, tamping down the urge to push it through a wall. "Nannette and Eliza have told me enough that I know the majority of vampires in Rider's nest were rescued from those sires by him. He killed their sires because of the way they treated their fledglings. Why would any of the people he rescued think he would suddenly start doing the same horrible stuff he saved them from?"

"That's just part of what the rumor mill is churning," Daniel told me. "Rider's nest isn't just comprised of vampires he's saved from shitty sires. He's got shifters and even humans in his mix, along with other stuff. His nest is more like a network that stretches far and wide to include witches and other paranormal beings who generally don't run in packs with vamps. All of these people have something to gain from working with Rider, and something to fear should he go dark side. Any way you slice it, turning two women in just over two months after living as long as he has without ever doing it before can easily be viewed as odd behavior. Throw in the fact that the women he has turned are sisters, and it's extra weird. Then there's the fact that you are, well… you."

"What's that supposed to mean?"

"You're a hot, flaming mess." He grinned.

"You think I'm a mess?"

"I think you're adorable, but you're a hybrid. You have this Bloom thing going on that only a few of us know the exact details about, but everyone knows there's something off about you. I mean, you had Rider stuck in his room with you for like two weeks. He had to leave Tony in charge of everything and although most of his people don't know the details, they know he spent that time with you. For all they know, he was having the time of his life, shirking his responsibilities to enjoy the sexcapades during that time. He's put a lot of his men on your protection detail and has lost quite a few. People know you're something special, but they don't know why. Now he's turned your sister, so that's got people thinking maybe he's not enamored with you after all. Maybe there's just something in your blood and now he's double dipping in that DNA pool. Maybe your sister is going to turn out like you and more people are going to lose their lives protecting Rider's toys."

"They think I'm a toy?" I asked, the indignation of that managing to help me not completely fall into a pit of guilt brought on by the reminder people had lost their lives protecting me from Selander Ryan. "Some sort of plaything?"

"They think a lot of things, none of them very flattering. They're concerned that Rider might be turning into the type of vampire they don't want to serve. Those who are loyal to him regardless are worried they might die serving him because you and now your sister are affecting his thinking. Of course, there's also the women he used to sleep with before you came along," he said, as if I needed that reminder. "Apparently he was an equal opportunity playboy before you, now he's stingy with the lovin' and he's pissed off quite a few females who were perfectly happy getting a little time with him as long as they weren't deprived altogether. Now they can't get so much as a look from him. They were already pissed off that it was looking like he'd found love with some hybrid newb, but now he's turned your sister and that's got them thinking he's going after a certain, I don't know, blood type or something. They feel like they've been tossed in the trash because they aren't special enough and they're resentful. The man already had problems after he turned you. Now he's got a whole shitfest."

I already knew the women in Rider's nest resented me, and I knew why, but I never thought they'd think he would sleep with Shana after turning her. Sure, I'd had the same thoughts earlier, but that was my succubus-side talking, and my succubus-side was kind of a crazy neurotic bitch. I'd also had Shana's beauty shoved down my throat all my life so my jealousy of her couldn't be helped. "It sounds like he'd be better off without me."

"Don't think like that," Daniel said, voice stern as he nudged me with his shoulder. "He'd be miserable without you."

"There'd be less trouble for him." I sighed. "Maybe I should take Shana and move to Australia."

"No. Wherever you go, I go, and I'm not moving to Australia. There's like a hundred different types of wildlife there that can kill you."

"I'm a vampire-slash-succubus. You can shift into a dragon. We'd be fine."

"I'm telling you, they have spiders there that can eat me in dragon form. I probably couldn't even burn them. I'd just piss them off if I tried. We're not going to Australia."

"If I left Rider, you wouldn't be my guard anymore. You work for him."

"That's what it says on paper." He looked at me. "I go where you go. Period. I would prefer you stay here so I can have the aid of Rider's resources in protecting you."

"I don't want to complicate his life."

"Sweetheart, it's far too late for that." He slid his arm around my shoulders and pulled me tight against his side. When he spoke, his lips brushed my temple. "If you ever truly want to leave him, I will help you in every and any way I can, but I think you'd put the man through a hellish world of pain if you did. I haven't been here long, but it only took a day to know that man is head over heels in love with you, and you're crazy about him too. It would be a tragedy to throw that away just to make shit easy. Plus, you have the Bloom to think about."

I groaned and lowered my head to my knees. "My life sucks."

"It could be worse," Daniel said, rubbing my back.

"What could be worse than repeatedly getting thrown into a cycle where I become a sex-starved beast?"

"Not going through the cycle, but just staying that way forever, which is what would have happened if Rider didn't bite you and redirect your change. In the grand scheme of things, being a hybrid is better than being a full succubus, and you have people who love you no matter what and will protect you." He dropped his hand and stood. "And you're not a beast. You're too hard on yourself."

I looked up to see him offering me a hand up. I took it and found myself standing directly in front of him, barely a breath away. Something fluttered in my belly. His gaze rove over my face, studying. His eyes told me there was something he wanted to say, but wouldn't. Maybe he couldn't. The silence stretched out, awkward.

"You're supposed to be kicking his ass."

We both turned, surprised by Rider's voice. He'd slipped into the room without a sound.

"I did. We finished up."

Rider stepped closer to us as we subtly moved apart. "He doesn't look too banged up."

"Maybe because he's a shifter?"

"Did he shift?"

"No."

Rider studied Daniel, and his lips turned up just a fraction at the corners. "You went real easy on her, didn't you?"

"She has girl parts," Daniel answered. "It doesn't feel right throwing punches at someone with girl parts."

"I saw you knock the hell out of three women in that alley behind Shana's reception."

"Them? They don't count. I don't care what they had on or how big their boobs were, I'm telling you those bitches had prostates. I'd bet money on it."

Rider grinned and tucked a lock of hair behind my ear, his knuckles skimming over the temple Daniel's breath had tickled a moment earlier. I felt a pang of guilt, but was unsure why. I'd done nothing inappropriate with Daniel. Okay, maybe I'd gotten a little tingle when he was on top of me, and maybe I'd thought about his abs, but I'd kept my hands and fangs to myself.

"He pulled his punches," I said.

"Tattletale," Daniel muttered. "I'll train her any time you want, and she's free to knock me on my ass, but I can't hit her like I mean it. No matter what you say, I know you'd be pissed if I did anyway."

Rider nodded. "Yeah, I would, but Nannette says it will help her control her succubus traits. I hope you taught her some good blocking techniques, because she'll need them when she works with Nannette."

"You said she wasn't going to kill me!"

"I said she wasn't going to kill you," Rider agreed. "I didn't say she'd go easy on you. You're going to get banged up."

"Oh, joy."

"You'll survive."

"She's actually pretty good at blocking," Daniel said, walking over to scoop his discarded water bottle off of the floor before stepping back over to us. "She's got one hell of a right hook too, natural instincts, but she could definitely improve on wrestling. Get her on her back and she's pretty easy to outmaneuver."

Rider looked at me, jaw set, nostrils flared. Daniel winked at me, clearly amused by the reaction.

"You were rolling around on the floor wrestling?"

"More like I got my feet swept out from under me and quickly put out of my misery," I said as I fought the urge to shoot Daniel with a death glare because that wouldn't be suspicious at all, now would it? The last thing I needed was Rider picturing me rolling around with Daniel, getting pinned under him. I felt heat fill my face as I remembered him lying on top of me, pressed so intimately against me. I hoped my cheeks weren't flaming red.

"Well, that's something we'll have to work on," Rider finally said, as he slipped his fingers under my chin and tipped my face up. "You worked hard enough to have grown pale. Venom check."

He put his thumb in my mouth and I bit down.

"All clear," he said before turning to Daniel. "Nannette says it's best for Danni if she drinks fresh blood from the source along with bagged blood, but I shouldn't be the only source. Have you eaten today?"

"Yeah." Daniel's brow creased. "I ate a couple of hours ago."

"Good. Allow Danni to feed and you can go. Grab a quick bite to replenish and try to sleep in tomorrow. You'll be reporting here at sundown, but I may need you earlier, depending on if anything comes up. I'll try to make sure you get to sleep until at least noon."

"Sure." Daniel turned toward me and held his arm out.

I took his wrist and bit down, aware Rider was watching. I'd drunk from Daniel once before and knew his blood was very spicy and came with a punch, but I still rocked back a little on my heels when the liquid spilled over my tongue. His blood wasn't as intense as Rider's, but it still packed a big wallop, especially after I'd been restricted to bagged blood for so long. Rome's blood had been delicious, but held no true power. Nannette's had been power with no jolt. Daniel's blood was like whiskey, forcing a tidal wave of heat into every part of my body.

"Danni."

Rider's voice brought me out of a gluttonous haze. I withdrew, then carefully ran my tongue over the puncture wounds, healing Daniel's skin and making sure I didn't leave any mess behind. He took his arm back, flexing his hand as he looked at the spot where I'd taken blood.

"Thanks," I said.

"Any time." He stepped back before dropping his arm and looked up at Rider. "See you tomorrow night, or … whenever."

"That put some color back in your face," Rider said, placing his hand at the small of my back to guide me out of the room.

"Blood straight from the source is a lot better than bagged."

"Yeah. You'll drink from me next, and tomorrow night we'll find you a female donor. I'd give you one of mine, but when they agreed to sell me their blood, it was with the promise I wouldn't turn them into a buffet line for other vampires. I don't want to break that trust."

"That was nice," I said, my tone a little clipped. Part of me loved that Rider had saved those women from selling their bodies on the street, but part of me was not thrilled they still provided him a service. "By female donor, you're not talking about the same type of arrangement you have with those hookers?"

"They're not hookers anymore, Danni." He gave me a disapproving look. "And that's exactly what I'm talking about. If you have the ability to help someone in the process of getting blood, why not?"

Well, he had me there. Still, my stomach felt squishy at the thought of drinking from someone who'd turned tricks to pay the bills. He clearly didn't see a problem with it, though, so I didn't say anything else until we reached the inside of his room. "There's still a few hours left until sunrise."

"Yes, but Shana is down for the count until the sun falls again, and we're going to need these few hours."

"For?"

"First, we're taking a shower," he said, and my shirt was whipped over my head. "Then I'm giving you a wrestling lesson."

# EIGHT

I slowly came awake, instantly aware something was wrong. My internal clock said night had not yet fallen, and Rider stood over me, dressed in a black button-down shirt, sleeves rolled to just beneath his elbows, and black slacks, his mouth set in a grim line.

"You pulled me out of sleep," I said as I sat up and stretched. "What's wrong? Is it Shana or are more hunters after me?"

"Shana won't wake until nightfall. You need to go down to the bar." He set clothes next to me on the bed. "Get dressed."

"I need to shower."

"You showered last night."

"We showered last night," I clarified. "Then we *wrestled*. I need another shower. Alone."

"You're fine. Get dressed."

"Fine. Pushy, pushy." I stood and dressed in the clothes he'd selected. "What's the rush?"

"I think you have a visitor and we need to know what she wants."

I groaned. "My mother?"

"No. Possibly someone worse."

"My grandmother?"

"No."

"There's no one worse than my grandmother and her gassy little dog."

"Your grandmother's gassy little dog wouldn't be allowed in my bar, and this visitor might be worse considering she's the woman who sent you to the bar to be attacked by my brother."

I froze with my jeans halfway over my ass, my jaw slack. I hadn't seen Gina since I'd left Prince Advertising, but prior to then I'd considered her a friend even if we mostly only socialized at work. She'd been the person who'd insisted we grab some drinks at Midnight Rider the night Selander Ryan had attacked me. She was supposed to meet me but got sidetracked by some guy and never showed. Later, I found out she'd been used. As an incubus, Ryan could visit women in their dreams and he didn't always kill them. Sometimes he used them for information or to do his bidding. Gina hadn't any idea she'd been Selander Ryan's puppet, setting me up to be viciously mauled when she'd suggested the bar. Even after meeting Ryan in the flesh, she'd been clueless. I certainly hadn't told her what he was, or for that matter, what I'd been turned into. "Why is she here? What does she want?"

"That's what we're going to find out."


If Jessica Rabbit dyed her hair blonde and suddenly became a real-life human, she'd be Gina, I thought as I stepped through the door leading to the bar and immediately saw her. It was hard not to zero in on her, as she appeared to be sucking up the majority of male attention in the room, which was one of the reasons I hadn't socialized with her very much outside of work. Gina was hell on my self-esteem.

She sat at a small table near the bar, smiling at one of

the men brave enough to approach her. Four altogether surrounded her, smiling and flirting. She batted her lashes and touched their arms as she responded to their questions or laughed at their jokes. She finished the small pink drink in her hand, and one of the men immediately flagged a server down to buy her another. The man opposite him took the opportunity to crane his neck for a better view of her abundant cleavage as it threatened to pour right over the neckline of her little black strapless mini-dress. Throughout the bar, men ogled her from afar. Even the ones on staff seemed enthralled.

"Go talk to her," Rider said, his breath tickling my neck.

"She looks busy," I said as I looked down at the jeans and navy blue stretchy T-shirt Rider had selected for me. "And I'm underdressed."

"We're in my bar. You're not underdressed. She's overdressed."

"She's *barely* dressed."

"Yeah." Rider grinned. "Why can't I get you to dress like that?"

"Because it would take three of my ass cheeks to make one of her boobs," I answered. "I couldn't keep the top of that dress from sagging down to my waist."

"Then we definitely need to get you one, but you can only wear it for me when we're alone. Go talk to her."

I gave him side-eye. "How am I supposed to get through her admirers?"

Rider placed his hand along the small of my back and walked me straight to her table. I noticed Gina's gaze latch on to him and slide appreciatively over his face and body before she noticed me and her eyes widened. "Danni! Oh my gosh! I've been thinking of you!"

She stood abruptly, nearly toppling a man leaning close to her and enveloped me in an overly excited hug. I was pretty sure I would have bounced back off her boobs if she hadn't wrapped her arms around me quick enough to keep me in place. "It's been so long!" She released me and looked at Rider. "Does this chunk of hotness belong to you?"

"I have some work to get done," Rider said before I could reply, and kissed me with enough heat to ensure there was no need for me to answer that question. "I'll let you catch up with your friend." He nodded at Gina and stepped away. We both admired him as he walked over to the bar where Tony was on duty as bartender.

"That's Rider?" Gina asked.

"That's Rider." I'd told her I'd met a man in the bar the night I was attacked and had given his name, but they'd never met.

"Nice." She made a fanning motion with her hand. "You lucky girl. Let's grab a booth in the corner where we can have some privacy."

"What about us?" one of the men, a ruddy-faced bald guy in a U of L shirt, asked.

Gina giggled and tapped him on the nose with her index finger. "Silly boys. I need to have girl talk with my friend, but keep it on simmer, all right?"

"All right," the man agreed, his face growing redder as his cheeks puffed up from the big smile spreading across his face. The other men nodded eagerly.

"Shall we?" Gina hooked her arm in mine and sashayed us over to a corner booth where we sat opposite from each other. My side of the booth put me in position to see the front door where Rome stood guard. He met my gaze and nodded a greeting before continuing to scan the bar for signs of trouble. I knew from experience his watchful gaze would stick to me like glue if Rider left the area. "So tell me what you've been doing. I can't believe how you quit. It's all anyone talked about for weeks. They're still talking about it. You're like a hero."

I grinned, remembering how I'd shoved my resignation letter into the new boss's mouth before leaving the company. "He had it coming. How's your harassment suit against him working out?"

"The little twerp settled out of court, not wanting to tarnish the family name. I got a nice chunk of money and a new position with my own office. I barely see that little rodent now. I preferred his brother." She quit fiddling with the little umbrella in her drink and leaned forward. I held my breath out of fear her boobs were going to spill right out of her dress, but they somehow managed to stay put. A nipple must have snagged on a thread or something. "Dex is still missing. Chad is telling people you had something to do with it, but of course, we know better. What do you think happened to him, though? Has he contacted you at all since that night? Are you sure he didn't say anything, mention anything weird?"

"He never said a word about going anywhere or gave any indication anything was wrong. I'm as clueless as everyone else," I lied through my teeth.

Gina frowned. "I'm sorry he just ran off like that. I know you really liked him."

"I'm just fine. I ended up with someone much better."

Gina smiled, glancing over at Rider. "You certainly did. If he's even half as nice as he is sexy, you aren't missing Dex at all. I just wish we knew what happened to him."

"I'm sure he's fine wherever he is. He has enough money to hide out as long as he wants." Of course he couldn't spend any of that money, I thought with a little grin. I'd killed the bastard after he'd tried to force himself on me. "That last night we were together, you were at the party with Selander Ryan of Nocturnal, Inc.," I said, targeting the subject I needed information on. "How's that going?"

"It went," Gina answered with an eye roll as she took a sip of her drink. "That jerk vanished right about the same time Dex did. I never even got a phone call and as you know, the Nocturnal, Inc. account went bust on us right after that. It's all so weird." She grinned a little. "Maybe Dex and Selander fell in love and took off together."

"Maybe."

"To hell with them." She raised her glass to toast and realized I was drinkless. "You're not drinking. We need to get you a drink."

"I'm not a drinker," I said as I forced myself not to laugh. If only she knew how spot on her comment was for Selander Ryan, who was currently burning somewhere deep down under, and for all I knew, maybe Dex *was* with him down there. I couldn't imagine a rapist getting into Heaven. "You said you've been thinking of me? Is that why you're here?"

"Kind of," she said, nodding as she looked around. "I've been having these dreams. Nothing weird or anything like that, just memory-like dreams of when we worked together. I've tried calling you a few times, but you never picked up. I was going to leave you a message but got a recording saying your voicemail was full."

I groaned inwardly, imagining how many irate messages I'd received from my mother and grandmother since Shana's reception. I really needed to clear out my voicemail. "My sister got married. Things have been really hectic."

"Oh, that's so nice for her. It'll be you next. Maybe Mr. Tall, Dark and Sexy over there."

Mr. Tall, Dark and Sexy had already said marriage wasn't an option for us. Marrying me would put a huge target on my head. He had dangerous enemies who'd stoop to any level to overthrow him. "I don't know. I'm not really thinking about marriage. How long have these dreams been happening?"

"Not that long," she said, her brow creasing a little as she thought about it. "Maybe about a week, maybe a little less."

A little ball of nausea started rolling around in my belly. Ryan had used her to get information on me and Rider before and had the ability to invade dreams. It was how he'd controlled her without her knowing the first time. I was willing to bet her dreams started happening after Seta had reassigned the soul stitch assignment he'd branded me with. The evil bastard might be roasting in Hell, but he was still up to something. I hadn't known a thing about the soul stitch until Ryan had started coming to me in my dreams after he'd supposedly been killed. I imagined he could have easily assigned an attachment to Gina as well.

"I've really missed you at work," she said as she finished her drink and made a show of pouting as she turned the glass and didn't get any sloshing of liquid inside. A fresh drink was placed in front of her, courtesy of the ruddy-faced man anxiously waiting for her to return to the table where he waited.

"You haven't paid for a single drink since you came in, have you?"

"I never pay for my own drinks." She batted her eyelashes at the man and gave him a flirty finger wave. "Seriously, we need to get together sometime and just talk or see a movie or something. I don't have many gal pals and guys are fun, but sometimes I'm just not in the mood for them."

"That'd be nice," I said, unable to produce any sincerity. I knew Ryan was behind her visit and he was fishing for something, but I had no idea what it was. I just knew it wasn't good.

A burst of energy flooded my body, signaling the sun had gone down completely. Shana would be coming awake. I looked over to see Rider headed toward the back door, no doubt on his way to her. A wave of jealousy and suspicion rolled through me. I gritted my teeth and fought to keep myself planted in the booth despite my body's aching desire to run after him and supervise the interaction between the two of them. In my brain, I knew I needed to chill out, but my heart usually ran the show and my heart didn't want to feel any pain. My heart remembered countless guys using me to get to my sister. It remembered crying myself to sleep at night, thinking I'd never have a man who truly loved me. My heart went crazy at the thought of losing Rider to my sister.

"Hellooo… Earth to Danni."

I realized I'd zoned out, staring at the door Rider had slipped through and picturing him with my sister. I turned toward Gina, along the way noticing a pair of servers huddled together, giving me serious evil eye as they talked about me. With a little vampiric effort, I could hear what the women were saying, but I knew it wouldn't be nice. Almost every woman in Rider's employ hated me from my very first day of being his fledgling. I chose to ignore them as much as possible.

"I'm sorry. I got distracted."

"I noticed." She smiled. "I was saying maybe we could check out this band at Pussycat Playhouse. They're new, but really good. I mess around with the drummer sometimes."

The last time I'd been at Pussycat Playhouse was during Shana's bachelorette party. Daniel and I had caused a male stripper pileup and nearly ruined her party. The place was loud, rowdy, and filled with people. It would be an easy place for Ryan's minions to get to me, although I knew Rider could put his own security in place. I'd have to clear it by him. I'd have to clear everything by him before agreeing to do *anything*. "I'll have to see. When did you have in mind?"

"They're playing this weekend."

"I'll have to see if I can make it and get back to you."

"Of course. I meant to ask what you're doing now. Are you still in advertising?" She frowned as she took in my attire, and I knew she was wondering whether I'd changed after work or if I hadn't been able to get another job of the same caliber.

"Um…" I glanced around the bar, wondering how to tell her the only thing I was doing since leaving Prince Advertising was a centuries-old vampire, which, of course, I couldn't tell her even if I wanted to. I was just scanning past the front door when Daniel stepped through it, said something to Rome, playful banter judging by their gestures, and zeroed in on me. He quickly strode across the room, headed my way. "I'm kind of in-between jobs right now. I know it's been a while, but I want to make sure I take a job I really like, not just something to pay the bills."

"I understand. You don't want to work a job you hate. That's worse than death."

"That's a little extreme," Daniel said, sliding into the booth next to me. He grinned over at me. "But I love my job so much, even the bad days are good days. Who's your friend?"

"This is Gina. We worked together at Prince Advertising before ... I got involved with Rider," I said once I finished rolling my eyes. "Gina, this is Daniel. He's a good friend."

Gina was quiet for a moment as she took in Daniel's multi-colored hair and silver nose ring, or maybe she was stunned by his good looks, which could capture a woman's eye and hold it hostage even while dressed in a faded black Soundgarden T-shirt and ripped jeans. "Geez, Danni. You've cornered the market on attractive men. Do you know the hunk at the door, too?"

Daniel snorted as I looked over at Rome. "Yes. He works for Rider."

"I was kind of hoping one of the guys hitting on me would go too far so he could swoop in and save me, then I could chat him up."

"I'm sure he barely ever gets laid," Daniel said. "You don't need an excuse to talk to him. It's only fair to warn you though, I think Danni made sure his junk is permanently out of order."

I elbowed Daniel in the ribs. "Ignore him. He and Rome are like bickering brothers. Toddler brothers," I added, narrowing my eyes at Daniel. His grin spread into a full smile, showing off straight white teeth. "And I'm sure he's perfectly fine. He was giving me a lesson in self-defense and I punched him where I shouldn't have. It wasn't that big of a deal."

"You got to, like, wrestle around with him?" Gina leaned forward, eyes wide, boobs threatening the limits of the fabric she'd poured herself into. "What was that like?"

"It was over before I knew it," I answered, pulling another snort of laughter out of Daniel, who'd thoroughly enjoyed seeing Rome hit the floor.

We were all watching as another man in all black approached Rome and shared a few words before doing one of those overly extra handshakes and taking his spot.

"Oh, no." Gina pouted. "Is he leaving?"

"He's not free for the night, but he's off door duty," Daniel said. "If you really want to get to know him, I can get him to walk you to your car."

"That would be wonderful." She smiled and did a happy little shimmy dance in her seat. "I'm sure none of those losers buying me drinks will try to follow me out if I'm with him. He's sooo big."

"I'm sure he has his small areas," Daniel murmured as he slid out of the booth, barely avoiding my hand as I swatted at him. He hit me with a devilish grin and walked over to Rome. He could have called him over telepathically, so could I for that matter, but Rome preferred more normal forms of communication and it would be weird if we'd been talking about him walking Gina out and he just popped over to our table to make the offer.

"You still have my number?" Gina asked.

"Yes, of course. I'm really sorry I didn't get any of your messages, but I'm going to clear out that voicemail."

"Don't worry about it." She made a hand gesture, indicating it was fine. "But if you're available Friday night, give me a call. I think we'll really have fun."

"Sounds great," I said, hoping my face didn't show how unenthused I was with the idea.

"I hear my services are needed." Rome stopped by our table and offered his hand to help Gina up as Daniel slid in beside me.

Gina wiggled as much as humanly possible as she slid across the seat and placed her hand in Rome's much larger one. I don't know how she managed to do it, but her breasts continued to dance a jig as she stood and smiled up at him. "It's so nice to have a big, strong man protect me on these dangerous streets. Surely I can repay you."

"It's my job," he said as he placed his hand on the small of her back and turned her toward the front exit, "and my pleasure."

Daniel stuck his index finger in his mouth, simulating gagging. I didn't even elbow him this time. They were both nauseating me. The men who'd been waiting for Gina to return to them looked pissed. The one with the ruddy complexion abruptly stood, but a hard warning look from Rome quickly stopped him from acting on his anger. His hand still at the small of Gina's back, Rome guided her toward the door. I noticed him crane his neck to check out Gina's rear view and shake his head before focusing on where he was headed, his chest not quite as puffed out as it had been when he'd first reached our booth.

"What was that about?" I asked.

"That was disappointment. Baby doesn't have enough back."

I rolled my eyes. "Gina's a perfect hourglass. She's all curves. The only thing flat on her is her belly."

"Yeah, she's curvy, and she has a decent ass, but she doesn't have a big *juicy* booty. Rome likes big juicy booty."

"What's juicy booty?"

"You know."

"I don't know." I looked at Daniel. "How would I know?"

He held my gaze and raised his eyebrows.

"You better not say I have a juicy booty."

"Okay, I won't say it… but that doesn't make it any

less true."

"Ugh, that sounds so gross," I said, "and you're from Imortia, a realm with no pop culture. You haven't been here that long. How do you know about Sir Mix-A-Lot songs and all the other pop culture stuff you know?"

"I told you we were given a ton of information to study before we were released into the wild."

"And rap songs from the nineties were part of your education about our realm?"

"We were taught your complete world history, learned about your technology, your music, books, pretty much everything. We binge-watched just about *everything* and listened to the Billboard Top 100 from every year since the Billboard Top 100 has been a thing. I really liked the seventies and eighties the best. The fifties and nineties were pretty good too."

I sat there for a silent moment as I tried to compute the hours such an endeavor would take.

"Judging by your scrunched-up face, you're either trying to figure out how all that was possible in the short time I've been in this realm or you really need to hit the bathroom."

"Wiseass," I said, and jumped a little as a server slammed a bottle of beer down on the table in front of Daniel much harder than necessary, glaring at me and barely holding back a snarl before turning away to deliver drinks to another table. I recognized her as one of the two shifters who'd been giving me the evil eye while I'd been talking with Gina. She had long brown hair, wore heavy makeup and jeans so tight I could count the coins in her pockets. "You ordered that?"

"Yup."

"Did you order the attitude?"

"Nope, that was all for you." He sighed and took a pull off the bottle. "Used to be, I protected you from psychos with flamethrowers. Now I'm protecting you from jealous women. It makes me miss the psychos. I felt manlier protecting you from psychos."

"I have to be hunted by psychos to help you feel manly?"

"Oh, there are other ways you could help me feel manly, but I don't think Rider would like them."

I looked down at the tabletop and feigned interest in the design of the wood. The memory of Daniel lying on top of me surfaced, and I squashed it down before I could put much thought into it. I wasn't the best at picking up on things, but there were times it really seemed like Daniel was flirting with me, but surely he couldn't be. I heard Daniel chuckle beside me.

"You blush so easily." He took another drink before setting the bottle back on the table and waving to someone. I looked up to see Eliza had entered. She smiled at me as she headed toward the back door, which would take her to the staircase leading to the lower levels. "We're supposed to go out and find you a female donor while Eliza does her vampire orientation thing with your sister. You're also going to have your first session with Nannette. Before all that, Rider wants you to check in with him to feed, and tell him what you learned from Gina."

"You knew who she was when you walked in, didn't you?"

"Rider told me and gave me tonight's itinerary when he called me to report in for duty. He didn't want you to talk to her long enough that she could get information out of you while you were getting information out of her. That's why I suggested having Rome walk her out when she showed interest in the muscle-bound turd." He finished his beer and turned to face me fully. "So... Rider taught you some *wrestling* maneuvers last night? He just had to do it after learning you'd rolled around on the floor with me."

My mouth dropped open. "He told you that?!"

"No, but it was easy to figure out." Daniel grinned, the laugh lines around his eyes wrinkling. "He's jealous as hell, and you stink like sex. You might want to shower before we head out."

I gasped and smelled myself. "I stink?"

"You don't stink, but I'm a dragon. I have a powerful sense of smell. I know when people have had sex." He turned his head toward the front and sniffed as Rome walked back into the bar.

"If Rome and Gina just had a quickie out there, I don't want to know."

"You're in luck. It smells as if he didn't get any. I told you he's damaged now."

"I did not damage him. They weren't out there long enough to do anything anyway."

"They were if he can't hold it long. I bet he can't hold it long."

I rolled my eyes. "You two are children."

"Keep rolling your eyes like that and you're going to give yourself a migraine." He looked at the clock on the wall over the bar before standing and offering me his hand to help me up. "Eliza's with your sister, so Rider's probably in his office or down in the Bat Cave. Let's go find him so we can do what we have to do before Nannette gets here for your training session."

"Do you think this training idea of hers is just a way for her to give me the ass-kicking she's been longing to give me?" I asked as we crossed the room, headed for the back door.

"Rider would never allow that," Daniel assured me. "Even if he did, I wouldn't, and Nannette isn't a problem. The jealous women in Rider's nest are the problem. If they try some shit, they're going to be sneaky about it. If Nannette wanted to kick your ass, she'd just go for it. She's pretty badass, but don't knock yourself. You're not so bad for an untrained warrior."

"Warrior?" I laughed. "I'm just a girl."

"Sweetheart, you could give Xena a run for her money when you're pissed enough."

He opened the door, and we stepped through, both coming to an abrupt stop as we looked up the stairs and saw a gorgeous, buxom woman walking out of Rider's private quarters. It wasn't one of his blood donors. I heard a low growl and realized it was coming out of my own throat.

# NINE

"Down, girl," Daniel whispered before stepping in front of me, partially blocking me with his shoulder. "Seta. We weren't expecting to see you tonight."

"I'm looking for Rider," she said, eying me with an expression that was half intrigue, half *try me, bitch, and I'll kill you where you stand.* "I popped into his room, but he's not there."

"Do you normally just pop into people's bedrooms?" I asked. "People could be naked."

She shrugged, the corners of her crimson lips slightly lifting. "I've seen it all before."

I felt myself go very still as everything in my field of vision went black except for my target. Rider had warned me the vampire-witch was one of the most powerful people he knew, that she could easily kill me, but in that moment I didn't care. Apparently, Daniel cared because I felt his hand tighten around my wrist, his energy pouring into me. Slowly, the blackness faded and the tunnel vision was gone. I saw Rider step through the door from the stairwell leading down to the sublevels. He looked at Daniel and me, eyes narrowed. His gaze softened as he noticed Seta.

"Thank you for coming, Seta. Daniel will show you to my office. Both of you can wait for Danni and me there." He smiled at her. "I won't keep you waiting long. I just need to feed Danni."

"Of course," she said, nodding as she brushed past me.

Daniel released my wrist, sent me a look that said *behave*, and escorted Seta through the door leading into the bar so they could go to Rider's office.

"Is your succubus side acting up?" Rider asked. "You looked like you were about to go for her throat and that would have been very, very stupid. I've told you before she's not someone you want to piss off."

"My succubus side is just fine," I answered. "She was coming out of your room."

"And you're mad about that?" He shook his head and started up the stairs, knowing I'd follow. "Danni, I wasn't even in the room with her."

"Your room is supposed to be spelled to only allow those you want in it."

"Seta's not my enemy. As long as she has no intention of harming me, the magic guarding my private quarters will allow her access."

"So just any woman can enter your room?" I asked as we walked through the door.

"No, but those I consider friends and allies can." He turned and stood in front of me, hands on hips. "I've told you before, Seta is nothing you have to worry about. She's here to help you. I want to keep the amount of people who know about the Bloom as small as possible to prevent anyone from using that information against you. I will continue working with her since she already knows. I realize you don't really know her, so I don't expect you to just trust her. I do expect you to trust *me*."

"You told her you had to feed me like I'm your poodle," I muttered, shoving my hands into my pockets as I dropped my gaze to the floor. I felt a little bad about acting all untrusting when, honestly, he'd never given me reason to, but I was too stubborn to just give up my indignation.

"I told her I had to feed you like you're my fledgling. She's also a vampire. She understood what I meant and wouldn't have any reason to think anything else. I would never insult you, Danni, especially not in front of a woman you feel threatened by."

I glared up at him. "I don't feel threatened by her."

He raised his eyebrows and cocked his head to the side.

"Well, who wouldn't feel threatened by her? She's gorgeous."

"She's a beautiful woman. So are you. So are several women currently walking this earth. I can see beautiful women and not desire them." He pulled my hands out of my pockets and laced his fingers through mine. "Except for you, which is why you should drink from my wrist and not my throat. We almost always end up naked when you drink from my throat and we don't have a lot of time. Seta isn't much for patience and she's got a lot going on with her own family. I need to get down to my office and see what she has for me before she gets pissed and leaves."

"I'm not thirsty."

"Drink anyway. Nannette thinks drinking from me can strengthen your vampire side as well as our bond, which will come in handy the next time the Bloom hits. Plus, we don't want another random incident like what happened at Auntie Mo's." He released my hands and raised his wrist in an offering. "Besides, you'll need it when you train with her later."

"Fine." My fangs dropped, and I began to drink. As usual, his blood delivered a powerful surge of energy, but I was too lost in my thoughts to truly enjoy it. I knew Rider loved me, but couldn't shake off the disappointment that there was a stunning, powerful woman waiting for him in his office. I had yet to see my sister, and Gina's visit still troubled me.

"What did you find out from Gina?" Rider asked as I

finished drinking and sealed the punctures.

"She said she's been dreaming of me, dreams that are basically just memories of us working together. I brought up Selander, and she said she hasn't heard from him since about the time Dex vanished, but she remembered him. She didn't seem to remember him much at all after the night you ripped his heart out. It was like he just left her life and didn't leave much of an imprint. Now she remembers him enough to be miffed he hasn't called her since that party."

"Like he left her life, but now he's slipped back in."

"Yeah."

"Dreams are definitely an incubus thing." Rider released a frustrated sigh.

"You thinking what I'm thinking?"

"Soul stitch attachment?"

I nodded. "Just like before, she doesn't seem to be aware she's being used, but she started having the dreams around the time Seta reassigned my soul stitch attachment to Daniel. It makes sense that if he can't creep into my dreams, he'd use someone else he'd marked with that symbol to get access."

"The evil bastard's always thinking ahead," Rider muttered. "What information did she try to get out of you?"

"Nothing, really. She asked about Dex, but Selander wouldn't care about him. She asked what I was doing now. Normal stuff you'd ask someone you used to work with and hadn't seen in a while. She wants me to go to Pussycat Playhouse and see some band Friday night."

Rider's eyes hardened. "He used her before to send you here so he could attack you. Who knows what he has set up for you?"

"I told her I'd have to see if I could make it and get back to her. I'm assuming it's a no?"

"It's a hell no." He kissed the top of my head. "He's not getting his hands on you again. I'm headed downstairs to see what Seta has and to give Daniel instruction. He'll be taking you out to find your female donor. Take a quick shower and meet us in the office."

My mouth dropped open, and I narrowed my eyes as Rider moved toward the door. "You … You said I didn't need one earlier. You talk about my jealousy, but you knew I'd be seeing Daniel and you know how powerful his sense of smell is. You had me skip the shower, so he'd smell you on me."

"Who, me?" Rider looked back at me, grinning.

"Good grief, Rider, next time you want to mark your territory, why don't you just raise your leg and piss on me?"

He was halfway out the door now. He scrunched his nose and fought to keep a straight face. "Geez, Danni. I didn't know you were into that freaky shit."

"You!" I grabbed a pillow off the bed and flung it at him, but he moved too quickly and it hit the door as it closed behind him. I rolled my eyes as I heard him laugh his way down the stairs.


I showered quickly, not wanting to leave Rider alone with the beautiful Seta very long, even if Daniel was allowed to stay in the office with them. I swapped out the clothes Rider had given me earlier for a dark gray T-shirt and black jeans. I had no idea where Rider was sending me to in order to find my blood donor, but he'd mentioned hookers before, so I was thinking somewhere on the street. I didn't want to wear bright, attention-grabbing colors if I was going to be prowling around unsavory areas. I added a swipe of light pink lip gloss and looked at myself in the bathroom mirror.

Before Selander Ryan had changed my life, I'd dressed better. I wore slacks, skirts, and flirty little dresses. I wore makeup. I paid attention to my hair. I lived on my own in a nice little apartment I'd worked hard to make cute. I'd had a decent job. Now I was an unemployed twenty-eight-year-old who practically lived in jeans and T-shirts, barely wore any makeup and finger-combed my hair. I hadn't been to my apartment in weeks.

As I moved out of the bathroom and sat at the foot of Rider's bed to pull on and lace black boots, I felt a little sad, but couldn't say why. I just felt something was missing. Shaking off the emptiness working to claw its way inside, I stood and left the room.

I was surprised to find Ginger leaning against the wall across from Rider's office. She was the vampire who'd been assigned to watch over me, along with Daniel, at my sister's bachelorette party. A lesbian, she wasn't jealous of my relationship with Rider. Female, she wasn't in danger from me if the Bloom hit while with her, which was a good thing because she had been with me when it hit. Unfortunately, I'd broken her nose when she'd tried to restrain me from attempting to jump Daniel's bones. I hadn't seen her since that night.

"Hey, girlfriend." She smiled at me, her crimson painted lips parting to reveal mostly straight white teeth. She was pale with hazel eyes, more brown than green, heavily lined in black liquid eyeliner, and her hair had been cut and styled into a shaggy pixie cut. It also appeared to have been dyed an almost black shade of brown, and fit her punk look, I decided as I took in her ripped jeans, black crop top, leather jacket, and combat boots guaranteed to leave a dent in anything or anyone she kicked.

"No longer rocking the auburn hair?"

"It's hard being a ginger Ginger. People make jokes or dirty old men use it as an opening. I crack their skulls, drama ensues…." She shrugged. "Speaking of cracking, you broke my nose. Not bad, newbie."

"Yeaaaahhhh…" I shifted uncomfortably. Although, as a vampire, she'd healed quickly from the damage, a broken nose wasn't a tiny little thing to easily be overlooked or forgotten. "I'm really sorry about that."

"It's not like you could help it. If I was mad, I wouldn't have agreed to go out with you and Daniel tonight. We're cool, sweet cheeks."

I smiled with relief. Ginger was extremely flirtatious but never crossed the line, and she was a really nice, fun person, not to mention one of few women in Rider's circle who'd actually bothered to get to know me before deciding whether or not she liked me. I'd hate to have lost having her around me because of something I'd done while whacked out of my mind thanks to the demonic crap Selander Ryan had stuck me with.

"How have you been?"

"Better," I answered. I didn't think she knew about my most recent succubus hiccup, and I didn't see any reason to tell her. I just wanted to forget about it. "I shouldn't do anything remotely like I did the last time you saw me, but just in case, I'm assuming Rider gave you one of those hawthorn oil shots to subdue me?"

"Yup." She pulled a syringe out of her jacket pocket and held it up for me to see before stashing it again. "And don't take this the wrong way, but if you go ho, I will stab the shit out of you."

We were both laughing as Daniel stepped out of Rider's office. "We're all good to go," he said, looking curiously at us as he pulled the door closed behind him. "Did I miss something?"

"Just girl talk," Ginger said. "I'm driving."

"I'm driving," Daniel said.

I gestured toward Rider's door. "I'm going to say goodbye first."

"No time." Daniel grabbed my arm and turned me away from the door before prodding me down the hall. "We have a lead on a good donor for you."

"But…"

"Danni, don't worry about it."

I looked back toward Rider's office, fighting the urge to

dig my heels in. He was in there with her, Miss Petite, Gorgeous, and Boobs Galore. "He said for me to meet you in his office."

"You met me close enough," Daniel said as he ushered me down the hall and started moving across the bar floor. "We have an appointment."

"Hey!" The ruddy-faced man who'd been buying drinks for Gina pointed at me as we neared. "I want to talk to you about your slut friend."

"Oh, she's a slut now that your dumb ass bought her a bunch of drinks and she didn't go home with you?" I asked, transferring my anger from the Seta situation over to the jerk as we moved past his table. "Get over it."

The man's chunky arm whipped out, and he grabbed my forearm. Without even thinking, I pivoted and rammed my fist into his throat. He made an awful half choking, half gurgling sound as his eyes bulged out of his head, his face resembling a red tomato. Still fueled by anger and in need of some way to release it, I yanked him up from the chair by the front of his shirt, rammed my knee into his groin, then spun with him. I slammed his face into the top of the bar and dragged him the entire length of it as patrons fled their barstools to get out of the way. At the end of the bar, I picked up a bottle and brought it down on his head, glass shattering around him. I let his body drop to the floor, stepped back, and took calming breaths, the worst of my anger spent.

"Sorry," I said to Tony, who was still on bartending duty, as he started wiping down the mess I'd made.

"He had it coming," the tiger shifter said and motioned for one of the security guards to come collect the man off the floor.

I looked around and saw a lot of gawking human faces, undoubtedly wondering how such a small woman had just beat the shit out of the hefty guy. The men who'd been at the table with him sat stone still, mouths gaping open. Apparently, none of them cared enough about the guy to defend him. Just beyond the table, Ginger and Daniel stood side by side, arms folded, watching me. Both of them were grinning.

"It's supposed to be our job to protect her, right?" Ginger asked.

"Yup," Daniel answered, his smile widening. "Sometimes she makes it really easy."

"And other times?"

"Other times she causes a clusterfuck of chaos, but she's never boring."

I rolled my eyes as I walked past them, suppressing a grin as I saw the server from earlier watching me with a bit of apprehension in her eyes. I bet she'd think twice before slamming another bottle on my table.


"Do you think Seta's hot?" I asked later as we were settled into Daniel's truck, stopped at a red light.

"Oh, yeah." He answered.

"I'd do her," Ginger chimed in.

I looked at both of them, feeling the heat of anger flood my face, but held my death glare on Daniel until he glanced over at me.

"What?" he asked. "Do you want me to lie or something? You're hot too."

"Am I hot?" Ginger asked.

"You're all right," he answered.

"Gee, thanks."

Daniel grinned and stepped on the gas as the light turned green. "Why do you care if she's hot, Danni? From what I've gathered, Rider's known her a long time. If he was going to hit that, he would have. Maybe he already did at some point, but that shouldn't matter either. He doesn't look at her like he looks at you."

"She's prettier than me." I sulked. "She's all gorgeous with those beautiful Latina features and that silky black hair, and geez, her boobs are like two planets."

Daniel laughed. "Actually, I think she's Native American and Spanish or something. She's very attractive, but that doesn't mean she's any better than you."

"Her boobs are a little too big," Ginger said. "You could suffocate in there… but then again, what a way to go."

This made Daniel laugh more as I rolled my eyes and sat back, sandwiched between him and Ginger in the truck. I looked down at my own meager chest and tried not to think of Rider alone with Seta, enjoying the view.

Daniel looked over at me and groaned. "Shit. Is this because your mother and grandmother sent you all those breast enhancement pills and that electro-tit-o-shocker thing?"

"Electro what?" Ginger asked, eyes bugging out of her head.

"Her family has some crazy obsession with big breasts," Daniel told her. "You know, this may come as a shock to you after all you've undoubtedly heard from them, but not all men are obsessed with big breasts."

I gave him a look.

"I'm serious. I'm an ass man myself."

"You got the ass part right," Ginger quipped, nudging me with her elbow and winking.

"Funny," Daniel said, grinning as he glided his truck down a one-way street and parked along the side of the road. I saw a man in a police uniform standing a few blocks up, outside of the opening to an alley. "That's Grissom," Daniel said. "He's a werewolf who happens to be a cop, but he's also on Rider's payroll. It helps him to have some of his own people in the police department. Rider asked him and his partner if they had any recommendations for a female blood donor you could use. They have one in mind, and that's why we're here."

"A hooker?" I asked as Daniel and Ginger opened their doors to exit the truck.

He shook his head as he helped me out and closed the

door behind me. "I don't think so. Rider knew you weren't thrilled with the idea of using a hooker and with the whole succubus thing you tend to not want to drink from women at all so he thought maybe if we found someone you truly cared deeply about helping, you'd struggle less with it."

We walked toward Grissom, my curiosity piqued. The man was tall, about Rider and Daniel's height, with dark hair cut short and gray, assessing eyes. He had a five o'clock shadow and filled out his uniform well enough, I knew he was no stranger to the gym. Then again, he was a werewolf, so there was some natural automatic muscle tone there too.

"Hi." He nodded his head toward us all in greeting and held his hand out to shake mine. His grip was firm, but not overly so. He didn't feel the need to prove anything. "Aaron Grissom. My partner, Amelia, is with the girl. When Rider asked us about a donor, we knew just the girl for the job. Poor thing's been through hell and back. Rotten parents. Rotten childhood. No future if things don't change."

"Wait," I said, digesting the information. "Exactly how old is this girl?"

"Today's actually her eighteenth birthday," Grissom answered, his eyes reflecting sadness. "Come see how she's celebrated it so far."

He turned and disappeared into the alley. I shared a look with Daniel and Ginger, and we followed behind. He led us down, carefully stepping over broken glass and assorted trash, and stopped before a nook that had been formed by three buildings being sandwiched together, the back of the center one not quite as long as the other two.

We stopped beside him and followed his gaze to two figures on the ground. One was his partner, Amelia. She had dishwater blonde hair pulled back in a loose bun. Her uniform didn't do much for her slender figure, but when she glanced back at us I saw she had a very pretty face and caring eyes radiating a mixture of sympathy, anger, and hope.

She was kneeling over a young girl huddled in the corner, her knees pulled to her chin. Between my vampiric ability and the moonlight spilling into the little nook, I was able to see bruised kneecaps poking out of ripped jeans, blood splatter on her grungy pale yellow T-shirt, goose pebbled flesh on slender arms, a split bottom lip, and the mother of all purple, blue, and black bruises surrounding her right eye. Long, stringy brown hair fell over the girl's face as she looked at me, brown eyes hollowed from surviving enough bad stuff to steal even the concept of dreaming from her.

"Shit," I whispered.

"Yeah." Grissom sighed. "Her name's Angel Cordova. She's not a bad kid, just fell in with the wrong people. Her older brother was a gangbanger. He got his ass killed, but not before getting baby sis on drugs. The parents were shit. Dad's in prison. Mom ran off with some guy to who-knows-where. Angel's been staying with assorted cousins, and none of those households were any damn good. She's been in rehab a few times. I'm pretty sure she's clean right now, but if we don't get her into a better situation, it's only a matter of time before she gets dragged back down. She doesn't have one single relative who isn't some kind of addict."

"Who beat the hell out of her?"

"The man who tried to rape her earlier. She left her last cousin's house because the situation got too bad to deal with and she's been out on the streets since. Afraid she'd go into the system because she was underage, she never called me despite having my card I gave to her after we'd crossed paths before. My partner's psychic. She had a vision of Angel being assaulted after Rider asked us if we knew of any good ideas for a donor, and that's how we found her. Unfortunately, we found her after she'd killed the sonofabitch. Rammed a sharp piece of metal she found on the ground through his throat."

I looked at Daniel and Ginger, and could tell they were both thinking what I was thinking. We would have loved to kill the bastard ourselves. I didn't see a body, but I smelled more blood than I saw on the girl's clothes. I sniffed, focusing on the smell, and followed the scent to a large dumpster.

"Yeah, his body is still behind it," Grissom said, following my gaze. "That's where he dragged her's where it happened. We haven't called it in yet because I figure she's had a shitty enough birthday without having to go to jail and suffer through a murder trial she'll probably lose because the court will take one look at her and think she's not worth saving."

"And you think she is."

"Yeah, and I'm hoping you do too, because if you take her as your donor, give her a safe place to live and half a chance, she might turn out to be someone really great. She deserves better than the sucky hand she got dealt."

"Does she know I'm a vampire?"

He shook his head. "No, but she's seen enough bad shit that I don't think she'll be too bugged out about it. Amelia can help you break it down to her, but if you're going to do it, you need to do it soon. I recognized the guy, and he's a well-known lawyer with money, the type of guy with family who won't stop pushing until his killer is caught and brought to justice. I have no intention of allowing that girl to go down for this, so as soon as we get her out of here, I'm shifting shape and doing what I have to do so I can call in the body found from a *dog attack*." He looked at me. "I'd rather he be as fresh as possible before I do what's necessary for that."

I grimaced, realizing what he was saying. I'd bitten through my share of throats, but I'd never ate flesh, or even drank from a body once it was dead. As far as cover-ups went, his idea was pretty good though. "I'll go talk to her, but what should I do if I tell her what I am and she freaks out? We're not supposed to just go around announcing what we are."

"We'll cross that bridge if and when we have to. Just do your best. She deserves a shot at a decent life."

I nodded my head in agreement and walked over to the girl. Amelia smiled up at me, mouth closed, as I approached. Angel shrank back against the wall. I squatted next to Amelia, not crazy about putting my knees on the dirty ground, and offered Angel what I hoped was a reassuring smile.

"Hey there, Angel. I heard you've had a pretty bad day."

"And you're supposed to make it all better?" she asked, defensive. She studied me a moment before looking at Amelia.

"I told her that you might be able to offer her a way out of this mess," the psychic told me before looking at Angel sternly. "Of course, she has to trust you and give this arrangement a chance. She can't be helped unless she allows it."

"You keep saying arrangement. That sounds weird." Angel narrowed her eyes at me. "Are you one of those weirdos who likes young girls?"

I felt my eyebrows shoot up into my hairline. "No, nothing at all like that. I'm someone who has been where you are."

She frowned, her eyes narrowing more. "You don't look like someone who's spent a single night on the street. I bet you've never done a drug, and look down on those who do. I'm not a charity case."

"No, you're not, but you need help. You're right that I haven't ever spent a night on the street and I've never done a drug. I have been sexually assaulted, and I did have to kill the man who hit me and tried to rape me."

Her eyes widened at this. "You didn't go to prison?"

"No. Someone helped me cover it up. We'd like to help you cover this up. That man got what he deserved and you shouldn't be punished for protecting yourself."

She glanced over at the dumpster before returning her gaze to me. "What's the arrangement? You want something from "

I nodded. "You said yourself you're not a charity case. I'm not offering you charity. I'm offering you a job. It comes with room and board, as well as protection. Officer Grissom told me a little about you. I know you need a place to stay, a place where no one can hurt you physically or persuade you to go back to old habits."

"And what is this job I have to do in order to get all that?"

"I have special dietary needs, and could use some help with that," I explained, figuring that sounded better than just telling her I wanted to drink her freaking blood. I glanced over at Grissom and saw him shuffling impatiently from foot to foot where he stood with Daniel and Ginger. I could imagine how anxious he was to stage the dog attack before the victim's body got too disgusting. "Tell you what, why don't you come with me and my associates so the officers can take care of things here? We can discuss the job over a nice birthday cake away from the scene of the crime, and you can get cleaned up."

She looked down at herself, her nose wrinkling as she stared at the blood. "Is there a uniform for this job?"

"No, but I have clothes you can wear after cleaning up. So, do you want to come along with us?"

"Yeah, you had me at birthday cake, but the clothes would be nice too."

I stood and waited for her to get up, then led her over to the group. Angel split off to thank Grissom and say goodbye.

Daniel raised his eyebrows as I walked over to him. "She agreed?"

"I haven't told her what I am yet, or what I want from her. I'm going to get her a birthday cake, let her clean up and get comfortable in new clothes first. We have to get her out of here so Grissom and Amelia can make sure she doesn't go down for this bastard's death."

"Do you think it's wise taking her back to The Midnight Rider before she knows? If she freaks out after finding out, she could reveal who you and Rider are. You know he can't allow that."

"I'm taking her back to my apartment. If she freaks out, she won't know anything about Rider, and I'll just deal with whatever happens myself."

"Not by yourself. I'm coming with you and not leaving your side."

"You just want to go to my apartment to see the Jug-Jolter."

He smiled. "Yeah, there's that."

# TEN

We dropped Ginger off at the grocery store to grab a birthday cake and continued on to my apartment. After the initial search of my apartment following the incident at Shana's reception, Rider's staff had reported no other visitors, and they had been relieved of duty after I'd made contact with my mother and assured her we were safe. I didn't see any of his people patrolling the street outside my building and the hall corner outside my door, usually occupied by a vampire wrapped in shadow, was vacant.

"Shit. I didn't bring my keys," I told Daniel as we neared my door.

Daniel stepped back, allowing Angel to pass him, then disappeared in a myriad of colors once he was out of her line of sight. A second later, he was back. "I think you left it unlocked," he said, and winked at me.

I turned the knob and the door easily swung open. It was handy having a shifter around, although I now realized a locked door would never keep Daniel out if I decided I didn't want to see him.

"Geez. I can count on you not to pop in on me in the bathroom, can't I?" I whispered as I stepped aside and allowed Angel entrance.

"If I want to see you naked, it won't be on a toilet," he whispered back. "I'm not a pervert."

"I was thinking more of in the shower."

"No worries. I never join a lady in the shower unless I'm invited. I do have a moral code, you know." He stepped over toward the coffee table where my mail had been placed by Rider's staff while they'd been guarding my apartment and plopped down on the couch to go through it, looking at the packages containing breast enhancement pills that had been ordered by my mother and sister, and of course the Jug-Jolter 2000 my grandmother purchased as an early Christmas gift because she felt it very necessary I have it as soon as possible.

Angel stopped in the middle of the living room, looking around. I looked around too, trying to see it through her eyes and tell what she thought. My apartment was a basic one-bedroom. The front door opened directly into the living room. I had a comfortable pale blue couch with matching armchairs. My coffee table was basic wood, as was the TV stand which supported my nineteen-inch flat-screen television. A small desk and a set of bookshelves lined the back wall and a combination of white blinds and pale blue curtains blocked out the view of the building next door and the narrow strip of parking lot between the two. A side table lined the left wall, and I was relieved to see whoever had been tasked with keeping an eye on my apartment the past several weeks had watered my plants. I'd decorated with cheap but pretty art I'd found here and there, and overall it wasn't too bad. My open kitchen with breakfast bar was to the right after you walked in, and was nothing to brag about, but it was clean and served its purpose. I had added a small round dining table with matching wooden chairs just outside the kitchen to add more seating for dinner parties, but had never thrown one.

My bedroom was off the left of the living room. A large closet was to the right of the entry door, a dresser and a mirror to the left. My queen-sized bed with floral sheets took up most of the room, and the small desk in front of my bedroom window was where I generally worked on my laptop. The laptop was at Rider's now. I only had one bathroom, a small boring all-white room with a bathtub with shower. It wasn't much, but it was nice and homey, and I imagined Angel would love it after being on the street. I missed it a bit myself after spending so much time in Rider's one-room apartment over the bar.

"I think you're about my size, so if you'd like, we can pick out some clothes and let you get cleaned up. Ginger should be here soon with your birthday cake."

She looked back at me and nodded. I showed her to my room and pointed out where I kept what, clothes-wise. "You're in luck. I went on a little shopping spree with my family not that long ago and I still have underwear that hasn't been worn. I imagine you're chestier than me, most are, but I have some sports bras that should work for you until we get you some clothes of your own."

"If I take the job."

"Right." I guided her to the bathroom and showed her where everything was. "I have alcohol, peroxide, and bandages, everything you need to clean up your scrapes. I have deodorant and spare toothbrushes still sealed in their packaging in that little drawer in the space saver there. I'll be in the living room when you're done."

"With the guy with the hair?"

I noticed the hint of fear in her eyes and offered her a reassuring smile. "Daniel's a good guy. You don't have to worry about him. In fact, if anyone tries to harm you, *they'll* have to worry about him. You're safe here."

She seemed to think about that as she looked at me, but said nothing. After a moment, she looked down at the T-shirt, leggings, and underclothes she'd chosen, held them tighter to her chest and entered the bathroom, closing the door behind her, the longing for cleanliness putting any lingering fear on the back-burner.

135

I reentered the living room to find Daniel playing with a gadget that looked like a breast pump but emitted an electrical pulse. He'd plugged it into the wall and set it on the side table, and was poking the inside of the cup with a piece of one of my plants, chuckling as it spat out sparks.

"You know, it's against federal law to open someone else's mail."

"Yeah, but you like me too much to put me in the slammer, and I wouldn't stay there anyway," he said, continuing to play with the Jug-Jolter 2000 he'd unpackaged. "This thing is ridiculous."

"You're putting a lot of faith in me liking you." I watched him zap the strip of leaf and chuckle, and shook my head. "Especially considering what you're doing to my Chinese evergreen."

"It's just a leaf, and it was dead already."

"I'm pretty sure it wasn't."

"Well, I'm pretty sure it is now." He lifted it up, and we watched it smoke. "Your grandmother really wanted you to use this thing on your breasts? Did she find out you were shipping her off to the nursing home or something?"

"She thought she was doing me a favor, correcting a hideous deformity," I said as I crossed the room to enter the kitchen.

"You're not deformed, damn it. Not physically, anyway."

I opened the refrigerator door, paused, and turned toward him. "What other deformed is there? Just what are you saying?"

"I'm saying you frustrate the hell out of me with all your negative body talk. Sometimes you make me want to grab you by the shoulders and rattle you until all the bullshit your family has told you about yourself leaks out your ears."

"Geez. Sorry I'm so annoying." I turned back to the fridge and grabbed the remaining bags of blood I'd left in it before I'd started spending my days and nights at

Rider's, and tossed them into the garbage.

"Vamp-proofing?" Daniel asked as he moved back over to the couch and sat.

"I guess. Those expired two days ago anyway. I'll have to get delivery set back up again if I'm going to stay here."

Daniel's eyebrows shot up into his multi-colored hairline. "You're going to stay here again?"

"Maybe." I finished discarding everything that had gone bad in my fridge and looked around the apartment. "I miss it. I miss doing what I want when I want, and I miss sitting on a couch to veg out in front of a TV. I actually miss having a job to go to. Now that the Quimbys have been dealt with and the soul stitch attachment linking me to Selander Ryan has been taken care of, maybe I can start posting for work again."

"It hasn't been that long since Seta reassigned the attachment to me," Daniel reminded me. "We can't be sure it matters that much yet. That Gina woman was just sent to the bar today. You know Selander Ryan is still out there somewhere, and he's not just going to forget about you because you bested him on the attachment thing. If anything, he's more pissed off than ever. You also have to remember the Bloom. You don't want to be in some office building working when you cycle through that again. Of course, it might make you very popular with the male employees."

"Funny," I snapped as I plodded over to the couch and sank down into the soft cushions. "Did you happen to notice if there were bills here while you were meddling through my mail?"

"I wasn't looking for bills," he said, eying me warily. "I'm sorry, Danni. I was just trying to make light of a pretty screwed up situation. I guess it's still too soon for jokes."

"It'll always be too soon for jokes as long as my life is held hostage by this stupid Bloom thing. It wouldn't be so bad if my body just wanted sex during it, but it wants nonstop sex. It lasted two weeks the first time, and I could have killed Rider."

"I know." He squeezed my shoulder. "Rider's using all his resources to find a way to help you. Nannette's been working nonstop on figuring you out, and I told you earlier that you shouldn't be worried about Seta. Her whole reason for being at the bar tonight was to help Rider with you."

"You heard her when I said she could have popped in on him naked. She said she's seen it all before, the smug bitch."

"You know, she could have meant she's seen a ton of naked people. I'm sure she's lived long enough to."

I rolled my eyes in his direction.

"Fine. What if she did mean Rider specifically? The dude is old. He's gotten around, but clearly he didn't care about anyone enough to keep them around. I haven't heard of him assigning security teams to any other women."

"There have been two men on my sister's door since she was turned."

"That's totally different." He sighed in exasperation. "Sometimes you're a real pain in the ass."

I stuck my tongue out at him. "Then why don't you ask for reassignment?"

"Because you're a cute pain in the ass. I like you despite your annoying tendencies, and it's fun watching you when you get mad and beat the shit out of people." He looked over at the Jug-Jolter 2000. "Besides, who else is going to have a titty-shocker I can play with?"

"Why don't you play with it on yourself?" I teased.

"Nah, all my body parts are more than sufficient in size."

I felt heat rise in my face and knew I was red when he looked at me and chuckled.

"You're a pain in the ass too."

"Yeah, I get that a lot."

Before I could respond, my front door banged open and six men dressed in all black rushed in, guns drawn. Daniel sprang from the couch and took a flying leap at the group, arms spread wide. He clotheslined two of them before his feet hit the floor and he immediately grabbed a third man.

Realizing these were not Rider's men, and we were under attack, I jumped over the back of the couch, using it as a barrier as I took a moment to assess the situation. So far no one had shot at us, two were on the floor groaning as they struggled to get back up, and Daniel was busy fighting three others at once. That left one burly guy for me, and he quickly realized I was the easier target.

"Where is she?" he asked as he moved toward me, the couch not going to be a deterrent.

"Who?" I asked, wondering who the hell the men were and why they'd come in armed to drag Angel away. Two were black men, the other four were white, none of them remotely favored Angel, who was Latina, so I didn't think they were any of the cousins Grissom had mentioned, but I knew it was still possible.

"Your sister! Where are you hiding her?"

"Shana?" Realization dawned on me. "Kevin sent you here *armed* to get my sister back?"

"Where is she?" the man repeated himself as he closed the distance and reached out to grab me, which really pissed me off.

I grabbed the man's beefy arm and spun with him, releasing him as we turned full circle. He fell back over the couch, banging his head on the coffee table as his ass hit the floor. He had a military style buzz cut, which made it easy to see the gash in the back of his head, but the new wound didn't stop him. He shook his head, took a beat to reorient himself, and stood. His dark gaze burned through me as he clenched his jaw tight and raised his hand to check the back of his head. When his fingers came away bloody, he growled a curse and advanced toward me again.

"Mr. White said we were to be very careful with his wife. He didn't say shit about you, bitch. You'll pay for that."

The two men Daniel had clotheslined were back on their feet, helping the three others trying to take Daniel down, Ginger still hadn't returned from the grocery store, and an innocent girl was in my bathroom. A girl I wanted to feel safe. I needed to get the men out of my apartment.

Reading the intention in the pissed off burly man's eyes, I positioned myself in front of the window and reached back to unlock it. The man leaped at me and I used my vampiric speed to raise the pane just in time for him to go sailing through it, taking the blinds I hadn't had time to draw all the way up with him. There was a panicked scream that sounded unnaturally high coming from the hefty guy, followed by a thud.

"Shit," a dark-skinned man said, staring at the open window. He split apart from the group still ganging up on Daniel and rushed me.

Acting on reflex, I braced myself and once he was within my grasp, I grabbed him by the collar of his shirt and the buckle of his belt, and lifted him over my head before tossing him out the window to join his friend.

Four men were still fighting Daniel. He was doing pretty well with the uneven odds, doling out a lot more damage than he was receiving, but it was taking him too long to get the men out of my home, especially considering there was a chance the two I'd thrown out the window would be back. I lived on the second floor. The worst damage they'd probably get would be a broken arm. If I was lucky, a leg.

I waded in to the battle, grabbing a light-skinned black man by his shoulders. I dug my nails into his skin and yanked him away from the group. He elbowed me in my stomach, spun and hit me directly in the face with his meaty fist. My head snapped back, pain screamed through my skull and I was blinded by bright stars dancing before my eyes. I didn't know if I flew through the air or stumbled back, but my back hit a wall. I shook my head to clear out the Fourth of July spectacular happening inside of it just in time to see the asshole running toward me, head down, no doubt about to ram me into the next three apartments over. I'd done pretty well fighting after being turned into a vampire-succubus hybrid. I'd beaten the big guy at the bar pretty easily, snapped my jackass former boss's neck without a ton of effort, and knocked trees down with a wolf I'd swung over my head as if she were nothing more than a towel, but this muscle-bound human had punched me dead in my face and I was scared of what he'd do next. My confidence suffering, I didn't trust my own hands. I grabbed the closest thing to me and rammed it into his face, gasping in shock as the man started convulsing, electricity dancing over his skin. I'd grabbed the Jug-Jolter 2000.

"What the hell's going on?"

I looked over to see Ginger standing in the front doorway with a cake box in hand. Daniel had a man in the air. He brought the guy down over his knee, snapping his back before dropping him to the floor next to the two other bodies he'd beaten the crap out of. I tried to pull the Jug-Jolter 2000 off the guy's face, but it was suctioned on for dear life, covering his nose and mouth, and the button on the side didn't seem to do a thing.

Daniel moved over and yanked the plug out of the wall, and the shower of sparks died out. The man's body fell back onto the floor and continued convulsing for about thirty seconds before it went still, the Jug-Jolter still suctioned on.

"You titty-shocked him?" Daniel asked, fighting a smile. He looked at me and the almost smile fled. "Shit."

"What?" I asked, still staring down at the man in shocked horror.

"You're bleeding."

I licked my painfully swollen, cut lip, healing the damage my saliva could reach, and looked at him. "Yeah, your lip is busted too, and you have a cut over your eyebrow."

He disappeared in a beautiful display of sparkling colors and reemerged flawless.

"Why the hell didn't you do that when they were all ganging up on you? You could have beaten the shit out of them in half the time."

"Yeah, but if they saw me do that, I'd have to kill them to keep my existence a secret. I figure we need to ask some questions and figure out why they were sent here to attack."

"They were sent to retrieve my sister, or at least that's what the one guy said before he took a dive out my window. We need to get them out of here and make it look like nothing happened before Angel finishes her shower. I want her to feel safe."

"We can't hide it from her," Daniel said as we heard the bathroom door open. "You're starting to develop a pretty bad black eye and that's not going to go away with saliva. You'll have to heal that with sleep."

"Fuck," I muttered as I heard Angel softly walking across my bedroom floor. "Just get them out."

Ginger had set the cake box on my dining table. She quickly rushed over, grabbed two of the men by their collars, and pulled them into the hallway in a flash of vampiric speed. Daniel picked another up and effortlessly flung him out into the hallway.

Angel appeared in the doorway to the living area and gawked. The man I'd electrocuted was still lying on the floor with the titty torture device stuck to his face, my window was open, the blinds gone, and the floor was littered with mail and everything else that had gotten knocked off of tables, including my phone. Her eyes grew round as she looked at me, taking in the damage to my face. "What happened?"

I sighed. So much for convincing her my apartment was a safe haven.

"We had a bit of a security breach," Ginger said as she stepped back into the apartment and closed the door behind her. "We quickly got it under control though, and hey, I got your birthday cake!"

Angel stared down at the guy on the floor and folded her arms, not so easily swayed by birthday cake when there was an unconscious man with a breast enhancement device stuck to his face in front of her. I guess everyone had their priorities. Personally, I would have run straight to the cake and lost myself in its moist, flavorful goodness, but I was also a newly turned vampire who couldn't eat a lot of things without getting sick. I'd kill to be able to eat a slice of that cake and not spend the rest of the night in the bathroom.

Daniel walked over to the guy, placed his foot on the man's chest and yanked the Jug-Jolter 2000 off. It released with a sickening plop, leaving the man's face much puffier than I remembered it being when I'd watched in terror as he'd barreled toward me.

"If he sprouts a titty on his face, I'm going to be turned off titties for life," Daniel said.

"It might be an improvement," Ginger said, moving over to get a better look at the guy. "A big titty will take the attention away from those scorch marks, and the fact his eyebrows look like two fried caterpillars. They're still smoking a little. I thought you said you were an ass man anyway."

"Just because titties aren't my favorite part doesn't mean I don't enjoy them."

"The next person who says titty is getting thrown out the window," I snapped as I ran my hands through my hair. *Shit.* I turned toward Angel. "I know this looks bad, but you really are safe here. We just didn't have our full security available because I haven't used this apartment for a while and we didn't have any reason to think someone would be watching it."

Angel looked around the room, taking in the aftermath,

and frowned as she looked at my face again. "There's three of you and this one guy managed to get to you?"

"There were six," I corrected her, realizing she now thought the three of us were incapable of handling just one guy and would never feel safe if she believed that. "And Ginger just got here right before you left the bathroom. Two men left via the window and we dragged the others out the front door."

"What did they want?" she asked.

"My sister. She got married but ran off during the reception and her husband apparently had someone watching my apartment. When we showed up, he sent in the goons."

"Families are crazy," she said, and stepped over the man to walk over to the table to look at the cake. "This is pretty. I haven't actually had a birthday cake since my mom left when I was little."

"I'll get plates and forks," Ginger said, moving across the room to root through my kitchen cabinets for what she needed.

"Well, she doesn't seem too bothered by this," Daniel said softly.

"It's the cake," I said. "Cake has a way of making every thought in your head disappear."

"I know how much you love cake," he said, grinning, referring to the one time since being turned that I'd been able to enjoy eating a cupcake thanks to a spell Rider's friend, Rihanna, had cast. Unfortunately, it was a temporary spell, so I'd only gotten to enjoy the one cupcake, but according to Daniel and Rider, I'd been almost pornographic with my enthusiastic enjoyment of the chocolate treat. "But it's not going to make this guy disappear. Do you want me to dispose of him or interrogate him?"

"I already know Kevin sent them to retrieve my sister. They were looking for her. Kevin's just a regular human guy, but with money. These men were just hired thugs."

"So get rid of him?"

"Yeah."

Daniel walked over to the window, stuck his head out, and looked down. "Looks like the ones you threw out the window are getting loaded into the back of a flatbed truck," he said before turning and lifting the guy in a fireman's carry.

"Technically, I only threw one out the window," I corrected him. "I just outsmarted the other. So nobody died?"

"I don't think so. I can feel this one's heartbeat going crazy. Must have juiced it up." He walked over to the window and dumped the guy out of it. "And tell your friends!" he yelled down to the men in the lot, making sure to give them the finger before stepping back and lowering the window pane.

I looked over to see Angel gawking at us. Ginger fought a smile as she cut cake and put it on plates.

"He'll be all right," I said. "His friends were down there to collect him."

"If we're going to hang here for a while, I'll see what's on TV," Daniel said, scooping the remote off the floor before sitting on the couch and powering on the television. "You might want to check in with that Kevin twerp to let him know we intend to break any more rent-a-thugs he sends over here."

"Yeah, as soon as I get this room cleaned up," I said, glaring at him.

He smirked. "I'd help clean, but I don't know how you like things. Besides, I fought more of them all at once. I earned a break."

"You can be such a jackass," I muttered as I picked my mail off the floor and tossed it back onto the coffee table.

"Yeah, but I'm good-looking, so most women let me slide."

"I'm not like most women."

"No shit."

I rolled my eyes and continued picking things up, straightening furniture that had gotten moved during the fight, as he flipped through channels.

"Oooh, I love *Underworld*!" Angel said as she carried her cake over to the couch. "Can we watch that? I haven't seen it in forever."

Ginger shared a smile with me as she helped me finish picking up. "A vampire fan?" she asked.

"Yeah. Vampires are cool," Angel said, eyes glued to the movie.

"I thought most girls your age liked that *Twilight* shit," Daniel said.

"Vampires that sparkle are pussies," she said around a mouthful of cake. "Everybody knows real vampires are dark and brooding, and vicious. Vampires kick ass."

"And apparently electrocute guys with boobie plumpers," Ginger whispered before walking back over to the dining table. She grabbed two plates of cake and handed one to Daniel before she settled into one of my armchairs to watch the movie.

I'd left my cell phone charging on Rider's nightstand, so I picked up the cordless handset of my landline and dialed Rider's office number as I walked to the bathroom.

"Danni?" he asked, picking up. "Why are you at your apartment and why are you calling me? You could just use our link."

"I'm still a little weirded out doing that sometimes," I explained. "I'm at my apartment because I needed to get Angel off the street and I thought this was a better place to bring her than your crowded bar." I'd reached the bathroom and let out a tiny squeal of anguish as I took in my reflection in the mirror over the sink.

"What? What's wrong?"

"Nothing," I said, gingerly touching my cheekbone. I'd healed my split lip with saliva, and thanks to my healing saliva there hadn't been any chance of an injury to the inside of my mouth, but I had one mother of a black eye forming and a bruise starting to color the left side of my face. "I need you to get Kevin's number from Shana."

"Who's Kevin?"

"Her husband," I reminded him.

"Why do you need his number?"

I sighed. "There was an incident. He had someone watching my apartment and sent men in after we arrived. We beat the hell out of them and sent them packing, and I'd like to call him and let him know how very stupid it would be for him to send more in case he gets the idea to."

Rider was silent for several beats. I didn't know whether he was using that time to telepathically get Kevin's number from Shana or if he was composing himself. I figured it was probably a little of both.

He gave me a phone number, and I ran over to my desk to write it down. "How many men?"

"Six."

"Are you all right? And I'll be seeing you later when you come for your session with Nannette, so don't lie to me."

"One of the men hit me. I have a black eye and a bruise forming, but it'll all heal when I sleep."

More silence. This time I knew for sure he was trying to compose himself. "Where the hell was Daniel? And Ginger?"

"Ginger was getting a birthday cake. Daniel had three guys on him when this guy hit me, and he couldn't shift shape because he didn't know if we'd need to question and release them. If he revealed what he was, we'd have to kill them. We have Angel here, so we didn't want to kill a bunch of men or use our paranormal abilities. She doesn't know what I am yet."

"Why the hell was Ginger getting a birthday cake, and are you telling me you've brought this girl to your apartment without confirming she's willing to be your donor?"

"Relax, it's not like I brought her to *your* apartment," I

snapped. "I'm not an idiot. I'm sure Grissom told you the deal with her. I needed to get her away from that crime scene so he could take care of things for her, and we're fine. I didn't even have to bite anyone. I zapped the guy with the Jug-Jolter 2000. There's a slight chance he might sprout a boob on his face, but other than that, we didn't give those men any reason to think anything weird about us. Angel's watching a vampire movie right now and she thinks Edward is a pussy and *Underworld* rocks so I think she'll be fine when I tell her I'm a vampire, especially once she's in a birthday cake coma. Everything is under control."

There was another stretch of silence before he spoke. "I don't know where to even begin with whatever the hell that was you just told me. *I'm* contacting your sister's husband and putting the fear of me in him, and I'm assigning a detail on your apartment again. Don't miss your session with Nannette and try to stay out of trouble."

"I always do."

"Yeah, well, try harder than you normally do. You're giving me an ulcer."

"I'm pretty sure vampires can't get ulcers."

"I was pretty sure about that too until I fell in love with you." And he disconnected.

I pushed the End button on the phone and walked into the living room to return it to its base, then sank down into the armchair not currently occupied just in time to see the end credits roll on *Underworld*.

"The second movie's about to come on," Angel announced, smiling, her eyes a little glazed from the huge chunk of cake she'd devoured. "It's a whole marathon."

"So," I said, "you really like vampires, huh?"

She nodded.

"You don't think they're monsters?"

"Depends on the writers," she answered. "Hey, why aren't you eating any cake?"

"Those dietary restrictions I told you about. It'll be a

while before I build up the ability to eat sugary things like cake without getting sick."

"That sucks," she said, frowning sympathetically.

"Yeah, it does suck. So what if vampires were real? Do you think they'd be monsters?"

"That's a weird question," she said. "But I think they'd be really cool. Why?"

"Because I'm a vampire."

# ELEVEN

Angel stared at me, barely blinking, before slowly turning her head to look at Daniel and Ginger, who were watching us instead of the television. She set her now empty plate on the coffee table and looked at me again. "Is this like a joke, or …?"

"No joke," I said, careful to keep my tone very even, my voice perfectly calm. "I told you I have special dietary needs. You can probably figure out what and why now. We're real, but we're not monsters."

She remained silent, staring at me, focusing on the left side of my face. She grinned. "Funny. I'm pretty sure a vampire wouldn't be getting a black eye and would have drank that guy who attacked you earlier instead of attacking him with whatever that thing was that was stuck to his face."

The second *Underworld* movie came on, snagging Angel's attention. I looked at Daniel and Ginger. They both shrugged their shoulders and watched along with her. I couldn't get into it. My face was starting to throb and I felt the pangs of hunger in my belly. My eyelids grew heavier. My body knew what it needed to repair itself.

"You have anything in the fridge?" Ginger asked.

I slowly turned my aching head side to side, knowing she was referring to bagged blood. She walked over and sat on the edge of the coffee table.

"You want her to know, so this shouldn't matter now," she said, holding her wrist out to me. "You need a drink and a little nap. I can see it in your eyes that the adrenaline rush has gone and you're really feeling that big meathead's punch."

I looked over at Daniel and could see the deep concern and a hefty dose of guilt in his eyes. "It wasn't your fault that guy got a punch in."

"I failed, but believe me, if I see him again, he's a dead man."

Angel glanced between us, eyes a little wide. "You kill people."

"Everyone in this room has killed someone, you included," Ginger told her, "but only when necessary to protect ourselves or others." She shook her wrist in front of me. "Come on, Danni. You need this. If she freaks out, we'll handle it."

My stomach growled, the offering too tempting to refuse even if it was coming from a woman, which my succubus side did not like. Both my succubus and vampire side agreed I needed any blood available to repair the damage inflicted from the fight, and even though Daniel was steadily growing more appetizing to me, I knew better than to go there without a venom check first. Whether or not I had venom didn't matter when drinking from women.

"In the room," I said, and stood. I led Ginger into my bedroom before grabbing her wrist and sinking my fangs into her flesh, greedily lapping enough blood to take the edge off the throbbing pain that had started creeping over to the right side of my face despite there not being any bruising there.

"I thought you wanted her to know you were a vampire," Ginger said as I drank. "You could have done this in there and she would have had no choice but to believe."

I finished drinking and pulled back. "I don't want to freak the kid out. She's had a shitty day."

"So, what are you going to do with her?"

I shrugged as I moved over to the bed and rested on top of it, shoes and all. "If I manage to actually fall asleep and don't wake up in time to head back over to the bar for my session with Nannette, contact Rider and have him pull me out of sleep. I imagine he can do that from a distance."

"Your body knows what it needs. You'll fall asleep."

"I don't know. I'm always pretty wired this time of—"

I opened my eyes to the sound of gunfire coming from the living room. Fortunately, it was only coming from the television. I sat up, swung my legs over the edge of the bed, and stood. The pain in my face was gone, and my reflection in the mirror over my dresser was bruise-free.

Two heads turned my way as I entered the living room. Angel was engrossed in the final scene of her movie.

"I told you she'd wake on her own," Ginger said.

"So you did." Daniel smiled at me. "Looking good, Rocky. Now you get to go fight Nannette."

That statement snatched Angel's attention as the end credits started rolling. "Who's Nannette, and why do you have to fight her?" she asked, turning her head toward me as I sat in the armchair I'd occupied earlier. Her eyes narrowed as she studied me. "You do makeup really good."

"Thanks," I said, "but I'm not wearing any. The lip gloss I started my night off with is long gone and I didn't bother with anything else. Nannette's one of my … trainers."

"You used something to cover that bruising," Angel said, studying me harder. "What kind of trainer? Like at a gym?"

"Something like that," I said, contemplating trying the vampire explanation again, but Daniel was pointing at his watch, and I really didn't want to make Nannette wait for me. She had enough of an attitude with me without giving her any fuel. I closed my eyes and widened my senses, a trick I hardly used, mostly because I didn't think of it and Eliza was still teaching me how to do it well. I sensed a vampire in the hall. "Rider's security detail is here."

"Yeah, they got here about ten minutes after you fell asleep," Ginger said. "It's the regular setup. One in the hall, two on the street. I checked in with them and they know you have company, so they'll stick around after we leave to make sure Angel is safe, but Rider sent a representative to speak with your sister's husband. He won't be sending anyone else here to speak with you."

I raised my eyebrows, but didn't say anything. I doubted Rider had done anything to bring negative attention to himself or his company, but it wasn't beyond the realm of possibility that he had. He had a temper.

"You're all leaving?" Angel asked, a hint of fear in her voice.

"We're Danni's security detail, so we go where she goes," Daniel explained. "There's a man out in the hall who will make sure no one gets past that front door except us. Grissom is covering for you for what happened earlier tonight, so you shouldn't expect anyone to come looking for you. No one knows you're here except the people protecting you."

"Who *are* you people?"

Daniel, Ginger, and I shared a smile as we stood. *Rise of the Lycans* popped on the TV screen and I saw there was still about a fourth of the birthday cake left in the bakery box.

"You have your marathon and cake," I told her. "Make yourself at home. You can have whatever you find in the kitchen, and sleep in my bed when you tucker out. Just, please, don't leave. I don't have to tell you how dangerous the streets are, and there's no need for you to be out there when you are more than welcome here."

"You still haven't told me what I have to do to stay here."

"We'll get to that later," I said as I walked over to the desk and jotted my cell phone number on a notepad. "I have some stuff I need to take care of right now. If I don't make it back tonight, I'll be here tomorrow night. We'll talk more then. If you should need anything, I've left my number, but I usually sleep through most of the day and might not answer right away."

Daniel had scooped up his keys and moved to the front door. He stared back at me. "We really have to go, Danni."

"I know." I joined him and Ginger by the door as he opened it.

"When you get back, you can show me how you did your makeup," Angel called after me.

I looked back to see her eying me with suspicion, and knew she was thinking over everything she'd seen and heard since meeting us, and remembering what I'd told her. "Sure," I said, smiling as we stepped out of the door, Daniel closing it behind us.

I looked over in the corner, peered through the shadows to see the vampire stationed there. It was Carlos, the same one who'd initially been assigned to watch my door after I'd first been turned. I'd never even known he was there until Rider taught me how to look through the shadow and find him.

"She's a nice girl," I told him. "Make sure she stays safe."

Carlos nodded at me. "Yes, ma'am."

"Rider's going to be upset you left the girl in your apartment and don't even know if she's going to be your donor or not," Daniel said as we moved down the hall and started down the stairs.

"I think she'll agree," I told him. "She's acting like she doesn't believe I'm a vampire, but I see the suspicion in her eyes. It's a hard thing to believe. We don't come from a world of magic like you did. She'll come around."

"She does enjoy those vampire movies," Ginger said.

"There's a big difference between liking vampires on screen and offering to be one's blood supply in real life," Daniel said.

"Yeah, but I'm offering her a safe place to sleep. That goes a long way."

"Don't forget the cake," Ginger reminded me.

Daniel opened the truck door and grinned down at me.

"Make one remark about me and that damn cupcake," I said as I slid onto the seat, "and I'll punch you right in the balls."

"There you go, obsessing about my balls again."


It was late, but The Midnight Rider stayed open until four in the morning, so it was lively when we entered through the front door. It was almost one in the morning, so there was still a good amount of humans hanging out with the shifters and vampires they mostly had no idea were in their midst. Music blared from the jukebox, a few couples danced on the floor, and the alcohol was flowing. The three of us walked through the bar and headed straight to Rider's office.

He was sitting at his desk when we entered, focused on his computer screen as his long fingers tapped away at the keyboard. He glanced at us, quickly finished what he was doing, and sat back, steepling his fingers in front of him as he studied me. "You drank?"

"From Ginger. The blood left in my fridge was old. I was able to sleep a little too, long enough to repair the damage done, which you knew I'd be able to do."

Rider grinned. "Which you should have known too."

"You took advantage of my flustered state and tricked me into telling you about my black eye and bruising, knowing I could have repaired the damage before you had a chance to see me. Did you think I'd lie about it?"

"You hesitated when I asked."

"Well, you tend to be overprotective."

"Yeah, and it's a damn good thing too." He cut his eyes toward Daniel. "How did she get banged up on your watch?"

"It's not his fault," I said.

"I didn't ask you," Rider said, his eyes dark. "I asked him."

"I wasn't using all of my abilities because of the circumstances," Daniel said. "I didn't know who the men were, but I could tell they were human and we had a young human girl with us. In the moment, I thought it best not to risk revealing we were more than human."

"And Danni got hurt."

Daniel nodded but still stood tall, shoulders straight, his hands clasped behind his back. "I failed. I have no excuse, but it's a mistake I don't intend to make again."

"Oh, for crying out loud, I'm a paranormal super-freak too," I said. "I fight. Nannette even told you to let me fight. It's not like I was shot or stabbed or anything."

Rider directed another dark look my way, and I promptly shut the hell up. "And you were off getting a cake?" he said to Ginger. "In what part of your job description does it say for you to be shopping for cake while your partner and your assignment are under attack?"

"In all fairness, I wasn't really given like a written description of my job," Ginger said, "and I didn't actually know they were under attack."

"I asked her to get the cake."

"Well, you're not her boss, are you?" Rider picked up a pen and tapped it on his desk as he held me in his sights with a hard glare. After an uncomfortable silence that felt very much like standing in the principal's office with my friends, Rider let out a disgusted sigh, tossed the pen down, and pointed to the door. "Ginger, you're done for the night. Daniel, Rome's waiting for you out back for a special assignment, and Danni ... I'll deal with you myself."

*Relax, if he punishes you, it'll probably just be a sexual thing,* Ginger told me through our telepathic link.

*Thanks so much for putting that image in my head,* Daniel shot back using the same link.

They continued grumbling at each other telepathically as they made their way out the door and I clamped my teeth down on the inside of my cheek to keep from laughing and giving our private conversation away.

"I don't know what they said, but I see you found it funny. For their sake, I hope they weren't disrespectful to me."

I blew out a sigh, my endeavor to keep the silent communication a secret from Rider an utter failure. "They're never disrespectful toward you, and they didn't do anything wrong. I was never in any real danger."

"You were hurt."

"And now I'm all better."

"You're kind of sassy, you know that?"

"If you don't like it, you can bite my ass."

Rider smiled.

"I didn't mean that literally."

"That's a shame." He stood and moved around the desk. "It's awfully tempting."

"Well, too bad. I'm off the menu for you." I folded my arms and gave him my best miffed face.

He stopped in front of me, planted his hands on his hips and gave his head a slight shake. "What the hell did I do now?"

"Seta."

"I didn't do Seta."

I rolled my eyes. "Maybe not in this decade, but she clearly has intimate knowledge of you."

Rider's brow creased. Either he was thinking hard or had a headache. I often got this reaction from him. "And you came to this conclusion, how?"

"I pointed out how rude it is to pop into people's bedrooms and advised people could be naked. She said she's seen it all before. Interesting."

"You pointed out her *rudeness*? I've told you before, Seta is not the grizzly you want to poke with a stick. Clearly, she didn't take what you said offensively because we're still standing here talking about this. You're damned lucky." He pinched the bridge of his nose and muttered a curse. "You're giving me angina. I'm going to be the only vampire in history to die of a stress-related heart condition."

"You didn't say anything about her comment. No surprise that she's seen it all? So you and her were—"

"Danni, think back to the first time you ever saw Seta. When was that?"

"During the Bloom."

"Where was I when she first popped into my room?"

I recalled the moment Seta and her witch partner first appeared and felt heat flood my face. "Oh."

"Where was I?"

"On the floor."

"And what was I wearing?"

"Nothing," I muttered.

"Well, there you go. She's seen everything. It's not a big deal."

"Really? What if Daniel saw me naked?"

"I'd kill him, but that's a totally different situation." He kissed my forehead and pulled me close. "Is that all that's bothering you?"

"Mostly."

"What else is it?"

"You mean, besides your brother still being out there somewhere, the Bloom hanging over my head, and all the mess with my sister?"

"Yeah, besides all that little stuff." He grinned. "Come on. You know I'll do whatever it takes to keep you safe. We'll get through the Bloom. That's why Seta was here in the first place. You shouldn't worry about her. You should be glad when you see her here."

"Now you're pushing it."

He chuckled and pressed another kiss against my forehead. "Nannette should be down in the training room waiting for you. Go get that over with and then you can check in with your sister before bedtime."

"I was actually thinking about staying at my apartment."

He frowned down at me, his eyes guarded. "I told you, Seta is nothing to me, just a friend who is helping to find a way to beat the Bloom."

"It's not about Seta." I sighed. "I just miss my apartment."

"You're not happy with me here?"

"I love you. I do…"

"But?"

"But you're a little controlling."

"I'm a lot controlling," he said, releasing me to shove his hands into his pockets. "I have to be. It's how I keep you safe."

"Rider, I really don't want to fight with you."

"Then you should head down to the training room and fight with Nannette." He moved back around the desk and took his seat. "Go on. She's waiting."

"You're mad at me."

"No." He gave his head a little shake. "Go on. Nannette thinks she can help you, so you should get down there to her."

I sighed and moved to the door, turning to look back at Rider before I stepped through. He wasn't mad at me. He was hurt. And it made me feel like crap.

I stepped into the training room to find Nannette in skinny jeans, brown suede ankle boots, and a brown crocheted top with spaghetti straps. Her lips were glossy,

159

her eyes were lined in black, and her ears were decorated with dangling hoops in earth colors. She leaned against the mirrored wall, her arms folded in front of her, ankles crossed.

"I was going to apologize for not being dressed in my normal workout clothes because it would have made me late," I said as I crossed over to her, "but I think mine are more suited for training than yours."

"We're not doing that kind of training tonight," she said, the corner of her mouth slightly curving up.

"I thought you were training me to fight."

"I am." She walked over to the corner of the room and grabbed the two chairs that normally stayed there, then walked over to me and set the chairs on the floor facing each other before dropping onto one. "Sit."

I sat in the remaining chair and looked around. "I don't get it."

"Not all fighting is kicks and punches, or guns and blades," she said. "None of that will help you fight when your biggest enemy is yourself."

"So... what are we doing? Are you going to train me how to talk to the succubus inside me or something?"

She slowly moved her head side to side, her mouth pinched, and her eyes strained with the pressure of wanting to roll but not being allowed to. "You need to be serious, Danni, because I'm not here to play with you. I'm here to give you a very much-needed lesson."

"I honestly don't understand."

She studied me for a moment. "Maybe you don't, but you're going to understand a lot of things when I get done with you. Yes, you're a hybrid and you're connected to Selander Ryan. That's some bad shit, but it's not what's screwing your life up. You are giving way too much power to your enemies and you're hurting yourself and making it that much harder for your loved ones to keep you safe. I'm going to make you a real fighter, Danni, but in order to do that, I'm going to have to rewire you."

I sat still for a moment, just looking at her, then I looked down. I didn't see a bag of tools with her and the training room only held the things it normally held. "I hope that's not as painful as it sounds."

"I suppose it could be painful, but not physically. You've been brainwashed, or conditioned, to hate yourself. I'm going to fix that."

"I don't hate myself," I said, sitting straighter.

"Are you beautiful?"

"What?"

"Are. You. Beautiful?" She stared at me, waiting for an answer.

I felt myself shrink under her appraising eye. I shrugged. "I'm all right."

"Just all right?" She nodded her head, her lips slightly pushed out as she thought about this. "Hmmm… but not beautiful? Like your sister? You think she's the perfect one, right?"

"Society thinks she's the perfect one."

"Oh, it's society that thinks this?" She smiled, seeming to enjoy this idea. "Society includes your mother and grandmother?"

"Society is everyone."

"Society is Rider?"

I looked down and started fidgeting with my hands. Warmth climbed up from my chest to crawl up my neck. I shifted. "What's any of this have to do with anything?"

"Until you learn to truly love yourself, you're going to remain prey to anyone who uses your self-doubt against you. Selander Ryan uses that self-doubt. The succubus part of you uses that self-doubt. *You* use that self-doubt."

"I don't hate myself."

"Maybe, but honey, you sure don't love yourself either. If you did, you'd have a lot more faith in who you are. You'd feel the confidence you should feel. The succubus part of you wouldn't make you obsess about losing Rider, because you'd know you could survive without his love and adoration. If you really loved yourself, you'd know the love of another is just gravy. You have to be your own damn meat and potatoes. Do you understand what I'm saying?"

"I think so," I said, covering my belly as it rumbled, "but can you drop the food references? I haven't been able to eat real food in a while and it's just cruel making me think of it."

She grinned. "Yeah, the whole not being able to eat much after first turning thing sucks, but it'll be over soon enough and it'll be just a tiny blip of time in your very long life."

"If I have a very long life."

"Stick with me and Rider, girl. We'll make sure you do."

"And here I thought you wouldn't care if I died," I said drily.

"I wouldn't be all torn up about it." She shrugged as she leaned back in her seat. "But Rider would be devastated, and that wouldn't be good for the community. I've served horrible masters and I don't intend on ever doing that again, which is why I'm here coaching your sad ass with all this Dr. Feel-Good-About-Yourself crap."

"Right."

She narrowed her eyes as she studied me. "Take your shirt off."

"Excuse me?" I instinctively folded my arms protectively before my chest, prompting her to roll her eyes.

"Girl, please. You're not my type and I can tell you're wearing a sports bra under that T-shirt. Take the shirt off. I have a point, I promise." She stood and gestured for me to do so as well as she walked over to the mirrored wall and stood in front of it. "Come on!" she barked when I remained sitting, "or I will turn this into a physical training."

"Rider would make you pay for that," I muttered as I

stood and walked over to stand at her side.

"He'd probably pay me *for* it if it helped fix you. Take the shirt off. It's just you and me in here and I'm not suddenly going to change my whole orientation and fall in lust with you. Come on. Let's go." She snapped her fingers impatiently.

I grabbed the hem of my shirt and started to lift it, but stilled as I got it halfway up my torso.

"Girl, what are you afraid of?"

"I don't normally prance around in my underwear," I snapped. "Some people are just modest."

"And some of you are just insecure. Take the damn thing off, you chicken."

"I'm not a chicken."

"Prove it." She stared at me as I stood stone-still, except for my trembling fingers. "This is sad as hell."

I growled a curse under my breath and pulled the shirt off, holding it in a tight ball in my hands as I clasped them together and tried to stop shaking.

Nannette grabbed my chin and moved my head, forcing me to look at myself in the mirror. "What do you see?"

"Me," I said.

"Describe yourself, based on only what you see right now."

I rolled my eyes. "This is stupid."

"Just do what I said!"

I huffed out a breath and looked at myself, feeling the heat of indignation crawling up my neck. This was by far the most ridiculous thing I'd ever done. "I'm brunette, kind of short, thin, and I have green eyes."

"Are they nice eyes?"

"I guess." I shrugged. "They're kind of a bright green. I guess they're pretty for green eyes."

"Is there something wrong with green eyes?"

"Most people like blue eyes."

"Do you?"

"I like Rider's, but I like Rider. I've never really gone for a specific eye color."

"So… why can't you just look at your own eyes and think they're pretty without having to add a qualifying statement about the color?"

I thought about that, unsure why I'd done it, and gave a one-shouldered shrug. "I don't know."

"Has anyone ever told you your eyes were pretty?"

I thought back, but couldn't think of anyone. "No."

"Not even Rider?"

"I don't think so."

"Well, men are stupid, so don't look too much into that. What about your parents?"

I shook my head. "My mother has never told me I'm pretty. Not my eyes, my face, definitely not my body. My sister soaked up all the compliments."

"What about your father?"

"He never said anything about my eyes that I can remember," I said as my mouth curved into a smile, and I grew warm from a sweet memory. "He never commented on my looks, but he didn't have to. He always called me his best girl and bragged about me to his friends. Looks weren't important to him."

"But they were important to your mother?"

I nodded my head. "Oh yeah. They still are, and I'm still not good enough. I'll never be Shana, their princess."

"Why is Shana so great?"

"Because she lucked out in the gene pool. Blonde hair, blue eyes, big chest, tiny waist, long legs. She's perfect."

"So if that's perfect, the rest of us are all just filling space with our unattractiveness?"

"No." I frowned. "I didn't say that."

"If you're not blonde with big breasts, you're not beautiful? You're not worthy?"

"I see where you're going, but you wouldn't understand."

"Oh, really?" She jutted her hip out, folded her arms,

and raised an eyebrow. "I wouldn't have a clue what it's like to feel inferior?"

"No," I said, looking at her. "Look at you. You're like a drop-dead gorgeous, strong... warrior goddess."

Both her eyebrows shot up for a moment, then she threw her head back and laughed a good spell before sobering. "My daddy never told me I had pretty eyes either. He never met me. He was put on one ship and my mother was put on another. I was born in a field and picking cotton as soon as my little fingers could grab it. Nobody told me my eyes were pretty. They were brown like the rest of me, and to the world that brown was the color of a shit stain and that's what the world told me I was. My own people didn't see me as beautiful because every last one of us was told we weren't."

My mouth fell open, and I just looked at her, no idea what to say. It was a big rule that vampires didn't reveal their age, so just the fact she was telling me she'd been a slave was a great deal of information I knew she didn't share lightly, and I'd take that information to my grave.

"The world, this society you speak about, it tried to destroy me. It told me I was nothing. It told me the blue-eyed blondes, and the green-eyed brunettes, and the pasty-assed redheads, and everybody but me was beautiful. I wasn't worthy of what they had. I was ugly. I was stupid. I was nothing. I was told this every day of my human life, and for the beginning of my vampire life as well."

"None of what you were told was ever true."

"It sure wasn't, and the bullshit you've been told about yourself is a damn lie, too. I found my strength, my power, my wisdom, and that's when I realized my beauty and there is no one in this world who will ever tell me I'm not one fine-ass, intelligent, strong as hell woman. You need to find your beauty too, because no one's going to find it for you." She grabbed my chin again and turned my face to the mirror. "Look at your damn self!"

Tears spilled from my eyes. "I've tried. It's hard when

165

you've been told you're not enough for so long."

"You think I don't know that?" She held her arms out as if to encourage me to look at her, all of her. "You think people were kind to me when I couldn't even drink out of the same water fountain? When people listed me as their property? I wasn't even treated like a human being and you're gonna boo hoo because your sister has bigger breasts than you?"

"Everyone has bigger breasts than me!" I snapped as I wiped away tears. I knew my insecurity seemed insignificant compared to what she'd been through, and in the grand scheme of things I'm sure it was, but for me, in the present time, in my life, it was a major deal. "No one is built like this! I'm deformed. My own mother and grandmother remind me every damn day. Even the few women who are built like this have themselves fixed. You never see anyone built like me on TV or in magazines. This isn't how a woman is supposed to look. I know you had a horrible start to your life and I'm not trying to take away from that or even compare, but you don't understand how hard it is to feel attractive when you're not built the way you're supposed to be built."

"Danni, look at me."

I wiped my eyes and looked over at her. "What?"

"Look at me." She gestured toward her chest. "Really look."

I stared at her, blinking. "Have you always stuffed your bra before?"

"Never."

"What are you, a B cup or…"

"Honey, I'm a 34A. I've always been a 34A, and if I'm correct, that makes me just like you."

"Shit," I whispered, shocked. "But you're so beautiful. You carry yourself like a supermodel. I didn't even notice we're the same size."

"The world is not as obsessed with the size of your chest as you are, or your mother and grandmother. I carry myself the way I do because I know I'm beautiful, every little and big part of me. People told me I was ugly and we both know why they did. You need to figure out why your mother and grandmother have spent so much time trying to convince you that you're not good enough. I assure you, it's not because it's the truth."

"What reason would they have to lie?"

"That's what you need to discover so you can heal the damage they've done to you and strengthen yourself from the inside out. Our session for tonight is over, but you have homework. Check out *Cinderella*. I think you'll find it enlightening."

She crossed the room and left. I stood in front of the mirror and really looked at myself. I couldn't see a beautiful warrior princess looking back at me, but I thought I could feel her a little bit, waiting for me to pull her out of whatever dark place inside me she'd been shoved into. "Hang in there," I told her. "I'm looking for you."

I pulled my shirt back on and headed toward Shana's room.

# TWELVE

The guards on Shana's door were the same shifters from the night before. They nodded respectfully at me as I approached, but said nothing as I entered the room. Eliza was gone, and Shana sat cross-legged on the bed, filing her nails. A blood-stained glass rested on the bedside table.

"What's up, sis?" she asked, barely glancing away from her work.

"I received a visit from your new husband's hired thugs," I told her. "We had to send them back damaged."

This caught her attention. She stopped filing to look me over, then laughed before resuming. "What, did you slap them around?"

"Something like that," I said.

"Yeah, I'm betting a sexy vampire guard did all the heavy work. So that Daniel guy is like your personal bodyguard? He's paid to hang out with you and keep you out of trouble?"

"He's my bodyguard, but he's also my friend," I said, defenses awakened. "He likes me."

"Well, of course he does. You're a very likeable person." She set the nail file on the table and eased back against the pillows. "That Eliza woman visited me tonight and talked to me forever." She rolled her eyes. "She'd be so pretty if she had some style. Anyway, I know all about the vampire stuff now, and what you did so, like, thanks for saving my life. That's really a great thing you did."

"You're my sister. What else was I going to do, watch you die in front of me?"

She shrugged. "I imagine not a lot of women would be willing to share such a hot sire."

I imagined little bubbles rolling along my bloodstream as it heated with jealousy. "I'm sure Eliza told you a sire-fledgling relationship isn't always a sexual one."

"Yeah, he's like our warden or something." She looked at her nails. "He's kind of uptight. I'm thinking he needs to get laid. I thought you were sleeping with him, or did you just tell Mom that to cover up the truth?"

"I never told Mom I was sleeping with him. I said I was seeing him, and I am."

"He's grumpy," Shana said, glancing at me. "I guess I could give away a few of my tricks to keeping a man happy."

"Not necessary," I said, "and Rider's fine. Your turning wasn't planned, and your husband has become a thorn in Rider's ass, and mine too. Then there's Mom and Grandma. Of course he's grumpy with everything going on," I said, not bothering to tell her he didn't like her and didn't want to save her, but the little devil on my shoulder really liked the idea. "Besides, the only man you should be concerned about keeping happy is Kevin, your husband."

She scrunched her nose. "If I knew I was going to be young and beautiful for all eternity, I would have set my sights higher than Kevin. He's still not a bad first husband, though."

"First husband?" I stared at her, gobsmacked. "How many husbands do you plan on having?"

"How should I know? I'm immune to death now and there's no telling how long this planet is going to keep on spinning. I'll marry as many rich husbands as I can get. At

169

least, until I have enough of my own money that I won't need to be married." She looked around the room. "So we're underneath Midnight Rider. Is this Rider's only property?"

"Why?" I asked as I fought not to narrow my eyes into tiny slits.

"Just wondering." She looked at me and sighed. "I'm so bored. I can't wait to get out of here. Rider said if I was a good girl, I could leave tomorrow."

I raised an eyebrow at this. "All by yourself?"

"I believe he said *us*, so he'll be going with me. I guess you too. Can you get some of my clothes?" She looked down at the shirt she'd been given. "And my makeup and hair stuff?"

"I don't think I'll be welcome at your new house all by myself. I did send your husband's hired help back to him all broken."

Shana rolled her eyes. "Sure you did. Ugh, did Rider keep you locked up after turning you?"

"No. I actually went to work right after finding out what I'd been turned into, but I didn't believe him when he told me I was a vampire."

Shana sat still for a moment, her brow creasing as she studied me. "You didn't ask to be turned? He just did it? Did you almost die too?"

I opened my mouth to answer, but couldn't find the words. I didn't want to tell her anything that might lead to her discovering I was more than just a vampire. Initially, I'd thought Rider was being far too paranoid about not trusting Shana, but the more I spoke with her, the more I was beginning to think he'd been right about a few things. For one thing, Shana did like being the queen bee. She definitely seemed to show interest in Rider, despite knowing he and I were together. Suddenly it felt like giving her any extra information on me would be like handing her ammo.

"Um, you spoke to Eliza tonight. I'm sure she told you

about how vampires don't really talk about their age or how they were turned. You know, for security."

"Yeah, she said something about how it could be considered a threat to ask another vampire's age and we should all keep our ages guarded. It sounds stupid, but whatever. Why can't you tell me how you were turned? You know how I was."

"It's just good to stay in the habit of keeping tight-lipped," I told her and changed the subject. "I have clothes here. I can loan you something."

She looked at my clothes and scrunched her nose. "Do you have anything cute here? From all the hotties I've seen around here so far, I want to look at least halfway decent."

"You're married now. You shouldn't care about impressing any of the men who work for Rider," I reminded her, barely suppressing the urge to threaten her life if she so much as thought of trying to cute herself up for Rider himself. "You are going to stay married to Kevin, aren't you? At least until he notices you aren't aging. You'll definitely have to make a decision then, but there's plenty of years before that will be necessary."

Shana twirled a lock of her hair as she thought about the dilemma. "It'll be a pain keeping all this a secret from him, but I suppose it can be done. I can always come here for my blood. I'm sure Rider takes good care of his girls. You've never seemed as if you've been starved for blood."

"We're not his *girls*," I snapped, then quickly collected myself. "Rider is our sire. It's important to treat him with respect."

Shana narrowed her eyes for a moment and a cold chill washed over me. She fluttered her lashes and the dark shadow that had covered her eyes seemed to evaporate. "Of course," she said, smiling full of saccharine sweetness. "I promise to be very respectful and show my appreciation every chance I get. After all, Rider saved my life. I owe him my devotion, or whatever he may want." She stretched and yawned. "It must be about that time."

I nodded, remembering that as a newly turned pure vampire she wouldn't stand a chance against morning. I realized what a hindrance her new condition would put on her marriage and felt panic rise in me. A married Shana was less of a threat than a loose Shana prowling around the bar looking to hook up with whomever she pleased.

"Shouldn't you be getting ready for bed?" she asked.

"Yeah," I said, and faked a yawn. "I best be on my way. I just wanted to check in with you first." I turned for the door. Maybe other sisters would have hugged goodnight. Such a thing seemed utterly ridiculous for us.

"If I'm stuck wearing your clothes tomorrow night, try to bring me something that'll fit over my boobs and not hang loose around my ass. You're quite a bit bigger in the ass than I am."

"Sure," I said and crossed the room as quickly as my feet would carry me without having to use my vampiric speed.

"Oh, wait. I meant to ask… is Daniel available?"

I turned with my hand on the doorknob, my back straight as a rod. "Available for what?"

"Whatever," she said, waggling her eyebrows. "Oh, what? You can't call dibs on both of them."

"You're married!"

"For now," she said and giggled. Her eyelids lowered, and she sank back against her pillows. "You can't expect a vampire to stay true to just one—"

I watched her fall asleep as my own body drew sluggish, and turned to leave her room, grateful to know she'd be dead to the world for the rest of the day. Unfortunately, she'd be up every night and, from the sound of things, ready to mingle. The shiny new wedding band on her finger might as well have been invisible for all the attention she paid it.

I quickly moved through the lower levels, nodding at members of Rider's staff as I passed them. With the sun rising, it was mostly non-vampires on deck. He employed some older vampires who were capable of remaining awake during the day, but even with that ability, most preferred to sleep until nightfall, when the energy surge made sleeping difficult.

I made it out the door leading to the ground floor just as Rome and Daniel stepped through the attached garage door, lugging what looked like an unconscious sludge-covered man with a bag tied over his head between them. Rome had a little grime on one of his arms, but Daniel was covered in gunk. Dark sludge encased his legs from his feet to just over his kneecaps. His T-shirt was wet, streaks of I didn't know what smeared his arms. I could see traces of whatever it was on his neck.

"What happened to you two?" I asked, waving my hand in front of my nose as the smell of them assaulted me. "Who is that?"

"This is the assignment Rider put me on," Daniel answered. "Or, I guess I should say this is my punishment. I failed to stop a man from hitting you, so your boyfriend decided to make me pay for that by having to track and capture this disgusting bastard."

"Hey, you didn't round this guy up all by yourself," Rome said. "And I didn't do anything wrong, so this isn't punishment. It's just a bad hand. We get dealt some of those sometimes."

"I might as well have been by myself for all the good it was having this oversized lump of shit with me."

"Lump of shit?"

"That's what I said," Daniel snapped.

"What the hell crawled up your ass?"

"What *didn't* crawl up my ass?" Daniel's voice elevated. "I still feel shit squirming all over me thanks to you, you defective asshole."

"Man, I am in peak physical form, you flying jack-wad."

"If you're in peak physical form, why couldn't you lift those fat sausages you call legs to climb in the dumpster after this guy or fit your wide, overgrown ass down the manhole when he slithered down into the sewer?"

"You wish you looked like me," Rome told him before flexing the biceps of his clean arm and planting a kiss on the bulging muscle.

"Nobody would wish to look like you," Daniel said, his nostrils flaring. "Who wants to look like a gigantic, crusty-assed turd?"

Rome's eyes grew wide, the whites bulging out of his head as the rest of his body tensed. "Who the hell do you think you're talking to? I know you're not talking that shit about me."

"Who the hell else would I be talking about? You're the only one here who looks like you just slid out of King Kong's ass!"

"Boys!" I clapped my hands, trying to snag their attention before they resorted to blows, which was about to happen judging by the red scald climbing Daniel's neck and the enormous fist Rome's free hand had tightened into. "Stop arguing. I'm sure you both have had a rough night. You'll feel better once you finish with whatever you're supposed to do with whoever that is and jump in the shower."

"Rome's not jumping into anything," Daniel said. "Rome can't get his fat feet off the fucking floor."

"You gonna see how far I can raise my foot off the floor when I ram it up your rainbow-colored candy ass," Rome said, releasing his hold on the greasy guy between them and stepping back. He whipped his shirt over his head, wiped the sludge off his arm and tossed it to the floor, leaving him in pants and a thin wife-beater strained to its maximum stretchiness.

"Oh, are we doing this?" Daniel asked, releasing his hold on the stocky guy, allowing his body to hit the floor. He didn't bother whipping anything off, and probably couldn't if he wanted to. His clothes appeared to be glued to him with whatever he'd had the misfortune of rolling around in.

"Hell yeah," Rome told him. "I'm about to beat your dragon ass all the way back to Honalee."

"I'm from Imortia, you dumb fuck!"

"Honalee's part of the song, dumbass. Puff the Magic Dragon lived by the sea, and he frolicked … somewhere… and he came from Honalee…"

"If you have to explain your trash talk, you're obviously not any damn good at it."

"That's it. I'm busting your ass!" Rome lowered his head and lunged at Daniel, who disappeared in a burst of sparkling colors just as I screamed for them to stop before they killed each other. Rome's head slammed into the wall and made a horribly loud banging noise as it cracked through the plaster. I gasped as Rome sank to his knees and fell onto his back, unconscious.

Daniel reappeared beside him, hands on hips as he looked down at him and kicked him in the side with the toe of his shoe. "Dumbass knocked himself out."

"Don't kick him!" I started to swat at Daniel, but instantly stilled, realizing there was no way to touch him without touching whatever was on him. "Is he dead?"

"He's fine. It takes more than a bump to the head to take down a rhino."

"He's not a rhino, he's a human. Rider's going to be so mad about this."

"I did the shitty job I was assigned," Daniel said as he walked over to the discarded man, bent over and picked him up in a fireman's carry. "Rome knocked himself out, and if Rider has an issue with that, he can kiss my scale-covered ass."

I stared after Daniel, mouth agape, as he disappeared through the door I'd emerged from, I assumed to deposit the man he and Rome had captured into a cell or the interrogation room.

The door leading to the bar opened and Rider emerged. He immediately zeroed in on Rome sprawled out on the floor, and moved toward him. "What happened?"

"He bumped his head on the wall," I said, being very careful not to actually lie while also trying to protect Daniel.

Rider stared down at Rome and toed him with the tip of his boot. When this didn't get a response, he kicked him a little harder.

"Don't kick him!"

"It's all right. He has a thick hide." Rider looked at the crack in his wall, frowning. "What really happened?"

"Do you promise you won't get mad?"

"I really hate when I'm asked that."

"It was an accident. Kind of."

Rider looked down at Rome, looked at me, then looked back at Rome. "You didn't do this, did you?"

"Nope. This time I didn't even touch him."

Rider sniffed, his lip curling. "I still smell the stench from the creature I sent them after and Daniel isn't here, so I'm going to go out on a limb here and say Daniel did this, and then he fled the scene of the crime?"

"Daniel and Rome may have been bickering at each other, and Daniel may have provoked him, but in all honesty, Rome knocked himself out. Who was that man you sent them after, anyway? He was foul, and Daniel was covered in some kind of sludge. He was griping about having to go into a dumpster and I think down in a sewer to go after the guy too."

Rider's lips curved slightly at the corner as he fought a smile. "Yeah, the particular type of creature I sent them after does like to travel through the nastiest places."

"So he was right that you sent him out on this errand as punishment?"

"Not deliberately, but I'm not mad that he had a rough time. They captured him?"

"Yeah. Daniel headed downstairs with the guy over his shoulders. Are you going to tell me what he was? They had a bag over his head and he stank worse than anyone I've ever smelled before."

"The bag was so he wouldn't know how they accessed the doors to get in here in case we let him go. He's a wererat. They're nasty creatures. We heard reports of some kind of beast trying to drag young women down into the sewer. Police tend to not believe tales of gigantic rats in the city sewer system, but I've seen this sort of thing before. Surveillance picked up a wererat, so I sent Rome and Daniel after it. He'll be questioned to see how many others there are, and if he's our culprit or not."

I stood there, blinking at him.

"What?"

"I'm sorry, but it sounded like you said wererat. Like, an actual rat."

"I did."

I tried to imagine a human-sized rat in my head and shuddered. "You're telling me there are people who shift into gigantic man-sized rats?"

"They're not quite man-sized when they shift, like werewolves are big but not ridiculously big, but… yeah, they're pretty big. Much bigger than regular rats."

"How big?"

"Like a dog."

"Like my grandmother's Pomchi?"

"No, like a real dog. Like a Rottweiler."

I felt myself sway, and Rider gripped my arm, steadying me until the room stopped spinning. He toed Rome with his boot again. "You'd tell me if Daniel knocked Rome out, wouldn't you? Because I can't have that."

"I swear Rome knocked himself out."

Rider looked at the crack in the wall again. "Rome launched himself at Daniel and Daniel did that twinkle shit where he bursts into colors and disappears?"

"Yup."

"I guess I need to get the poor dumb bastard out of the way." He looked at me again, his eyes softening. "The sun's on its way up. Are you staying with me?"

"Yeah," I said on a sigh as I thought of Angel all alone in my apartment. I had missed my apartment when I'd visited, but I only had one bed and if I was going to share a bed with anyone, I'd prefer it to be Rider. Plus, he'd told me he sleeps better with me. We'd been apart for a few weeks after his showdown with Selander Ryan and the poor guy had looked like hell when I'd finally given in to my urge to see him again. "Do you really need me with you for you to sleep well?"

He reached out and ran the back of his finger down the side of my face. "I worry about you too much to sleep when we're apart."

"I have a personal bodyguard now."

"Thinking of Daniel watching over you while you sleep, or worse, sleeping close to you, isn't going to help me sleep," he said as he bent down to pick up Rome, effortlessly tossing the muscular man over his shoulder, which was an impressive feat. Even for a vampire. "I need to get Rome situated and check in with Daniel and I'll be on up. I'm really glad you're staying with me."

I smiled involuntarily, touched by the sincerity in his blue eyes, despite part of me still wanting more independence. Then a rumble erupted from the vicinity of Rome's ass, forcing both Rider and me to stagger back.

"Geez Louise," I said, fanning the air in front of my face, but it seemed too thick with stench for my hand to do any good.

"It's burning my eyes," Rider said, half-gagging. "Head on up and save yourself."

He stepped toward the door, and I ran for the stairs to take me to Rider's room. "It's following me!" I cried as I jogged up the stairs. "What the hell did he eat?"

"I don't know, but he instantly felt about twenty pounds lighter after he let 'er rip," Rider said, and then he was gone, moving in a flash of vampiric speed. I couldn't blame him, considering how close his nose was to Rome's ass.

I entered his room and stripped down to my T-shirt and underwear as daylight steadily sucked away at my energy. I looked longingly at the bed, but out of habit I checked my cellphone which was still hooked up to the charger on Rider's nightstand where I'd left it. I saw I had a massive amount of voicemail notifications and I knew they'd be from my mother and grandmother, and maybe a few from Kevin. I deleted them all and checked my call history, noticing I'd received calls from my landline while I'd been with Nannette, and again while I'd been speaking to Shana.

I pressed the button to dial the number back despite it currently being the ass crack of dawn. The last call hadn't been that long ago, and it wasn't like Angel had a job to go to. She picked up after two rings.

"Danni?"

"Yeah, it's me. I didn't have my phone on me earlier and I was busy. Is everything all right? You should be asleep by now."

"I've gotten used to staying up all night. Even when I found shelters, it was safer to catch naps during the day."

"I can imagine," I said, my heart going out to the girl. "You're safe to sleep now. Despite what happened earlier, no one will get into that apartment to get to you. You should get some rest."

"You're not coming back?"

"Not until tonight. I'm actually about to go to sleep myself. I'm staying at my boyfriend's place."

"The guy who assigned security to watch your apartment?"

"Yes."

"The guy who assigned Daniel and Ginger to guard you?"

"Yes."

"You must be pretty important."

I thought about that. "My boyfriend is a bit overprotective, but the security does come in handy."

"Most people don't need their own personal security," she said.

I remained silent, not sure how to respond. She had a valid point. I wasn't famous or rich. My apartment was very simple and not exactly loaded with expensive merchandise or rare collectibles.

"What you were saying earlier, about being a vampire… Were you serious?"

I took a breath and thought about how best to answer. It had seemed safe earlier, but now she was alone in my apartment. It would be easier for her to run away if she freaked out, but then again, did it really matter? She could freak out with me there with her. Either way, if she ran, she ran. I certainly wasn't going to kill the girl if she chose not to be my donor. I'd probably have to move, but despite missing my apartment, I wasn't so attached to it that moving would kill me. Mostly, I missed my space, not the actual apartment itself. It was replaceable. "Are you asking because you believed me, or are you wigging out because you've been watching a vampire movie marathon all night?"

"I'm asking because I threw away a paper towel earlier, and I saw bags of blood in your garbage can."

"Oh." I sighed. "Yes, I was telling the truth. I'm a vampire. I drink blood, but vampires don't have to kill for it. We don't turn into bats and garlic doesn't repel us. We're pretty human, except we need to drink blood and we have this fountain of youth thing going on."

"And you heal with blood and sleep."

"Yup."

"You want my blood, don't you?"

Man, that sounded gruesome. I sat on the edge of Rider's bed and chose my words carefully. "I need a donor who is available to give me fresh blood on a regular basis. The blood will be given freely in exchange for compensation, which includes shelter and security. I need a donor who will keep my lifestyle and the lifestyle of those like me secret. You don't have to give a lot, and it's a very easy process."

She was silent for a long moment, and I allowed it, seeing no reason to rush her. I wasn't asking for a simple favor and I didn't want to come off pushy. If she decided to be my donor, great. I'd have a donor and I wouldn't have to move. If she fled, I didn't have a lot of stuff to pack. However, she'd be back on the street and I was more worried about that than anything else.

"This is crazy," she finally said.

"Yeah, I thought it was pretty nuts when I got turned, so I understand where you're coming from," I told her as Rider entered the room, his eyebrows raised. He stood at the foot of the bed, listening. "I'll tell you what. It's daytime, so I really need to sleep and you probably haven't gotten a good stretch of sleep in a long time. Get some good sleep, think about it, and you can let me know your decision tonight. Just … don't freak out and run. You were lucky last night. If that happens again, you might not find a weapon in time or have cops who care so much be the first on scene. I'd feel terrible if what I am caused you to run away and get into that type of situation again, so please, just don't do that. You're safe. I promise."

"I'll be here," she said, and hung up.

"I'm guessing that wasn't your mother," Rider said as I set the cell phone back on the nightstand.

"It was Angel. She's still deciding if she wants to be my donor or not." I pulled back the bedsheets and crawled under them, exhausted. "It didn't take long for you to take care of Rome and check in with Daniel."

"I got the hell away from Rome as fast as I could," Rider said as he started to undress for bed. "He let out more gas as I took him downstairs. He was like a deflating balloon and what came out of him had to have smelled worse than whatever the wererat made him and Daniel go through."

"Did you actually speak with Daniel? I think he'd

disagree, and he smelled pretty bad. Though, now that you mention it, I think Rome's gas actually was worse."

"Daniel was in the men's locker room scrubbing himself raw in the shower. It's awkward talking to another man when he's doing that, so I'll check in with him later. They got the man I sent them out for squared away and that's the most important thing." Rider dropped the last of his clothes and slid under the sheets beside me. "So you took the girl to your apartment without even telling her what you are, told her over the phone, and now she's there considering her options?"

"Sort of, and if you're going to nag me about any of that, save it. You didn't give me any instruction on what I was supposed to do or say to sign up a donor."

He grinned. "That's true."

"How did you go about getting yours?"

"Found them being beaten or sexually assaulted while out on patrols. I saved them, told them what I was, and offered them the job on the condition they never told anyone, never sold their bodies again, and never took drugs. They were so happy to be safe and off the streets they jumped at the opportunity."

"Well, that was easy. You sent me to a teenager. I had to try another approach."

"Birthday cake?" He smiled.

"Never underestimate the power of birthday cake."

"Oh, I know how much you love cake." He studied me. "You're not banged up. I take it the training session with Nannette went well?"

"We talked about our feelings and compared our breasts."

He sat still, blinking at me a moment before he nodded his head, his mouth curved with amusement. "Ohhh-kay then. Well, if that's the training you need, I say we do some more of that. As you can see, your breasts are much plumper than mine and I'm feeling very friendly." He moved over me. "How are you feeling?"

"Tired. The sun's up and we're vampires. Aren't you tired?"

"Babe, I'm never *that* tired."

# THIRTEEN

I woke cocooned in Rider's arms, his heart thumping steadily against my back. I rolled over to find his eyes open, the slightest hint of a smile playing about his mouth. Energy zinged through my body, indicating I'd slept the whole day away and had awakened naturally with the rise of the moon. "Hey."

"Hey." He kissed my nose. "Sleep well?"

"Yeah. It's been a long time since I woke up on my own and found you still in bed with me." I narrowed my eyes. "Were you here all day?"

He was silent a moment. "Most of it," he finally said as he brushed a lock of my hair back from my face and kissed a spot under my ear before working his way down my neck. "I'm here now. Isn't this nice? You can't wake up like this if you go back to your apartment."

"You could spend the day at my apartment."

"It's not as secure as my place, and you know I run all my businesses from here and have to get up during the day sometimes."

I started to sigh in frustration, but his mouth had made its way from my neck to even better places and frustration was giving way to anticipation. Maybe staying with him wasn't so bad. My apartment was average at best and he was right. Waking up alone didn't come close to waking up with Rider.

*Hey Danni! What are you doing?*

"Eeeeyikes!" I jerked upright and jumped off the bed, my knee connecting with Rider in the process.

"What the hell?" He asked, bent at the waist, hand pressed against his groin. Teeth clenched. "I was just going south. You like that."

"Not with my sister in my head," I told him as I snatched my shirt off the floor and pulled it on. "Are you all right?"

He glared at me. "Yeah, getting kneed while you have a hard-on feels amazing."

*Danni. I'm bored already. Bring me some cute clothes. I can't wait to go out tonight! Bring me a dress. A short one.*

"Get out of my brain!" I yelled, smacking the heel of my hand against the side of my head.

"Stop hitting yourself. You look crazy." Rider eased himself out of the bed and limped over to me. "What's she want anyway?"

"Clothes. She said you told her she could get out of here tonight if she was a *good girl.* Did you actually say that?"

"Does that sound like something I'd say to her?"

"No."

"Well, there you go."

I growled, remembering all her commentary on how hot Rider was and how he needed to get laid. "She was flirting with you, wasn't she?"

"If you can call it flirting."

"What would you call it?"

He shifted uncomfortably, and not because I'd accidentally kneed him. "Doesn't matter. I'm not interested and you can ask any guard. They'll tell you I haven't gone into that room alone since she's awakened. I don't trust her not to pounce on me and you'll get all pissed off if I use my power to slam her into a wall."

"If she pounces on you, I don't care if you put her *through* a wall," I snapped. "So what's with the going out stuff? Did you tell her she could leave?"

"I told her I would allow her to leave the room if she could control her hunger and her attitude. I sent a rep to speak with her husband to make sure he doesn't send anyone else after you, but since he already sent men to your apartment, he knows you're in the area. I don't see him sitting on his hands, waiting patiently for her when he knows she's, or at least he knows *you're* close. It's best we have her speak with him and put all this to rest, but I want it to be in person and for us to be there to make sure she doesn't reveal anything about us that shouldn't be revealed."

"Are we moving in with them too? She's married to the man now. She lives with him."

"Yeah, I'm thinking that's not the best idea. I'm her sire so I can sense if her bloodlust gets out of control, but you yourself know I can't just teleport to wherever she is if she attacks someone. If I release her into the world, I'm responsible for her, and she could kill someone if I release her too soon."

"Like I did."

Rider tipped my chin up with his finger. "Stop wallowing in that puddle of guilt. It's my fault. I knew you were having trouble believing you'd been turned. I shouldn't have assumed you'd come to me when the hunger overtook you. Let's just agree it was a teachable moment for both of us and move past it."

"You're afraid Shana will kill someone if she's left alone."

"That's just one thing I'm afraid of. You lived alone and didn't seem like a party girl, so although I wasn't entirely comfortable leaving you on your own, I wasn't afraid you'd cause complete chaos. If Shana stays married, she'll have to live with her husband and keep what she is a secret. She doesn't seem bright enough to do that, and she likes to party. I don't see her hiding being a vampire for long or resisting telling people about it. Does she work? She hasn't said anything about a job."

"She has a blog with a ton of followers and makes money off of that."

"A blog? That's just great." Rider placed his hands on his hips and groaned. "Just what I need. A vampire who can't keep her mouth shut … who blogs for a living."

"Shana's kind of spacy, but she's not a complete idiot," I assured him. "I'm sure Eliza told her about hunters and how dangerous it would be for us if we became common knowledge."

He looked down at me, frowning. "This is the woman who thought she couldn't possibly be a vampire because she had a bowel movement."

My nose scrunched all by itself. "I'll be sure to stress the dangers to her. I really don't think it's wise to have her break off the marriage. If you think she's hard to control now, imagine her out there single and ready to mingle. Besides, she said Kevin's a workaholic, and he's not that great looking. The man always shows her off like a trophy. He probably won't care if she sleeps all day as long as she's available to him at night."

"How will she explain the sleeping all day?"

"Partying all night."

"And the barely eating?"

"She's never been a big eater," I told him. "She practically lived off of water, salad, and yoga."

"I don't know."

"You have humans on your staff," I reminded him. "Clearly, some can be trusted. Kevin might not even care that she's a vampire. He practically worships her. I'm sure he'd be willing to keep her secret if it meant he still got to stay married to her, and she's never going to get old. Her boobs are never going to sag. He'll love her even more for that. Men are disgusting."

"Thanks," he said, frowning down at me.

"You know what I mean."

"No, but I'm naked and close enough to your knee that I'm not going to press the subject and make you angry. Let's see if we can figure this out in the shower," he added with a lascivious smile.

I had clothes at Rider's, but most of what I had was basic. Mostly jeans, leggings, and T-shirts. I had the dress I'd worn to Shana's bachelorette party, but I shuddered, imagining her ample breasts squeezed into the very revealing neckline. There was no way she could pull it off without looking absolutely pornographic, which she probably wouldn't mind, but I would.

"Just grab something," Rider said, pulling on his shoes. He stood, kissed the top of my head, and headed out. "I'll be in my office scolding the children."

I turned to ask what he meant, but he'd already exited the room. He hadn't had trouble getting ready for the night, opting for black pants and a black polo shirt. Knowing we'd be going somewhere at some point, I'd chosen black leggings, a sleeveless, white crocheted tunic, and my black combat boots. A little dressier than jeans and a T-shirt, but I could still maneuver well enough to kick ass if the occasion arose. I'd even added small hoop earrings and a swipe of rosy lip gloss. Shana would probably still find me dowdy.

I grabbed leggings and a pretty blouse, then realized I had no underwear for Shana. Even if I was comfortable sharing mine, it wouldn't be possible. Shana had big breasts and no butt. I had the opposite body type. *You're going to have to wait for clothes*, I told her telepathically. *I'll have to go buy some underwear for you.*

*Buy me some clothes too,* she responded. *Wait! Take me with you!*

*You have no underwear!*

188

*So?*

*So I'm not taking you shopping for clothes with your massive boobs swinging all around. You'll poke someone's eye out!*

*Don't you have a tank top I can wear? A little nipple showing through won't kill anyone.*

I imagined my impressively endowed sister in a tank top and no bra. It might not kill someone, but I could just imagine all the gawking men getting smacked upside their heads by their significant others. *Just be patient. I'll get you some clothes you'll like.*

*But you don't know how to —*

*I can pick out some damn clothes!* I snapped. *Besides, Rider won't let you leave here with just me and he's not going to want to go shopping with you, so just be patient like I said.*

She didn't respond, but I could feel her fold her arms and jut out her bottom lip in a huff through our link.

I slammed my dresser drawer shut, grabbed my cell phone, and headed downstairs to Rider's office. I entered to find him sitting behind his desk. Daniel occupied one of the chairs in front of the desk. He was dressed in a black Led Zeppelin T-shirt, worn jeans, and his boots. He nodded at me, but said nothing.

"What's up?" Rider asked.

"I realized Shana won't fit my clothes. Well, underwear anyway. I'm going to have to go shopping for her."

"She's not going with you."

"I figured as much."

"Daniel and Ginger can go with you when I'm done with this meeting. Have a seat and wait for the others. They should be here, but Rome's moving a little slow tonight."

I sat on the leather couch, keeping the other chair open for Rome. I now understood what Rider had meant by scolding the children.

"What time are we meeting Kevin? I need to check in on Angel."

Rider watched me while he thought. "I just had blood

sent to your sister, so all she needs are clothes. It'll be late by the time you come back with them. Why don't you go by your apartment first? If Angel agrees to be your donor, you can take her shopping with you. I'm sure she needs some clothes too."

"True," I said as I mentally calculated the hit my bank account was about to take. I'd gotten all my unused vacation pay when I'd quite Prince Advertising and had a decent little savings built up, but I hadn't actually put any money into my account since quitting and my rent and utilities were taking a toll.

"Put it on my card," Rider said. He opened his desk drawer, grabbed a credit card, and slid it across the desk. "If she agrees to be your donor, she'll be on my payroll anyway."

"But she's my donor," I said as I reached over and picked up the card. It had my name on it underneath his.

"And you're under my care," he said. "Babe, you don't have a job."

I started to remind him I didn't have a job because he threw a hissy fit every time I brought up the idea of applying for one, but remembered he had a valid reason, no matter how irritating it was. "Well, if you'd figure out how to cure me of this Bloom thing, I could get one."

"I'm working on it, and I've told you before you don't need a job."

"I thought she was going to be working with us," Daniel said. "I thought that was why Nannette was training her."

Rider glared at him. "We'll see about that. Nannette isn't finished with training her." To me, he said, "Get Angel, get clothes, and come back here. I'll have Kevin come here for the meeting so we still have the upper hand, and Ginger can take Angel back to your apartment while we're meeting with him. I assume that's where you want her to stay?"

I thought about it and nodded. I was paying for the

apartment anyway. "I think she'd be most comfortable there."

"That's fine. I'll cover the rent and utilities as part of her compensation."

"Rider…"

"This is non-negotiable," he said.

I sighed as the door opened and Rome stepped in, a large bump on his head. Ginger helped him into the chair, then sat next to me on the couch. "What's up, buttercup?"

"The usual," I said and sat back, getting comfortable to watch the show.

"Were you released to work, or do you need time off?" Rider asked Rome.

"The doc says I'm all good as long as I don't take any more blows to the head," Rome said, handing Rider some papers.

"Do you boys have anything to say to each other?" Rider asked as he picked up the papers and looked them over.

"He started it," both men said, pointing at each other.

"Sometimes I regret the fact that I never had children," Rider said, setting the papers aside. "Then I remember I have you jackasses. When I send you out on a job, I need to have confidence that you will carry that job out without endangering one another. What the hell happened?"

"Daniel got all mad because he got all nasty chasing the wererat and got an attitude," Rome said. "He was calling me names."

"He called you names?"

"Yeah, he said I was too fat to climb in the dumpster or crawl down the manhole." Rome folded his arms and jutted his lip out like a petulant toddler.

Rider stared back at him for a moment before running his hand down his face and shaking his head in disgusted disbelief that he was dealing with this. Ginger and I glanced at each other and quickly looked away, knowing we'd erupt into laughter if we didn't.

"Did you climb into the dumpster or go down the manhole?" Rider asked.

"No," Rome said.

"Why not?"

Rome shrugged. "Daniel got there before me, and he did fit better. I'm not fat though. I just got a lot of muscle."

"Could he fit in the dumpster and the manhole?" Rider asked Daniel.

"Yeah," Daniel answered. "If he wanted to."

"I'll ask again, Rome. Why didn't you do at least one of those things with your partner? You were both tracking the wererat. You both should have been chasing him."

"Well, I didn't see why we both had to get all disgusting," Rome mumbled.

Rider stared at Rome as he nodded his head, considering what to do. After a moment, he sat back and steepled his fingers. "Rome, since we can't risk you getting another head injury right now, I'm putting you on janitorial duty. I want the bathrooms kept spotless and I better not find a single drop of blood or viscera left on the interrogation room floor this week. Understood?"

Daniel's lips twitched as Rome groaned but nodded his understanding.

"If someone gets sick in the bar, I expect you to be there with a mop and a bucket before the vomit hits the floor."

"I understand."

"Good. And Daniel, scale back on the teasing. Clearly, Rome's testicles haven't come back down from when Danni rammed them up into his stomach and he's a bit of a pussy who can't handle name-calling."

"Yes, sir," Daniel said, fighting back the urge to laugh as Rome stewed beside him.

"Good, now I think you both have something to say to each other."

"I'm sorry I didn't help with the dirty work," Rome

muttered.

"I shouldn't have called you a chocolate-covered hemorrhoid," Daniel said.

Rome turned toward him. "You didn't call me that."

"Well, I meant to."

"I could have beat your ass if you didn't do that disappearing shit."

"Too bad you knocked yourself out like a dumbass."

"I went down like a man."

"You went down like a rag doll," I said, "and you farted."

They both looked at me. Daniel broke out into an ear-to-ear smile as Rome's cheeks reddened. "I didn't fart."

"Yes, you did, and for the record, what comes out of your ass should be declared a nuclear weapon," Rider said, sighing in frustration. He pointed to the door. "Get out of here, both of you, before I give in to the urge to just kill you and hire new employees."

"You seem to be in a better mood than you were in last night," I said ten minutes later as we climbed into Daniel's truck and set off for my apartment.

"I normally don't get that angry without being physically assaulted," Daniel said, "but the combination of crawling through a dumpster, chasing that disgusting bastard through a sewer, and listening to Rome joke about it while he didn't bother to lift a finger to help just got to me."

"Was that all that got to you?" Ginger asked, raising an eyebrow.

Daniel glanced over at her. "Yeah. Why?"

"Rome said he was teasing you to try to get you out of the funk you were in because Danni got hit while with you."

"Rome talks too damn much," Daniel muttered.

"It wasn't your fault that guy hit me," I told him. "I

grabbed him and he reacted. I should have expected him to swing on me, but I guess I was thinking of him as a normal human guy, not a trained ... whatever he was. Was he Kevin's regular security? I know he has money, but I wasn't under the impression he had his own security team."

"Judging by the way they fought, I'd say they were trained, but they could have been freelancers. What does your sister's husband do anyway?"

"She said he's a financial manager or something."

"What's that?"

"I have no idea, but he makes six figures, which is what drew Shana to him."

"Sounds like a nerd," Ginger said. "I'd die if I had to live in the business world. What kind of life is it if you can't punch anyone every once in a while?"

"Did you punch a lot of people before you were turned?"

"I punched a lot of people before I graduated elementary school. All my teachers said I had an attitude problem."

"Did you?"

"No, I just knew who needed to be punched, and I punched them. I provided a valuable service, just like I do now."

"You're lucky to have found a profession that allows you to use your natural talents."

"Damn skippy."

Daniel parked the truck in the lot in front of my building and we all climbed out.

"Did you bring your keys this time?" he asked.

I pulled my keychain out of the side pocket of my leggings and held it up to show him as we headed toward my apartment. "No need to do your magic tricks tonight."

"So far anyway," he said. "So, are you going to go through with it tonight, and actually convince her you're a vampire?"

"I spoke with her on the phone early this morning after Rome knocked himself out. She found the blood bags in my garbage can. She knows what I am."

"She's not freaked out?"

"She didn't sound like it on the phone, but she wasn't ready to commit to being a donor. I told her to sleep on it and let me know tonight. And here we are." I looked through the shadows in the corner of the hall and waved at Carlos, who was on duty guarding the exterior of my apartment and the occupant inside, and slipped my key into the lock.

I turned the key, tumbling the lock, and pushed the door open to find Angel standing behind the couch, my butcher knife tightly clasped in her white-knuckled fist. Her eyes were wide, wary, and trained on me.

"I think she's freaked out," Daniel said, stepping around me.

"Stop," Angel said, her gaze moving from me to Daniel as she pointed the knife at him.

"You actually would be better off with a paring knife," Ginger said, closing the door behind her. She moved to my other side. "The butcher's knife is big, but it's not that sharp. Not that it matters much anyway. We're vampires, kid."

Angel's eyes grew wider. "All of you are vampires?"

"Just me and Danni. Daniel's a whole other kind of freak."

"I'm taking it a good day's rest didn't ease your mind about this arrangement," I said. "Angel, if we wanted to hurt you, we would have easily done it last night. I think you know that or you wouldn't still be here."

"I trust Amelia and Grissom, and they told me I could trust you. I called Grissom tonight, and he said he knew what you are and you won't hurt me."

"Good," I said, wondering if Grissom had revealed what he was, but didn't ask. One issue at a time. "So, what's the problem?"

"I want to know how this donor thing works."

"That's understandable." I moved over to the chair and sat. Daniel and Ginger also moved forward, taking the same seats they'd taken the night before. Even if Angel attacked us, she wouldn't be fast enough to do any real harm. Seeming to realize we weren't intimidated, and maybe realizing she couldn't really do anything if we did decide to lunge at her, Angel lowered her arm, but she kept the knife gripped tight like a security blanket, which I thought was a fair comparison. "I told you I have special dietary needs."

"No shit. I figured that much out after peeking into your garbage can."

"Well, I don't just need blood. I need a *variety*. I need bagged blood, and I need fresh. I've taken blood from gangbangers, and once from a man who tried to rape me. I can't count on people like that falling into my lap often. With a donor, I have a convenient supply that I can take with no violence necessary."

"How much will you take?"

"No more than would be taken if you were to donate at a hospital. That's what this would be. A donation. Only instead of donating to a sick person or someone who has been in an accident, you'll be donating to me. Both types of donations help extend a life."

"Why me?"

I smiled at her. "Because I like you. You seem like a good person who was dealt a shitty hand and needs some help. Grissom is a friend, and he knew I needed a donor, and he thought of you. You can live here where you're safe enough to sleep at night, where you have a kitchen full of food. All you have to do is allow me to drink some of your blood and keep the existence of vampires a secret. That means no more asking anyone if they know what I am. Fortunately, Grissom already knew. It would have been very bad if he didn't and you told him."

"I didn't say vampire. I asked if he knew you drank

blood, and he said he knew what you were and what you needed me for, and that I was safe with you."

"Close enough. You can't do that anymore and you can't have guests here, but you can call this home. You can go out and shop, jog, whatever you want to do. Just be here at night when I may need you. You will be compensated for rent, utilities, food, whatever you need. It's not a bad deal."

She looked at the three of us and shifted uncomfortably. "Who all do I have to feed?"

"Just me. You will never be asked to provide blood for anyone else."

She held my gaze for a moment and nodded. "All right. It beats living on the street. So… do I need to *donate* now?"

"I drank before I headed here, but I can take a sip now to show you what it's like, unless you'd prefer to wait until I need it."

She bit her lip as she thought about it. "I guess a sip now. I don't want to wait until you're too hungry."

"Smart girl," Daniel said, grinning as I shot him a glare. "Just kidding. Danni only goes full animal kingdom on chocolate cupcakes."

"You can eat cupcakes?" Angel asked as I stood and moved toward her.

"Unfortunately, no, but I was able to eat one once thanks to a spell a friend put on me, and apparently I made quite a memorable scene of it."

"That must suck," she said, stepping backwards as I approached her. Her legs shook.

"It does, but I'll be able to eat again, eventually. We don't have to do this right now."

"Where are you going to bite me? You're going to bite me, right?"

I nodded. "I'll only drink from your wrist."

"Then let's get this over with." She stuck her arm out and turned her face away. "Do it."

197

I reached out for her wrist and the moment my fingers touched her arm, she hit the floor like a ton of bricks. Ginger and Daniel jumped up and walked over to us.

"I think she's nervous," Daniel said, standing over her with his hands on his narrow hips.

"Yeah, I gathered that." I crouched next to her. "Now what do we do?"

"Ooh!" Ginger walked over to the side table and grabbed the Jug-Jolter 2000. "A little zap should get her up."

"I'm not zapping anyone else with that thing," I said. "Throw it away."

"Really?" Ginger pouted as she twisted to look at her rear end. "I was kind of thinking of using it on my booty. No matter how many squats and lunges I do, I can't seem to get much junk in my trunk."

Angel's eyelashes fluttered. "Whuh… uhn…"

"Hey. Are you all right?"

She opened her eyes and looked up at me. "What happened?"

"I took a drink from your wrist and your nerves got the best of you. You fainted, kid."

"I never faint." She sat up, rubbing the back of her head. Then she realized what I'd said and lowered her hand to look at her wrist. "You did it?"

"Yup."

"I don't see anything. I don't remember anything."

"It was really quick, and we don't leave wounds. We'd never live undiscovered then."

"That makes sense," she said, turning her wrist to inspect it thoroughly. "I guess it wasn't so bad. Next time I won't be nervous."

"Of course not. You're a brave girl." I helped her up. "We're going shopping. I have to get an outfit for my sister, and I thought you might need some clothes and stuff of your own. You up to it?"

"Sure. I'm going to just go grab some Tylenol for my

head. It's starting to throb."

"Slick," Daniel said as she left the room to raid my medicine cabinet.

"I can't have her faint every time I try to drink from her. Hopefully, my little fib works." I turned to see Ginger still holding the Jug-Jolter 2000, studying it and her bottom. "If you use that thing and end up having to milk your own ass, don't come complaining to me."

# FOURTEEN

We'd managed to reach the mall before closing, but didn't have a ton of time to look around so I went straight to H & M and grabbed a slinky little baby blue lace dress with thin straps I hoped were strong enough to hold all of Shana's chest in, and strappy heels in her size.

Then we left and went to Wal-Mart for the rest of our shopping because, unlike Shana, Angel and I weren't snobs. I grabbed a cart and let Angel fill it with whatever she needed and grabbed some underwear for Shana.

"Please tell me that isn't what you wear," Daniel said over my shoulder as I grabbed a plain white pair of granny panties and proceeded to look through equally unflattering bras.

"Nope. These are for Shana," I said as I selected a very plain beige bra that looked like it could hold two soccer balls. "Must you hover?"

"I was hoping this would be entertaining."

"Is it?"

"Yeah, but not in the way I was hoping." He walked over to a display stand, picked up a scarlet red thong, and held it in front of him. "I'll give you fifty bucks to try this on and wiggle around a little bit."

"I'll tell Rider about your little indecent proposal for free just to watch him kick your ass," Ginger said as she looked through a rack of nightgowns nearby and stuck her tongue out at him.

"You're just mad I didn't ask you to do it," Daniel replied, then he shot the thong like a rubber band, hitting Ginger right between the eyes with it.

"They're kind of fun," Angel said, watching as Ginger chased Daniel down the aisle. "I didn't expect vampires to be so playful."

"They're supposed to be watching over us," I said, looking around to make sure no one had heard the vampire comment. Fortunately, we had the lingerie department to ourselves. "Try not to use the V-word in public."

"Sorry." She blushed as she put the last of her selections in our shopping cart. "I think I have everything I'll need for a while."

"All right. I have one more thing I need to get." Angel pushed the cart because, for some reason, she really enjoyed doing it, and we walked over to the electronics and entertainment department. I found the Blu-Rays and looked through the Disney movies until I found *Cinderella*.

"Um, shopping for a niece?"

"No, this is for me. My trainer wants me to watch it as homework."

"Why?"

"I'm not sure. I think it's supposed to be enlightening or something. I already know the story, but I haven't watched it in a long time, so why not?"

"What exactly are you being trained for?" She eyed the movie curiously.

I thought back to my last session with Nannette and laughed. "I have no idea. I thought it was to be a better fighter. I think she's doing some kind of Mr. Miyagi psychology with me or something, but she's a total badass, so if I can learn from her, I'll do whatever she asks."

"That's cool." Angel moved to my side and picked up a copy of *Lady and the Tramp*.

"You want that?"

She looked over at me and grinned sheepishly. "I know it's stupid. I remember watching this with my brother when I was little, back before he started running with the gang and he was nice to me."

I took the movie out of her hands and put it in the cart. "We'll have a Disney double feature."

"Who'd have thought I'd end up watching cartoons with a vam..." She looked around, noticing we weren't alone in this section of the store. "V-word."

"Who'd have thought you'd see one strangling a man with a thong," I said as Daniel came into view walking down the aisle, Ginger riding on his back as he pried at the thong she'd wrapped around his neck.

"You're attracting a crowd," I told them as they reached us.

Daniel looked around, noticing the people watching them, and ducked behind a display. I saw a shimmer of color and then heard a grunt as Ginger hit the floor and Daniel appeared next to me in a flash of movement. He shook the thong out, revealing it had been stretched out of shape during whatever they'd been doing. "Well, that's no good now," he said, and tossed it behind him where it landed in the kiddie movies.

"Did the two of you get all the juvenile antics out of your systems?" I asked as Ginger stood and dusted herself off.

"I don't know." Daniel shrugged. "The night is young, but your boyfriend is old and cranky. We need to get moving."

Daniel parked in the bar's lot and we transferred Angel and the majority of our purchases over to Ginger's Mustang so the two could go back to my apartment. We watched them exit the lot and turned for the bar, the small bag with Shana's clothes in my hand.

"He's already here," I said, noticing Kevin's Porsche in the lot.

"We're not late, so he must be eager to see his wife. I imagine I would be too if I got married and my wife just disappeared at the reception. This whole thing is a big mess."

"I know, I know," I muttered as we walked toward the bar.

"Danni, I would have done the same thing if someone I loved was about to die." He squeezed my shoulder. "It's a shitfest, but it's not like you tried to cause such a clusterfuck."

"You're really not that great at the motivational speaking thing, you know?"

He grinned. "I'm strong, sexy, funny, intelligent, and charming. I had to be subpar at something or else it would just be unfair to the rest of the world."

"And so humble." I rolled my eyes.

He winked at me and opened the door to the bar, allowing me to enter before him, although he stuck close to my side in bodyguard-mode. The place was starting to fill up, but once I passed the guard at the door, a shifter I wasn't familiar with, my gaze went straight to Rider. He was standing at the bar talking to Tony, who was on bartending duty again.

Rider caught my gaze, inclined his head toward the right, where I saw Kevin waiting impatiently at a booth, crumpling a napkin. Two large men stood near him on either side of the booth. I recognized one as the guy I'd Jug-Jolted. His face was still puffy from the nose and cheeks down, and his eyes were bloodshot. They narrowed as he noticed me. I gave him a little finger wave as Daniel and I walked over to Rider. His hands tightened into fists and I could imagine how hard he must have been struggling not to flip me the bird, or run across the room and choke me out.

"Shit," Daniel murmured.

Rider looked between him and the man. "What?"

"That's the guy Danni electrocuted with that breast enhancement thing. He still shows evidence of that, but she doesn't look like she ever got hit."

"Shit," I said. "I hadn't even thought of that. He hit me way too hard for me to not have damage. He would have at least broken the nose on a purely human woman."

Rider glared at the man, jaw clenched. I felt the fury spill from his pores and placed my hand on his arm in an effort to calm him. "He was doing what his employer told him to do."

"I don't give a damn what he was told," Rider replied, his words even and controlled. "He believed you were a human woman, and he punched you in the face. Fucking piece of shit, coward."

"I electrocuted him in the face," I reminded him. "Look at him. He barely has eyebrows and there's scorch marks on his face. He paid for what he did. Our concern now should be making sure he doesn't figure out why I'm not all bruised and puffy myself."

"Makeup," they both said.

"You guys really overestimate the power of makeup."

"I could always eat him," Tony said, leaning over the bar to look at the guy. He caught my reaction, which I imagined screamed shock, and shrugged. "What? He can't talk if he's being digested."

I leaned in close and lowered my voice. "Do you actually eat… everything?"

He smiled and looked at Rider. "She's cute," he said before tossing his towel on his shoulder and moving down the bar toward a man signaling his request for another drink.

Rider ruffled my hair. "Come on. Let's get those clothes to your sister so we can get her up here and get this over with. Daniel, stay here and if that asshole gives you any reason whatsoever, take him out back and destroy him."

"Is his presence enough?"

"Unfortunately, no. He'd have to at least bump into someone or something."

"Got it." Daniel folded his arms and leaned back against the bar, his sights firmly latched on to the man.

Rider slid his arm around my waist and guided me toward the back door, never taking his murderous glare off the man, who now shuffled his feet nervously. It didn't take a rocket scientist to know we'd been talking about him and the men with me weren't very happy with him. I almost felt sorry for him. Almost. That bastard had hit me hard.

Rider pushed through the door and we took the stairs down to the sublevels. "Have you spoken with her today?" I asked.

"I haven't been to see her directly. I've made sure she'd been fed and told her telepathically that we would be meeting with her husband today."

"Are you still thinking she should leave him?"

We were on the second sublevel now. Rider squeezed my hand. "I know you have reservations about that. The initial hunger she showed after turning has tapered down, but I still don't feel confident unleashing her into the world."

"Unleashing her? You make her sound like some sort of beast."

He grinned, but there was no humor behind it. "Let's see how she does tonight."

"All right," I said. "So… what about Kevin? What exactly are we telling him?"

"We'll see." Rider nodded at the men guarding Shana's door and they stepped aside for us to enter.

"About time," Shana said, sitting up in the bed. Her gaze fell to the bag in my hand, and she frowned. "H&M? That's where you shopped for me?"

"It was this or Wal-Mart," I said. "We're kind of limited to shopping at night and we didn't have much time before the mall closed. The boutiques you like to shop at close even earlier."

Her shoulders sagged. "I didn't think of that. This vampire thing is going to put a serious crimp in my style."

"You can always shop online," I told her, passing her the bag.

She grabbed it and looked inside, pulling out the dress. Her nose wrinkled. "I guess it isn't hideous, and the blue shows off my eyes." She looked into the bag and her lip curled. "Did you buy underwear for me or Grandma?"

"Just wear what she got you," Rider told her. "Your husband is upstairs in the bar."

Her brow furrowed as she looked at us. "Why is he in the bar? I thought we were going out to meet him."

"You are going out… to my bar."

"I want to go out somewhere nice."

"Well, that's insulting," Rider said to me before returning his attention to her. "Your husband sent men to Danni's apartment, and they got rough. I'm not meeting him anywhere else where he can set up some sort of stunt like that. We are meeting him in a location I can control, and if you're not happy with the location, you don't have to go at all. You're more than welcome to spend another night confined to this room."

"Fine," she snapped. "So do I get to leave with him? He is my husband, after all. We're supposed to be on our honeymoon."

"You can't go on a honeymoon right now," Rider told her. "You are dead to the world during the day, and you're going to be that way for quite a while until you build up the ability to stay awake during the day. Have you thought of how you will explain that to him?"

"I figured I would just party all night and sleep all day." She shrugged. "He works a lot of hours anyway, so he's gone most of the day."

"So he sleeps at night?" Rider asked.

"Yes."

"And he's going to be fine with his wife out partying all night long without him?"

"He adores me," Shana said, straightening her shoulders. "He'll let me do whatever I want. He's thankful to have me."

"I think you overestimate your appeal," Rider said. "No normal man is going to be happy with his wife out partying all night. There are two options here. Option one would be to leave him. Option two would be to trust him to know what you are and not reveal that secret to anyone else. How long have you actually been with him?"

"About six months," she answered.

"Shit," he muttered, and looked at me. It wasn't a very hopeful look.

*You and I haven't known each other even that long,* I reminded him telepathically.

*Yes, but that's just this lifetime, and may I remind you I've apparently been waiting centuries for you.*

"Do you want to stay married to him, or do you want to start a new life?" Rider asked, returning his attention to Shana.

"I wouldn't have married him if I didn't want to be with him," Shana said, looking genuinely affronted, but I'd talked to her about the subject enough to know she really didn't care all that much. Not to mention she'd had sex with other men at her bachelorette party.

Rider studied her for a moment, but it was hard to tell what he was thinking. "We'll see how it goes. What would you do if you were allowed to leave with him?"

She shrugged. "Shop, hang out with my friends, live like I normally do, just mostly at night."

"You cannot blog about being a vampire."

"Well, I know that, silly. Eliza told me about hunters. I'm not going to broadcast what I am to the world and invite those psychos to come kill me."

"You can't tell any of your friends. You shouldn't have anyone at your house where they can find your blood supply. It's hard to explain bagged blood in the refrigerator."

"Understood."

"You cannot, under any circumstance, tell your family."

Shana shot a glance my way before nodding. "Understood."

Shit. I hadn't thought of how she'd keep being a vampire a secret from my mother and grandmother. She was their favorite, and they were always taking her shopping or out on lunch dates. It wasn't that hard for me to hide my vampirism because being hybrid altered my physiology, enabling me to function during the day regardless how new of a vampire I was. With a ton of specially made sunscreen Rider provided his people, I could move about in the daylight. It wasn't the most comfortable thing, but I could do it. My family hadn't a clue anything had changed in my life.

Rider blew out a sigh. "Get dressed and we'll see how this goes, but I'm not making any promises right now."

"All right," Shana said, and she started unbuttoning her shirt despite the fact we all knew everything she'd been wearing except for a very flimsy pair of panties had been ruined when she'd been shot.

"Whoa!" Rider and I both said at the same time.

She paused and looked up at us innocently despite an excessive amount of cleavage being revealed. "What? I'm getting ready."

"I'll be waiting in the hall when you're ready," Rider said. He shook his head in disbelief and quickly left the room, closing the door behind him.

"What the hell was that?" I asked. I felt anger, but unlike the usual raging fury that flooded me from time to time since being turned, this was manageable.

"What was what?" Shana stood from the bed and dumped the rest of the contents out of the bag, looking over the makeup I'd bought her at Wal-Mart.

"He's mine," I said, careful to keep my tone free of anything that could be perceived as jealousy. "I wouldn't undress in front of your husband. I'd appreciate it if you'd show me the same respect and not undress in front of my boyfriend."

"I thought we were all like a little vampire family or something," she said as she finished unbuttoning the shirt, dropped it to the floor, and pulled the blue dress on, opting to go braless and remain in the same tiny scrap of underwear she'd been wearing on her wedding day.

I couldn't help but notice her breasts stayed perky despite their size thanks to the damned vampire enhancement. I started to fold my arms over my chest, a defense mechanism when I felt insecure, but remembered my conversation with Nannette and forced myself to stand defiantly in the presence of Shana and her supermodel body.

She slipped her bare feet into the shoes I'd bought for her and smoothed the dress over her hips before planting her hands there and turned toward me, smiling sweetly. "You could undress in front of Kevin and he wouldn't notice, but if you feel you don't have the same kind of adoration from Rider, that sounds like something you might want to think about so you don't end up heartbroken. I'd hate to see that."

She picked up the makeup and hairbrush I'd brought her and took it into the bathroom, throwing a smug smile back my way before she put everything down on the sink and started her beauty routine. I realized I was standing there with my mouth gaping open and snapped it shut. I had no comeback and my anger was starting to move toward the uncontrollable range. Deciding against raking my fingernails down the side of Shana's pretty face like I desired, I clenched my fingers into fists, turned, and left the room.

Rider's eyebrows shot up as I reached him at the end of

the hall. "Everything all right?"

I looked at him. He was perfect. Tall, beautiful without being feminine, intelligent, powerful, and he'd seemed to care about me from the moment we'd first met. He'd seemed attracted to me as well, despite the fact a man like him could have anyone he wanted. "Do you think I'm pretty?"

"No, I just like to bang ugly chicks," he said, frowning down at me. "Of course I think you're pretty. Actually, I think you're beautiful. Did she say something to you? Don't let her get in your head."

I thought back to my training session with Nannette and covered his eyes with my hands. "What color are my eyes?"

"A very bright and gorgeous shade of green. Like emeralds. Why?"

I lowered my hands and smiled. "Just seeing how much you pay attention."

"Honey, I have every inch of you etched into my brain." He lifted my chin with his index finger. "Again I ask, is everything all right?"

I nodded. Rider loved me. He'd left Shana's room and her big overstuffed boobs without the slightest hesitation. "Has she tried that stunt before? The undressing in front of you thing?"

"No. I think that was a power play. I warned you she'd do that."

"What do you mean?"

"You're both my fledglings. The part of her that is accustomed to being number one and feeds on being adored wants to be adored by everyone. I've tried keeping my feelings for you secret for your own safety, but I've never managed to do that well. I'm assuming she senses it and she doesn't like it." He looked toward the closed door. "Do you believe she wants to stay married to her husband?"

"I believe she wants to stay married to his money," I

said. "He's a smart guy. No matter how enamored he is with her, I'm sure he made her sign a prenuptial agreement. If they divorce, she'll lose that income."

"Is the money enough to make her play the role of loving wife and stay on her best behavior if I let her leave with him?"

I thought about it. "I don't know about her best behavior. I'm sure she'll have affairs, but she'll stay married as long as poor Kevin is bringing home the big bucks."

"Do I need to remind you that poor Kevin sent men to your apartment to attack you?"

"Oh yeah, right. I keep forgetting I should hate him. He's so dorky and pitiful, and completely getting screwed over, but then again, I'm sure his supposed love for her is just as shallow as hers is for him."

"Maybe they deserve each other," he murmured, staring off into space.

I recognized that look. "What are you pondering?"

He grinned. "Who says pondering?"

"Fine. What are you in deep thought about?"

"There's a third option I didn't tell her about," he said. "Rihanna will be in the meeting with us. She's going to see if Kevin is susceptible to persuasive magic, and if he is, she can work a spell that will make it possible for Shana to live with him without him questioning any vampire-related oddities. I felt kind of bad doing something like that to a person, but after he sent men to your apartment, I started liking the idea a lot more."

Hope blossomed in my chest. After the near-striptease in Shana's room, I wanted her out of Rider's building as soon as possible. "It's not a bad thing, is it? It won't hurt him?"

"No. The way she explained it to me, it'll just blur his perception a bit, so if he sees blood in the refrigerator, he won't think anything of it. He won't question why she sleeps all day or think anything's unusual if he sees her drop her fangs."

"Well, that's not bad at all. I mean, he married her so by doing this you'll be helping a married couple stay together."

"I'm not sure it's a nice thing to help a man stay with her," he said, grinning mischievously, "but like I said, he sent men to your apartment and I don't really feel that bad for the man anymore."

"So do that. Problem solved."

"We'll see," he said, the humor fading from his eyes. "First, we need to see if he's susceptible to the magic required, and I need to see how she does around people. I can't let her loose on the world if she's going to destroy it."

"Is it really necessary to be that dramatic?"

"Danni, it's happened before," he said, his eyes haunted. "Seta's son turned a woman he loved and had to kill her the very first night."

"Why?"

"She killed almost an entire village. She was about to kill a baby when he stopped her the only way he could."

Cold invaded my body at such a terrible thought. "That's horrific."

Rider nodded. "I know. That's why we can't turn just anyone. That's why I have to make sure your sister is fit to leave here before I allow it."

"That's why you might have to kill her," I whispered, looking down.

The door to Shana's room opened, and she emerged, hesitating when she saw the two guards. They moved aside, allowing her to pass. She looked beautiful as always, and curious as she looked around. I couldn't help but notice she gave a lingering glance at one of the guards before turning her full attention to us once she reached the end of the hall. "How do I look?" she asked, batting her lashes at Rider.

"Presentable," he said, sliding his arm around my waist. "Let's get this over with, and remember, you say nothing about being a vampire, or any of us being what we are. You mention nothing you've seen here. You're unsure about the marriage, afraid you might have rushed into things, and you need more time. Do you understand?"

"Yes, sir." She snapped him a playful salute.

Rider's face morphed into a mask of complete seriousness. "I can kill you without touching you. I will kill you to protect my people. Now, do you understand what is expected of you and what will not be allowed?"

Shana straightened her posture and nodded, all trace of humor gone. "I understand."

"Good. I wouldn't recommend forgetting." He led us through the sublevels, to the bar, me at his side and Shana trailing behind.

*Guys*, Daniel said in both of our heads as we neared the door leading to the bar. *Someone else has joined the meeting and you're not going to be happy about it.*

Rider and I shared a look as he pushed through the door. We immediately looked over at the booth Kevin had been sitting in and found him still there, guarded by the two men. Rihanna had arrived and was sitting at a nearby table with turquoise streaks in her dark, curly hair, a low-cut turquoise tank top revealing a lot of mocha-hued skin, and skin-tight jeans hugging her curves. She winked at us covertly and went back to sipping her drink.

"Shana!"

My heart stopped as my mother's voice registered. Rider and I both turned toward the voice to see her moving across the room, headed our way. Daniel looked at us as she passed him, his expression a mix of sympathy and amusement. He knew the rest of the night was going to be entertaining, but possibly pure torture for me.

"If I had balls, I'm sure they'd be crawling up into my stomach right now," I muttered.

"Mine are doing that for the both of us," Rider said, rubbing my back.

"I was so worried about you!" My mother enveloped

Shana in a suffocating hug, squeezed the life out of her, then turned toward me. "And *you*, how dare you—"

Rider stepped forward, a low growl rumbling from his throat. My mother backed up a step, gasping. Kevin saw what was happening and rushed over, his guards with him. Daniel moved in closer, and I caught Shana winking at Tony.

"So," I said, easing between Rider and my mother. "Anyone want a drink?"

# FIFTEEN

We managed to get everyone moved over to the booth before things got out of hand. Kevin sat on the inside of one side, my mother next to him. Shana sat across from Kevin. I sat next to her, and Rider sat next to me. Rihanna remained at her table, but sat angled so she got a good look at Kevin. Kevin's guards stood far enough away from the booth to give us privacy, but close enough to come to his defense if needed. Daniel leaned against the bar, keeping a watchful eye over us and Kevin's men. He didn't bother trying to look inconspicuous, not that a man who looked like him could pull inconspicuous off anyway.

"Explain," my mother said, almost growling as she glared at me and Rider, "and it better be good. I could have the cops here in five minutes."

"Shana," Rider said. "Are you here against your will?"

"No," she said as I held my breath.

"Why are you here?" Kevin asked, and I didn't imagine the hurt in his voice, buried under anger.

"She's here because of Danni," my mother snapped as she pointed her finger at me. "You couldn't let your sister be happy."

"When have I ever stood in the way of Shana being

happy?" I asked.

"You've always envied her."

"You've always told me I should," I snapped back.

"This meeting was supposed to be with Kevin," Rider said, jumping in with a tone much calmer than my mother and I had been using.

"I'm Shana's mother. Her welfare is my business."

"What about Danni's welfare?"

My mother frowned, looking between the two of us. "What about her welfare? She's fine. Jealous and spiteful, but—"

"You heard gunshots and noticed Shana was missing. You called the police in to search for her. Her husband wanted to go on the news and put up a reward for information on her whereabouts. Danni was missing too, but no one was worried about her. No reward was considered for information on her. You have a lot of nerve to sit there and call yourself a mother, lady."

"How dare you—"

"He's right," Shana said, surprising the hell out of me. "You should have been worried about both of us. And my husband should have offered a reward for me *and* my sister."

Kevin's already big eyes widened as he realized he'd failed to do the right thing and was quite possibly in big trouble for it. "But, honey, all I could think of was getting you back safely as soon as possible. I didn't even know Danni was missing. We just thought she'd left and wasn't answering her phone."

"Sure, that's why the police were sent here to question me," Rider said.

"Well, clearly we had good reason to," my mother said. "You've been harboring them."

"Do I look like I've been abused?" Shana asked. "I needed some time to think, and I was going to just run off on my own somewhere, but Danni stopped me and made me stay here instead of running off and getting into trouble, like a good sister is supposed to do."

We all just looked at Shana, not sure what to say. It wasn't often she sang my praises. I turned toward Rider and could see the suspicion in his eyes, but the other two almost looked ashamed of themselves.

"Why would you run away from your own reception?" my mother asked. "You've been planning your dream wedding forever."

*Like that was my dream wedding,* I heard Shana think and realized she was too worked up to block the thought. Rider had warned me early after my turning that, if not careful, my thoughts could leak out to him and anyone in his nest close enough to hear.

"You've been planning my dream wedding forever," Shana told her. "Pushing me."

"You don't want to be married to me?" Kevin asked, his voice barely above a whisper.

Shana muttered in her mind about what a clingy pain Kevin could be, but reached across the table and squeezed his hand. "Aww, Kevvy-kins, you know I wuv you."

Rider and I slowly turned our heads toward each other and I'm sure I wore the same *don't you dare ever call me anything like that* expression as he did.

"So, it's settled," my mother said, smoothing her bleached-blonde hair. "Kevin, collect your wife and let's go home."

"Excuse me?" Shana's voice raised by at least four octaves. "Have you moved yourself in already?"

"It's just an expression," my mother said. "Now let's go."

"No."

"Excuse me?"

"I said no." Shana pulled her hand away from Kevin's, straightened her shoulders, and folded her arms defiantly. "I have a lot to consider, and I need some time away from certain influences."

"What is there to consider?" Kevin asked as my mother

sat shell-shocked. "I asked you to marry me and you said yes! We had the ceremony. We're married right now. This is ridiculous. What could have possibly changed?" His eyes darkened. "Did you meet someone else?"

I felt the vibration of Rider's silent laughter and discreetly elbowed him in his side. Now was not the time to even hint at Shana hooking up with random guys at her bachelorette party. She stared at Kevin, deep in thought, but apparently she'd remembered to throw her mental wall up because I couldn't hear anything rolling around in her head.

"There's no one else," she finally said. "I agreed to marry you because I wanted to, and I intend to stay married to you."

*You can't go home with him just yet*, Rider told her through our link.

"Good, so let's go," my mother said, grabbing her purse.

"You can go home," Shana told her. "Kevin and I need to discuss a bit more."

My mother's mouth dropped open. Shana had always listened to her. She might not have always followed the rules, but she'd always been careful to appear as though she had. She certainly had never openly defied my mother before. As if thinking the same thing, my mother pointed her perfectly manicured finger at me again. "This is your fault. You've been a horrible influence on her."

"Mrs. Keller, I'm going to ask you nicely to leave now," Rider said, voice even, eyes dark.

"And if I don't?" She straightened her shoulders and attempted to make herself look more threatening, but at barely five feet four inches, she wasn't successful.

Rider opened his mouth to answer, but Shana beat him.

"If you don't leave and allow me to handle my own life, I'm going to stay with Danni much longer," she said. "If you want this marriage to work, and better yet, if you want to eventually live with me, you need to give me some space now."

"Well, I never!" My mother slid out of the booth with about as much grace as a water buffalo, held her purse tight against her chest, and declared, "I'll be back, and the both of you better find your manners and remember I'm your mother. I will not have this disrespect."

We watched her turn and storm across the bar, snapping at the guard on duty as he held the front door open for her. We all let out a breath of relief as the door closed behind her.

"She's planning on living with us?" Kevin's face grew paler than usual.

"She'd like to," Shana told him, "but just because she wants to doesn't mean she'll get to."

His shoulders lowered as he let out another relieved breath. "Shana, when are you coming home? I don't understand this. And why are we having this discussion here with these two? This should be private."

"You lost your shot at private when you sent goons after Danni," Rider told him, a threatening edge to his tone.

Kevin glanced at me before lowering his gaze to the table, his expression sheepish. "I didn't send them to hurt anyone. They were told to watch her apartment and grab Shana if she showed up there. I did tell them they could use force with any captors holding her hostage. I didn't mean for them to barrel into the apartment without proof Shana was there, and I definitely didn't tell them to attack her sister. Of course, your guy started it when he—"

"Your guys started it when they barged through my door," I snapped. "Daniel and I only defended ourselves against strange men with guns who'd just broken in."

"You told them to grab me?" Shana folded her arms and glared across the table at her new husband.

"I thought you'd been abducted," Kevin snapped. "We'd just gotten married. If you were going to run, I figured it would have been before we exchanged vows.

None of this makes sense. Why are we here instead of on our honeymoon?"

Her glare softened. She unfolded her arms and reached across the table for Kevin's hand. "I'm sorry. I think everything was just rushed. I just need a little time to sort things out without worrying about you sending someone after me or my sister."

"I didn't mean for that to happen," he mumbled as he looked at their hands. "I love you Shana-bear. Come home with me. Better yet, let's just go on our honeymoon."

She squeezed his hand. "I can't right now, and I can't really put into words why, but I'll be home soon."

Kevin cut a glance to Rider.

"No one is keeping me here against my will," Shana quickly said. "Do you trust me?"

"Always," he said.

*Poor dumb bastard*, Rider said telepathically, earning another jab from my elbow.

"Then go home and I'll call you soon," Shana said. "I just need a little time, and what's a little time when we're going to spend the rest of our lives together?"

Kevin's mouth twisted into a semblance of a smile. It was sad, yet hopeful at the same time. "All right, Shana-bear, but don't make me wait too long. There are a lot of people wondering what's going on."

"I understand."

Kevin looked at Rider. "If anything happens to her—"

"You'll do nothing," Rider finished for him, "and I'll break whoever you send after me or my people. In fact…" He stood and stared at the man I'd hit with the Jug-Jolter 2000 until the man turned toward him. "You're going to leave this one here. We have unfinished business."

"Jamal has been reprimanded, and your guy did enough damage to him, as you can clearly see."

Rider smiled. "He told you my guy did this to him?"

"Yeah," Kevin said as Jamal's puffy face flushed with color, and pointed at Daniel. "The rainbow-haired guy. He

220

doesn't even have a scratch on him. My security got the worst of that incident."

"Tell him the truth," Rider said to Jamal. "Tell him who really kicked your ass and why."

I almost felt sorry for the guy as he turned teary, bloodshot eyes toward the other security guy he was working with, a man who hadn't been at my apartment and probably had no clue what really had happened. Then Jamal looked at me with a glare mean enough to kill. "If she didn't want to get hit, the bitch shouldn't have grabbed—"

Rider's fist smashed into Jamal's face in a burst of speed, and the man flew back at least six feet, landing on a table, which broke on impact. His partner moved forward, but having watched the entire scene play out, Daniel anticipated the move and had already been on his feet before Rider's fist had connected. He stood a breath away from the second man, silently daring him to make another move. The man backed away, raising his hands in defeat, clearly seeing something in Daniel's eyes that warned him this was a fight he wouldn't win.

"Holy crap," Kevin said, sliding out of the booth. He stood next to Rider, gawking, as two muscular members of Rider's security staff each grabbed Jamal under an armpit and dragged him out the front door. His bloodshot eyes were closed and his face had gone from puffy to flat, his nose broken.

"He really shouldn't have called my woman a bitch," Rider said, turning toward Kevin, "and you really shouldn't send anyone near her again. Also, you should leave now."

Kevin's Adam's apple bobbed as he swallowed hard and quickly nodded his head. He turned back and blew a kiss to Shana. "I'll be waiting for you to call, sweetie." Then he gestured toward his remaining security guard and they made their exit.

"Well, that was entertaining," Rihanna said, getting up from her seat as Rome passed her to clean up the broken table, which had fortunately been vacant when Jamal landed on it. I hadn't seen him earlier, but he seemed to come from the direction of the bathrooms, so I assumed he'd been keeping them spotless as ordered.

Rider took my hand and pulled me to a stand, then directed me to sit on the other side of the booth. He slid in next to me as Rihanna took a seat across from us, next to Shana, and Daniel took the spot next to her. Every eye in the bar had been on Rider after he'd hit Jamal, but sensing the fight had ended as soon as it began, patrons went back to drinking or whatever they were doing before the incident.

"So?" Rider asked the mocha-skinned witch.

Rihanna pulled her gaze away from Daniel, who she'd been hungrily ogling, and nodded. "He's susceptible, so it's up to you how you want to handle this. Hey girl," she said to me.

"Hey." I smiled. "This is my sister, Shana. Shana, this is Rihanna, a good friend."

"Yeah, I heard all about the newbie," Rihanna said, looking over at my sister. Shana looked at her with a hint of disdain I knew to be a touch of jealousy. Shana didn't show it much, but Rihanna was very pretty and had killer curves, not to mention she reeked of power, not as strong as Rider's, but as a witch hers kind of leaked out more whereas Rider's stayed under the surface unless he chose to display it. If she picked up on Shana's jealousy, she didn't say anything. Instead, she turned toward Daniel and batted her eyelashes. "How's my sexy dragon boy doing tonight?"

Daniel's gaze met mine, and he threw me a look that begged for help.

"So, what are we going to do about the situation?" I asked, getting everyone back on track. "Shana, do you want to stay married to Kevin?"

"Yes." She nodded matter-of-factly, but her eyes were curious. "Vampire or not, I assume I still need money to live off of, and he has plenty. Plus, he adores me. What's this about him being susceptible? Susceptible to what?"

"Rihanna is a witch," Rider explained. "She can work a spell that will help your husband not pick up on any peculiarities you have so that you may stay married to him without us having to worry about him revealing our existence."

Her eyes widened as she looked at Rihanna again. "You can do, like, magic?"

"Bet your ass," Rihanna said. "This isn't even that major of a spell since your hubby's all smitten with you and he's the susceptible type. It just makes his mind a little fuzzy about vampire things he might see or hear, like if he sees you drinking blood, he'll think it's like a fruit drink or something. If he catches a glance of your fangs, it'll be no different than seeing regular teeth. Now, I can't just blanket the whole state of Kentucky with this spell, or anyone whose chemistry makes them unsusceptible, so you still need to be careful not to reveal yourself to any other friends or family. For example, your mother is not susceptible to spells of this level. Casting the spell on her won't do diddly."

"Not surprised," I muttered. Nothing was ever easy with my mother.

"So I'm free to go home?" Shana looked at Rider hopefully.

I sensed the tension inside him as he stared at her, considering. I understood his fear of the world discovering us and how that information could endanger us, but saw no reason to keep Shana locked up under the bar. Despite what he'd said about her having bad characteristics for a new vampire, she'd actually kind of defended me to my mother. That didn't seem like the action of a purely evil vampire to me.

"You can't tell anyone what you or any of us are," Rider finally said, his tone brooking no room for argument. "You absolutely cannot blog about any of this.

You can't go on your honeymoon. I don't care what excuse you have to come up with, but if you don't stay in the house playing the role of loving housewife, I will track you down and drag your ass back down to the basement. I am your sire. There is no hiding from me. Do you understand?"

I felt a shiver of lust go through Shana and bit down on the inside of my jaw.

"Perfectly," she said, her eyes a little heady as they rolled over Rider.

A low growl started in my throat. Rider quickly squeezed my thigh under the table. *Don't let her know we're picking up on her thoughts and feelings,* he said through our mind link. *I don't want her blocking us out. I still don't trust her.*

*Are you going to let her go?*

*You think I shouldn't?*

I thought about it. Shana wouldn't do anything that threatened her own well-being, so I couldn't see her exposing us to the world if she knew the dangers. I could, however, see her taking advantage of the vampire benefits like immortality and never-ending youth to cheat on her poor husband left and right, which was good reason to get her out of the building and far away from Rider and Daniel. Er... far away from Rider. Daniel was free to sleep with whoever he wanted, although the thought of him with Shana made me a little nauseous.

"Shana, you know you became a vampire because you were shot by men hunting me and Rider," I said, pushing back the thoughts of Shana wanting those closest to me for her personal toys. "Those hunters may have been killed, but there are more where they came from and they are always searching for our kind. If our existence became common knowledge, we would never be free to live in peace. It's important that you stay mindful of this. Any slip-up could bring hunters down on any or all of us. Are you grasping the severity of this?"

Shana's jaw clenched, and I got the impression it was

taking a lot of willpower not to roll her eyes. "Eliza told me all of this. Both of you are repeating yourselves from earlier tonight. I'm not dumb enough to do anything to bring murderers my way or give crazy conspiracy theorists any reason to fear me and try to take me out. I can keep this a secret. I'm great at keeping secrets, maybe one of the best." She grinned mischievously, then quickly adopted a completely serious look. "I will take the secret of our existence to the grave, and I don't plan on ever going to my grave, so you can all relax."

I looked over at Rider and sighed, letting him know the ball was in his court. It was, after all, his show to run.

"You can go home tomorrow night," he told my sister, the hint of mistrust heavy in his eyes, "but you will be under surveillance and if you choose to believe anything in this world, believe this: I am not a man you want to upset."

"Of course not." She batted her eyelashes coyly, as if Rider hadn't just delivered a very clear threat to her, and turned her attention to Rihanna. "So, how does this spell work?"

Rihanna closed her eyes, spoke some words that sounded very Latin, did a little flourish with her hand and a bottle of wine appeared. She handed it to Rider. "Make sure he drinks from this when you arrange for him to come back to retrieve his bride."

Shana's mouth dropped open. "That just appeared out of nowhere. What else can you do?"

"Honey, what can't I do? I'm the shit." Rihanna laughed and flipped her hair back from her shoulder before holding her hand out, palm up. Rider heaved out a sigh, counted out a sizeable amount of bills from his pocket, and forked the money over.

Shana's gaze stayed glued to the money during the exchange and again I could feel the desire run through her as she sized Rider up. It didn't escape me when her gaze shifted to assess the rest of the bar. I could practically hear the cash register chime in her head as she estimated how much money Rider had.

"So are you born a witch or is magic something you can learn to do?" Shana asked her.

"There are some who learn a little magic, but to have any true power, you have to be born with the gift."

"What a shame," Shana murmured. "It seems like a lucrative way of life."

"We can't do just anything for money," Rihanna told her. "Everyone wants love spells, but those are a big no-no. Some witches specialize in dark arts, but I'm not willing to pay the price for that, no matter how much people offer to pay me to do it. I make most of my money from protection-related spells and cosmetic magic."

"Cosmetic magic?"

Rihanna nodded. "Boob jobs, nose jobs, hair coloring. My way is so much easier than going to a salon or getting all cut up in some surgeon's office."

Shana looked at me. "Did you know about this, Danni?"

I shook my head as Rider's hand firmly gripped my thigh. *No*, he said in my mind.

"Danni had a breast augmentation all scheduled but then canceled out because she couldn't risk the bleeding." Shana lightly smacked her forehead with the heel of her hand. "Duh, you canceled because you got turned, and that's why you couldn't have it done. But if there's no cutting, you can still have it done this way."

"Oh, I do it for vampires all the time," Rihanna said, frowning at me. "You poor thing. You've really had a rough introduction into the paranormal world. That whole messy situation when we met," she said, referring to how she'd cleaned up the mess I'd made of Dex Prince after he'd attacked me not long after I'd been turned, "and you had to cancel your surgery. My way is better anyway. It's much safer."

"It's unnecessary," Rider said.

"Oh, I'll do it as a freebie," Rihanna said, waving her hand as if to say his money was no good. "Every woman should be able to feel confident in her own skin, and it's so simple. See!" She snapped her fingers, and I looked down to see what had to be at least a 34C chest where my formerly 34A chest had been. "I can go bigger or smaller, but with your frame, I wouldn't recommend bigger."

I felt my mouth hanging open, matching the look on my sister's face. I tried to speak, but no sound would come out. Looking down at myself in the sleeveless crocheted tunic, all I could see was a line of cleavage sticking out the top and two protruding mounds stretching out the fabric. I hadn't felt a thing.

"Change her back."

We all swiveled our heads toward Rider.

"It's no charge," Rihanna told him. "And there's no side effects or anything—"

"Change. Her. Back." His eyes started to glow as power leaked out of him. He clenched his fist, fighting for control of his temper. "Put her back exactly as she was right now."

Rihanna's eyes grew round as saucers and she gulped as she quickly nodded. She spun her shaking hand around in a circle and snapped her fingers twice. Again, I felt nothing at all, but my chest deflated back to its normal size.

Rider pulled his power back in and did a little wavy thing of his own, snatching shadows to wrap around us as he pulled out the collar of my shirt and looked inside.

"What are you doing?"

"Making sure everything's been returned correctly," he said. Seeming to find everything as it should be, he fixed my shirt, released the shadows and glared at Rihanna. "Never do that again. You are not to change one single thing about her. Not ever."

*What the hell?* I heard Shana think. *Oh, he has to be messing with Danni's mind to make her dependent on him. There's no way he'd take those little non-breasts over a real woman's curves.*

Rider snapped his head toward Shana and opened his

mouth. This time, I dug *my* fingers into *his* thigh. *Don't*, I said through our link. I may have growled a bit as I also fought the urge to kick Shana in the shin.

"I'm sorry," Rihanna said. "I thought it was a nice gift, but Danni is beautiful just the way she is. To make up for this little misunderstanding, I'll give you something else. Just name it."

Shana rolled her eyes and made to move. "Excuse me. I need to use the ladies' room."

"For what?" Rider asked.

"What, do you like, want a number?" Shana asked him before reining in her irritation and pasting on a phony smile. "I have to make tinkles," she whispered. "You can trust me. You have security all over this floor anyway."

Rider studied her a moment before looking at Daniel and gesturing with his head for him to allow Shana out of the booth. Daniel and Rihanna moved over, allowing Shana out. Rider caught the eye of a shifter he had on security duty and I sensed the silent communication between them before the man nodded and discreetly followed Shana, where I was sure he'd stand outside the bathroom to make sure she didn't try anything.

Rihanna sighed and flagged down a server. "I'm hungry. I'm going to order some food while you decide on an appropriate gift."

"Give me that," I said, realizing this was another opportunity for me to eat actual delicious food, not the bland stuff my new vampire tummy could actually handle. Bland food was so worthless I didn't even bother with it unless I was forced to eat something to keep up appearances.

"Bar food?" Rihanna asked.

"Yes," I said, "and the ability to eat it without being sick."

"Oh." Her eyes widened, catching on. "That spell only lasts an hour."

"That's fine. Just give me that and let me feast. I've

been eying the fried food in here too long to not get to enjoy it."

Rihanna looked at Rider for approval and he nodded, insinuating the temporary spell was a suitable gift to make up for her snafu.

The server who'd slammed Daniel's beer bottle on our table the other night came over, glaring at me until she noticed Rider's own narrow-eyed gaze on her. "What can I get you?" she asked, suddenly all bright-eyed and merry-voiced.

"One of everything on the food side of the menu," Rihanna said, winking at me. "We're going to have a buffet. Add a couple of beers for me and my dragon cutie, and three, uh, whatever you have on tap for my nocturnal friends."

"Is the bakery open?" Rider asked Daniel, remembering how Daniel had run for it the last time Rihanna had worked the same spell on me just to grab me a chocolate cupcake I'd been dying for.

"I already checked the time," Daniel answered, grinning. "Sadly, the bakery is closed, so we won't be entertained by cupcake porn this evening. Maybe the onion rings will do something for her."

"Your food and drinks will be right up," the server said, cutting me a quick glare before turning on her heel and walking away to put our order in.

"I'll be right back," Rider said before kissing me on my temple and sliding out of the booth. He headed toward the server.

"Somebody's in troublllle," Daniel sang, watching along with me as Rider approached the woman and directed her toward his office. "That was really stupid looking at you like that right in front of Rider."

"I hope I'm out of trouble," Rihanna said softly. "I'm sorry, Danni. I thought you really wanted the augmentation, and after everything you've been through since turning, I thought it was a nice gift."

"I did really want it," I told her. "I was turned right before the date I had scheduled to get it done and was really disappointed when I had to cancel." I looked down at my chest, comparing it to how it had looked with Rihanna's magical help, and frowned as I tried to sort through my feelings. I'd wanted a decent sized chest since puberty had come and gone without leaving me anything, but in that moment when I'd looked down to see an abundance of cleavage, I'd actually felt a little... disappointed. Now, how the hell was that for weird?

"So why was he so mad?" the witch asked.

"Because Danni's perfect just the way she is," Daniel answered, staring at me.

I averted my eyes, feeling a little exposed as the heat of a blush climbed my cheeks. With a deep breath, I pushed the awkward feeling away. Daniel was my friend and my protector. He cared about me, but not in *that* way. I knew he still mourned the loss of his fiancé, who had been killed right after accepting his proposal back in Imortia, before he'd been turned into a dragon shifter.

"If it makes you feel any better, Rihanna, I'm kind of relieved you could undo the spell. I didn't feel right looking down and seeing all that cleavage. It just wasn't me."

Rihanna smiled. "Honestly, you don't need it. I'll always help a woman feel confident, but magically helped confidence is never as strong as the confidence of a woman who accepts and loves herself as she is. That's why I haven't reduced these fun bags, no matter how often I'd like something a little smaller."

I gaped at her. "You have the power to mold yourself into anything you'd like and you don't use it?"

"Honey, we all have the power to mold ourselves into whatever we want. The way we look has nothing to do with that. And no, I don't judge the women who come to me for cosmetic spells, but when I look in the mirror, I want to see the me that God created. I want to see the way the DNA from my family tree mixed together so I can see and connect with my ancestors."

"That's deep," Daniel said, nodding his approval. "I like that."

Deep indeed, I thought as a different server came to our table with beers, three dark mugs of blood, a basket of fries and a basket of onion rings.

"The rest of your food will be brought out as it comes up," she said, smiling, before turning away and crossing the room to another table.

"Wait," Rihanna said as I reached out for a hot, greasy french fry, my mouth already watering. She murmured in Latin, flicked her wrists, and winked at me. "Now you can eat. I want you to get your full hour's worth."

"Thanks," I said a second before filling my mouth with fries. The flavor of delicious, fried, lightly salted potatoes hit my tongue, and I let out a soft moan.

"Oh boy. More food porn," Daniel said, laughing as he helped himself to an onion ring.

"Shut up," I said, not bothering to swallow my food first. Who gave a crap about manners when you only had an hour to eat and you wanted everything?

"We can eat that?"

I looked up to see Shana returning. Her eyes practically dilated as she stared at the food.

"Yup, we sure can," I said, spearing Rihanna and Daniel with a look that said not to utter a single cautionary word as they slid over, allowing room for Shana on their side of the booth.

Rihanna raised an eyebrow as a small grin played around the corners of her mouth, and Daniel shook his head while reaching for his beer, which he used to hide his smile.

My conscience nudged me a little as I recalled how horribly sick I'd been after making the mistake of eating heavy food after turning, but then Shana smiled seductively at Daniel as she scooted as close to him as she could possibly get.

"We have more food coming," I said. "Eat as much as you want."

# SIXTEEN

By the time Rider returned to the booth we'd downed the fries and onion rings, and had moved on to sliders, buffalo wings, mozzarella sticks, soft pretzel sticks, chicken tenders, and shrimp among other things, none of them particularly good for a newly turned vampire's stomach.

Rider slid in next to me and watched Shana pop a shrimp into her mouth. He raised his eyebrow as he looked over at me. I returned an innocent closed-mouth smile and finished chewing my chicken tender. He shook his head and picked up his mug of blood, sharing a grin with Daniel as they met each other's eyes.

*You know Rome's on bathroom cleaning duty tonight*, Rider reminded me through our mind-link.

I winced, recalling the horror scene I'd once turned a restaurant bathroom into after eating food I'd been warned not to eat, but then Daniel's body jerked a little and he reached under the table to forcefully shove Shana's hand away from him. The poor guy had been getting harassed from both sides, but Rihanna's flirtation amused me. I didn't find any amusement in Shana's manhandling of him, and suddenly, I didn't feel so bad for Rome. Rome was a big boy. He could handle mopping up puke.

"Everything all right?" I asked Rider, changing the subject. "Was there a problem with the server?"

"Her name's Myra," he answered after finishing one of the sliders. "She needed an attitude adjustment and a reminder of how stupid it would be to blow the good job she has here."

"She hates me?"

He shared a look with Daniel before shrugging. "She doesn't know you, and it doesn't matter. It's taken care of."

*She's one of the women you slept with before you met me, isn't she?* I asked him telepathically and felt his body grow tense next to mine.

*It doesn't matter*, he finally answered through the mind link as a loud gurgle erupted from Shana's stomach, giving me the answer I'd feared without actually admitting to anything.

"Excuse me," Shana said, covering her flat belly with her hand. Her face grew pinched as she reached for her mug and took a sip of blood. Her hand trembled as she set the mug back down and gripped the edge of the table.

Daniel tried to slide away from her, expecting her to erupt like Mount Vesuvius, but this only smooshed him tighter against Rihanna, who took the opportunity to fully press herself against him. The man couldn't look down without getting a face full of cleavage.

I felt Rider's amusement next to me in the form of a barely perceptible rumble of silent laughter, and I should have been feeling it too as Shana's skin turned an unflattering shade of green, but I'd sought out the server in the bar and was too busy studying her. She was taller than me, thinner than me, but her breasts were at least two cup sizes fuller than mine. I didn't think she was that pretty, but that might have been my jealousy talking as I imagined her wrapped around Rider, his mouth on her tanned skin. She was a shifter. Who knew what she could do in bed?

"I can feel your hurt and anger," Rider whispered softly. "You can't hold sexual encounters I had before you against me, Danni. It's not fair, and I've told you they meant nothing. She means nothing. I don't even think of her, but if it makes you feel better, I can have her assigned somewhere else."

"And if you start reassigning women you've slept with, how many would be left to work here?" I whispered back.

A mixture of irritation, wariness, and dread flitted through his eyes as he stared at me, carefully choosing his words. The amount of time he took just thinking of how to answer the question answered the question for me and left a pit in my stomach that had nothing to do with the food I'd just devoured.

A gurgling sound escaped Shana's mouth before she clapped a hand over it and ran for the bathroom. I saw her cover her rear with the other hand before turning the corner and felt a little better. Maybe I was horrible for that but I didn't really care that much. I only wished Myra felt the same nausea rolling through her body. I caught the shifter in question's eye and saw that although she wasn't feeling nauseous, she wasn't in a good place either. I wouldn't go so far as to say she was hurt like me, but she was definitely not happy.

The sound of violent retching carried over the music in the bar, reaching our booth, and I knew Shana hadn't made it to the bathroom before losing a good portion of fried goodness she'd happily stuffed into her mouth, so happy she could eat whatever she wanted without fear of it sticking to her hips, thanks to the vampire metabolism. We could gain weight, or lose it, but from what I'd been told, it was damned difficult.

Having slid over to the edge of the seat as soon as Shana left it, Daniel raised his hand and snapped to grab Rome's attention as the hulking human leaned against the corner of the bar, a watchful eye on the room looking for spills to clean up until he was notified of messes elsewhere. He looked Daniel's way and the dragon shifter pointed toward the hall Shana had run down. "Better get on that!"

"Get on this," Rome called back to him, flipping him the meatiest bird I'd ever seen.

Rider turned, looked at him, and although I couldn't see his face from where I sat at his side, I knew his expression was dark enough to set Rome into instant motion. It didn't stop him from grumbling a few choice profanities at Daniel as he passed our booth.

"I heard you made quite a scene when you ate at Adore shortly after turning," Daniel told me. "Knowing that Rome has to clean up after your sister, I'm really hoping the story wasn't exaggerated."

I glared at Rider.

"He didn't hear about it from me," Rider said. "So why did you set her up like that? You knew she was going to be violently ill, and she ate a lot more than you did at Adore, and what she ate was a lot worse."

"Do you feel sorry for her?" I felt my eyes narrow involuntarily.

"No," he answered coolly as a pair of women barreled out of the bathroom hallway, gagging. They grabbed their purses and the men they'd left watching them before they fled the building. "I may have to fumigate that hall. Could cost me some of tonight's business. That'll come out of my pocket. I'd like to know it was worth it."

"It's going to get that bad?" Daniel asked, a mischievous smile spreading across his face. "Definitely worth it. I swear if she went for my balls one more time, I was going to stab her with a fork."

"That's why you did it?" Rider's hand tightened around his mug as he held my gaze. "Because she was touching Daniel?"

"You know why I did it," I told him, my voice low. "You heard and felt what I heard and felt."

"I didn't, don't, and won't ever reciprocate those

thoughts or feelings."

"It's the principle of the thing," I explained. "She's my sister. She knows there's something going on between us. She shouldn't even be thinking about thinking about you like that, plus she insulted me."

"I feel like I'm missing something here," Daniel cut in, looking between the two of us, his forehead deeply creased. "What did she say that was insulting?"

Rider and I frowned at each other before returning our attention to Daniel. "You didn't hear her thoughts leak out?" I asked him.

"Leak out?" His nose wrinkled in disgust. "That sounds nasty, but no. I didn't hear her thoughts. She didn't direct any my way. You're talking about the telepathy stuff, right?"

"Shana's guard came down a few times, and we were able to pick up on her thoughts and feelings," Rider explained, grinning when he noticed Daniel's face pale. "It's a vampire thing. I had to force a mind-link between you and the other members of my nest so we could talk telepathically. It's just for communication. Your thoughts won't leak like hers. The bond between sires and fledglings is much stronger and the mind-link is automatic. If my fledglings don't guard their thoughts, I can hear everything. Danni was able to hear Shana's thoughts too, being that they are both fledglings of the same sire, not to mention they shared the same blood prior to being turned. I imagine that increases the strength of their bond."

"After I turned, you warned me that my thoughts could be picked up by anyone in your nest," I reminded Rider. "That doesn't sound like what you're telling Daniel about Shana. Was that not the truth?"

"You know I don't lie to you," he answered without a trace of emotion, but I felt the frustration simmering within him. "You tended to drop your guard when you were afraid or insecure. Your thoughts can be loud. If not careful, you very well could project out to other members of my nest, but not the entire nest. Except for the ones I trust the most, you'll only ever be able to speak with most of them. Tony, Eliza, and Nannette can pick up on your emotions and thoughts if unguarded. If they'd practice more, Daniel and Rome could too."

"But my thoughts and emotions won't leak out?" Daniel sat back, arms folded, gaze steady on Rider. I saw the distrust in his eyes.

"You're Imortian. I was able to create a mind-link for communication, but no, I don't think your thoughts or emotions will come through it."

"You've tried to read my mind."

Rider nodded, one firm movement. "Yes."

"And you got nothing."

"Right."

Daniel grinned. "Good. I'm not a fan of people just traipsing around in my neurons."

"You said Daniel could pick up on my thoughts though. Why didn't he pick up on Shana's?" I looked at Rihanna. "Did you pick up on her thoughts?"

"Mind reading isn't my thing," she answered.

"Rihanna isn't an actual member of my nest," Rider clarified. "She's more of an associate, and as for Daniel not picking up on Shana's thoughts, I'm not that surprised. As I said, your guard usually slips when you're upset, mostly when you're scared or insecure. Your thoughts are loud, panicked. Certain members of my nest can pick up on your thoughts then, because we have an emotional connection that's there for security. If something happens that is dangerous enough to scare you, I want my team able to pick up on that. That's why you have to really protect your thoughts when you feel that way. The same goes for Shana, being my fledgling, but she wasn't afraid or insecure when her thoughts slipped earlier. She was irritated. That wouldn't grab the attention of anyone else in my nest, but I'm her sire so I caught it, and you're her sister, in more than one way."

"Are you saying you're like their daddy?" Daniel's nose wrinkled in disgust as my stomach did a little roll.

"Don't get perverted, jackass." Rider shot him a dirty look. "It's nothing like that."

Daniel laughed. "Just checking. Wait, so… are you saying I'd have picked up on Shana's thoughts if she was scared?"

"No." Rider sighed, mildly frustrated. "It's complicated. You actually shouldn't ever pick up on Shana's thoughts, but you and Danni may eventually be able to pick up on each other's thoughts, especially if you give her blood enough times. You also have that other bond," he said, referring to the soul stitch attachment we shared. "There's no telling how that may affect your mental bond."

Daniel downed the last of his beer. "Weird."

"You come from a realm of magic and you're weirded out? Well, you can imagine how I'm processing all of this." I popped the last shrimp into my mouth and it was on its way down my throat when Rome approached the booth.

"Boss, I know I'm on janitorial duty, but Shana's in the bathroom making all kinds of sounds. There's enough smell coming out under the door I know I need to get in there and clean, but she's making some scary sounds. I can't just go in there. She's a woman. I'm a dude. It's a woman's bathroom."

Every head at the table turned to me, including Rihanna's. "You're a woman," I reminded her.

"Honey, there's not enough money in the world to get me in that bathroom right now," she said. "And she's your sister."

"And you're the one who food-poisoned her," Daniel added around a wicked grin.

I stuck my tongue out at him, getting a laugh in return.

"Somebody has to check on her," Rider said. "I'd make Rome do it, but I'm afraid he won't be much help."

I made a show of looking at the time on my cell phone.

"I have to get back to my apartment and do some homework before my next session with Nannette."

"Danni."

"Fine," I said. As I slid my phone into the side pocket of my leggings, I noticed the server again. Myra. The shifter… who'd done some *shifting* on top of or underneath Rider. "I'll check on her, but I really have to leave and handle some things. You're going to have to get one of your other women to babysit her the rest of the night."

"One of my other women?" His tone could chill blood.

I smiled at him sweetly, imagining how evil it must look, considering I knew damn well my eyes were as far from sweet as possible. "Your female employees. Maybe Myra, unless for some reason you don't want to inconvenience her?"

Rider sat still as death, staring at me, simmering below the surface. If his annoyance burned any hotter, steam would rise out of his scalp. I got the impression he was using a great deal of willpower to not go off in front of company. Finally, he slid out of the booth. "We're not that busy tonight. I can spare a server. I'll assign Myra to help Rome with Shana, but you should go check on her now. You knew this would happen, so you can at least help get her back down to her room before you go."

"Fair enough." I slid out of the booth, thanked Rihanna for the food and the spell that allowed me to enjoy it, and headed for the bathroom, Rome two steps behind me.

"I'm sorry this happened while you're on janitorial duty," I told him, guilt creeping back in as I noticed the slumped set of his usually proud shoulders. The guy was in for a long, awful night.

"I thought you all weren't supposed to eat food for a while after you turned, except for like, salads and fruits and stuff."

"We're not." I sighed and stepped carefully around the wet floor sign Rome had set up after cleaning the spot where Shana had thrown up. A cart with cleaning supplies stood just outside a small janitorial closet near the bathroom doors. "I shouldn't have let her do it. If this is anything like the night I got sick from eating she'll expel everything, get a little reprieve which will allow time to get her down to the room Rider put her in, and she'll be sick the rest of the night but I asked him to put that Myra woman on her so you'll have help. He can't expect you to stay cleaning up after her if you have to keep the bar and the interrogation room clean."

"Myra doesn't deserve the job of cleaning up after her either. No one does." He took a deep breath through his mouth as we neared the women's restroom and braced himself with one hand on the door, which was just barely holding back the rotten stench of stomach upset. Strangled moans of agony came from within. "I'm not going in there until she's out. If you're not back out in ten minutes or less I'll assume you've been knocked out by the fumes and notify Rider. Good luck."

He pushed the door open and the foul odor knocked me back a few steps. My eyes watered and the back of my throat clogged. I'd never thought of smell having a color before, but the air smelled green. Putrid green, the kind of green that erupts from a demon-possessed child's mouth as her head spins violently.

"What *is* that?" I heard Shana wail from inside the bathroom. "*What's coming out of me?!*"

Rome gagged, covered his mouth with his forearm, and used his other hand to shove me into the bathroom before letting the door close behind me, saving himself.

I stumbled forward, deeper into the fog of funk, tears running the length of my face. This was definitely worse than the time I'd gotten sick. Guilt took another stab at me as I looked over to see Shana's knees on the tile floor. That was all I could see under the stall, but it was enough to know she was hugging the toilet bowl for dear life as I had done when in the same predicament. Her underwear was around her ankles. Apparently, there'd been no time to pull them up before she'd had to switch positions.

"Shana? It's me. Are you all right?"

"I've been poisoned!" She retched, and I waited for her to finish throwing up.

"You weren't poisoned. We all ate the food. It's just not agreeing with you." I pulled my shirt up to cover my nose, thankful I'd had my boobs shrunken back down so I had enough fabric available to do so, and took a look around.

There were six stalls, all empty except for Shana's, three sinks, two automatic paper towel dispensers on the wall, and a small window that wouldn't allow a body through, but thankfully would allow air. I crossed the room, stood on my tip-toes, and jimmied it open.

"Why aren't you sick?" Shana cried before groaning and switching positions.

"I guess my stomach is stronger than yours," I lied, keeping my face toward the blessed air I knew was beyond the window. I focused on it, trying desperately to not listen to the sounds coming from the stall, sounds much worse than the ones Shana had made while vomiting.

"I think I've burned a hole in my ass," she cried.

"No, I'm pretty sure you already came factory equipped with one there."

"Funny," she snapped. "I'm dying!"

"No, you just wish you were." I glanced under the stall and grimaced, seeing where she'd missed the toilet and splashed vomit on the floor and baseboard. I grabbed a small stack of paper towels and wet them in the sink. "I got sick like this once right after I turned. You're going to throw up everything you just ate and then you're going to be all right for about fifteen to twenty minutes. We'll get you cleaned up and moved downstairs during that time. After that, you'll need a steady supply of blood to keep your strength, and you'll still be sick, but once the sun comes up, you'll be out like a light and will wake up tomorrow night feeling just fine."

"Are you going to take care of me?"

"I have something I have to do." I turned off the water and rang the excess out of the paper towels. "How are you doing in there? Do you think the first wave has passed?"

She released a loud fart potent enough to peel paint from the walls and started crying like a two-year-old who'd just gotten spanked in the middle of a grocery store. "What have I done to deserve this?"

Lusted after the wrong woman's man, sweetie, I thought to myself as I wondered why I was suffering right along with her.

Twenty minutes later, Shana was back in her room, changed into a clean T-shirt and knit shorts, both borrowed from me, lying in the bed, one hand resting over her gurgling stomach.

"You have to stay," she told me. "Someone has to take care of me, and I can't be seen like this by the men here."

There'd been a few moments I'd felt the pangs of guilt as she'd voided her body of the human food I'd tricked her into eating far too soon into her new vampire life, but with the reminder that the men she feared seeing her in such a condition included my boyfriend the guilt slipped away.

"You'll be fine. Rider is assigning a woman to help you get through the night," I told her as I fluffed her pillows harder than necessary and leaned in close. "Just remember, if it feels like you have to fart… it's not a fart."

Shana started up another sobfest which was my cue to leave. Myra entered the room as I exited, and we held each other's gazes as we passed, our dislike for one another clearly mutual.

I made my way to the stairwell and found Rider in the hall behind the bar, waiting for me as I came out on the ground floor. He stood near the recently repaired wall Rome had rammed his head into, hands thrust into his pockets, scowl on his face. "What's this homework you have to do?"

"I have to watch *Cinderella*," I told him, instantly feeling stupid. "Don't ask."

He stood still, staring at me, but didn't ask. "Are you coming back before sunrise?"

"Do you want me to?" My tone came out snippier than I intended.

Rider's jaw clenched in annoyance and he raised his hands, gesturing he was done. "I don't know why I bother telling you anything. None of it ever seems to stick. Daniel will escort you. Try to stay out of trouble." Then he turned and left.

"Hey."

I turned toward Daniel to find him looking over at me expectantly. I'd been so wrapped up in my thoughts I hadn't heard him speaking to me. "What?"

"I asked why you look so bummed," he said, returning his focus to the road as he drove us in the direction of my apartment. "You successfully made your sister sick and got Rider to assign Myra to watch her. Why aren't you on a vengeance high?"

I rolled my eyes and might have growled a little. "I don't know. I should be. They deserved it."

"Did they?"

"Shana's my sister and she's lusting after my boyfriend, and you, and winking at Tony and insulting me in her head. Yes, she deserved it."

Daniel grinned. "I wasn't aware you were so bothered by her lusting after me."

"She's a married woman. She shouldn't be lusting after anyone, especially not my... men I'm close to," I said. "It makes things awkward."

Daniel appeared to think this over and nodded. "And Myra? She's not the only woman in that bar who's given you the evil eye. Why are you making her pay such a crummy price?"

I looked out the window and lost myself in the same thoughts his question had dragged me out of. I felt bad, and if I was being honest, I felt disappointed in myself, and I wasn't really sure why. I hated the feeling. My eyes burned, and I grit my teeth as I forced the image of Rider walking away from me into the back of my mind. The image of him with Myra popped back, front and center, and I sighed. It made no sense why he seemed so against me changing my body when he clearly enjoyed more generous curves. "Why do you think Rider got so mad when Rihanna put her whammy on me and gave me a bigger chest?"

"I told you. He knows you're perfect as you are."

"Oh, come on." My voice raised two angry octaves as my temper got the better of me. "He's slept with Myra before. That's why she hates me. He probably slept with Seta. He obviously finds big-chested women attractive, so how am I supposed to believe he thinks I'm perfect?"

Daniel pulled off into an alley and cut the engine before turning toward me, his eyes dark. "Rider doesn't love you because he thinks you're perfect. He thinks you're perfect because he loves you. It's that simple, and it doesn't matter who he slept with before you. As long as he's been alive, I guarantee you he's slept with women of all shapes and sizes. You need to quit fixating on it. I know your family put a shitload of insecurity in you, but you're a grown woman now, Danni. It's time to get the hell over it. You're too fucking beautiful to do this shit to yourself."

My mouth dropped open, and a tear leaked out of my eye.

"Shit. I didn't mean to yell." He closed his eyes and took a moment to gather himself. When he reopened them, the frustration was gone. "I honestly don't think Rider cares what size your chest is, whether you gain weight, lose weight, cut your hair, wear makeup, or go barefaced. He loves you. The reason he got so mad was the same reason I really didn't like her doing that spell on you either. He wants you to love yourself as much as he loves you. If you need the help of magic for that, you'll never really love yourself, and that would be a tragedy because you're pretty damn special just the way you are."

Damn. I stared at Daniel, unsure how to respond. I didn't feel any better about the childish way I'd behaved after figuring out Rider had once been intimate with Myra, but I no longer felt the overwhelming need to cry.

A loud scraping noise down the alley captured our attention. Following Daniel's lead, I turned my head toward the noise and saw a dark humanoid shape appear to crawl out of the ground.

Daniel retrieved his cell phone from the dash and punched a button before holding it to his ear. "Did you interrogate the rat?" he asked a moment later. "Because that mind-talking stuff feels weird," he said, and I deduced he was speaking to Rider. "What did the rat say? Was he our guy? I think I just saw another one… She's right here with me… It's in the area… No… No… Yes… We can catch up to him if we move now… He'll be in the wind by then… Nannette said she should be trained to… I won't let anything happen to her… If you really want to take a chance on this being the guy and another woman being taken… Yes… All right… Yes… I will." He disconnected and slid the phone into his pocket.

"What was all that about?"

"I got you a job. We're going to go catch us a giant rodent."

"What?"

"I'm pretty sure that was a wererat. The one Rome and I caught might not be the one snatching women, so we're going to go grab that one."

I gawked at him for a moment. "Rider agreed to let me capture a shifter with you?"

"Yes, with the understanding that if anything happens to you, he's going to let every vampire in his nest drain me dry before turning me into a dragon nugget buffet for his shifters. I have faith in you, and I think Nannette was on to something about allowing you to do security work, but it's your call. You in?"

I swallowed past the nervous fear lodged in my throat and nodded. "We need to be quick though. I have to watch *Cinderella*."

He barked out a laugh. "Of course."

"It's not funny. Nannette gave me homework, and she's scarier than any wererat. Let's go."

"Not so fast." He reached over, rubbed the lacy material of my top between his fingers. "This is pretty. Take it off."

# SEVENTEEN

"Excuse me?" I automatically inched closer to my door.

Daniel barked out another laugh as he turned and reached behind his seat. "Calm down. You're not in any danger."

"A lot of these particular shifters seem to have hygiene issues and you just saw the one we're going after come up from the sewer system," he said as he turned back around, a black T-shirt in his hand. "We're probably going to get at least a little dirty. A lacy white shirt isn't a good fashion choice for this job. Hurry up. We need to catch up to him."

Daniel handed me the shirt, grabbed a gun and nylon belt from under his seat, and stepped out, turning his back to allow me privacy.

I switched out my shirt in record time and climbed out of the truck to meet him. He grinned as he gave me a slow once-over.

"Black pants, black T-shirt, black shoes. About to go catch a bad guy. All you need is a SEALS cap, and you'd look like that guy in those books you have all over your apartment."

I frowned, wondering when Daniel had time to really look at the books in my apartment, and actually read enough of them to know about the characters. "The Stephanie Plum books? You think I look like Ranger?"

"Sure."

"Ranger wouldn't be caught dead in leggings, and if I looked remotely like Ranger, I wouldn't have all the problems I have. I'd be stuck inside my bedroom all day, staying busy fornicating myself."

Daniel's eyes dilated as his grin widened.

"What?"

"I'm just visualizing that scenario."

Now it was my turn to grin. "You realize in this scenario I'd look like Ranger, so you're basically picturing a guy playing with himself."

Daniel grimaced and turned away. "Well, that took an ugly turn."

"Serves you right. Are we going to catch this guy or not?"

He'd already clipped on the nylon belt and the gun was positioned on his hip. He extracted a switchblade from his pocket and handed it to me. "You don't want to use your fangs. Not just because of the whole venom thing, but because if he's anywhere near as gross as the guy Rome and I brought back last night, you don't want that in your mouth. Put the knife in your side pocket and use it if you have to."

"Are you really going to shoot him?" I asked, placing the knife in my pocket as instructed.

"If I have to. The last guy was easy to knock out once I could get my hands on the slimy bastard. Let's go."

Daniel took off at a run and I quickly rushed forward to catch up. With his height and lanky form, he seemed to lope effortlessly. I had no idea what I looked like running, but I knew if it wasn't for the gift of vampiric speed, I'd have been left in the dust. Of course, with the use of my vampiric abilities always came the hunger for replenishment in the form of blood, so I hoped we'd catch up to our prey and snatch him up quickly.

We ran the length of the building Daniel had parked by and turned the corner, spotting the silhouette of the man several feet ahead. He glanced back at us and took off running. I briefly questioned why he would instantly run, but realized if Daniel could sense he was a shifter, he could most likely sense what we were too and maybe word had gotten out one of his friends had been taken. Then again, we were barreling toward him. Who wouldn't run from two people chasing them down a dark alley at night?

"Is he Imortian?" I asked Daniel as we continued the chase.

"No," Daniel answered, not even out of breath, which was pretty impressive. I mean, I wasn't either, but I was part vampire. I was pretty sure I only breathed at all because of muscle memory or something. "I believe rat shifters were created by a virus similar to lycanthropy."

Great. Between Eliza and Daniel, I'd learned a great deal about shapeshifters during the short time I'd been part of the paranormal community. Werewolves had been created when an Imortian was cast out of that realm several centuries ago. She'd been cursed to take on the spirit of a wolf, an animal she loved, an animal that the evil queen of Imortia had slaughtered to force its spirit on her. She had been the first werewolf and when she gave birth, she created the entire race. Daniel had been made into a dragon shifter by the same horrid ruler, but much later. Weres could transform into the animal whose spirit they shared, but they couldn't half-shift, taking on characteristics of man and beast at the same time. Lycanthropes and shifters born of a viral blood condition, on the other hand, could. From what I'd heard, they were particularly nasty with a tendency to fight dirty.

The rat shifter could move, and he'd made good time. I grew concerned when I saw him nearing the mouth of the alley. Once he made it to the main streets, it would be more difficult grabbing him. It was late, so there wasn't a ton of traffic, but it only took one concerned citizen to see what they would probably assume was a mugging for things to go bad. Also, I could see another manhole just before the street and I didn't want to have to chase him down there.

"If he turns around, don't let him get past you," Daniel said, and then he disappeared in a burst of multi-colored sparkles. The buildings closest to the opening were smaller, causing the narrow alley to widen just enough for Daniel to shift into his dragon form, which he did just before landing at the mouth of the alley and turning toward the rat shifter. He blew out a stream of fire, cutting off our quarry's exit.

"Fuck!" I heard the shifter cry before skidding to a stop and turning. He stumbled, but quickly regained his footing and headed straight in my direction. I got a better look at him as he neared. He was short, maybe a few inches taller than me, and he was thin enough I didn't feel terribly intimidated. He wore jeans and a dark, long-sleeved shirt, both of which appeared grimy, which wasn't a major surprise since he'd been coming out of a sewer when we first saw him. He appeared Caucasian with dark, beady little eyes, a sharp nose, and dark, shaggy hair cut short and slicked back with what I hoped was actual hair product. As he neared me, I caught the unmistakable scent of urine and realized he'd wet himself.

Having never slowed down, I had the necessary momentum to take Mr. Ratface McPottyPants down, so I gave in to the probability that I was going to come out of this smelling like a toilet and dove for his midsection.

He veered to his right, but I'd extended my arm mid-air and caught him in the ribs. He hit the side of a dumpster and bounced off as my knees connected with the ground. I quickly spun, acting on instinct, and got off the ground a second before the bottom of his grungy shoe connected with the pavement where my head had been.

That pissed me off.

I heard Daniel's footsteps as he ran back toward me in his human form, but couldn't wait. I balled my hand into a fist and landed a decent punch in the center of the rat shifter's face, knocking him off balance. He grabbed my arm as he went backward, though, pulled me to him, and sank his elongated front teeth into my arm. I cried out in pain, and a whole lot of rage, and after that, everything was a flurry of bites, kicks, and punches.

"What's your problem, lady?" the shifter yelled as he disentangled and quit biting me long enough to crawl up the side of the dumpster.

"Get back here!" I jumped up the side, dropping into the mess to snatch him before he could escape me. I grabbed the back of his shirt and pulled him down before unleashing a series of punches into his face, trying my damnedest to knock loose at least one of the rodent teeth that had drawn blood from me. We slipped and fell, and the more we tried to grab or punch each other, the deeper we seemed to sink into the bags of garbage, busting some open in the process.

The rat shifter scurried over a pile of bags and slipped over the lip of the dumpster. I dug my hands into his back and fell over the edge with him. We landed hard, and he was on his feet before the stars could clear from before my eyes. Dizzy and disoriented, I acted strictly on impulse and dove for his leg. I grabbed him below the knee with one hand and yanked him under me. I groped around with my other hand until my fingers wrapped around something and I beat the hell out of him with it, until whatever it was busted and chunky liquid splashed in my face, snapping me out of my rage-filled haze.

The rat shifter lay unconscious underneath me. I looked over to see Daniel, Tony, and Rome standing to the side, looking down at me, mouths hanging open.

"When the hell did you two get here?" I asked, wiping thick yellowish gunk off my chin and shaking chunks of it off my shirt. "What is this all over me?"

"Rider thought you might need some backup and sent us," Tony answered as Daniel stepped forward and toed aside the busted thing I'd beaten the rat shifter with. It was a jug. "We got here about the time you dove into the dumpster."

"This is buttermilk," Daniel said, reading the label on the jug, "and by the looks and smell of it, it's about a month past its expiration date."

"Thanks for the help," I snapped as I held my hand out. They all stepped back.

"You seemed to be doing all right," Daniel said. "Then things got hairy and we couldn't find a way in."

"It was like someone flung a cat into a pool," Tony said.

"Yeah, you were one pissed off kitty," Rome added. "Screeching, scratching, punching, and kicking, and getting covered in more and more mess." His lip curled as he looked me over. "I'm kind of glad to be going back to janitorial duty after this. Cleaning you up is going to be a hell of a lot worse than cleaning up after your sister."

"So I rolled in some garbage," I snapped, growing angrier by the second as the wet garbage started to really set into my clothes and grow cold against my skin. I stood on my own, realizing they weren't going to be courteous and give me a helping hand, and looked down at myself. I was covered in filth and as I turned to try to check out the back of myself, I got a whiff of something extremely foul. Worse than the spoiled buttermilk. "What is that?"

"One of these buildings is a daycare," Daniel said, grimacing as he nodded to an area behind me.

I turned to see a busted open Hefty bag on the ground with what looked like a hundred crap-filled diapers that appeared to have been steamrolled. My bottom lip trembled.

"It's just on the back of you," Daniel said. "And a little of it is in the ends of your hair."

"I'm not going to cry," I half-whispered, then burst into tears.

"We're out," Tony said, stepping forward. He grabbed the rat shifter by the scruff of his neck and started pulling him down the alley.

"Yeah, I gotta get back to work," Rome added. "We'll take care of the rat dude and you, uh, handle that," he said, pointing to me before jogging to catch up to Tony, who was walking extremely fast for someone dragging an unconscious body.

"Thanks," Daniel yelled at his back, his tone not very thankful at all before placing his hands on his hips and watching me. "I'd wipe your tears away, but there's not a spot on you not covered in God knows what."

I started crying harder.

"Shit." He pulled his T-shirt over his head and used it to wipe my tears away. "If it makes you feel any better, you caught the bad guy, and this was a totally Stephanie Plum-worthy apprehension."

"Stephanie Plum can eat donuts," I cried.

"You'll get there." He finished wiping my face and pulled the shirt away, giving me a clear view of his half naked body.

The tears stopped. I was covered in baby shit, reeked of urine and spoiled buttermilk, and probably had cooties from rat-man bites, but it was hard to be upset when presented with Daniel's shirtless chest. Daniel's shirtless chest was a work of art.

"Feel better?"

I nodded. I might not feel that much better, but I was starting to feel warmer.

"Good." He tossed the shirt into the dumpster and turned to walk back to where he'd left his truck, gesturing for me to do the same. "Do you want to clean up at Midnight Rider or risk tracking all that gunk into your apartment?"

My heart nearly stopped at the thought of Rider seeing

me covered in baby shit and assorted other nastiness. "My apartment."

"All right. Don't take this the wrong way, but you're not getting in my truck. You're riding in the back. Even if I put something down on the seat, I'll never get the smell out of the cab."

"You know, some of this smell is from when you literally scared the piss out of him."

Daniel grinned. "It's a gift."


Thankfully, the streets were dark and there wasn't a lot of traffic. Those who were out driving gave me weird looks as I got caught in their headlights. I guess it wasn't every day you saw a garbage monster riding in the back of a Ford.

Daniel had found another shirt in his truck because when he parked and walked around the back to retrieve me, his chest was covered with a Black Sabbath logo. "I'd give you my shirt, but there's no point. You're going to have to hose down before you even bother changing."

I nodded, completely understanding. I was pretty sure some of the gunk I'd rolled around in had actually seeped into my pores to coat my bones. It felt like it had anyway.

"Maybe you should just ditch the shoes," Daniel suggested after I got down from the truck bed. "Or I could call Ginger down here, have her bring a Hefty bag and I could carry you up in it."

I looked down at my shoes. They'd never be clean again. "I'll ditch the shoes," I said, and walked over to the curb. I didn't want to touch the shoes, and I didn't think there was anything I could offer Daniel good enough to get him to, sexual or otherwise, so I dragged my heels along the edge of the curb until I got the shoes to pop off.

An ungroomed dog that had been resting on the grassy patch of lawn outside my building trotted over to investigate. It sniffed one of the shoes, let out a startled yelp, and ran like hell down the sidewalk. I looked over at Daniel and saw the corners of his mouth twitch. "Laugh and I'll wrap myself around you and shimmy up and down like you're a stripper's pole."

"It would be worth it if not for the baby shit."

I rolled my eyes and slunk toward the building, every move I made causing wet fabric to touch my skin. I almost gagged three times before we were in the building and up the stairs to my floor. I looked in the corner and saw Carlos was once again the vampire on guard duty outside my door. His mouth started to curve upward as he took in my appearance. His humor fled as I bared my teeth, fangs and all, and growled low in my throat.


"What the hell happened to you?" Ginger asked, looking up from the television as we entered the apartment. Angel sat next to her on the couch, staring at me with her mouth hanging open. They both covered their noses in synchronized movement. My stomach rumbled, my blood thirst awakened by the reminder I'd reached my source. I'd skinned my knees and managed to collect at least six bite wounds during my tussle with the rat shifter, all of which were bleeding. I needed to take in what I'd lost.

"We caught a bad guy," Daniel answered. "It wasn't exactly what you'd call a smooth operation."

"Well, I'm glad you finally showed up to do this Disney double feature thing. She's got me watching this *NCIS* marathon in the meantime and if I have to watch this Latino guy another minute, I might just have to turn in my lesbian card. He's doing things to my nether regions men aren't supposed to do."

I looked over at the TV. "Wilmer Valderrama?"

"You call him Wilmer Valderrama, I call him Wilmer Valdemakemeyobabymama." She rolled her eyes. "Good grief. Listen to me. Get cleaned up so we can get these movies going. I don't want to turn hetero."

"What's wrong with being hetero?" Daniel asked.

"If I was hetero, I'd like men," Ginger answered.

"And?"

"And no offense, but you're a bunch of dumbasses, you fart too much, and you got those stupid-looking knobby things hanging out where your vaginas should be."

Daniel grinned over at me. "She's a nut, but I like her."

"Put the first movie in while I scrub myself down," I told them. "I have to watch *Cinderella* before sunrise. I'll have to miss the beginning of *Lady and the Tramp*."

I was in my bedroom looking at my dresser, wondering how I was supposed to get my clothes or open my bathroom door without contaminating everything, when Daniel stepped in with a garbage bag. He grabbed my robe off my bedpost and opened the bathroom door. He hung the bathrobe on the back of the door, placed the bag on the floor, and turned the shower knobs, adjusting the water until he found the temperature sufficient.

"I'll close the door after you step inside. Toss everything into the garbage bag. You can decide if you want to wash it or toss it all later, and you can pick out new clothes after you're clean." His gaze lingered on the blood drying on my arms and the assorted bite wounds it still seeped out of. "You need to feed from the girl. If she passes out again, feed from Ginger, or hell, feed from me. I'll tell Ginger to knock me out if you inject me with venom and I get too happy. Can you seal those bite wounds up with your saliva?"

"Yeah, but I don't want to until I'm clean."

"Understandable." He stepped aside and waited for me to pass him. "Don't take too long. If I think you've passed out from blood loss, I'll come crashing through this door to save your ass whether it's naked or not."

I turned toward him. "You could send in Ginger."

"And let her have all the fun?"

257

I sealed my wounds as soon as I got the surrounding areas clean, then adjusted the water until it was as hot as I could bear and scrubbed the rest of myself until I was just shy of removing my top layer of skin. I washed my hair three times and conditioned it, then stood under the spray watching the last slimy remnants of my first security assignment go down the drain. I wanted to fill the tub with water and soak, but I wasn't sure whether Daniel had been playing when he said he'd crash through the door and I didn't want to risk getting caught in the buff.

I turned off the shower, dried off, and slipped into the robe. I was towel drying my hair as I stepped out of the bathroom to see Daniel depositing Angel atop my bed.

"She fell asleep," he whispered, straightening back up. "Ginger left so she could get back to her place before sunrise. Do you want to head back to the bar or stay here and watch the movie?"

I looked at the clock on my nightstand. There was no way I'd finish the movie before sunrise. Hell, I was already growing tired so might not manage to stay awake to watch it, but Nannette had told me to. I needed to try. Drinking much needed blood to replenish the blood and energy I'd lost would help me stay awake and focused, but my donor was asleep and looked too peaceful to wake up. "Rider doesn't have anything I can play movies on, so I'm going to stay here and watch it."

"You've sealed your wounds, but you need blood. I checked your fridge, and it hasn't been restocked yet. Probably, Rider didn't think you'd need it here because this is where you're keeping your donor."

I looked at Angel and sighed. "I'm fine. I'm going to let her sleep."

"Danni."

"I said I'm fine. I need to get dressed."

Daniel shook his head in frustration and left the room. I finished towel-drying my hair and slipped into cotton bikinis, an under-wire bra, gray yoga pants and a stretchy white T-shirt. When I entered the living room, I found Daniel sitting on the couch, the remote in his hand. He looked over at me, set the remote down, and stood.

"Wake her up and feed."

"No."

"I'll wake her up. You need to feed."

"I said no. She's resting. I don't want her thinking of me like some creepy monster who feeds on her while she's half out of it."

"Then you're going to feed from me."

"You know that's not a good idea."

"You've lost blood, you expelled a lot of energy, and you're pale." He stepped in front of me. "Where's the knife I gave you earlier?"

"I set it on the sink before I got in the shower."

He stepped around me and left the room, returning shortly after with the switchblade in hand. "Do you feel the need to jump my bones right now?"

"No," I answered, possibly fibbing a little. Who wouldn't want to jump Daniel's bones? They were mighty fine bones.

He opened the knife and put it in my hand. "If you're not feeling the desire to attack me, you're probably fine. If by chance you do have venom right now and I try to attack you because of it, stab me."

"What? Are you crazy? I'm not going to stab you!"

"I'm a shifter. I'll live. Just do it."

"This is insane. I'm not going to drink from you and I'm definitely not going to stab you."

"Then I'm taking you to Rider." He grabbed my wrist and moved toward the door, not seeming to care I didn't even have socks on, let alone shoes.

I planted my feet and yanked him back. "The hell you are. I already have Rider bossing me around. You're not going to do it too."

"I will if it keeps you alive. Wake the girl up and drink

from her or drink from me. You have two seconds to decide or else I'm going to toss you over my shoulder and—"

I moved forward, fueled by frustration, and sank my fangs into his throat. If I was going to drink from him at all, I knew I should have done it from the wrist, but I'd been focused on the pulse point throbbing away in his neck while he'd been threatening me, his emotion seeming to cause his blood to pump harder. He fell back onto the couch and I went with him, ending up straddling him. A soft moan escaped, but for the life of me, I couldn't tell if it came from him or me. His spicy blood spilled over my tongue and I gulped it heartily, savoring the rich flavor and the burst of Imortian power that came with it. His hands gripped my hips, and I felt a tremor of panic. What if I'd injected him with the venom? Could I stab him? Did I even want to?

# EIGHTEEN

*Where the hell are you two?*

Daniel's hands instantly released my hips as I jerked away from his throat and looked around in a panic, feeling as if I'd been caught doing something I really shouldn't have been doing.

"I hate when he pops into my head like that," Daniel muttered, cluing me in that he was looped into the telepathic conversation with Rider and me.

*We're at my apartment*, I answered for the both of us and quickly licked the bite mark on Daniel's throat, sealing it closed. *I have to watch this movie. Homework for Nannette.*

*You haven't finished it? The sun will be up soon. You're safest here during the day.*

*It took me a while to get cleaned up. I'll be there once the movie is over.*

*You have sunscreen there?*

*Yes.*

*Be careful. I was given a report on what happened tonight. Drink well from the girl.*

I felt him withdraw, but didn't move, waiting to see if he returned. I also waited for guilt to pass and wondered why I felt it. I'd drunk from Daniel. So what? I'd drunk from him twice before, both times with Rider standing right beside us watching.

"Danni."

"Yeah?"

"Not that it's a major hardship or anything, but, uh, you're kind of in my lap."

Oh. That was where the guilt was coming from. I scrambled off of Daniel and settled as deep into the edge of the couch as I could. "Sorry."

"It's all right." He smiled, almost bashfully, as he situated himself, getting comfortable. "I just don't think Rider would approve or understand you were just feeding. Perfectly innocent."

"Perfectly innocent," I said, ignoring the disapproving clucking noise coming from the little angel on my shoulder as the little devil on my other shoulder purred and did a little shimmy dance.

"Your color is returning. You feel stronger?"

"Yeah," I answered. "I think I might actually be able to keep my eyes open and watch the movie. I didn't take too much blood, did I?"

"No, I feel good. We had a pretty decent sized buffet of bar food tonight and I had a big lunch. I guess that matters."

"Yeah, well, I appreciate it, but don't try that provoking me into drinking from you stunt again," I said, tossing the switchblade onto the coffee table. "Things could have gone horribly wrong if I'd had venom." I sighed. "I'm thankful though. I was afraid I was going to have to sleep in order to fully recover, especially from the…" I gasped, realizing I'd been bitten by a wererat.

"What?" Daniel sat forward, concerned.

"That wererat bit me. You said he was like a lycanthrope. Don't they spread their disease through bites?"

I saw real fear flit through his eyes for a moment, then he leaned toward me, grabbed me by my neck and pulled me close to sniff me, his nose tickling my skin. "I only smell vampire and succubus," he said, still sniffing, his lips grazing my neck as he spoke. "You're safe. Vampires and succubi are impervious to disease, but with you being a hybrid, I know there's room for shit to go wrong, but I'd be able to smell the virus if you were carrying it."

He pulled away and visually relaxed. "Well, that was a terrifying half-second."

"You could really smell if I'd been infected?"

He nodded his head, looked at the switchblade on the table, and laughed. "You beat the hell out of that man. Punched him, clawed him… but when you decided to go for a weapon, why in the hell did you beat him with a jug of rancid buttermilk? I gave you a knife."

"I was caught up in the moment. Why didn't you shoot him?"

He grinned. "I was a little stunned. It was like watching a train wreck."

"Turn the damn movie on."

I watched the movie and was still trying to figure out what I was supposed to find so enlightening about it as Daniel drove me to Midnight Rider. I'd lathered myself generously with the special sunscreen Rider gave to the vampires in his nest and smelled like aloe and whatever else was in it instead of baby crap, so Daniel allowed me to sit in the cab with him.

"Is the sun bothering you?"

"No. Why?"

"You're squinting."

"Must be my thinking face." I yawned as daylight tried to drag me into a deep sleep. "Nannette thought *Cinderella* would enlighten me."

"Enlighten you how?"

I shrugged. "I don't know. My first training session had nothing to do with actually physically fighting. I think she's trying to help me out with my self-esteem, which I know isn't that great."

"No kidding."

I raised my middle finger, earning a wide smile in return. "I think it was supposed to help me understand my mother and grandmother, why they criticize me so much, but it didn't."

"Why were Cinderella's stepmother and stepsisters so mean to her?"

I looked over at him. "Her stepmother was an evil bitch like every wicked stepmother in every Disney movie, and her stepsisters were dramatically ugly. She was beautiful and sweet as an angel. Of course they were jealous of her."

"Well, it's a cartoon geared toward children. Of course it's going to be overly simplified. You have to dig deeper and look for parallels. Forget what the stepsisters looked like. Even if they were drawn attractive, the story would have played out the same. What did they want more than anything? What was their big goal?"

"The prince. The sisters wanted to marry him and the stepmother wanted one of them to marry him."

"And they tried to keep Cinderella dirty, give her the worst clothes, and do everything they could to ensure she'd stay home from the ball. Why?"

"They were jealous because she was prettier."

"Their jealousy wasn't all about looks. They were afraid of her before she was all glammed up and they could have sent her to that ball in rags, or shaved her head or something. And it wasn't even so much that they wanted the prince. Did they genuinely love him?"

"No. They wanted the status of being his princess. And this relates to the relationship between my family and me how?"

"I see a lot of parallels." He glanced at me a moment before returning his attention to the road. "Your father loved you and he died while you were young. Your mother isn't your stepmother, but she desires material things and status all the same. Shana may be what many would consider to be aesthetically pleasing, but her attitude isn't much better than the wicked stepsisters. I get the impression her marriage is all about money and status, and your mother definitely encourages it."

"They never dressed me in rags or made me do all their chores."

"They criticize and belittle you every chance they get. The way they constantly attack your confidence isn't much different than dressing you in rags."

"Why do they do it? Shana is beautiful. She's never had trouble finding men to drool over her. Cinderella's wicked stepmother didn't care which daughter got the prince. Why would my mother choose Shana over me? That's where I'm stumped."

"I don't think they were jealous of Cinderella so much as they were afraid of her," Daniel said as he pulled into the parking lot by Midnight Rider. "Cinderella was treated horribly, but she never let it break her. Yeah, the fairy godmother dressed her all up, but the prince didn't care when he found her and she was in rags again. Your mother, grandmother, and sister are threatened by you, just like the wicked stepmother and stepsisters were threatened by Cinderella. It didn't matter that they had better clothes and a better station. Cinderella had genuine love from her father. She had the love of her animal friends. The prince fell for her instantly. No matter how she was treated, no matter what they took from her, she survived and came out on top. The help she got from the fairy godmother gave her a needed boost of confidence, but it disappeared and she still got the prince. From what I've seen of the women in your family, they're all boobs and no … anything else. That's why they're fixated on breast size. It's all they think they have to offer and they have no aspirations further than using their mammary glands to land a man to take care of them. They criticize the hell out of you because they wish they were more like you, and your mother most likely seems to prefer Shana because she can manipulate her."

Daniel got out of the truck, as I sat stupefied, trying to process his theory. Giving up, I got out and rounded the truck. "More like me how?"

"You're smart. You had a job and your own apartment and you got all that without help from anyone. Yeah, you have your moments of thinking you're inadequate, but that's always their voices in your head. When it comes down to it, you don't need anyone to take care of you."

That sounded good, but there was a major flaw in his assessment. "Rider takes care of me, and you're my bodyguard."

"Rider takes care of you because he loves you, not because you can't survive without him, and honestly, you tend to beat the shit out of most guys before I even get a chance. You beat the shit out of that wererat."

"That was a disaster."

He nodded in agreement as he opened the door to the bar. "Yeah, but you caught the bad guy. You didn't act helpless and cry for me to do it for you."

"I cried some after."

"You rolled in baby shit. I would have cried too."

I laughed as I entered the bar. "Well, I guess it's a good thing I made you watch the movie with me. You got a lot more out of it than just magic and talking animals."

"I'm a pretty deep guy."

"Yeah, I could tell by all the fun you had playing with the Jug-Jolter 2000."

The bar was quiet and empty, having closed hours earlier, but I knew the building was alive with activity. Rider ran his security business from the property and the sublevels would be full of people. MidKnight Enterprises never slept.

"I guess you're off the clock now," I said as we crossed the room. "What do you do with your free time

266

anyway?"

"Sleep. Try to prepare for whatever chaos I know will occur when I report in to guard you again."

"With the exception of the calamity that occurred with the wererat, am I really that bad?"

He smiled wide, his eyes sparkling with laughter as he ruffled my hair and stepped back. "Yeah, but you're a hell of a lot of fun. Get some sleep. I'll see you later."

I watched him leave and heard a heavy lock engage after the front door closed behind him. I frowned, recalling how we'd just walked in without a key and no one was in the bar. Rider was too concerned with security to leave his bar unlocked and unguarded. I closed my eyes and opened my senses. He wasn't upstairs in his bed. He was in his office. I traveled down the hall and opened the door to find him at his desk.

"I heard you had an interesting night," he said, looking up from his computer.

"I can think of other words to describe it. Why are you down here?"

"If I'm going to be up all day worrying about you, I might as well try to get some work done."

I thought about what Daniel had told me. "Maybe you shouldn't worry about me so much. I'm not incompetent. I took down a wererat."

"You rolled in baby shit."

"Rome really tells you everything, doesn't he?"

"He wants to keep his job." He looked at me, grinning despite the tiredness in his eyes. "Did you really expect him not to tell that story? Even Tony couldn't stop laughing."

"I'm so glad my humiliating experience brought joy to your men." I folded my arms and perched on the edge of his desk. "I heard the door lock behind Daniel. Was that you?"

"Yes."

"You can lock and unlock doors with your mind?"

"Some doors. Are you ready for bed?"

I yawned.

"I'll take that as a yes. Did you learn anything from *Cinderella*?"

"No, but Daniel did a pretty deep analyzation. He thinks my family is intimidated by me."

"He's not wrong." Rider stood from his seat and stretched. "Wait until he sees you help me interrogate the wererat later. The wererat is terrified of you."

I woke drowsy, with Rider standing over me holding a mug of blood. He was dressed in black slacks, a black T-shirt, and black boots. His hair was neatly pulled back into his usual style of low ponytail, and he didn't look happy.

"You're mad at me."

He frowned. "No. I'm not. Why do you think that?"

"Well, you certainly don't look happy," I said, sitting up. I took the mug and sniffed. It was fresh enough, but I feared where it came from. "This isn't wererat blood, is it?"

"I'd drink battery acid before I drank from a wererat, and I certainly wouldn't feed their blood to you. And I don't look happy because I'm tired and frustrated. It has nothing to do with you."

I looked up at him. "You didn't try anything when we came up to bed this morning."

"*You* didn't seem all that happy with *me* when we parted ways earlier in the night, and you had a rough night after that. I was afraid that if I tried anything, you'd separate my testicles from the rest of my person."

I grinned. "So you still like me?"

"Unfortunately." He sat on the chaise and leaned back, arms folded. "You're a pain in my ass, but I'm infatuated with you. Lucky me."

I stuck my tongue out at him and took a sip of blood. "It's not nightfall yet. Why did you pull me from sleep?"

"Your friend is back."

"Gina?"

He nodded. "She came in about twenty minutes ago and ordered a drink. A few men have tried to talk to her, but she's shooed them away. She asked a server if you were around, and prior to entering the bar, I received a report from the man I have stationed outside your apartment. She swung by there first. Your donor told her she didn't know where you were or when you'd be returning and offered to take a message. She didn't leave one."

I drained the mug of blood and set it on the nightstand next to my cell phone. I picked up the phone and saw three missed calls. "She's been calling me. The last time she was here, she mentioned going to Pussycat Playhouse with her Friday night and I told her I'd get back to her. It's only Wednesday. She's a little impatient, or Selander Ryan's a little impatient."

"That's what I'm thinking. She's wearing a lot of makeup, but there's definite discoloration underneath it."

I looked at him. "A bruise?"

"Don't trust her, no matter what story she sells you."

My stomach suddenly felt very empty. "Would he hurt her physically?"

"I wouldn't put it past him, but from what you've told me about her, she isn't that picky about the men she goes out with. Anyone could have hit her. She could have tripped over her own feet. We won't know until you talk to her. Just stay aware that she is more than likely Ryan's puppet, here to get information out of you or try to figure out a way to get to you without me being there to protect you."

"Are you going to be there with me when I speak to her?"

"Do you think she would speak openly around me?"

"I don't know." I sighed and stood from the bed, stretched, and walked over to the dresser. "I feel bad. She

269

would have never met Selander Ryan if he hadn't been hunting me down."

"He wouldn't have been hunting you down if not for me."

"I still had the blood type incubi go for. Even if he didn't know about me being your soulmate, he would have probably found me eventually and killed or turned me."

"Maybe, but what he's doing with Gina now is all because of me, his need to make me suffer. It's awful that he's using her, but you didn't cause this. It's not your blame to feel."

"It's not your fault, either. He was evil, and beyond sick. He needed to be stopped."

"Then let's agree that all of this is on Ryan's shoulders."

"All right." I grabbed a pair of jeans and a pink T-shirt with a flowery Pigeon Forge logo on it from the dresser. "I'll see what I can get out of Gina."

"One more thing. The server she asked about you is Myra. Myra's shift ends at midnight. She took care of your sister last night, and it was rough. I gave her clear warning that she wasn't to give you any attitude, but are you going to be cool? I can reassign her somewhere you won't ever see her, but I can't ask her to play nice with you if you're going to be hateful to her for no reason. That's not fair. I have a responsibility to take care of everyone in my nest. She's one of my people. My people need to know they serve a fair and loyal leader or I will lose their trust. So what do you want me to do?"

I took my clothes over to the bed and sat across from Rider, thinking about everything Daniel had told me. "You've slept with a lot of women."

"Yes. I've never lied about that."

"A lot of those women are in your nest."

He nodded.

"And they mean nothing?"

"I have a duty as their leader to protect them in the

same manner I protect any of my people, including Rome, Tony, and Daniel. As long as they are loyal in return, they will have a job and protection. That's as far as it goes."

When I pushed aside my insecurity, what he said made sense. I could understand it. Still, I struggled with the knowledge he employed women he'd slept with, women who were clearly upset with my existence. I didn't see that level of animosity coming from a simple one-night stand. "How long did you have something going on with Myra?"

His brow creased. "I never had something going on with Myra. I've told you before, I never let things get serious with anyone."

"How many times did you sleep with her?"

"Once." He shrugged. "I've rarely slept with a woman more than once, especially in the last century, and if I did, they were usually older vampires who were just as determined to avoid emotional attachment as I was. I've never made promises, and I've never lied to get a woman into bed. Any woman who slept with me before I met you knew it was a onetime thing and purely physical."

"Then why do I get so many death glares from Myra and some of the other women who work for you? They don't behave like women who were cool with a one-night stand."

"Babe, some of the women in my nest who don't like you never even slept with me. I didn't do them *all*." He grinned. "I've never claimed to completely understand women. I don't have all the answers. All I know is I've never loved anyone like I love you, and you have nothing to worry about. I have feelings for no one but you."

"I don't understand that. I don't understand how you can sleep with someone and feel nothing, especially when you still see them."

"Good. I hope you never understand it, because it's a hollow feeling. It's like eating food for the sustenance, but not getting any flavor. It was easy for me to do before you because I never allowed myself to even think of growing an emotional attachment to anyone, but since being with you, I could never go back to that. And I would never hurt you." He leaned forward and took my hand. "What do you want me to do?"

I looked into his eyes and saw only truth. I might not understand it, but that didn't make what he told me any less honest. "You've operated your business for a long time. I'm sure you've put people in the best positions and locations for them, and I won't ask you to change things. I'll play nice with Myra as long as she plays nice with me. I have just one more question."

"What is it?"

"Why were you so mad when Rihanna did that spell?"

"Would you want Rihanna to work that spell on me? Make me taller? More muscular?"

"Of course not. I love you just the way you… are."

He kissed my forehead as he stood. "Then you understand where I was coming from. Get dressed. You need to talk with your friend."

Rome was at the bottom of the stairs when we left the room. He was dressed in his usual uniform of black slacks and T-shirt, and carrying a bucket of cleaning supplies.

"Seta's in your office," he told Rider as we took the stairs down. "Your vehicles have been washed and the gas tanks filled."

"Thank you, Rome." Rider waited until he left to turn to me. "I need to speak with Seta, then I'll be dropping in on one of my donors. That's why I didn't feed you directly from myself after waking you up. I haven't had a full day's sleep in quite a while so my power is draining faster than normal. I need to replenish."

"I understand." I didn't like it. I didn't like him being alone with a woman as gorgeous as Seta, and I didn't like thinking about him taking blood from another woman, but he had to feed. I wasn't a fan of bagged blood and couldn't expect him to live off it any more than I could. I also knew fresh blood was more powerful, and he needed that power more than I did. Also, I'd drunk from Daniel and ended up in his lap. I had no right being upset by the thought of Rider drinking from a woman's wrist.

His eyebrows raised. "No commentary? No narrowed eyes? No steam coming out of your head?"

"Would you like to see steam come out of my head?"

"Not particularly."

"Then shut up and do what you have to do."

He grinned. "Yes, ma'am. Tony is bartending, but he'll keep an eye out for trouble. Rome knows to watch for trouble as well. Find out what you can, but be careful."

He walked me through the door to the bar, brushed his lips over mine in a quick kiss, and left me to meet with Seta in his office. I pushed the thought of Seta out of my mind and crossed the room to where Gina sat alone at a table, sadly twisting a little umbrella around in her drink. She was wearing a low-cut navy blue long-sleeved shirt that clung to her like a second skin, and equally tight black slacks with black heels. Her long blonde hair hung freely and her makeup was heavier than usual. I could see the purple and blue splotches of color over her cheekbone. She'd done a pretty good job with the makeup, but not good enough to fool vampire eyes.

"Gina?"

She looked up from her drink. "Danni! I was hoping to run into you here. I called you but you didn't answer. I went by your apartment." Her gaze drifted back down to the table. "Gosh. I sound like a stalker."

"You're fine," I said, taking a seat across from her. I noticed a few men watching us, but none walked over. The bar wasn't packed, but still, I found it odd. "I'm not used to seeing you all alone. Did you actually buy your own drink?"

She nodded. "I guess there's a first time for everything. I don't feel like talking to any men right now, but I do feel like getting tipsy." She raised her glass, giggled a little, and knocked it back. She released a delicate burp and raised the glass again, signaling for a refill.

"How many of those have you had?"

"Not too many. I can hold my liquor. Been practicing for years."

Myra brought a fresh drink over to the table and switched it out with Gina's empty glass. She didn't give me a death glare or slam Gina's drink down.

"I was told you took care of my sister last night," I said, deciding maybe I'd been wrong to ask Rider to stick her with the gross job. Karma had certainly tossed my ass in a dumpster for some reason. "Thank you. I know it couldn't have been the best job."

"I do what the boss says." She glanced at me and walked away.

"She doesn't seem friendly," Gina observed, already sipping on her new drink.

"She had a rough night." I could relate.

"What's wrong with your sister?"

I barely suppressed a groan. I probably shouldn't have mentioned my sister around Gina. For all I knew, I wasn't even talking to Gina. If Selander Ryan had carved a soul stitch attachment into her as we suspected, he could be controlling her.

"Nothing. What brings you here?"

"I wanted to check in with you. So, are you going to make it to Pussycat Playhouse Friday night?"

"I doubt it. Things are kind of busy right now."

"Did you find something? A new job?"

"Yeah, it's in, um…" I looked around the bar. I didn't want to say I worked for Rider and I really didn't, except I had caught the wererat. "Animal Services."

Her nose scrunched. "Really?"

"Yeah." I shrugged. "I might not stick with it. We'll see."

She frowned and opened her mouth to say something,

but something beyond me caught her attention. I turned to see Rider and Seta emerging from the hallway where his office was located. They parted, and Rider looked over at me. He winked, and made his way through the back door, headed to his blood donor. Once the door closed behind him, I turned my attention to Seta to see her eying Gina. She glanced my way as she reached our table and tipped her head in passing.

"Who was that?" Gina asked, watching her leave.

"A business associate of Rider's."

"You trust him alone with a business associate who looks like that?" She placed air quotes around business associate and shook her head as she swirled the liquid in her glass and took a sip. "That seems to be asking for trouble."

My hand balled into a fist completely on its own as I imagined grabbing Gina by the neck and slamming her into the table. I felt the air shift in the room and looked over to see Tony standing at the bar, staring at me. One hand rested on top of the bar and his posture said he was ready to pounce over it at any moment. I took a deep, calming breath and subtly shook my head, letting him know I was fine. Rider was right. His nest could pick up on my emotions if I didn't lock them down.

*Everything all right? I felt a surge of anger.*

I grinned. Speak of the devil. *I'm fine*, I told Rider through our link. *I think I'm just tired and the reins on my mood are kind of loose. No worries. No danger here.*

*Be careful.* I felt his presence leave my mind.

I wanted to address Selander Ryan directly, to let him know his usual games weren't going to work with me, but I wasn't sure if Gina was being outright possessed or just influenced by him, and I didn't want to look in her face and talk to Ryan. If she was only being influenced, I'd look like a crazy person. And if I gave in to my temptation to physically assault her, well, I'd be physically assaulting her, not the evil man I suspected of pulling her strings. I really should have drunk from Angel, calmed my temper with female blood.

"I trust Rider." I yawned, unable to control it. "I'm sorry. I was up all night and I'm very tired. Gina… are you all right? It looks like you have some bruising on your face."

Her hand rose to her face, covering her cheekbone. "It's nothing. I'm fine, just a bit klutzy."

"I've never known you to be klutzy." I leaned forward, searching her eyes, wishing for some way to see inside and know if I was talking to her or Ryan. "How did that happen?"

"I fell."

"Falls don't usually end up in that kind of bruising. What really happened, Gina?"

She guzzled down the rest of her drink and lowered her eyes to the table. "You wouldn't believe me."

Tiny alarm bells rang out in my head. "Try me."

"I've been having these dreams, and there's a man. I can't see him. He's in shadow, but he comes to me at night and we have sex. It's great, but it's taken a turn. Now he hits me, and last night he did this." She pointed to the bruise. "I can't explain it. It was a dream, but it was real. He said he's going to kill me."

Shit. "You don't recognize him at all? I know you said he comes to you in shadow, but does he feel familiar?"

"I guess." She wrapped her arms around herself and gave a little shudder. "I can't place him, but when the dream starts, we seem to know each other. It feels like I've been waiting for him and then he's inside me, and it's pretty hot, but it changed a few nights back, and last night I swear it was real, and I woke up with a bruise where he hit me. What's happening?"

I stared at her and shook my head, at a loss for words. I had a pretty good idea what was happening, but no idea how to explain it to her. She was a human and although Selander Ryan had used her before, she didn't know about it, and I doubted she knew she was being used again. I wasn't even a hundred percent sure how she was being used. Getting information through her was one thing. Why did he need to hurt her? "Have you told anyone else about this? A doctor?"

"You think I'm insane." She lowered her head, covering her face with her hands.

"No, but I think this is dangerous and you need help."

"That's why I came to you."

The alarm bells started clanging harder. "How can I help?"

"I don't know, but you're brave. The way you stood up to Chad when you quit Prince Advertising, I wish I could be like that. I don't have a lot of friends. I don't get along with most women, and men only want one thing. I could really use a friend."

She reached across the table to take my hand and I instinctively sat back, putting distance between us, and lowered my hands into my lap, out of reach. My heart went out to Gina. The poor woman was completely innocent, but the monster using her wasn't, and I felt like touching her would be touching him. I couldn't let him get his hands on me. I'd nearly killed Rider the last time he'd gotten his evil claws on me.

"Danni?" She sat back, eyebrows raised over desperate eyes. "I'm scared. I need help."

I nodded, but I knew there wasn't anything I could do to help her without endangering someone else I loved. This reeked of a trap.

"Maybe you could stay with me a while, watch over me when I sleep?"

And there was the trap. Selander Ryan wanted to get me away from Rider. "Gina, I work nights, and I don't think there's anything I could do."

"I thought we were friends."

"We are." I started to reach for her hand, but thought better of it. "I know that you have power in your dreams.

If this… person… comes to you in your dreams, you have the power to cast his ass out."

"I'm not that strong."

"Yes, you are."

"I'm not. He's going to kill me." She grabbed her purse, dropped a few bills on the table, and stood. "Thanks for nothing. I guess I shouldn't have expected much. You think I'm crazy, but you'll see. You'll see when he kills me."

She left the bar, moving fast, leaving me sitting at the table feeling like the absolute worst. I turned toward the bar and saw Tony watching me as he dried out a glass. He raised his eyebrows in question. I shook my head, not even sure where to begin. I wasn't in immediate danger, so there was no need to give him the details.

I got up and returned to Rider's room, Gina's parting words haunting me. Selander Ryan was a real bastard, and he fought dirty. Gina didn't deserve to get caught up in the feud between him and Rider. I had to get her out of this mess somehow, but I had no clue how. I wished Rider had stayed behind. I could speak with him telepathically, but just thinking about it tired me. I'd had a rough night, stayed up past my bedtime, and Rider's bed was so inviting.

I kicked off my shoes, dropped my jeans and fell face first. If I was going to save Gina, I needed a nap first.

# NINETEEN

I smelled rain and knew Rider was with me. He always smelled like fresh, clean rain. I opened my eyes to see him lying on his back, looking over at me.

"You have clothes on."

He grinned. "Is that a problem?"

"It's unusual. I'm used to you being naked when you're in the bed."

"I was too tired to undress and I don't particularly care if my clothes are wrinkled for what appointments are on my calendar for tonight. Night just fell. Kevin should be downstairs. I need to get Rihanna's spelled wine into him while you go downstairs and retrieve your sister." He rolled onto his side and ran his finger under the elastic of my underwear. "How'd it go with Gina? Tony said she looked upset when she left."

"She told me a man has been coming to her in her sleep, having sex with her. Last night he hit her and she woke up with the mark on her face. She asked me to stay with her, to protect her while she sleeps."

Rider stilled, his eyes darkened. "I hope you refused."

"That's why she left upset. It's your half-brother up to his tricks, isn't it?"

"Sounds like him."

"He can actually do that? I remember him coming to me in my dreams and I know I could feel him. I remember him choking me, but he was one of my sires. He can do that stuff to someone who isn't one of his succubi?"

"If he's marked her with the soul stitch attachment, there's no telling what he can do."

"I told her she could cast him out, that she has that power since it's in her dream. Did I lie?"

"I don't know. I imagine she'd have to have a strong will. I don't know her well enough to know if she does."

"I have to save her. She doesn't deserve this."

"I'm sure she doesn't, but you can't play into his hands either. He could just as easily kill her after getting what he wants from you. I'll reach out to Rihanna and Seta, see if they have any ideas. I do not want you with that woman alone." He kissed me just over my temple. "Try not to worry. There's nothing you can do right now and you'll only drive yourself mad. We have other things to focus on right now, like the wererats abducting women, and releasing your sister. That's immediate. We need to take care of that right now."

"Right this moment?"

"Yes."

"Then why are my panties halfway down my legs?"

"Apparently," he said, rolling me onto my back and moving over me, "we're going to be late."

We'd opted to use the big bathtub instead of the shower before redressing so our hair wouldn't get wet. One thing led to another, and by the time Rider was dressed, he was an hour late for his meeting in the bar with Kevin. I was still dressing as he left to deliver the spelled wine, and despite what Rider had said, I was worried about Gina.

I adjusted my clothes, ran a brush through my hair, and

rolled on a coat of lip gloss. I remembered seeing some saying before about no matter how you feel, get up, get dressed, and get out there… or something like that. I figured it applied just as much for hybrids who'd accidentally dragged their friends into danger as it did for normal humans who were having a rotten day.

While Rider entertained Kevin, making sure he drank Rihanna's wine, I took the stairs down two sublevels to Shana's room. The guards, the same two shifters who'd been on duty her first night awake, allowed me entrance without a word. I entered to find Shana pacing the floor in tight designer jeans, strappy heels, a low-cut white off-the-shoulder-blouse, and dangly diamond earrings. Her hair was long and flowy around a perfectly made-up face.

"About time," she said, clearly agitated, interrupting the pacing to jut a hip out and glare at me with her arms folded. "I'd like to get back to my own home while there's still night left for me to enjoy it."

"You haven't lost that much time. Where did you get the clothes and makeup?"

"Myra went out and got me a few things."

I stood there for a moment, stunned. Except for Eliza and Ginger, none of the women in Rider's nest had been kind to me. Even Nannette had taken time to thaw through the ice cold shoulder she'd initially given me. "Myra?"

"Yes. She's a dear. She took such good care of me while I was sick." Shana narrowed her eyes. "You left me."

"I had something I had to do. I actually asked Rider to have Myra watch you, so you wouldn't be alone."

"How thoughtful." She studied me. "It's funny you didn't get sick at all. We ate the same food."

"I've been turned longer than you. If it makes you feel better, I had an even worse night than you."

"I doubt that, but I'll be free of this dump soon, and I'll know better than to trust someone offering food." She passed me, headed toward the door.

"Shana." I turned toward her and, for a moment as she looked back at me, I caught a glimpse of the little girl who played dolls with me and wished on dandelions. "I'm sorry you got sick." I actually was. I'd been hurt when I'd overheard her criticism and disbelief that Rider could find me attractive as I was, but she'd been raised in the same household with me, had listened to my mother and grandmother pick me apart while bragging about her. What I'd done was spiteful. She was my sister. Even at her worst, she would always be that.

"I'm ready to go."

"I know. Kevin's in the bar with Rider. I'll take you up there and you can leave with him, but please be careful. There are all kinds of dangers for us, far worse than human food. If you need help with anything, ask. I had a lot of bumps after my turn. You've already experienced one. I can help make sure you don't suffer any others."

She studied me for a moment before flashing a dazzling smile. "Sure thing, sis. Now let's go. This princess has had enough of the dungeon."


"I hope this wasn't a mistake," Rider said later as we watched Shana walk toward the front door, arm in arm with her husband. "But I am glad to have her out of here."

I frowned as I noticed Myra smile at Shana as they passed, as if they were old friends. "Did you send Myra out to get Shana clothes?"

"No. I only instructed her to take care of her while she was sick, keep her full of blood until the sun rose and pulled her under."

"Shana said Myra brought her those clothes and makeup. She would have had to do that today, maybe before her shift started? Why would she be so nice to Shana?"

Rider looked over at the shifter in question. "I don't know. Maybe they just get along."

Unease slithered in my gut. It couldn't be that simple. Myra hated me, and she knew Shana was my sister. Supposedly, the women were worried about Rider creating a harem. It seemed to me they should loathe Shana with the same gusto they loathed me with.

"I've set up a blood account for her, and I can monitor her from afar. As with you, if she goes blood-crazed or has any extreme emotional shifts, I'll feel it. It'd be best if you stay in touch with your mother since she, and most likely, your grandmother, aren't susceptible to the spell Rihanna worked. You may need to get involved to keep them from figuring out something's up with Shana because if they do figure out what she is, we can't fuzzy up their minds with wine."

"Oh, joy."

"It's a horrible job, I know, but somebody has to do it." He hugged me against his side and kissed the top of my head. "Unless you just wanted to take them out of the equation."

"I hope that's a really macabre joke."

"Yeah, for the most part." He grinned.

Daniel entered the bar, spotted us, and ambled over. He was wearing faded jeans, Nike cross-trainers, and a T-shirt with the Ghostbusters logo.

"Now that the gang's all here, let's move this into my office," Rider said, leading the way.

Once we reached Rider's office, he took his seat behind his desk, and Daniel and I sat side by side in the chairs in front of the desk.

"Around ten women have gone missing in the past month," Rider said, reaching into a desk drawer. He retrieved a file and placed it in front of us, turned so we could read its contents. "It was brought to my attention this week after a woman escaped what she called a large rat-like beast that tried to drag her down into the sewer system. We started searching street and security cameras and caught a glimpse of what we believed to be a wererat, and that's when Daniel and Rome were dispatched to locate it and bring it to me for interrogation." Rider opened the file and pointed at a picture caught on street camera of a very unattractive man who reminded me a bit of Joe Pesci, if Joe Pesci had gone ten rounds with an angry woman wielding a frying pan. Next to it was a police sketch given by another woman who'd gotten away from a man who attempted to drag her down a manhole. It looked almost identical to the security camera footage. "This is Mortimer Jones, who Daniel and Rome picked up. We haven't got much out of him yet, but he's either not our guy or he's got help because they picked him up Monday night, but another woman was almost grabbed yesterday morning. Last night, you grabbed this guy." He flipped the picture and revealed a mugshot of the wererat I'd taken down. "Mickey Poletti."

"Mickey?"

Rider looked up at me. "Yeah. Mickey Poletti."

I looked over at Daniel to see him silently laughing, catching the same thing I'd caught. "Yup. We took down Mortimer and Mickey Mouse."

I rolled my eyes and groaned. "What are the odds? I guess it's better than Lil' Peanut," I said, referencing the last guy I'd had the pleasure of seeing in interrogation.

This brought a full laugh out of Daniel, who'd been struggling, and I couldn't help but join in. I mean... I'd kicked Mickey Mouse's ass. I felt terrible thinking it, but how could I not laugh?

"Can the two of you be serious, please? There's a wererat abducting women, and we don't know if these two are in on it or not."

Daniel and I sobered and apologized.

"Daniel, you caught Mortimer. Danni, you took down Mickey." Laughter escaped me, earning an irritated look from Rider, so I quickly swallowed it down and apologized. "As I was saying, the two of you caught these guys. I've questioned them, but haven't really gotten anything. My usual method involves a lot of blood, but wererats are particularly vile and I honestly don't want to bite them. If I kill them, I'm not getting anything out of them. Danni, the guy you caught started screaming when he woke up, screaming to keep the crazy bitch away from him. I'm pretty sure he meant you. I'd like you to interrogate them, and Daniel, you can back her up."

Daniel groaned. "Both of us were covered in God-knows-what after dealing with them. They're disgusting."

"They've been hosed down and given clean clothes. They're cuffed with silver. You know yourself, shifters can't get out of pure silver cuffs."

"Why can't they get out of silver cuffs?" I asked.

"Most shifters, whether weres, skin-walkers, or lycanthropes, can't get out of silver cuffs, and if you pin them with silver, they can't shift. That part of the Hollywood werewolf story is true. Silver is like a deadly poison."

I didn't ask about skin-walkers, which was a new paranormal creature to me, and not one I really wanted to know existed because it sounded icky, but I did look at Daniel. "So Imortians aren't bothered by silver?"

"We can get out of the cuffs, but we can't shift if it's in us."

I pointed to his nose ring. "Explain that then."

"It's not silver. It's imortium, a metal found only in Imortia. If you've never been to Imortia, it appears silver. To see its true beauty, you must visit Imortia or be of Imortian blood."

I sat there, blinking at him for a minute, before turning toward Rider. "Can you see it?"

"It looks silver to me too, but I knew it wasn't because he wouldn't survive having silver in him all the time. He definitely wouldn't be able to shift."

"Trippy."

Rider grinned. Clearly, I'd amused him.

"So we need to find out who is taking the women and

why, and where they're being taken to?" Daniel asked.

"Exactly. The sooner the better. If they aren't killing them, we may be able to save them."

I shuddered, picturing the women huddled together somewhere in the sewer system or someplace even nastier, frightened to death as disgusting giant rats held them captive.

"Are you going to be all right doing this?"

I looked up to see Rider looking at me, eyes full of concern. I thought about the women, what they were feeling, and what the families they left behind were feeling. "Definitely. I might even have a little fun."

Rider's interrogation room was on the second sublevel and it looked a lot like any interrogation room you'd see on television, except it had a drain in the floor to help clean up spillage. Things tended to get messy in Rider's interrogation room.

Daniel and I stepped inside, pulling the door closed behind us. Mortimer and Mickey sat in the little metal chairs at the long metal table, their hands cuffed behind them. They'd been hosed down and dressed in light blue jumpsuits. Mortimer was thicker in the middle than Mickey, with a skinny mustache and a nose that seemed more likely to be found on a pig than a rat.

"Is this room supposed to scare us?" he asked, grinning, and I realized that although Rider said they'd been questioned, he clearly hadn't brought them into the interrogation room, which made sense. Rider had once told me no one left his interrogation room alive. I looked at the one-way mirror along the back wall. I couldn't see Rider through it, but knew he was there. I raised my eyebrow, questioning.

*You have free rein,* he told me telepathically. *Do what it takes to find those women.*

"Where are the women?" I asked Mortimer.

"Suck my dick, sweet-tits."

Daniel stepped forward and punched him in the face, knocking him clear out of the chair. He hit the mirror and slid down the wall, where he farted.

"Geez, Mort," Mickey said, looking back at him. "You're an embarrassment."

I walked over to Mickey, noticed him tremble, and wrapped my hand around the back of his chair as I leaned toward him. "Hey Mickey."

"H-hey. I didn't do anything. I was just minding my business last night. You attacked me."

I growled.

"Which is fine. It's a free country. You can attack anyone you want. It's a woman's right."

"Who's the embarrassment now, numb-nuts?" Mortimer glared at me. "We don't know anything about any women. We just want to live in peace like you do. You attacked us."

I pulled Mickey's chair away from the table, giving me enough room so I could sit on the table and lean forward in Mickey's space. "Your friend is mouthy."

"Yeah, it's one of his charms."

"I don't find it charming. I also don't find it charming when men abuse women."

"I've never laid a hand on a woman."

"You tried to kick me last night," I reminded him. "Actually, you tried to stomp on my head, and you bit me several times."

"It was self-defense!" he cried. "Your friend tried to barbecue me, and then you were beating the crap out of me!"

"Would you like me to beat the crap out of you again?" I asked him, ignoring Mortimer's laughing.

"Not particularly. It doesn't do much for my ego."

We'd brought Rider's file in with us. I reached over and picked the police sketch up, held it in front of Mickey's face. "A woman escaped a giant rat. Another woman was grabbed by a man who looked like this and we spotted your friend over there on a security camera. Your friend happens to be able to shift into a giant rat. You know what I'm thinking, Mickey?"

"You're thinking Mortimer's been a very bad boy."

"Yes, I am. I think this sketch looks a lot like him. What do you know about that, Mickey?"

"I think you're right." He looked over at Mortimer. "What did you do to those women, Morty?"

"You sonofa—" Mortimer launched himself at Mickey, knocking the other wererat out of his chair. They rolled around on the floor, hissing and biting despite being stuck in their human forms.

"This doesn't really seem to be going anywhere," I whispered to Daniel as the rats rolled around, trying their best to beat each other without the use of their hands. "We know Mortimer snatched at least one woman, but he's not going to tell us anything."

"Yeah, he's a real jackass," Daniel murmured, half-sitting next to me as we watched the two wrestle. He folded his arms and ran his thumb over his chin, thinking. "Mickey is scared of you. We need to get Mortimer that scared of you."

"Why me?"

"I beat the hell out of him. He took it and he survived. He strikes me as a man who can take a beating without losing his shit. Getting beaten by a woman, however, might just rattle him." Daniel picked up the chairs, settled them next to each other, and stepped over to the men. He grabbed each by the scruff of their necks, plopped them into the chairs, and rammed their heads together. "Enough!"

"He started it," Mickey said, grimacing in pain.

Annoyed, I stood and leaned in front of Mortimer. "Where are the women?"

"Why? You want to join them? Take a ride on my—"

I punched him hard enough to whip his head back.

Blood poured out of his nose as it snapped back. I saw him start to spit and backhanded him. "Where are they?"

He laughed. "Hit me all you want, bitch. I know what you are. You're monsters just like us, but you try to tell yourselves you're the good guys. You're like hyped up social justice warriors caring about the precious humans, protecting the special little humans." He leaned forward and yelled, "Don't you know they'd kill you if they knew what you were? Fuck them!" He laughed harder. "I did, you know. I fucked them all. Fucked them real good. There's not shit you can do about it either because you need me to find them. Mickey doesn't know where I keep 'em. If you let me go, I'll feed them. If you keep me here, or you kill me, they'll starve. That's a horrible death, don't you think?"

I fought past the bile threatening to rise in my throat and looked over at Mickey. His eyes bulged as he stared at me. His lips quivered. Sweat coated his skin. "I don't know nothin'. I swear."

Mortimer laughed. "Come on, sugar-tits. Take these cuffs off. I got scared little bitches to fuck."

I felt a surge of heat flow through my body as I grabbed Mortimer by the collar of his jumpsuit and slammed him onto the table. I reached my hand out. "Daniel, give me your switchblade."

I sensed his hesitancy, but a moment later felt the metal in my palm. I flipped the blade open and held it to Mortimer's throat.

"Tell me where they are, Mortimer, or you'll never fuck anything again."

"If you want the bitches to die, that's fine with me," he said. "A dead bitch is a quiet bitch, and they sure weren't quiet when I was giving it to—"

I brought the blade down into his left testicle. His eyes widened in grotesque horror as he let out an ungodly howl of pain. Mickey began screaming and fell out of his chair, trying to escape. I heard a soft "fuck" come out of Daniel and sensed the shock from Rider all within the second it took to twist the knife in deeper.

I waited for the initial panic-filled screaming to stop, and once Mortimer started crying like a frightened baby, I leaned in real close. "Lefty's a goner. You're about to lose the right one."

"You... crazy... red-eyed bitch," he gasped out as he whimpered in pain.

"Oh, sweetheart, I haven't even pulled back the lid on my crazy yet. After I cut your balls off, I'm going to slice your little weenie and make your friend eat all the pieces. Unless, of course, you tell me where the women are."

"There's an abandoned building on Mellwood. The sewer leads right to it. They're there."

"Are they alive?"

"They're alive."

I looked over at Mickey. He'd backed into the corner and was shaking, his knees pulled up to his chin. "Is this true, Mickey?"

He nodded. "Yes. I didn't hurt them. I swear on my life. I knew what him and Jimmy was doing, but I didn't hurt no one. I'm not part of it."

The surge of heat left me. I looked down, saw the red stain spreading from Mortimer's crotch as blood dripped off the sides of the table, Daniel's knife stuck in his testicle, and nausea rose. I clapped a hand over my mouth and ran out of the interrogation room, into the women's restroom across the hall, barely making it to the toilet before everything I'd eaten the night before and drank since came up.

I heard the door open and footsteps move across the floor, but didn't look up until I was sure I'd heaved everything in me into the toilet, and flushed it down. I turned to see Nannette leaning against the counter, watching me.

"Damn, girl." She grinned as she turned on the water and grabbed a handful of paper towels. "Let's get you a little less green. Maybe we can get you out of here before the guys stop throwing up."

"You saw?"

She nodded as she wet the towels and motioned me over. "I was in the observation room with Rider the whole time."

I walked over to the sink and allowed her to dab my face with the cool towels before I leaned over the sink and rinsed my mouth. "I stabbed that man right in the balls."

"I know. I'm impressed. The bastard had it coming, so don't you go feeling guilty about it either."

I finished rinsing and turned off the water before looking at my reflection in the mirror. I was pale, but otherwise I appeared fine. Except, of course, for the blood on my shirt. "He called me a red-eyed bitch. I felt a surge of something hot burn through me. It was the succubus in me, wasn't it?"

She nodded. "Your eyes flooded to red like they did that night with Rider. I've been studying, and I had a suspicion you just made a lot stronger. I think the vampire is your dominant beast, and when your succubus takes over, it's like a shift, like when Daniel shifts from man to dragon. That's why your eyes turn red. Some shifters do that when their emotions are extreme."

"But I didn't want to have sex with him." I gagged at the thought.

Nannette laughed. "Thank goodness for that. Succubi don't just lust for sex. They're nasty fighters. That man was hurting women. The succubus part of you didn't like it, and I told you already that part of you needs to feed, not just on sex and blood, but on violence. That's why I told Rider he needs to put you in the field."

"I'm a monster."

"No, you're a badass that shouldn't be messed with. What happened in that room was vicious, but it was controlled. You got the information out of him and as soon as you did, your vampire side took the reins back. If you keep both of your beasts fed well, they can work together. Just don't forget to feed from your female donor. You want to keep your succubus side controllable."

I nodded my head as my face heated with a guilty flush. I had yet to feed from my female donor and my succubus side had surfaced. Things could have gone to hell pretty quick in that room. I'd gotten lucky. "Is Rider upset with me?"

"No, honey. He's a little green around the gills, but you did what was needed to be done. You got the location of those women."

"Green? Rider? I've seen him rip a man's spine out."

"Honey, I don't care how tough a man is, he sees a guy take a knife in the ol' hushpuppy and he's going to be a little sick."


Rider was outside the interrogation room when we left the bathroom, instructing one of his men, Juan, not to leave his post until he returned. I could hear Mortimer and Mickey wailing and begging beyond the door. Rider turned and took a good look at me. "Are you all right?"

"I think my shirt is ruined." I looked down at the shirt. I'd gotten it during our trip to Pigeon Forge, a trip I recalled rather fondly. "I love this shirt."

"A little tip; don't wear anything you really love into interrogation." He grinned. "When Daniel gets out of the bathroom, we're going to go check that building out, see if the women are there. Rome's on janitorial duty, so he's in charge of laundry. Get the shirt to him right away and he might be able to save it for you."

I frowned. "You don't want me to go with you?"

"Babe, you got the information we needed and stabbed the bad guy in the nuts. You've gone above and beyond."

"You're leaving them in there?"

"I want to make sure the information is good first.

First, we save the women, then we kill the rats."

Daniel walked out of the men's room, one hand over his stomach. He looked over at me, his face a little pale. "What is it with you and balls?"

# TWENTY

I washed up, changed into black leggings, a gray tank top, and cross-trainers, pulled my hair into a ponytail, and handed my dirty clothes off to Rome, praying for a laundry miracle, before I headed down to the training room. Nannette had been dressed in leggings and a T-shirt with sensible athletic shoes, so I assumed we were ready to progress to the physical part of our training, but I entered the training room to find her sitting in one of the two chairs. The second chair faced her.

"Oh boy. We're doing the psychological stuff again tonight."

"A little bit," she said, smiling slightly as I took my seat across from her. "Did you do your homework?"

"Yep."

"And?"

"And I didn't really get anything out of the story, but Daniel did some analyzation and made a little sense."

"Only a little?"

"I get that Cinderella's step-family was jealous of her, and I get why, but when applying the story to myself I had trouble figuring out the jealousy part. Shana is beautiful and has a supermodel's body, so the jealousy thing wasn't working for me, but Daniel suggested they weren't so much jealous as intimidated by me."

Nannette nodded, her eyes shining. "Very good."

"I don't understand where the intimidation comes from. Except for tricking Shana into eating human food last night, I've never done anything to remotely harm my family."

"I've never met your family, but I've heard enough about them and listened to you enough to have made some assumptions. Where does your mother's power lie?"

I laughed, the thought of my mother having power absurd. "My mother has no power."

"If your mother had no power, she would have never succeeded in making you an insecure mess. Power isn't always about magic or physical strength. What does she do to make you doubt yourself?"

I looked down at my hands, my face a little warm. I knew I was insecure, but it never felt good when other people pointed it out.

"Has your mother actually told you that you were ugly?"

"No."

"What has she said to you?"

I sighed. "Every woman in my family except for me is big-breasted. My whole life, they've criticized me because I'm not built like them. They wanted me to get a boob job. I had one scheduled, but I was turned right before and had to cancel. They comment on my weight, always suggesting a diet to reduce my backside."

"Do they struggle with this?"

"My mother has struggled with her weight since my father died, but otherwise, no. And every woman in my family has an ass flat as a pancake."

Nannette smiled. "Ever think maybe they wish they had a little more back there?"

I shrugged. "As much as they comment on my ass, I wouldn't think so. I don't really get the jealousy angle because they actually wanted me to get a boob job. They've bought me enhancement pills and a device that was supposed to plump my breasts up. Why would they do that if they were jealous of me?"

"Not all jealousy is about looks, and intimidation works differently than jealousy. Why are big breasts so important to them?"

"I guess because they think it's their best feature. All I've ever heard was how men love a big-breasted woman and how terrible it is that I never had them, and how I'll never land a decent man without them."

"Rider loves you. I've known him a long time, and he's never looked at any woman the way he looks at you."

I felt a goofy smile start to spread across my face and fought it back. "Rihanna offered to give me a magical boob job, and she actually did it. He got so mad, demanded I be put right back exactly as I was."

Nannette's eyebrow rose. "And how did you feel about that?"

"A little confused about his anger, but relieved. I looked down and actually didn't like what I saw. It wasn't me. I kind of like me. And I guess Rider really likes me." I frowned, remembering Shana's reaction.

"What is it?"

"Shana accidentally let her thoughts slip. Let's just say they were pretty insulting. She couldn't believe a man would find me attractive as I am. That hurt."

"Do you think your sister hates you?"

"No." I shook my head. "We were pretty close when we were little, but as we grew older, she became more my mother's child, and I guess I was more my father's child. We grew apart, but I've never felt she hated me. She says some insulting stuff, but she says it good-naturedly most of the time like she doesn't even realize she's being insulting."

"So you were more a daddy's girl. How did that make your mother feel?"

I laughed a little. "She hated it. My father's been dead for years and she still gets in her little digs whenever she can. He's even been blamed for my body. 'Act like a boy and you'll look like a boy' was a favorite of hers. I really wasn't even much of a tomboy. I just liked going to monster truck rallies with him." I shrugged.

"Shana and your father weren't close?"

"He loved us both, but my mother has always had her claws deep in Shana. Shana has always been gorgeous, so in my mother's eyes she can do no wrong. She's stood up for me a few times, but other times, like last night, she's just as bad."

"Did you regret not keeping Rihanna's magical help after hearing what Shana thought?"

I thought about it and shook my head. "What Shana said hurt, but not because I agreed with her. It hurt because she's my sister. She should be supportive."

"Why do you think she has those moments of being just as hurtful as your mother?"

"I guess it's all she knows. My mother taught her everything her own mother taught her. It's like this never-ending cycle of mean girls."

Nannette sat still, staring at me, the gleam of knowing something in her eyes. I thought back over what we'd just said, sensing she was waiting for me to catch on. Finally, it clicked. "Shana learned from my mother, who learned from her mother. It's all they know. Shana is dominated by my mother like my mother is dominated by her mother. The women in my family believe everything their mothers say to be gospel, but I followed my father more. I'm not built like them. I don't think like them. I actually wanted a rich, powerful husband for a while just to prove to them I was as good as Shana, but deep down, it wasn't that important to me. I've always wanted to be loved as I am and to be happy, the way my father made me feel. They treat me the way they do because they don't understand me, and because they can't control me. That scares them."

"Stand up and face the mirror, please."

I stood and faced the mirrored wall as Nannette rose and stood next to me. She angled her head to the side, looking at my reflection. "What do you see?"

I took a deep breath, stood straight, and exhaled as I looked at the woman in the mirror. I saw her laugh, cry, and scream. I saw her run after a shifter in a dark alley, hold her own against a werewolf, and get up every time she got knocked down. I saw her alone, and I saw her surrounded by a few good friends. I saw her make love, make friends, make enemies, and never lose herself. I saw her steadily get stronger. "I'm pretty. I have nice, bright green eyes I'd like to think are friendly and honest. My body is strong. My legs can move fast when needed, my hands can comfort a friend or beat the crap out of someone who really deserves it. My chest is small, but there's a pretty decent heart inside it. I don't look like a supermodel. My chest is too small, my hips too wide, and a little too much junk in my trunk for that, but my body does everything it's supposed to do, and I don't want to change it anymore."

A tear leaked out of my eye, quickly followed by three more. "I'm sorry. It took me a long time to love the girl in the mirror."

Nannette pulled me into a hug. "By the way, the *Cinderella* assignment was just to get you to think. You are so much more than Cinderella. You have greater purpose than snatching up a prince. Maybe your family will realize they've mistreated you someday, maybe they won't, but it really doesn't matter. All that matters is that you looked into that mirror and loved who you saw. As long as you keep doing that, no one else's thoughts or opinions can hurt you, and their reasons don't matter. You've taken back your power from your family, from Selander Ryan, from enemies you haven't even met yet."

She pulled back, wiped my tears, and held my face in her hands as she looked directly into my eyes. "It doesn't matter why anyone has ever said anything hurtful to you. You don't need those reasons because they won't make or break you. It doesn't matter why anyone loves or loathes you. You don't need negative people in your life. Hell, you don't even *need* Rider. All you need is that badass bitch in the mirror."

I laughed and wiped my eyes.

"Are you good? Feeling strong?"

"Stronger than I've ever felt," I said, answering with complete honesty.

"Good." She lowered her hands and stepped away. "Because now I'm going to have to rough you up. You're good at using your anger and fear to defend yourself, but if you're going to go out with Rider and his nest on jobs, you need to learn how to fight strategically whether you're scared or not. It's a good way to keep the succubus side of you in check."

I followed her to the center of the room and braced myself. "I've worked a little with Rome and Daniel. Are we using the dummies?"

Nannette grinned. "No, honey. You're going to fight me, and unlike Rome and Daniel, I'm going to try my damnedest to knock you out."

Nannette didn't knock me out, but after an hour spent training with her, I kind of wished she had. My lip was busted, my gums hurt, if my nose wasn't broken, it sure as hell felt like it was, and I was starting to develop a black eye. Then there were my ribs. My ribs hurt like a bitch.

"Are you all right?" I asked, looking down at Nannette.

She lay on her back, wheezing. "If I didn't like you, I'd fucking kill you," she said, raising her fist to flip me the bird.

I smiled wide despite my split lip. "You like me?"

"Like is probably too strong. Let's just say I wouldn't smile if you died."

Coming from Nannette, I'd take that as a yes to my question. "Need help getting up?"

She held up both hands, and I bent as far as my ribs would allow to grab them and help her stand. She held her side and ran her tongue over her top row of teeth. "I'd be really pissed if you knocked a tooth out. You came close."

"You almost knocked mine out, too. Thank goodness for the healing properties of our saliva. Is training supposed to be this horrific?"

"I had to see what you had in you."

I started to ask how she could see at all with one eye swollen shut, but thought better of it. "Sorry I kicked you in the face. I just reacted."

"You have good instincts. I'll recommend Rider send you out more. I don't know why he's so protective of you. Once you got over being intimidated, you were mean as hell."

The door opened and Rome stepped in, cleaning supply bucket in hand. His eyes widened, and he paled to a degree I'd never seen a black man pale as he took in the sight of us and the smears of blood on the floor.

"Holy shit," he said.

"Girls' night got a little wild," Nannette said, looping an arm around my shoulders, grimacing with the effort. "Think you can go grab us some blood?"


We each downed a pint of bagged blood before Nannette left, moving better with the help of the life-sustaining nectar. I returned to Rider's room, earning my fair share of double takes as I walked past a variety of Rider's employees, from security to tech geeks. The blood started healing immediately, relieving the pain I'd felt in my ribs so it was bearable to breathe, and a swipe of my tongue over my lip and gums healed my mouth instantly. I looked at myself in the bathroom mirror and winced at the bruising still marring my face. I wasn't sure, but I thought Nannette might have actually broken my cheekbone.

Sleep called to me despite daybreak being hours away, but I fought against its pull, remembering what Nannette had said earlier about the effect of drinking from my female donor. After what had happened in the interrogation room, I didn't want to risk my succubus side getting out of control. I was thankful it hadn't chosen to come out in the training room. I closed my eyes and reached out to Rider.

*Are you all right?* He immediately asked, his tone heavy with concern.

*Yes. I wanted to swing by my apartment and check in on my donor, get my fresh female blood requirement. Will you and Daniel be back soon?*

*Not that soon. We found the women, but we've got a mess here. I'll send Ginger to you. Do not leave the bar without her.*

I looked at myself in the mirror, noting the way my eyelids drooped. Even if my car was parked in Rider's garage instead of my apartment parking lot, I wouldn't dare drive it, and I wasn't walking the distance either. *No worries. Be careful.*

I felt him smile through our link and figured I'd amused him. *You too.*

I sensed him ease out of my mind and started getting ready. For the second time that night, I peeled off a bloody shirt to pass along to Rome and hope for the best.

I heard a knock at Rider's door and opened it to find Ginger dressed in jeans, combat boots, a crop top with a smiley face that looked like it had been poisoned, and a leather jacket. Her short brown hair was spiky, her lips the color of blood, and pretty hazel eyes heavily lined in charcoal widened at the sight of me.

"Shit. I heard you had a big night, but I was under the

impression you dished out all the pain."

"I trained with Nannette. I looked and moved worse before a pint of blood."

"How's Nannette look?"

"One eye was still swollen shut when she left."

Ginger barked out a laugh. "Well, I guess if anyone could swell Nannette's eye shut, it would be Danni the Teste Slayer."

I started to roll my eyes as I double checked my pockets, making sure I had my cell phone and keys, but the action hurt. "You heard about that?"

"Honey, *everybody* heard about that," she said as we moved down the stairs. "Juan gave us all the gory recap."

"I don't think he actually saw it."

"No, but that's not going to stop him from telling the tale."

"Great." I eyed Ginger's clothes. She wasn't fancy, but she looked far less casual than me in my jeans, sneakers, and ladies' cut white T-shirt. "I hope it wasn't a bother for you to have to give me a ride to my apartment."

"No, I was in the group Rider took to rescue the women those wererats took. Man, the place was a pigsty and then there were the women. I can kick ass all day long, no problem, but I'm not good with dealing with heavy emotional stuff. Those women have been through a lot."

We'd made it to the parking lot. Ginger beeped her Mustang unlocked, and we got in.

"Did the rat tell the truth about raping the women?" I asked, hoping he'd been lying.

"I don't know. Like I said, not good with the heavy emotional stuff. I kept my distance." She started the car and pulled out of the parking lot, headed for my apartment. "Rider called in Rihanna to do her thing. The women saw that their captors shifted in and out of rat form and that's something we can't afford for them to tell the authorities. Rider's usual protocol in situations like this is to get as much information as he can out of the victims without traumatizing them further, then bring in a witch to alter their memories."

I thought about the amount of money I saw Rider give Rihanna the night she'd cleaned up the mess I'd made of Dex Prince after he'd tried to rape me. "Rihanna must be making a killing tonight."

"Rihanna doesn't charge for this, not when some evil paranormal bastards prey on humans and do what they did. She offers her services in these situations not only to protect the rest of the paranormal community, but to help the human victims heal mentally and emotionally. She's a good witch."

I nodded my head in agreement. I knew there was a reason I liked her.

Carlos was on duty outside my front door when we arrived at my apartment. He covered his privates as he faked a mask of fear, then winked.

"I see the news reached Carlos," I said as I inserted my key in the lock.

"He was one of the first to order a T-shirt."

I turned to look at Ginger. "What T-shirt?"

"The one I'm having made."

"You wouldn't dare."

"You stabbed a guy in the nut. You have to have a T-shirt for that."

I rolled my eyes and winced at the pain the movement caused as I pushed the door open and entered my apartment.

Angel sat on the couch, a bowl of popcorn in front of her on the coffee table and what sounded like an action movie on the television. I recognized Wesley Snipes's voice muffled by fake fangs.

"*Blade*?" I asked, as I moved over to the couch.

"Yup. It's a marathon," she said, looking up at me. Her eyes widened. "What happened?"

"My training session was very intense tonight," I answered, plopping down next to her. "I need fresh blood to heal."

Her eyes stayed wide, her skin paled a little. "From me?"

"Yes. You've done it before," I fibbed. "You know I won't hurt you."

"What if I faint again?"

"You're on the couch. You won't fall."

"You gotta toughen up, kid," Ginger told her, grabbing a handful of popcorn. "Besides, what self-respecting vampire fan is afraid of getting bit?"

"I'm not a kid," Angel said, narrowing her gaze.

"Prove it."

Angel thrust her wrist out in front of me. "Go for it. I'm not afraid."

I grinned at her bravado. "Did you eat well today?"

She nodded. "I had a big plate of pasta for dinner."

"All right then. This may pinch a little." I held her hand firmly but gently, but my fangs didn't drop.

"Problem?" Ginger asked. "A little performance anxiety?"

I used my free hand to flip Ginger off and thought about Nannette's warning. I needed the fresh female blood to mellow out my succubus side and keep it from taking over. I did not want another incident of attacking Rider like I had in the alley behind Auntie Mo's. I focused on my fear of that and my need for what flowed through Angel's veins until my fangs dropped and I sank them into her small wrist. Her blood was bland and didn't hold the slightest jolt of power, but I forced myself to drink it, knowing it was my succubus side that didn't care for it. My vampire side needed it. In fact, I felt the dull throbbing in my face ebb with each swallow. Mindful of the fact my donor was a teenager, I drank no more than what seemed equal to what a person would volunteer at any Red Cross event and withdrew. I swiped my tongue over the punctures and sat back, relieved to see Angel was fully conscious and perfectly fine. "See? Not so bad, huh?"

She looked at her wrist in amazement for a moment, then returned her narrow-eyed attention to Ginger. "I told you I wasn't scared."

"Yup. Didn't faint or whimper or anything," Ginger replied. "Peer pressure works again!" She pumped her fist in the air and grabbed another handful of popcorn before looking at me. "Your discoloration is gone. How do you feel?"

I poked at my face gingerly. "The area around my eyes isn't hurting as bad, but my cheek is still sensitive. I think Nannette broke bone."

"You're going to need sleep to heal that kind of damage. You're lucky she didn't smash your whole face in. Nannette's no slouch when it comes to fighting."

"Yeah, I picked up on that the first time I saw her fight."

"So, is she going to be your regular sparring buddy from now on?"

"I hope not."

Ginger laughed.

"Why do you have to train?" Angel asked. "Aren't vampires just naturally good at fighting?"

"I don't believe so," I answered, remembering what Rider had said of Eliza. "I've heard some aren't fighters at all."

"Very true," Ginger said, licking butter from her fingertips. "Some of the biggest wusses I know are vampires and shapeshifters."

"Shapeshifters?" Angel's mouth dropped open.

"There's a whole world of paranormal out there, kid." Ginger gave up on licking her fingers clean and walked over to the kitchen to wash her hands.

"You don't need to be afraid," I said, noticing the wariness in Angel's eyes. "Just like there are good vampires, there are good… other paranormals."

"And bad ones?"

"And bad ones." I nodded. "But you have security. There's been a guard in the hall since you came here. He has a direct link to my sire, who is very powerful. Nothing will happen to you here."

"I'm just a girl. Why would they care if something happens to me?"

"Well, because I would care, and my sire is my boyfriend. He does a lot for me, like protect my donor and pay for this apartment so you can stay here where you are safe."

"Wow. That's pretty generous."

"He's a great guy."

"And a vampire."

"Yes."

She blinked a few times as she processed this information. "So there are shapeshifters and what else? Witches? Fairies? Wendigos?"

I grinned. "You like *Supernatural*, don't you?"

"Hello, have you seen Jensen Ackles?"

I laughed. Angel was a girl after my own Dean Winchester loving heart. Realizing this, my laughter stopped. I wouldn't be happy kept up in an apartment, doing nothing but watching movie marathons and donating blood to a vampire. "Angel, what do you want to do? Go to school? Travel? Learn a skill?"

She shrugged. "I never thought about it."

"You never thought about what you'd like to do? Not once?"

"I was always busy thinking of how I was going to get my next meal or avoid getting slapped around." She chewed her bottom lip. "I worried about what important, not what I thought was pretty much a fairy tale."

I looked over at the kitchen to see Ginger watching us. I was pretty sure my eyes were as hard as hers. I reached for Angel's hand. "Angel, you can do or be whatever you really want. I'll help you. And no one will ever hurt you again."

"And if they try, we'll eat their asses," Ginger added, returning to us. She sat near us in the armchair and stilled. "Wait. Not literally, I mean. We won't *eat* their asses. That's disgusting. We'll just beat the pulp out of them and maybe kill them. Depends on what they do and our general mood at the time."

"I think she gets the point," I said, shooting Ginger a warning look. "You're going to make her think we're merciless."

"Girl, you stabbed a dude in the nut tonight."

"You stab guys in the nuts?" Angel leaned in, enthralled by this idea.

"One guy!" I said. "I stabbed one horrible, cruel kidnapper in the testicle. It's not like I just go around doing that."

"Too bad," Angel said. "I bet there are lots of guys who deserve to get stabbed in the nuts."

"Fuckin' A," Ginger agreed.

I sighed. "Think about it, Angel. What do you want to do? Sky's the limit. Let me know what you come up with next time I drop in and call me if you need anything. We have to head back now."

I grabbed Ginger and ushered her out the door.

"What's the rush?" she asked as I prodded her down the stairs to the parking lot.

"I'm getting you away from my young, impressionable donor before you encourage her to become some sort of serial nut-stabber. I have enough problems without whatever karma I'd get from turning a teenager into that kind of monster."

"She's killed a man already. How is stabbing a guy in the nut worse?"

"Have you ever met a man?" I asked. "Nine out of ten would choose to be murdered over losing a testicle if given the choice."

"Men are stupid. The more I learn about them, the happier I am I only do women," she said as we slipped into her Mustang. "Where to now?"

I looked at the clock on her radio. It was late, but Shana would be up. "One sec," I said, pulling out my cell phone. "I'm going to check in on Shana."

Shana answered on the third ring with an irritated "Hello?"

"Hey, it's me. I'm just checking in. I know it's late, but it's not like we sleep at night."

"My husband does," she said. "It's our honeymoon, although we're not spending it where I'd planned."

I bit my tongue before I snapped out my impulse reply that honeymooning at home was better than being dead. "I can imagine how disappointing it is not honeymooning somewhere nicer, but as time goes by, you'll be able to travel, even stay awake during the day. You can go on a honeymoon later, like on an anniversary."

"Hmm… I noticed you got the whole awake in daylight thing pretty quick. I realized when we were talking with Rihanna that you must have turned before your breast augmentation was scheduled, but you were out in daylight with Mom, Grandma, and me. You didn't seem tired at all. Word on the street is you're special."

I felt a growl rise in my throat and fought it down. I was pretty sure I knew where she'd gotten her information. "Don't believe everything you hear. A lot of women in Rider's nest aren't happy he's turning women now. If they're talking about me, you can believe they're talking about you too. I just wanted to check in on you, see how you're adjusting. If you need me to stop by, I will."

"Adjusting to being unshackled? I'm just fine. I have a mini-fridge full of bagged blood, some special sunscreen that I can't even use until I'm able to hold my eyes open during the day, and Kevin is clueless. I don't need anything."

"Good. Be very careful around Mom and Grandma,

308

and please don't give them this number. You can use it if you need me. I'm not a fan of the whole talking inside each other's minds thing unless it's necessary."

"Tell that to your boyfriend. I can feel him watching me in my head, like an obsessed lover."

I heard the click, indicating she'd disconnected, and let out a frustrated growl.

"Someone's been talking out of class?" Ginger raised an eyebrow.

"Myra, I'm sure. She was acting all chummy with Shana. I tried to give her the benefit of the doubt, even be nice to her earlier, but something's up. I can't see her being nice to Shana when all I've ever gotten is a cold shoulder. Do you know her?"

"I know of her. We don't exactly hang in the same circles."

"Do you trust her?"

Ginger laughed. "Honeybun, a vampire doesn't live long trusting a lot of people. I keep my circle small for safety reasons as well as personal. I trust you because I trust Rider, and you're pretty damn important to him. You have trust by extension, and I trust Daniel to do his job, but I'm not sharing secrets with him. Rider mostly uses me for solo jobs, a lot of them not around here, but he's keeping me close to help guard you, which is fine. I like you. I've never worked with Myra and we've never had any heart to hearts."

I sighed. I was tired, both physically and mentally, and wondering what was going on between Myra and my sister wasn't helping my mood. "Take me home."

# TWENTY-ONE

I'd fought to stay awake, anxious to hear what Rider had discovered in the building, and how the women were doing, but my injured body needed the sleep to mend and I was dragged under well ahead of sunrise.

I woke several hours later in Rider's bed, startled out of a nightmare where Shana tried to cut off my head and Angel had been captured by Rider's men after stabbing several men in the balls. Rider jerked up into a sitting position next to me.

"What's wrong? I felt your fear."

I saw the worry in his eyes and felt bad for causing it. "Nothing. I just had a nightmare."

The worry appeared to grow stronger. "The last time you had a nightmare, my brother was in your dream with you, trying to kill you. Is he back?"

"No. I'm pretty sure this was just a regular nightmare," I assured him. I looked down, noting he was naked as usual, covered from the waist down by the bedsheets we shared. Apparently, he'd had time to come home, clean up, and slip into bed. "I tried to wait up to see how everything went last night, but I couldn't keep my eyes open. I'm sorry I woke you. You must be tired."

"No apology necessary." He rubbed the sleep from his eyes and puffed the pillows up along the headboard before settling back against them, pulling me close against his side. We sat there together, his arm draped around me, as the last remnants of drowsiness caused by waking up too early slowly drifted away.

"Did you find all the women?"

"We found all the women reported missing, and then some. The fact there were others not reported there is disconcerting. Hopefully, that was the only building they were being kept, but I still have a team tracking all wererats in the area in case there are more."

"Were they all right? Did he actually do what he said he did?"

Rider was silent for a moment, his body tense. "I'll spare you the details, but some women really went through hell there. Rihanna used her magic to heal them from the psychological and emotional damage the best she could. After she adjusted their memories, taking all the paranormal aspects out of their ordeal, I called in a tip to some paranormals I know within the police department and any medical treatment was taken care of from their end."

"Grissom?"

Rider nodded. "He's a good cop, and a damn good guy. That part was all done within a couple hours of finding the women at the building Mortimer told us about, but we discovered their underground travel route. That dumpster you and Mickey tussled in was part of it. If he'd gotten to the bottom, he would have been able to escape through a sliding panel that led to a hole in the ground underneath. They use the sewers to get around, but also those underground tunnels. There was a dumpster right by the building the women were in. They came up into it from underground, and there was another hole that led right into the building. No one ever saw them moving about, so the building appeared vacant, allowing them to hide the women there without any suspicion."

"Smart," I said. "Disgusting, but smart."

"Yes. There are multiple tunnels going in different directions. I traveled down one with a team, but once we came to a point where tunnels branched out, I split the team into sub-teams and sent them to see where the tunnels went. So far, I've heard back that some lead to other buildings, but no women were found in any of those."

"That's good news."

"It is. I'd feel pretty good right now, except there's at least one more guy out there who needs to be captured and removed from existence. After you stabbed Mortimer, Mickey mentioned a Jimmy. We didn't find a Jimmy in any of the buildings. I came back and interrogated Mickey further."

"What about Mortimer?"

"Mortimer had already bled out by then. He couldn't shift shape while cuffed so he couldn't heal himself."

"So I killed him?"

Rider studied me. "You don't have to feel guilty about that. He did horrible things to those women."

I nodded, knowing he was right. Also, I knew if I hadn't killed him, Rider would have. Those found guilty during Rider's interrogations always received the death penalty. "So Mickey gave up this Jimmy person?"

"Not until I threatened to bring you down there and set you loose on him," Rider answered, grinning. "Apparently, you're more intimidating than I am now."

"It's the testicle thing."

"Yeah, I know." Rider winced. "I'm trying really hard to not think about the testicle thing. He spilled his guts. Jimmy is an older wererat that's been grabbing women for a few years now. He never crossed my radar because the rats have been traveling. By the time they hit our area, he'd taken Mortimer under his wing and taught him the ropes about how to grab and torture. I have a couple of men sitting on the building where we found the women, and a few stationed throughout the tunnels and other buildings. If he comes by, we'll get him and kill him too."

"Mickey's dead?"

Rider nodded. "He may not have actually hurt the women, but he still knew what was going on and did nothing to help them. For that, he didn't deserve to live."

I thought about what Mortimer had claimed to do to the women and agreed. There are some things you just don't condone.

"How are you feeling?" Rider gently touched my cheekbone with his fingertips. "I heard Nannette and you had a little cage match last night."

"Something like that." I grinned, completely pain-free thanks to the sleep. "We beat the hell out of each other. Is it weird that it was kind of fun?"

Rider laughed. "I spend so much time worrying about you and how I'm going to keep you safe, but you're pretty tough, aren't you?"

I shrugged. "I like that you care so much. It's always nice to know you mean something to someone."

"You mean *everything* to me." He leaned in and kissed me, sparking a flame deep inside my body. His eyes were full of heat as he pulled back enough to look at me. "You know I love when you wear nothing but one of my shirts like this."

"I have a feeling you'd say that about anything I had on right now."

"Guilty." He leaned in to kiss me again, one hand inching up my thigh below the shirt as his tongue slid inside my mouth. Suddenly, he stilled, then pulled away, his head cocked to the side. I'd seen him do this enough times to know someone was speaking to him inside his mind.

"Shit," he muttered, then tossed the sheets back and stood.

"More women were found?" I asked, a ball of nausea

unfurling in my belly.

"No," he answered as he crossed over to his closet and removed clothing. Black slacks and a dark gray button-down shirt. "The man I have posted outside your apartment for the day shift intercepted a package," he explained as he quickly dressed and sat on the chaise to put on his shoes. "He hasn't opened it, but he can smell the decay inside."

A cold chill swam through my blood as I realized why he'd smell decay inside a wrapped package. "Is Angel safe?"

"Angel is fine. She's inside the apartment, clueless. I'm headed over there to see what's inside the box."

"I'm going with you." I tossed the covers back and crossed to the dresser to find a pair of jeans to slip into.

"Danni, I'd rather you—"

I planted my feet and fisted my hands on my hips as I stared him down. "I said I'm going with you."

He stared back at me and sighed, holding his hands up in surrender after a moment. "Fine." He finished putting his shoes on and reached over to the nightstand to pick up a bottle of the special sunscreen he provided to all the vampires in his employ. As he slathered it on his exposed skin, he muttered, "Of all the women in the world, I have to be in love with the one who might stab me in the damn testicle if I don't let her have her way."

Rider pulled his Ferrari into the space next to my Taurus and cut the engine. He exited and glanced at my car as he rounded the front of his to open my door, ever the gentleman.

"Something you want to say about my car?" I asked as I got out.

"No. I just realized you don't use it much now. You're always with me, Daniel, or Ginger, and we all have our own vehicles."

"And you never let me go anywhere by myself."

His eyes narrowed a little as he closed my door and peered down at me. "My psychotic half-brother wants to kill you and we never know when your succubus side is going to go haywire. I may be overprotective, but I think my cautiousness makes sense."

"It does," I said, recalling what had happened after my visit with Auntie Mo. "And I'm appreciative. I'm just tired of having to be so on alert all the time. I really wish someone would figure out how to end this Bloom thing, and it'd be great if your brother would have the courtesy to stay dead the next time one of us kills him."

"Yeah, it was rather rude of him to pop back up like that," Rider said, grinning as we walked toward my building. "I have the brightest people I know working on the Bloom and ending Ryan's reign of terror is at the top of my to do list. Of course, you're always going to have to be careful. It's simply the way our kind must be, and it goes double for you. You're two types of paranormal."

"Lucky me."

"I tried to transition you into a full vampire," Rider said softly, as he held the door open for me to enter the building. "I'm sorry. Ryan and I were too close in age and power. His mark held on pretty damn good."

I sighed as I raised my hand to cup Rider's cheek. "I know, and I don't mean to be such a whiner. I could have died that night. You saved me. I appreciate it, even if I don't sound like it."

We walked up the stairs in silence. A slender, but well-toned man was positioned in the corner near my apartment. He had light brown skin, Asian features, silky black hair cut short on the sides with the top longer, but that was braided down the center of his head except for one lock that hung loose, sweeping over his left eye. He wore jeans, a dark V-neck T-shirt, and combat boots. He held a square package in his hand, wrapped in craft paper.

"This is Jon," Rider told me by way of introduction.

"Jon, you know who Danni is."

Jon nodded, the corners of his mouth curving up in the slightest hint of a smile. "The Teste Slayer."

I groaned. "Is there anyone who doesn't know about that?"

"Probably not," Rider answered. "Jon barely even talks to anyone, so if he knows, everyone knows."

I looked at the man and found him watching me, the almost-grin stuck on his face. It was a nice face. He was a very attractive man and although I got the sense he wasn't someone you'd want to mess with, he didn't radiate any shifter or vampire vibes, yet he didn't seem all the way human either.

He blinked slowly, breaking the staring spell, and handed the box to Rider. "It was delivered by a young boy, about fifteen years old. He said some old woman gave it to him about three blocks away and paid him fifty dollars to bring it to Danni's door. I attempted to read his mind, but whoever gave him the box wiped it of all trace. He was a mess of confusion and his instructions were playing on repeat. It had to have been a witch."

"And you sent him away?"

"As I said, he was just a kid. He knew nothing and after I sent him on his way, he didn't even remember this happening. I left a little something in the corner of his mind, though. If he's contacted by whoever sent him with this box, I'll know."

"Very good." Rider took the box and studied it as I tried to figure out what the heck Jon was. "This is safe to open?"

"I don't sense anything explosive or magical. I just know it's not good because the box can't contain the smell."

My nose wrinkled. I'd smelled the rot as we came up the stairs, but it seemed to intensify once someone spoke out loud about it.

"Let's open this inside," Rider suggested as he placed

his hand over my doorknob. I heard the lock tumble, and he pushed the front door to my apartment open.

"Seriously? You can just unlock my front door without a key?"

"Yes." Rider extended his arm, gesturing for me to precede him.

I stepped inside, finding the living room empty. Rider stepped in behind me and closed the door as Angel appeared in the bedroom doorway, rigorously drying her hair with a towel. She yelped and jumped back, then peeked at us from around the doorframe. "You scared the poop out of me! I wasn't expecting you in the daytime." She looked past me at Rider, and her eyes took on an appreciative glint. "Who's the pretty guy?"

"This is my sire, Rider." I smiled at Rider, enjoying the unhappy expression on his face.

"I'm not pretty," he said, taking offense. "I'm a man."

"Well, there's no hiding that," Angel assured him, "but you sure are a pretty one. Like those guys who model underwear."

"I don't wear—"

"All right," I said, grabbing Rider's sleeve. "You can be pretty and manly. It's a good thing, I swear." I prodded him toward the kitchen. "I guess we should open that in the kitchen. Maybe in the sink, in case there's a mess?"

Angel held her nose as we passed her with the box. "Ew, what's in that box? It smells like infected ass."

"I sure as hell hope it's not." I looked at the box as Rider set it in the sink, with what I was sure was a mask of complete horror on my face. I mean, anything was possible, right?

"I'm sure it's not infected ass," Rider said, a hint of *I-worry-about-you-sometimes* in his tone. "It is undoubtedly a body part, so maybe you should step away and let me handle this," he added, voice low.

"No way. It was sent to me, so I'm going to see what it is, no matter how disgusting." I saw Angel moving toward us and pointed my finger at her. "You, don't come any closer. Go into the bedroom and finish getting dressed," I ordered, noting she was in a bathrobe. "I'll let you know when it's safe for you to come back out."

Angel looked like she was about to say something, but her gaze shifted to Rider and she thought better of it. Nodding her head in silent agreement, she moved to the bedroom, closing the door behind her.

I returned my attention to Rider. "Must you always be so intimidating?"

"I literally did nothing but stand here." He reached for the box. "Last chance to back out of this."

"Let's just get it over with so we can do something about that smell before it kills my olfactory system."

Rider unwrapped the box as I stood at his side, staring down into the sink with my hand covering my nose and mouth.

"You know you don't actually have to breathe while we do this," he reminded me softly as he parted the craft paper to reveal a small brown box constructed of heavy cardboard. Reddish splotches had just started to seep through in a few places.

"I keep forgetting." I forced myself to stop breathing and lowered my hand.

"It's the hardest human habit to let go of," he said, "and honestly, not breathing wouldn't kill us, but we could slip into a coma if we went long enough without oxygen, but at times like this it's nice that we can turn it on and off for much longer than humans." He grabbed the lid of the box and looked at me. "Brace yourself. This will not be pretty."

Understatement of the year, I thought as he opened the box to reveal what I could only describe as horror pudding. A large blob of something floated in a thick stew of blood and who knew what other dark liquid, along with locks of blonde hair thrown on top like a garnish. This was all bad enough, but what really got me was the whole mess was looking back at me.

I clapped a hand over my mouth as bile quickly rose and used my vampiric speed to reach the bathroom and drop to my knees in front of the toilet before I erupted like a volcano. I heard gagging from the bedroom and groaned. Poor Angel. She was trapped between a vomiting vampire in the bathroom and human ratatouille in the open kitchen.

"Sorry," I croaked after I was sure I'd hurled all I was going to hurl and flushed the toilet.

She'd been sitting on the bed when I'd sped through the bedroom, but now stood in the doorway, dressed in jeans and an olive green T-shirt. "Are you all right?"

I managed to stand and rinse my mouth in the sink before grabbing a toothbrush I'd left there before pretty much moving in with Rider. "Nothing some toothpaste won't fix," I croaked.

"Vampires brush their teeth?"

I grinned, my mood lifted just a little. "The ones with fresh breath do." I brushed vigorously, swished around some mouthwash for added measure, and took a cleansing breath, willing my stomach to settle.

Once I worked my way through the disgustingness of what I'd seen, the fear slammed in. The pair of eyes I'd seen on top of the gunk in the box were blue. The hair not stained with blood and muck was blonde, and something had been written on the inside of the lid, but my eyes had gone straight to the freakfest inside and hadn't bothered to read any of the message. "Stay in here," I commanded, maybe with a little more force than required, and rushed out of the bedroom to find Rider washing his hands with a ton of liquid soap. One of the coolers I received my blood shipments in sat on the counter next to the sink.

"I wrapped everything in plastic storage bags I found and now it's all on ice. That should keep it all fresh so we can get it to the lab for analysis." He rinsed his hands, turned off the faucet, and grabbed a paper towel to dry off as he looked over at me. "Are you all right?"

"Rider, those eyes were blue. The hair was blonde."

"It's not Shana," he said, reading my mind. "Believe me, I'd have felt her fear and pain long before whoever Ryan has doing his dirty work got even one piece of that mess."

Right. He could feel Shana like he could feel me. Whenever I'd been in true danger or extreme emotional distress, he'd always felt it. But, still … "Gina."

He lowered his gaze as he threw the paper towel away and sighed. "Maybe. Call her and see if she answers. For all we know, what's in that box could be from more than one person. I poked around and found the eyes, hair, some intestine, and the big lump was a heart. There's no telling if it all came from one person or not."

My stomach started protesting right around the moment he mentioned the heart, so I moved into the living area and settled onto the couch. Lowering my head into my hands, I waited for the nausea to pass. I sensed Rider lower himself to sit on the coffee table in front of me and felt his comforting hand settle over the back of my neck. "I can just send someone to check on her if you know where she lives."

"No." I shook my head and sat up straight. Rider watched me carefully, eyes filled to the brim with concern. A little too much concern. "What did the message on the lid say?"

His gaze lowered, but not before I saw the hesitancy in his eyes. He didn't want to tell me.

"Just tell me. Sitting here imagining what it said has got to be worse than actually knowing."

Slowly, his gaze rose to meet mine, and he took my hands in his. "It said 'I don't need her anymore.'"

"It definitely came from Selander Ryan," I said as if there were any other possible sender, and clenched my teeth as another wave of nausea rolled through me. I freed my cell phone from my jeans pocket, found Gina in my contacts, and handed the phone to Rider, too freaked out to make the call myself. I wasn't sure I wouldn't hurl again the moment I opened my mouth if she did answer.

Knowing what I wanted, Rider thumbed the button to make the call and rose from the table. He stepped away as he made the call. Only a few feet to give me space, but still there with me for support. Between the frown lines creasing his forehead and his silence, I knew Gina wasn't answering. He lowered the phone and disconnected the call. "Voicemail."

"It's Gina." I stared at the cooler holding her beautiful blue eyes and willed myself not to fall apart. Not yet.

"We don't know that for sure. You have her address here. Is this current?"

"I think so."

Rider handed me back my phone and crossed the room to pick up the cooler. I felt his power pulsing as he did and figured he was communicating with his people. When he returned to me, his mouth was set in a grim line. "Do you want to go to her apartment with me, or do you want to stay here?"

"I'm going," I said without a moment's hesitation. Did I want to see what I feared I'd find? No way. But I had to. If Gina was dead, she'd died because she knew me.

"You should feed from your donor first. You were just sick."

"And I'll probably be sick again if we find what I'm afraid we're going to find, so why waste her blood? I can feed later after my stomach has settled."

Rider studied me for a moment and I got the feeling he was going to argue, but knew it wasn't the best time to get confrontational with me. "Fine, but you're feeding as soon as we check out her apartment, no matter what we find there."

"That sounds fine." I took a deep breath and stood, smoothing my hair as I did. I called for Angel. "We're leaving, Angel. You can have the apartment to yourself again."

I heard her feet patter across the carpet, and the bedroom door opened. She looked at us, then at the cooler, her eyes going wide. "Did you … leave anything?"

"No," I answered. "Some air freshener should take care of any residual stench. Sorry about that."

She nodded her head slowly, staring warily at Rider for a moment before returning her gaze to me. "Will you be coming back tonight to, uh, drink?"

"I might. I'll check in either way, and you have security right outside the door. You'll be fine."

She stared at me for a moment, a thousand thoughts flitting across her eyes, then nodded. "Be careful out there."

I grinned at the thought of her, an innocent teenager, warning two paranormal beings to be careful, and nodded at Rider, letting him know we were good to go. He led me to the door, opened it for me, and made sure it was locked as he pulled it closed behind us. He handed the cooler to Jon, who'd been standing just outside, waiting. "You know what to do as soon as your replacement arrives."

Jon nodded and offered me a look of sympathy. "On it."

Even with the special sunscreen we used to keep from burning alive, the sun felt hotter against our skin than a human's skin, but I was so chilled with fear I didn't even notice its warmth as we made our way to Rider's Ferrari.

"She's food, you know," he commented quietly after we'd settled into the car and he'd left my building's lot.

I looked over at him. "What?"

"I picked up on some maternal vibes in there with the girl. As your donor, she's entitled to compensation and security. It's not necessary that you check in with her. She's not your dependent, or your friend. She's food."

I stared at Rider, felt my eyes narrowing into a glare as

I thought about what he said. "She's an eighteen-year-old girl who's had a shit life, and I'm helping her out in exchange for her blood. I don't see how that's any different from what you do with your donors, unless you lied to me."

"I never lie to you." His gaze turned dark. "I'm just saying, don't get emotionally involved with her. She has to keep our existence a secret for the rest of her life. It's very important she knows her role and doesn't get comfortable questioning you. Humans push the limits with their friends and family. They don't do that with their masters. You're not her friend, and you're not her guardian. You're her master."

"Whatever," I muttered, my mood worse than before. Now I was afraid, disgusted, *and* irritated.

"Hey." Rider used his free hand to grab mine and stared at me until I finally looked at him, afraid we'd wreck if I didn't. "I love you."

"I know." I turned his face toward the direction we were headed. "Now pay attention to where you're driving. Jackass," I added in a low murmur.

This got a wide smile out of him, but he said nothing for the rest of the drive.

"It's not too late to back out," Rider said as we sat inside his car, parked in Gina's lot. The apartment building loomed before us, giving off an ominous vibe despite the bright morning sun shining all around it. "You can wait here while I check things out, or I can send in someone else and stay with you."

"No," I said, past the ball of fear in my throat. "I need to do this."

Rider opened his door and stepped out. I heard his defeated sigh as he closed his door and rounded the vehicle to open mine. I knew he wanted to protect me, not just physically, but mentally and emotionally, and I loved him for that. But if Gina had died because of me, I owed her the decency to see what happened and suffer the trauma of it.

Rider helped me out, and we proceeded to the building in tense silence. I felt his need to throw me over his shoulder and take me far away, but he allowed me the freedom to do what I needed to do. I squeezed his hand, silently thanking him for that as we entered the building and climbed the stairs to the fifth floor. According to the information I had for Gina, her apartment was 5E. We were about a foot away when the door swung open and Jon stepped out, his pity-filled gaze locking on to me before he shifted to meet Rider's eye.

"I really don't think you want her to go in there. It's bad. It's *really* bad."

My hand grew clammy and slipped out of Rider's. I backed up a few steps as my brain flooded with questions. What was inside the apartment? Where was Gina? How the hell had Jon beat us there?

"Is Gina in there?" Rider asked.

"Yes, and… *yes*," Jon answered, which I thought was a strange way to answer, but it wasn't as strange as the way the two men looked at each other, silently communicating, before both turned their attention to me, hitting me with looks that sent a shiver down my spine.

Suddenly, I was very afraid of whatever was inside that apartment.

# TWENTY-TWO

"Stay here while I check things out," Rider commanded me before turning his attention to Jon. "You make sure she stays here."

"Gina's my friend. I'm going in—"

"I said stay," Rider snapped, his eyes growing darker. "Don't make me make you."

We stared each other down, or more like we glared each other down, for a heated moment before he gave one last warning look to Jon and stepped inside, closing the door behind him.

"This sucks," I grumbled, fighting the childish urge to stomp my foot, cross my arms and stick out my bottom lip. I love Rider, but the treating me like a delicate child thing he does sometimes really burns my ass.

"You're telling me. He just put me in charge of the Teste Slayer."

I focused my frustration on the handsome Asian man leaning against the wall, arms crossed over his chest. Again, I wondered what he was, unable to put my finger on his paranormal flavor, but I knew it was there despite the strong sense of humanity also coming from him. "I assumed Rider gave you that cooler to take directly to a lab for analysis."

"He did, and I did." He held my gaze, his own revealing nothing. We could have been talking about the weather for all the emotion he showed.

"And you still beat us here?"

"Yes."

"You waited for a replacement to take your post at my apartment, dropped the cooler off at the lab, and you still not only beat us here, but had time to get into the apartment and look around?"

"It would appear so."

I narrowed my gaze on him. "What are you?"

"A person."

"You know what I mean."

His eyes lit up momentarily. I wanted to say I amused him, but his mouth remained a straight line. "I'm... complex," he finally said, then went into silent mode while we waited.

Rider returned, stepping out of Gina's apartment with a ruddier tint to his skin than he'd had before entering. He was angry and upset, I realized as he focused on me with sorrowful eyes. "I'm sorry, Danni. Your friend is dead. The eyes were definitely hers, and most likely the heart. Maybe all of it. We'll know after the lab finishes."

A loud whirring erupted in my head. The hallway spun as I processed the news. Rider gave instruction to Jon, but I didn't hear it. All I could think of was Gina. Gina was dead. I'd figured she was after ruling out Shana, but knowing it for a fact hit me harder than expected. She was dead, and it was my fault. Suddenly, I remembered the odd way Jon had answered when Rider had asked if Gina was in there. "Why did you say yes twice when Rider asked if Gina was in there?"

The men stopped talking and looked at me, but they didn't quite meet my eyes. I stepped toward the door.

"Danni, no." Rider blocked me. "You don't need to see her like this. I've already called this in to Grissom. They'll be very respectful with her body, I promise you."

"Move."

"Danni…"

"*Move!*" I called up every ounce of vampiric strength I had in me and shoved him aside, then used my speed to burst through the door.

I ran through the apartment in a blur, following the scent of blood, and stopped in the doorway to Gina's bedroom, where her dead body lay mangled atop the red silk sheets covering her bed. Her eyes were gone, blood leaked out of her mouth, nose, and the crater in her chest where her heart had been. But despite how horrible the image was, that wasn't what chilled me to the bone. A translucent Gina also stood beside the bed, glaring at me.

"You!" She raised her arm and pointed a see-through finger at me as footsteps pounded through the apartment, getting closer. "You didn't help me when I asked. You're the reason he did this to me!"

I gasped. My hand automatically rose to my mouth to stifle the scream I felt threatening to burst free, and I felt myself fall backward, but was stopped by strong hands. As Rider murmured reassurance in my ear, Jon stepped past me into the room, stopping a foot away from Gina.

"I can take you to Heaven," he told her ghost, "or I can throw you into Hell. Play nice. This wasn't her fault."

She glared at him, her eyes burning bright red as the same color swirled through her form like smoke. "You think I haven't already been to Hell? I felt what he did to me. I was asleep, but I felt it. I asked her to help me." Her face crumpled as she began crying. "I was so afraid."

"Gina, I'm so sorry," I said, pulling free of Rider's grasp to step fully into the room. My chest ached with the pain of her death and the guilt of my part in it. I blinked, warm tears sliding down my cheeks. "I didn't know how to help you. The man who did this to you, he was using you to track me. I think he wanted me to stay with you while you slept, so he could get to me."

"He would have still killed you if Danni had stayed with you," Rider told her. "Maybe he would have killed both of you. That's why I wouldn't allow it. I'm very sorry this happened to you, Gina. You didn't deserve this, but it is not Danni's fault. The same man who killed you wants to kill her. He wormed his way into your mind before he even met Danni. He used *you* to get to *her*. You are both victims of his cruelty."

The red smoke faded until it was gone, leaving Gina's body completely translucent as she looked at me. "I led him to you?"

I nodded as I wiped away tears so I could see better. "I've never blamed you. I never will. I'm so sorry."

"I had so much left to do," she murmured as she stared at her remains. Her jaw hardened, and she looked back up at me. "Make him pay for this."

"I will," I promised her, and I meant it with every fiber of my being. I'd hated the man before this. Now, hate wasn't nearly strong enough of a word. "I will make him pay, but, Gina, there has to be someplace better for you than here. You've suffered enough."

"There was a light," she said, frowning, "but I was so angry. I didn't want to leave. I wanted you to know what happened. I wanted… to blame you."

"I understand," I told her.

"I'm sorry." She sighed, the action causing a ripple to travel the length of her ghostly form. "I was wrong, and now I'm stuck here."

"I can take you to a better place," Jon told her. He looked at Rider. "Do you need any information from her first?"

"I already spoke with her while you and Danni were outside," Rider answered. "It didn't take very long to find out what I needed to know. Stop by my office when you're through."

Jon nodded and held his hand out toward Gina's ghost. His eyes started glowing bright white. "Come with me,

Gina. Your grandmother is waiting, and she has a Labrador wagging his tail next to her."

"Rusty!" she exclaimed, smiling with complete joy as she took his hand and they disappeared. No magic sparkles. No shift in the air. They were just gone.

"What the hell is he?" I asked Rider, turning toward him.

"I'm honestly not sure," he answered as he gently gripped my shoulder and turned me away from the body of my friend. "Grissom and other officials are on the way. Jon and I both did a quick scan of the apartment and found nothing implicating you, not that there should be, but you never know what Ryan's got up his sleeve. She was your friend, so we're going to say you had an early lunch date with her and found her like this. They should be here soon. Let's wait in the hall."

Questioning didn't take long, which I attributed to Grissom having already known what he was walking into and that the police department would never find the murderer because he wasn't human. He'd actually asked me more questions about how Angel was doing than he'd asked about Gina. Still, between discovering what had happened to Gina, being questioned about it, and the fact I'd awakened far before nightfall and had vomited up my morning feeding from Rider, I was exhausted by the time we returned to The Midnight Rider.

"I called ahead to have one of my donors picked up," Rider said as he opened my door. "She should be in my office now. I want you to drink bagged blood and get some sleep before nightfall. I'll be up to join you after I feed."

"All right." The normal pangs of jealousy I got from thinking about Rider drinking from one of his donors didn't strike me. I was far too tired. Physically, mentally, and emotionally.

329

"There was nothing you could have done," Rider assured me as he opened the door leading to the hall behind the bar.

"Mmhmm." I didn't agree, but I didn't want to argue. I didn't want to talk about it. I just wanted to go to bed and drift off into a dreamless sleep and not feel a damn thing.

We stepped into the hall and met two of Rider's men as they came up from the lower levels. I recognized them as the shifters who'd been guarding Shana's room. Both were dressed in black T-shirts and pants, the usual attire of Rider's security staff.

"We just took Jimmy to interrogation," they informed Rider. "Rihanna took care of the woman we found him with, and she was taken to the hospital like the others."

"You found the main wererat?" I turned toward Rider, suddenly feeling a second wind of energy. "When?"

"I was informed of the capture while we were speaking with Grissom."

Telepathically. I was starting to get annoyed by the way the majority of Rider's nest communicated with him. It kept me out of the loop. "So, what? You were going to have me sleep while you interrogate him?"

"We both are going to feed and get some sleep, then Jimmy will be taken care of."

"I want to do it."

"Later."

"Now," I said, moving toward the door. Both shifters' eyes widened, and they quickly moved out of my way. No doubt, they'd heard about what I'd done to the last wererat in interrogation and they didn't want to be the dumb fools who tried to stop me.

"Danni!" Rider called after me as he barreled down the stairs in pursuit. The shifters followed.

I continued, using my vampiric speed to reach the interrogation room, then I turned, coming face to face with Rider, who'd been right on my tail the whole time. The shifters were at the end of the hall, fast, but not as fast as vampires.

"This can happen later," Rider told me. "You're upset and you'll do something you don't want to do."

"I want to kill him. I couldn't save Gina and I can't do anything to your brother until we figure out how to get to him. I can put my hands on this bastard now. I can at least avenge the women he hurt. I *need* to kill him."

Rider studied me a moment, then sighed, defeated. "Find out if there are any other women before you kill him."

"You're not going in with me?"

"Yeah, I am. I'm just not sure if I can stop you if you jump the gun, so I'm making sure now that you know what we need." He opened the door and gestured for me to enter.

I stepped inside the interrogation room, Rider right behind me. The shifters didn't join us, but I was pretty sure they'd taken seats in the next room, behind the one-way mirror.

A short, squat man with a sharp nose and razor thin lips that almost got lost in the pudginess of the rest of his face sat at the table. He wore gray sweatpants and a T-shirt advertising beer. Both articles of clothing, along with his busted sneakers, held various stains, and he reeked of trash and sweat. He smiled, seeing me, revealing a few missing teeth. "Here I thought I was in some kind of trouble, yet you brought me a gift."

Rider snorted. "Be careful what you wish for," he warned as he moved away from me to stand with his back against the opposite wall. "Are there any other women we need to know about?"

Jimmy laughed. "Hell, if you need a woman, I can find you a woman."

Already tired of conversation, I moved forward and grabbed the disgusting man by the fat of his throat, digging my nails in as I pulled him half out of the chair. "Are there any other women out there that you've abducted?" I asked

331

before I released him.

He gasped, massaging his neck as he looked between Rider and me, goggle-eyed. "I don't know what you mean. I was just coming home when your guys grabbed me."

"You had a woman with you," Rider reminded him.

"She was my sister!"

"My men grabbed you in the tunnel leading to the vacant house we found several sexually assaulted women in," Rider said. "When they found you, the woman was half naked, and you were all over her. You still want to claim she was your sister?"

Jimmy grinned. "Why not? I hear siblings and cousins get freaky all the time in Kentucky." He looked at me. "Is this one your sister? You do her? I'd do her. She's feisty. Come a little closer, sweetheart. I got something to—" His eyes grew wide, and he whispered a curse as I felt pure rage flood my body and I knew my succubus side was taking over. I looked at the one-way mirror to confirm the cause of his fear. My eyes were flaming red.

"Are there any more women?" Rider asked quickly, sensing what little control I had.

"No!" Jimmy shook his head. "If you found the vacant house, you found them all. The one with me was a new one I was bringing to the house. Call this demon woman off of me!"

"Now, that wasn't a nice thing to say," I told him before I grabbed him out of the chair and slammed him onto the floor. I rammed my fist into his pudgy face repeatedly, not stopping until the crunching of bones stopped, then I stood, bringing him with me. "This is for every woman you hurt!" I yelled as I threw him across the room. He slammed into the one-way mirror, breaking the glass to reveal the shifters standing on the other side with their mouths hanging open, eyes wide.

Anger still coursing through me, I grabbed the chair Jimmy had been sitting in and beat him with it until I was drained of every drop of rage-filled energy I had.

"He's dead," I said, flinging the chair aside as I stepped away from his mangled, blood-covered body.

"Babe, he's been dead," Rider spoke softly as he crossed the floor, gently wrapped his hand around my wrist, and led me out of the room.

We got a few curious looks as we traveled the lower level to the stairs, and I realized I had blood on me, but no one said anything. Rider remained quiet as he led me up the stairs to the ground floor, then up the stairs to his apartment. He didn't release my wrist until we were in the bathroom and he needed it to adjust the water in the shower.

"Are you angry?" I asked.

"No. You needed to release that fury, and he needed to die. Two birds, one stone." Satisfied with the water temperature, he moved back. "Take your clothes off and get his blood off you. I'll leave blood on the nightstand. Drink it and get some sleep. I'll be right back to join you as soon as I finish feeding."

Then he was gone.


I woke with a heavy weight on my chest and a ravenous hunger burning in my belly. Looking down, I discovered the heaviness was due to Rider's arm slung over me. I was covered in his bedsheets, and judging by the feel of things, I was naked beneath them. I turned my head to find him watching me.

"You fell asleep in the shower. You didn't even drink the blood I left for you."

"Then you'll understand and forgive me for this," I said as I rolled onto my side and leaned over him to sink my fangs into his throat right over the pulse point I'd been eying since I'd turned my head to look at him.

I drank more deeply than I normally would, but he'd fed before coming to bed and, as an older vampire, he didn't need to refuel as often as I did, except for when he pushed the limits too often. Judging by the way he moaned and gripped my hips to pull me tighter against him, I didn't think he minded. Then he was inside me and I *knew* he didn't mind.

"You need to come to bed naked more often," Rider murmured a while later, after I'd finished feeding and we were lying together, recovering.

"It wasn't my choice."

"Well, it's what you get for falling asleep in the shower. I had to make an executive decision." He muttered a curse and sat up. "I have a meeting in my office. I have half a mind to play hooky from responsibilities and just stay in this bed with you."

"I'd be flattered, but why do I get the idea you want to stay in bed with me just to make sure I stay out of trouble?"

"Because you know me so well." He leaned over and kissed my shoulder before getting out of the bed and moving across the room to get clothes out of the dresser. "Nannette's working a double at the hospital tonight, so she won't be training with you. Is there anything you need to do?"

I thought about that as he dressed. I needed to find Selander Ryan before he harmed anyone else, but I had no idea how. Gina had been my only lead, and he'd killed her. My veins iced over as I thought back to the message in the box. "Why doesn't he need her anymore?"

Rider finished fastening his slacks and looked at me. "What?"

"The message. He said he didn't need her anymore. Why doesn't he need her anymore?"

Rider appeared to mull this over as he pulled a dark, long-sleeved T-shirt on and pushed the sleeves up to the middle of his forearms. "I don't know, but I do know he's a very sick monster, and he likes to play cruel games with people. He's taunting you."

"Yes, but he could have done that without the message.

Actually, there are far worse messages he could have chosen. He could have said it was my fault or he could have said I'm next. He said he didn't need her anymore. That means he needed her for something until that point, so what did he get from her that he no longer needs?"

"He used her to get you into the bar the night he attacked you. After that … I think he used her to try to get information on you, possibly lure you away from me."

I nodded, knowing that was all true. He hadn't lured me away from Rider, though. I hadn't taken the bait to see Gina alone, so why would he kill her? I smacked my hand to my forehead, remembering the short conversation I'd had with Myra in front of Gina the last time she'd visited the bar. He could have just sent me Gina's heart, but he'd included her eyes and her hair, her blue eyes and blonde hair. It was all part of his warning. He didn't need Gina because he'd found a new blue-eyed blonde he could use to get to me. "He's doesn't need her anymore because he found a replacement. He knows about my sister. He's going after Shana."

# TWENTY-THREE

"I just checked on her and she's fine," Rider assured me. "I told you, if she were in danger, I'd know."

I thought about how I'd purposely thrown up a wall to block Rider out of my mind early into our relationship, the night I'd almost been raped by my former boss. He hadn't known anything then, not until I dropped the wall. Supposedly, I was able to do that sooner than most due to me being a hybrid, much like my ability to stay awake longer through the day. As a newly turned pure vampire, Shana shouldn't be able to do these things, but I wasn't willing to take chances. I needed to see her. "I'm going to her apartment."

Rider sighed. "Not alone, you aren't. Let me take this meeting and I'll take you there."

"I can take Ginger or Daniel."

"Ginger is busy with another assignment tonight, and I'd rather go with you. Daniel will come with us. My meeting won't last long. Get dressed and wait for me. You can wait in the bar if you like."

"Fine." I tossed aside the bedsheets and stormed into the bathroom for a quick shower, not sure I'd actually washed before falling asleep in there earlier.

I quickly washed up, dried my hair, and dressed in jeans and a stretchy red T-shirt before pulling on black boots. I tried Shana's number, but my call went to voicemail. She was on her honeymoon, I reminded myself, and cringed at the thought of what that might entail. I nixed the idea of reaching out to her telepathically, never comfortable doing that. I always feared catching someone while they were on the toilet, or worse. Still, I needed to make sure she was fine. I didn't even want to imagine Selander Ryan doing to her what he'd done to Gina.

I left Rider's room and traveled downstairs to the bar, noting the loud music as I entered through the back door. Between that and the murmur of voices, I knew the place was busy before I even set foot on the main floor. I glanced down the hall leading to Rider's office, realizing I'd never asked who his meeting was with. I was tempted to find out, but entering his office while he was in a meeting would make him appear unprofessional, so I headed out onto the bar floor instead.

Tony was bartending, and Juan was posted at the front door. I didn't see Rome, but if he was still assigned to do janitorial work, he could be anywhere in the building. Myra didn't appear to be working, but there were plenty of other servers moving about, taking and delivering drink orders. A few glanced at me, but I didn't see the open animosity I usually saw in their eyes. I knew word had gotten around about what I did to Mortimer. Maybe they also knew about Jimmy, or maybe Rider had warned them to back off the attitude like he'd done with Myra.

I moved toward the bar, figuring I'd sit and chat with Tony, or try to. He wasn't the chattiest guy in Rider's nest, but he wasn't rude. Halfway there, I noticed a lone man sitting in shadow in a corner booth near the front of the bar. He also didn't strike me as the most chatty guy, but I had questions and I knew he had answers.

Jon looked up from his drink as I slid into the other side of the booth. "I prefer to be alone," he said. His tone wasn't rude or hostile. He spoke as if merely stating a fact.

"Tough," I said. "I want to know what you are and if you say complex, so help me, you'll learn firsthand why they call me the Teste Slayer."

"That would be a shame. These testicles have hopes and dreams."

Humor? Huh. I really hadn't expected that. "You're mocking me."

"I wouldn't dare." He took a drink of the amber liquid inside his glass. "Your reputation precedes you, or I should say, your temper."

"I'd like to say the same about your reputation, but I've never heard of you until I met you today. What did you do with Gina's ghost?"

"Her spirit, not her ghost, and I delivered her to the afterlife. She died horribly, but I assure you she is in a much better place now. No harm will come to her. She is quite happy, and you have no need to mourn her or continue to feel bad about what happened. She is in peaceful bliss now."

I stared at him a moment, processing his words. I still couldn't sense what he was. He wasn't quite human, and he wasn't quite paranormal. He unnerved me. "How can you do that? Are you an angel or something?"

He sighed and took another sip of his drink, never breaking eye contact. "I am a man with a very special, very unique set of skills which I employ as needed. I am not a part of Rider's nest, which is why you haven't seen me before. I do some work for him as needed, as I do for others in need of my abilities."

"You were on guard duty outside my apartment," I said. "That's a special skill?"

"I knew I needed to be there, so I was."

"What's that mean?" I leaned forward, my blood warming. "Are you saying you knew that package would be arriving? You knew Gina would be killed, but instead of going to her, you took up a post outside my door to wait

338

for her body parts?"

"No. That's not what I'm saying." He glanced toward the back of the bar, threw back the rest of his drink, and dropped some bills on the table before he stood. "All you need to know is I'm here to help you."

He walked away, meeting Seta as she headed for the front door. They walked out together, their heads close together in conversation.

"You were speaking with Jon?"

I looked over to see Rider standing next to me. "Am I not supposed to?"

Rider shrugged. "Speak all you want, but don't expect much response. The man makes Tony look like a blabbermouth."

"Your meeting was with Seta. Again."

"Yes." He frowned down at me. "I told you I was working with her on resolving the Bloom issue and also my brother."

"And Jon is a part of that?"

"He came highly recommended."

"But you don't know what he is?"

"He's a human, but he's more than that. He doesn't reveal much of himself to others, so it's hard to say. I know he's trustworthy. I've crossed paths with him a few times and he's always been on the right side of things. He likes his solitude, doesn't socialize much, but he's a damn good ally." Rider's gaze shifted to the front door. "Daniel's here. Are you ready to check in on your sister?"

I looked over to see Daniel walking toward us. He was dressed in worn jeans, a Metallica T-shirt, and scuffed combat boots. He looked considerably better than the last time I'd seen him.

"You're looking less green than the last time I saw you," I said as I stood from the booth to greet him.

"Yesterday was rough. I lost my favorite switchblade in some guy's nut." He grinned. "I'm not loaning you any more of my blades."

339

"You could have kept your knife."

"No thanks. I don't want a knife that's been in some gross guy's sac. There's not enough bleach in the world to kill those cooties."

"Fair enough," I said. "Let's go."

I rode with Rider in his Ferrari while Daniel followed behind in his truck. Most of the ride was spent in silence, Rider not speaking until we pulled into the parking lot. "You know she's on her honeymoon. There's a good chance she hasn't returned your call because they're busy doing what honeymooners do."

"Please. It's not like they hadn't had a ton of sex before they got married. I'm half succubus and even I would have to come up for air sometime, not counting the Bloom."

Rider grinned. "I'll be sure to put that to the test the moment I get a week off from chaos."

I rolled my eyes, but said nothing as he got out and rounded the car to open my door.

We met Daniel at the front doors. My sister and her new husband lived in the penthouse of an upscale apartment building and the doorman's judging eyes were hard to miss as he studied the three of us walking in. Rider looked fine in his black slacks and dark button-down shirt, but Daniel and I could have dressed better. Fortunately, the man didn't stop us as we entered and crossed the marbled floor of the lobby to the elevators.

"I'm surprised we don't have to sign in or something," Daniel said as I pressed the up button to call the elevator.

"I had my tech team ensure we'd have no problem getting in," Rider explained, nodding toward a camera facing the doors. "They use a facial recognition system. If you're in the database, they let you glide right by."

The elevator dinged, and the doors opened. We stepped inside and I pressed the button for the top floor. A short ride later, the doors opened to a white marbled lobby and a large door with a genuine gold knocker. Two large black men in dark suits stood on either side of the door, shoulders straight and hands clasped before them. One of them was Jamal. His face was purplish and puffy, he had scorch marks that might never heal, and his flattened nose was bandaged, but his eyes were no longer bloodshot. They were, however, glaring daggers into me.

"The Whites are honeymooning and are not to be disturbed," he said.

I blinked, momentarily confused, then recalled Kevin's last name was White, and now, so was Shana's. "I'm her sister. I need to speak with her, and I need to speak with her now."

He grinned. "You'll have to make an appointment."

Rider squeezed my shoulder and shook his head before I saw the concentration in his eyes. Shortly after, the door swung open to reveal a pissed-off Shana, dressed in a flimsy white silk gown and a sheer white robe. "It's fine, Jamal. My rude sister and her obnoxious friends may enter."

"Great to see you too, sis," I muttered as I led the way inside. I cast a sideways glance at Rider and he nodded, confirming my suspicion he'd ordered Shana to open the door. I suppose that was easier and less messy than beating the hell out of the men guarding it.

"You know, most people don't entertain company on their honeymoon," Shana complained, closing the door behind us before she moved across the open living area, stopping in the center to turn toward us, her arms folded under her ample chest.

The penthouse was beautiful. The floors were polished wood. An ivory leather sectional and sofa sat atop a fluffy white rug, a round glass table between them, with a beautiful ivory and onyx statue of an angel. A white grand piano sat at the back of the room, in front of the wall which was floor to ceiling window. I could see the kitchen from where I stood, all black and shiny chrome. The walls that weren't all glass were painted a creamy white and decorated in gold accents. I was sure Kevin had hired a designer before Shana ever moved in. She'd have the penthouse covered in hot pink and looking like a Barbie mansion in no time.

"I wouldn't have come by if you'd answer your phone and talk to me."

"Oh, that's rich coming from you. You never answer the phone when Mom or Grandma or I call. I never even had your cell phone number until last night and you don't want them to have it at all. But I'm supposed to answer the phone on my honeymoon? My lame-ass honeymoon, by the way."

"Where's your husband?" Rider asked, looking around.

"In bed, gearing up for our next round of monkey sex," she snapped. "Where else would he be?"

Daniel stepped closer to her, his nostrils slightly flared as he circled behind her. He moved a couple feet away from her and looked at us, shaking his head.

"You haven't had sex tonight," Rider told her.

Her mouth dropped open as she looked between the two of them. She sputtered a moment before taking a deep breath and stood straighter, rigid with anger. "Ridiculous. Not that I need to confess every time I have sex with my own husband, but—"

"I can smell when people have had sex," Daniel interrupted her, "and, sweetheart, you haven't had any at all tonight. You don't smell fresh from the shower either."

"I can sense the presence of humans," Rider told her. "I only sense the two outside your door. Where is your husband, and more importantly, why would you lie about him not being here?"

I opened up my senses. Rider was right. I sensed no one besides us and the two guards on the entire floor. My gut twisted. "Why would you lie about that, Shana?"

"Unbelievable!" She threw her hands in the air and spun around before marching over to the windows to look

342

down on the city that lay beyond. "We got into a spat, all right? The spell Rihanna worked to keep him from questioning what I am now worked, but he's upset I slept all day. He just left not that long ago, but he'll be back and I'd rather you all not be here when he gets back. You're not his favorite people."

"Why wouldn't you just say that?" I asked. "Why wouldn't you answer your phone?"

"Forgive me if I wanted a little privacy after being held captive underneath a bar!" She took her time glaring at each one of us before focusing on me. "What do you want?"

"I was worried about you."

She rolled her eyes and stomped out of the room, returning a moment later with a bag of blood. "I have my own little locked refrigerator in my boudoir filled with these, so I'm not going to go bloodthirsty and attack anyone. I haven't told anyone about what happened, not even Mom and Grandma, despite their constant calls to check up on me. I haven't blogged about any of this, not that I could if I wanted to. Don't think I don't know you hacked into my site!"

I looked over at Rider, and he shrugged. "I told you, a vampire with a blog is dangerous. I had to take safety measures."

I sighed. "I'm sorry you got into an argument with Kevin, and that this isn't the honeymoon you planned for, and I'm sorry about the extra security measures, but they're necessary. I wasn't worried about you attacking anyone, Shana. A friend of mine was killed this morning, or last night, I'm not sure, and the man who killed her… I'm afraid he might attempt to kill you next."

She stood still, blinking at me for a moment. "Who? And why?"

"Because he left a message," Rider jumped in. "We have reason to believe he may be looking for another blue-eyed blonde close to us. We're not sure what exactly his plan is, but it would be in your best interest to stay alert and to contact one of us immediately if you sense any danger."

She narrowed her eyes at Rider. "I thought you were supposed to know when I'm in danger. That's how Eliza explained our bond."

Rider nodded and looked at me, eyebrow raised as if to say, *See? Even she knows that much.* "I will sense if you are frightened or in pain, both of which can alert me to you being in danger. Selander Ryan is a tall man with blonde hair and dark brown eyes. I'm told he's considered to be very attractive and charismatic. He has the ability to slip into women's dreams and harm them. Have you had any strange dreams about such a man?"

"No," she answered, looking at Rider oddly. "What is he? One of the hunters Eliza warned me about?" She turned toward me. "Why would he be after me? There's a lot of blue-eyed blondes."

"He might not be," Rider answered before I could. "Danni just got worried when you didn't answer your phone. Do us all a favor and just answer when she calls."

"Fine. Now, would you please leave before Kevin returns?"

My gut twisted. I couldn't put my finger on it, but something was wrong, and I didn't want to leave, but I had no concrete reason to stay and I clearly wasn't wanted there. Not to mention, the guards outside were a problem. I wouldn't put it past Shana to call on them and that would be a bloody mess. "Just be careful," I said as I turned for the door. "Call us if anything odd happens. Anything."

"How much do you want to bet she wanted us out because she has another guy coming over?" Daniel asked a few minutes later as we walked out the front of the building.

"That would probably make more sense," Rider said softly. "Rihanna's good at what she does. Kevin should be more accepting of Shana's sleep schedule, even if he

344

doesn't understand why."

"So, you think she was lying?" I asked as we moved toward our vehicles.

Rider looked down at me, pulled me close, and kissed the top of my head. "I don't know. I couldn't imagine a man leaving his wife on their honeymoon for such a petty reason, especially after just getting her back from what he thought was an abduction, but then again, I couldn't possibly understand the thought process of a man who would willingly marry your sister."

Daniel snorted. I glared at him as I elbowed Rider in the ribs. "I understand you don't want her to know what I actually am, but shouldn't we tell her more about your brother? Maybe if she knew who he was and why he's doing what he's doing, she'll take this threat more seriously."

"You're talking about a woman whose primary concern after getting shot and turned was her dress. I don't think knowing about the history with my brother would help her show any more caution, and I don't trust her to know information that could be used against you. You've warned her about a man after women like her, which should be sufficient. We don't even know for sure that she's a target."

"Can you assign men to guard her just in case?" We were at our vehicles now, but we didn't get in.

"This building has security," he answered. "I've had my tech team hack into the video surveillance so we can see who enters. There's no way I can put a man on her floor when they already have security in place. Those men are employed by her husband, not her. I can't replace them with my own men."

I sighed in frustration and leaned against the Ferrari. "Why does she have to be so hard-headed?"

He looked at me pointedly.

"I might be a bit stubborn, but not when someone's clearly warning me I might be in danger."

Daniel cleared his throat. Now they both looked at me pointedly. Annoyed, but unable to think of a comeback because as much as I didn't want to admit it, they had a point, I stuck my tongue out at them, pulling a smile out of both.

"I have a lot of boring work to do tonight," Rider said, "so I'm going to head back to my office. You don't have any training unless you want to train with Daniel."

"I'm not training with her the night after she stabbed a guy in the nuts," Daniel said. "I need some time to work through the trauma of witnessing that."

Rider grinned and shook his head. "So that's out. I'm sure Rome feels the same way. Do you want to come back with me and hang out in the room, or do you want to drop in on your donor? You're supposed to be mixing your blood sources so it wouldn't hurt feeding from her tonight. You should stay tanked up given Ryan's latest attack. I'm not sure he's going after your sister, but he sent you that message for a reason. It's best we all keep our guards up."

It suddenly hit me that Angel might be in danger just as much as Shana. I thought the blue eyes and blonde hair might be a hint that Shana was in danger, but even if it was, Selander Ryan knew where my apartment was and clearly knew I'd still receive his cruel gift there. He must know I still rented the apartment. For all I knew, he might send someone there for me and find Angel instead. I doubted her innocence would be enough to keep him and his minions from hurting her.

"I want to go to my apartment."

"All right. Daniel, guard her with your life."

"Always do." Daniel gave a little salute and walked around his truck to open the passenger side door for me while Rider kissed me goodbye.

"I want to tell you to be careful, but it doesn't seem enough," Rider said, voice low. "Come back to me safely. Check in if you're going to be away from me for long and stay alert."

"I will. I'm too skeeved out not to be."

Rider kissed my forehead and prodded me toward Daniel, his hand on the small of my back. "If there's even the slightest bit of trouble, Daniel, you fly her back to the bar."

Daniel nodded his agreement and waited until I climbed into his truck to close my door.

"Why would Shana lie about Kevin not being there?" I wondered aloud as Daniel drove us to my apartment.

He looked over at me. "I told you my theory. She wanted us out so she could sneak some random guy in and she didn't want to answer any questions."

I shook my head. It didn't feel right, but the reason she gave didn't either. Kevin adored her. "That wouldn't explain how she got rid of Kevin. Rider made sense tonight. Her sleeping all day shouldn't have been enough to spark an argument bad enough to make him want to leave her, not even for half an hour. He offered a huge reward for her when he thought she'd been abducted. And why would she risk bringing a man to their home? She would go somewhere else if she were hooking up with some other guy."

Daniel didn't say anything. I looked over to see him eying me. "What?"

"Rider filled me in on your morning. You've had a very rough day, and I can only imagine how frazzled your nerves are right now, but you're going to drive yourself crazy if you keep worrying about your sister so hard."

"Parts of my friend were sent to me in a box. She overheard me mention my sister the last time I spoke with her, and I know Selander Ryan was using her to get information on me. How can I not worry?"

Apparently not having an answer to that, Daniel returned his attention to the road, and we remained silent

347

the rest of the way to my building.

"I'm sorry," he said after we reached the parking lot and walked to the building. "I'm not making light of the situation, and I can imagine how freaked you are right now. I just hate seeing you so upset when there's nothing I can do about it because the bastard I'd need to kill to make sure you stay safe is already dead."

"You're here. That's enough," I assured him as I replayed his words and remembered the warning Jon had given Gina's spirit when she'd been blaming me for what happened to her. "Do you know Jon?"

"Jon who?" he asked as he opened the door to my building.

"Rider didn't tell you about the man posted at my door when the package arrived, or how that same man took Gina's spirit to the afterlife, or Heaven, or whatever?"

Daniel's brow creased as we started up the stairs to my floor. "He told me about the package and about the ghost, but he didn't tell me anything about anyone named Jon. What do you mean, he took her to the afterlife?"

We reached my floor, and I looked deep into the shadows in the corner of the hall until I could make out which one of Rider's men stood guard. "Hey, Carlos. How's it been?"

"Quiet," he said. "No packages. No visitors or odd lurkers."

Clearly, he'd been informed of earlier events. I thanked him and used my key to unlock the door. Angel looked up from her spot on the couch, a large bowl of popcorn in her lap, and a movie on the television. "Just in time," she said. "There's a Stephen King movie marathon on. *Firestarter* is about to start."

We sat next to her and vegetated through four movies. I fed from Angel's wrist between *Misery* and *Pet Sematary*, and asked her if she had an answer for me about what she wanted to do during a commercial break. She wanted to travel, see the beautiful parts of the world. I thought that was a great idea and was thinking up a plan as she fell asleep during *It*.

"Think I should put her in the bed?" Daniel asked as she started to snore softly.

I glanced over at her slouched form and grinned. "Yeah, she'll wake up with a crimp in her neck for sure if you don't."

He effortlessly scooped her up and carried her to the bedroom as gently as he would a child. I picked up the remote and switched the channel. I was a Stephen King fan, but I'd had enough horror for one day. I found a channel playing back-to-back *NCIS* episodes and left it there.

"So tell me about this Jon," Daniel said as he returned and settled next to me on the couch.

I told him everything I knew about the mysterious man. "You've never met him?"

"No, and Rider never mentioned anyone by that name to me."

"What kind of person can take a spirit to the afterlife, and how did he beat me and Rider to Gina's apartment and still have time to drop the box off to a lab?"

"Someone who can move through realms," Daniel answered. "If he can take a spirit to the afterlife and disappear like you say he did, zapping himself to a lab, then to the apartment wouldn't be complicated for him. Rider said he's human?"

"Yes, and I sensed the human in him as well, but he's more than human. I just can't put my finger on what exactly he is."

"I wouldn't worry about it too much. He's on your side, right? That's all that matters."

I turned my attention back to the television, but couldn't concentrate, not even when Wilmer Valderrama graced the screen. Ginger was right about him. The man was hot, but his hotness couldn't ease the worry inside me.

Between Shana's strange need to lie about Kevin,

Rider's meetings with Seta, and the mysterious Jon's appearance in the middle of things, I couldn't kick the feeling that something major was brewing and if I didn't figure out what it was, I might lose another loved one, maybe even myself.

# TWENTY-FOUR

Daniel drove me back to the bar about an hour before sunrise and saw me inside before leaving to rest. The bar was empty and so silent you could hear a pin drop. I felt Rider's presence coming from his office and knew he was still there working.

"Working late?" I said, as I entered the office a moment later.

He looked up from his computer and gave me a small smile in greeting. "Yes. Thanks for checking in. I worried less. You fed well?"

"Yes," I answered as I took a seat in one of the chairs opposite him. "What are you doing?"

"Work stuff. Just got the lab results. Everything in the box came from Gina." He shut down the computer and leaned back in his seat. "I thought about the Shana situation. We may not know for sure she's a target, but with Ryan, anything is possible and I don't like for you to worry. I can't assign men inside her building, but my team already hacked into the building's security to monitor through their cameras, and I've just assigned a security detail to watch the building from outside and track her if she leaves it."

"Thank you!" I quickly moved around the desk and leaned down to kiss him. "I know you don't like her. This means so much to me."

"I have to keep you happy," he said, pulling me onto his lap.

"If you make a Danni the Teste Slayer joke, I might smack you."

He laughed. "It's going to take a while for that to die down. I think my men are more afraid of you now than they are of me."

"You've ripped men's heads off and pulled their spines out."

"Stabbing a guy in the nuts trumps all that."

I rolled my eyes. "Ridiculous."

"Face it. You're a terrifier of men and a legend among women."

I shook my head. "I'd trade all that just to be free of the Bloom. I'd really like to find a way to get rid of it before it cycles around again. I could have killed you. What if the next round is even worse?"

He kissed my temple. "I'm working on it."

"You've met with Seta multiple times. Does she know something or not?"

He just looked at me for a moment, then finally said, "She's working on something. This isn't something a simple spell will cure. Seta has made multiple trips to check in because we're all working together. Nannette, Rihanna, Seta… Everyone's working together to help you."

"And she has to visit you to check in?"

He raised an eyebrow.

"I'm not about to go on a jealous tirade, I swear. I just don't understand what's going on, why she has to come here unless you're actually *doing* something when she drops in and if you are moving forward with something to help me, I should know what it is."

"Trust me. If there was anything you needed to know, I would tell you immediately. Just try not to worry about it."

He kissed my forehead, then stood, bringing me out of the chair with him. "The sun will rise soon and lately it seems like we can never be sure how much day sleep we're going to get, so why don't we head up?"

"Sure," I said as he led the way out of the office. "Is Jon helping? He said something about being here to help me."

"Jon arrived with Seta earlier and offered his services."

"What services? What is he here to do?" I asked as we reached the stairs leading up to Rider's room.

"Jon has a lot of unique skills and talents. He does whatever is needed whenever it is needed. I'm not sure how he comes into play in helping you, but I'm not going to refuse his help. He's a damn good man to have around when things go sideways." He raised my hand to his mouth and kissed my knuckles. "Don't worry about anything, Danni. You have a really good team working on this."

Sure, I thought. That would be a lot easier to accept if it didn't feel like they were all hiding things from me, Rider included.

I woke alone, full of the energy nightfall gave. I assumed that was a good sign. Nothing major must have happened to cause Rider to wake me during the day. He, however, was not in the bed so he'd had need to awaken sooner. I opened my senses and felt him near, somewhere in the building.

I kicked off the covers, grabbed clothing for the night, and padded into the bathroom. After a quick shower and blow-dry, I dressed in a white T-shirt, gray drawstring joggers, and cross-trainers. Figuring Shana had had enough time to wake up and join the living, I detached my cell phone from the charger and called her.

"What?" she snapped upon answering.

"Well, good morning to you too."

"It's evening. I probably won't see morning for another several years."

I rolled my eyes and sincerely hoped I hadn't been so damn bitchy about being turned. "Well, you have a very long life ahead of you and it will be full of daylight if you choose. You just have to be a little patient."

"Was there something you needed?"

"Damn, Shana. Can't I just call and check on you?"

"I'm a big girl, Danni. You don't need to check on me and honestly, I wish you, your vampire lover, and the rest of you freaks would leave me alone."

"Well, pardon the hell out of me for caring. Maybe Rider was right, and I should have left you to die." I gasped, realizing what I'd said.

"Screw you, Danni."

"Shana, I'm sorry. You made me mad and—"

The call dropped, and I growled in frustration. Damn it, I really hadn't meant to say something so awful, but her attitude really pushed my buttons. I slid my cell phone into my pocket and went downstairs in search of Rider. He came out of the stairwell from the lower levels as I reached the bottom of the stairs leading to his room.

"Hey," he said, his brow creasing. "What's wrong? You look like you're about to cry."

I moved to him and he enveloped me in his arms. "I called to check on Shana and she had an attitude. I snapped and told her maybe I should have let her die."

"Hmm." He rubbed my back. "Surprised you said that, but I'm sure she deserved to hear it. Your sister is one of the most ungrateful women I've ever met and I've lived a long time."

I sighed and looked up at him. "It's still a horrible thing to say to someone, especially when that someone is my sister. She just makes me so mad."

"Don't beat yourself up about it. She needs to be put in her place."

"But what if she stops talking to me and I need to warn her about something? What if Selander—"

Rider pressed his index finger over my mouth. "If it comes down to it, I can *make* her talk to you. Don't worry about it."

"Easy for you to say. You hate her. You don't care if I hurt her feelings." I folded my arms and huffed out a frustrated sigh.

"Honey, I'm not sure she has feelings. I have the team in place watching her building. She will be fine. Do you want to get in some sparring with Daniel? Physically assaulting people seems to cheer you up."

I gave him a look and his mouth twitched as he fought a smile. "I thought I was supposed to be training with Nannette."

"Yes, but she's busy tonight, and according to her, you've accomplished a lot in your two sessions."

"What exactly am I training for?" I asked. It seemed to me Nannette's training had a lot to do with overcoming my poor self-esteem, not that I was complaining. I'd needed the help. With Daniel and Rome, I felt like they were just letting me beat on them. "Are you going to give me assignments?"

Rider shifted his feet uncomfortably.

"Nannette said it would be good for me, and I brought in that wererat. I've been pretty good at interrogation."

"You've been a maniac in interrogation, but I won't complain. And Nannette did say it would be good for you. I still don't like the idea of putting you in danger."

"So you're going to continue to keep me under your thumb?"

"I'm going to continue doing everything in my power to keep you safe. We haven't resolved the Bloom issue yet. We can talk about putting you on assignments after we deal with that." He pulled me in close and kissed my forehead. "You're supposed to go in for your weekly session with Eliza tonight. Daniel will take you. After that, you can train with him, feed from Angel, or do whatever you need to do. Speaking of feeding…" He held his wrist to my mouth. "Take some now and you can have bagged blood later. You know how to order blood from the bar if you want it."

My fangs lowered, and I sank them into Rider's wrist, drinking what I assumed was about a cup of blood.

"You could have taken more," he told me as I sealed the wound and pulled away.

"I fed pretty well yesterday."

"I want you to feed very well every day. It's better to be overfed than underfed if something happens and you have to use a lot of energy." He turned me toward the bar and started walking with me. "I'm calling in Daniel. You can wait for him in the bar. I got some new contracts in today and I need to iron out the details so I'll be in my office working."

"Contracts?"

"Yes. I run a security business covering multiple states, remember?" He grinned. "Sometimes I have to actually work."

"When you're not spending all your time protecting me, you mean?"

"I'm not complaining." He kissed my temple as we walked through the door leading to the bar. "You're going to hang out here?"

I nodded. The bar wasn't packed, but there were enough people that I wouldn't feel alone.

"Drink some more blood while you wait." He brushed a kiss over my mouth and turned to go down the hall to his office.

I walked over to the bar and slid onto a stool. Tony was on bartending duty and Juan was once again posted at the front door. He nodded at me as I looked his way. I nodded back and waited for Tony to finish fixing a drink for a lanky man at the other end of the bar. He finished that up, grabbed a dark bottle from beneath the bar and brought it to me along with a dark glass.

"Fresh from today," he said in a low voice. "Haven't even had to put it in the cooler yet so it's a good temperature."

"Rider told you to give me this?"

He pointed to his temple, indicating he'd received the request telepathically, and walked down to the other end of the bar to refill a pretty redhead's drink. She flirted with him a little, but he didn't seem to overtly respond, simply offering her a friendly smile before stepping away. He refilled peanut bowls and wiped down the bar.

"I think the redhead likes you," I said as he neared me.

"Yes, I've noticed." He continued wiping down the bar.

"You don't like her?"

"I like my girlfriend."

"Oh." I couldn't picture Tony with a girlfriend. I could picture him with a woman, no problem, but he wasn't the most open type, which was a little more required when in a relationship, plus he seemed to always be on call. "I imagine your girlfriend enjoys all the long conversations you have."

He looked at me, his mouth turned up slightly at the corners. "I satisfy her in other ways."

"Well, all right then, Tony." I waggled my eyebrows, drawing a rare chuckle from him. Noting no one seemed to be requesting drinks at the moment, I took the opportunity to see if I could get him to talk a little more, maybe give me some information. "So, do you know that guy, Jon? He was in that booth over there in the front corner last night."

"I know of Jon," he answered. "No one actually *knows* Jon."

"Do you have any idea what he is?"

Tony looked at me, eyes narrowed like he was trying to figure out what I was getting at and I realized I was asking an Asian man if he knew what another Asian man was, and in a way that sounded really rude. "I mean supernaturally. I know he's human, but he seems a lot more than that."

He nodded his head, his face softening. "Like I said, no one really knows Jon." Then he moved away to wipe down another section of the bar and replace peanuts.

Great. No one knew Jon, yet he was supposedly here to help me, and Rider was cool with it. Rider, the overprotective vampire who didn't trust many when it came to me. It just wasn't adding up.

I poured the blood into the glass, careful to hold the bottle close enough to the dark glass that no one would see and question the thick red liquid. I could have drank from the bottle, but I thought the glass appeared classier. Of course, I was dressed in a T-shirt and joggers, so I wasn't exactly fooling anyone, but oh well.

I was on my last sip when Daniel walked through the front door, dressed in jeans and a Princess Bride T-shirt. He zeroed in on me and walked over.

"Need another?" Tony asked, coming by to collect my glass.

"No thanks," I told him.

"What's up?" Daniel asked, reaching me. "Are we just visiting Eliza or are you knocking me around?"

"I only knock you around because you pull your punches with me."

He grinned. "I just can't bring myself to really hit you. Sue me."

I eyed his shirt. "Do you own any T-shirts that aren't rock bands or movies?"

"I have some solid colors. What's wrong with what I wear?"

"Nothing. It suits you. Have you actually listened to all the bands and watched all the movies on the shirts you wear?"

"Yup, and a million others."

I watched him for a moment. He didn't crack a smile. "You're serious, aren't you?"

"Well, maybe not a million." He shrugged. "I've listened to a lot of music and seen a lot of movies, though."

"During your training on fitting into this realm?"

He nodded.

"How? How in the world could you listen to that much music and watch that many movies in such a short span of time?"

He grinned. "If you're nice to me, I might tell you someday."

Great. Another person knowing something and not telling me. I got up and stormed across the bar without a word. Juan raised an eyebrow as I marched past, but said nothing. I pushed the front door open harder than necessary and headed toward the parking lot.

"Hey!" I heard Daniel's footsteps running to catch up to me, then his hand wrapped around my biceps.

Acting on impulse, I twisted and used my other arm to throw a punch aimed at his head. He ducked, pressed me against the wall of the bar, and held me there with his forearm against my neck.

"Whoa. I might not willingly hit you, but I sure as hell am not going to let you swing on me for real. What the hell's the matter with you?"

We stared each other down until he apparently felt I was no longer a threat and loosened his hold. I used the opportunity to shove him. "I'm tired of people keeping information from me!"

"You're pissed because I didn't tell you about my training?"

"I'm pissed because something's happening and nobody is giving me a clue what."

He frowned. "Okay, you're going to have to give *me* a clue what you're talking about, and why you're taking it out on me."

Guilt washed over me, leaving me to feel pretty cruddy. "I'm sorry. You're not to blame for any of this, and if you want to keep your training a secret, that's your business. I just wish people wouldn't keep stuff involving me a secret."

I continued on to the parking lot and Daniel fell into step beside me. He opened the passenger door for me before taking his seat behind the wheel and starting the truck. He looked over at me and shook his head. "The training we were given when we came from Imortia isn't some huge secret. I just liked teasing you, making you wait a little bit, but if it bothers you, I have no problem telling you. We could learn so much in such a short time span because we were taken to the Njeri realm, a realm where time works differently. It felt like we were there forever, but it was only a week. During that time, they crammed a lot of information in so when we mingle with people here, we can blend in as if we've lived in this realm our whole lives."

I let that sink in as he pulled out of his parking space and headed to Eliza's. Daniel had come from the realm, Imortia, and he'd been imprisoned for some time in Hades, which turned out to be another realm. "How did you get into these realms? Can anyone go to another realm if they know about it?"

"I was cast into Hades through a spell. I got out through a portal that was opened when Zaira, the mother of the werewolf race, and her mate, Addix, rescued us after freeing Imortia from the queen who worked the spell to cast us into Hades. We came here through a portal opened by Zaira and we went to the Njeri realm through a spell cast by Zaira. You have to have some magical ability or be with someone of magical ability to find or open a portal."

"So Jon would have magical ability to travel from here to the afterlife?"

Daniel nodded. "He has to have some magic or power to do that, especially if he just disappeared the way you said he did." He looked over at me. "Is that what you're angry about? Not knowing what Jon is?"

"Partially. He's supposedly here to help me, but everyone acts like they don't know what he is, yet they're fine with him being here. Seta has dropped in on Rider multiple times, supposedly working with him to help get rid of the Bloom and find Selander Ryan, but wouldn't she just call him or do that telepathic thing if she needed to ask him something or update him? Why does she actually have to come here if they aren't actively doing something, and why am I not being told what they've been discussing?"

"He hasn't told you anything?"

"Just that they're working on it and don't worry. I'm so sick of hearing that. And with Shana, all I get when I voice my concerns is 'Don't worry' but I'm telling you something is weird. Something was up last night. I know it was. There was no reason for her to lie about Kevin not being there. And why did Myra bring her clothes? Shana has been bitchy to everyone since turning, but she's all buddied up with a woman who hates me? If Myra hates me because Rider turned me, she should hate Shana too."

"Myra's jealous of you because you're sleeping with Rider. He wouldn't touch your sister with a ten-foot pole."

"Still… I don't trust her. I don't trust Shana. I don't trust Jon, and I'm almost to the point of not trusting Rider."

Daniel parked his truck along the curb in front of Eliza's house and turned toward me. "In the time I've been here I've never come across this Jon person so I can't help you there, but I know Rider loves you and wouldn't harm you or let anyone around you who would harm you, and as for your sister … if she's not talking to you, talk to someone she is talking to."

"Who? Myra? Kevin? Neither of them like me."

"Didn't she speak with Eliza?"

I looked toward the house, then back at Daniel. "Eliza gave her a crash course in being a newly turned vampire. Do you think Eliza would know something?"

"It's possible, and doesn't she have to do the weekly

sessions with Eliza just like you?"

"Yes, but I don't know that Eliza would tell me anything. Client confidentiality and all that."

"I don't know. Eliza likes you. Not many people like Shana. Give it a try."

Eliza lived in a small gray brick house with white shutters, softly colored flower bushes, and a butterfly welcome mat. She was tall and willowy with long blonde hair and gentle cornflower blue eyes. She gave off a strong flower child vibe and as far as I knew, was the sweetest vampire to ever walk the earth.

She greeted us with a smile and ushered us into the office she used for counseling sessions. She took her usual spot in her chair. I sat on the sofa facing her and Daniel wiggled his bottom down into the cushy beanbag chair to my left. The mouse she'd had on her shoulder the last time we'd visited ran across the room and disappeared behind a bookcase.

"He'll warm up to you with time," Eliza said, settling in. "How have you been coming along with your blocking technique?"

"Pretty good, I think." Once we'd moved past the vampire newbie basics, Eliza had started focusing on helping me block my thoughts since I had trouble doing so while my emotions were high, and after I'd first been turned, my emotions pretty much stayed high. I looked over at Daniel and he nodded encouragement. "Actually, there's something else that maybe you can help me with."

"Anything, Danni." The brightness in her eyes dimmed as they filled with compassion. "You've been through so much. I was given enough detail about the Bloom cycle you went through to know it must have taken a heavy toll."

"Yes." I lowered my gaze and shifted uneasily. What I'd done to Rider during those horror-filled weeks was known by both people in the room, but I still felt exposed, knowing there was no way they could think of it and not actually imagine it in their minds. "And I know you've been doing research, working with Nannette and Rider, and the others he's tasked with that, but right at this moment, I'm concerned about my sister."

Now Eliza lowered her eyes a little. Odd. "Of course you are. Watching her bleed to death on what should have been the happiest day of her life must have been hard, and I understand she was resistant to the turning. You were, as well, but look how well you're handling it now, and you're a hybrid with so many more hurdles."

I frowned. "So… you think Shana's fine?"

Eliza's face paled a little. "Do you think something is wrong with her?"

I looked over at Daniel and found him frowning at Eliza, no doubt noticing the subtle uneasiness I'd noticed.

"Honestly, I'm very worried about her. She's … well, she's *mean*. I understand being surprised and upset, but what Rider did saved her life. I know I was ungrateful at first myself, but Rider was a stranger. I'm her sister. That should get an easier acceptance. Now that she's been allowed to leave the bar, she has made it clear she doesn't want anything to do with me. I could understand a little better if it was truly because she's trying to enjoy her honeymoon with her husband, but we stopped by their apartment last night and he wasn't even there."

"Which she lied about," Daniel interjected.

"Yes. There was no reason to lie to us about that. It was strange, and it's been giving me a weird feeling ever since. Plus, I imagine Rider informed you about what happened to Gina."

"Your former co-worker," Eliza said, nodding. "He did, and I'm so sorry you had to go through that."

"Gina was my former co-worker, and technically the woman who led me to Rider's bar so Selander Ryan could attack me, but I know that wasn't her fault or anything she did intentionally. I've never had many friends, especially not really good ones, but I considered her enough of a friend that I cared. I still care. I think my fear that Shana might meet the same fate is the only thing keeping me from falling apart over Gina's death. It'll hit me soon enough, I'm sure."

"I'm sure it will. Our mind has tricks to get us through hard times. We grieve in different ways, at different times." She leaned forward and squeezed my hand before settling back in her seat. "You're worried about Shana because you think Ryan knows about her?"

"That, and I'm afraid she won't heed my advice to stay cautious. I told her she was in danger last night and she didn't react the way I expected her to. I know I can be stubborn about needing protection, as has been pointed out to me multiple times," I said, sensing Daniel's amusement, "but Shana has always been terrified of being harmed. She can't fight her way out of a paper bag and she can't even handle scary movies. Telling her someone killed my friend and that someone may be after her should have bothered her a lot more. I called her tonight to check in and she was irritated from the moment she picked the phone up."

I raked my hand through my hair. "I know none of this seems that big a deal, which is why everyone keeps telling me to not worry, but no one knows Shana like I do. Pre-vampire Shana would be begging me to stay with her if she thought there was even a sliver of a chance she was in danger. I know the turning couldn't have changed that. You and Rider both have told me it doesn't change people so much as it heightens attributes already in them. The turning wouldn't make Shana suddenly no longer fear such a threat, and the things she's said to me, even worse, the things she's thought about me.... There have been times I swear I think she'd do Rider in a heartbeat if she had the chance. I'd never do that to my sister, and I thought she'd never do that to me, but it's really starting to feel like she just doesn't care about me at all anymore. It's like she just wants me gone."

All the remaining color drained out of Eliza's face.

"What the hell do you know, Eliza?" Daniel asked, sitting forward.

# TWENTY-FIVE

Eliza licked her lips and looked between us as color slowly returned to her face. "As a counselor, I can't divulge what's said in—"

"Bullshit," Daniel cut her off. "I know you'd spill everything to Rider if he asked."

"Have you told Rider something about my sister?" I asked her. "Please," I added, feeling sorry for her as she seemed to wilt under Daniel's hard stare. Daniel was second only to Rider in fierce protection and, at the moment, didn't seem to care that Eliza was only trying to do what she felt was right. "I know this must put you in a hard place, but no one is telling me anything and worse, I don't think anyone is believing me when I try to tell them something is wrong. I can feel it in my gut that something is brewing, something horrible, but I have no idea what it is because everyone's withholding information." A few tears slipped out of my eyes. I wiped them away. "If I don't know what it is, I can't stop it. Worse, I might not survive it."

Eliza chewed her lip for a moment, then took a deep breath. "I'm not a fan of lying, and I generally don't encourage it, but newly turned vampires need to know they can trust me. If I tell you anything, they can't find out."

"We won't tell anyone what you tell us." I looked at Daniel and he nodded his head in agreement as he eased back on the threatening vibe he'd been emitting.

"Thank you for that." Eliza twisted the daisy bracelet on her left wrist as she spoke. "I've been what I am for a long time. I've helped many newly turned vampires and I've become very good at getting a feel for people. I believe in good in all people, supernatural or non. There have been very few times I've come across a person I've felt harbored true wickedness. Selander Ryan is one of those people."

Nausea swam in my belly. "And my sister?"

She nodded slowly. "Sometimes there are bad turns. People with certain characteristics, temperaments, or people who have been through trauma don't always successfully transition."

"Rider said she was too thirsty at first, but he wouldn't have allowed her to leave if he still thought that, and it's not like he can't feel her thirst. She's mean to me, yes, but she's not violent. She seems to have transitioned through the turning well. She just blames me for it and wants nothing to do with me."

"My fear is she transitioned too well." Eliza shifted uncomfortably. "As for the high bloodthirst she woke with, this isn't always a sign of a bad turn, but it is often enough to be of concern. What worries me is she asked a lot of questions about you and Rider, about your personal relationship."

I looked at Daniel to find him watching me carefully. "She had just turned and found out we were vampires as well. There would be curiosity. I asked a lot of questions."

"Everyone asks a lot of questions. Am I going to live forever? Can I have children? Can I tell my family? Do I really have to drink blood? She didn't have any questions like that. She seemed very focused on why Rider turned you, if you were in love first, what attracted him to you, and what made you so special. I'm afraid in my habit of always seeing the best in others, I chalked it up to a sister looking out for a sister, but now I think it was something much darker. She wanted to know how much power Rider had, what it meant to be his fledgling, and if there was a ranking system."

"A ranking system?"

"Yes. Among fledglings." Eliza stopped twisting her bracelet and smoothed her hands over her long skirt. "It's not unusual for some fledglings to feel a need to please their sire, so it didn't set off alarm bells, but if she asked me that and she's acting like she doesn't want you around, that isn't a good sign. You just said yourself you felt she would sleep with Rider if given the chance."

"True," I said, my voice coming out very soft. "I did, but she acts like she hates him now too."

"Not surprised," Daniel said. "She wants him. He doesn't want her. She obviously married Kevin for money, not love. Maybe what she really wants from Rider is his power, and she's behaving in the typical fashion of a spoiled child who can't have her way, because as long as he's faithful to you, she knows she doesn't have a shot."

"She was definitely interested in the paranormal hierarchy, and in what makes you so special to Rider," Eliza said. "I evaded her questions about you because I was already told by Rider not to disclose why you were turned or what about your turning makes you special, but there's always a chance she could have obtained that information from someone else."

Daniel and I shared a look. "Myra," I said.

"Does Myra know the actual details of what you are?" Daniel asked. "Rider's been careful to keep the circle of people who know about you small."

"They may not know about the Bloom or what my actual complete paranormal makeup is, but they can piece together enough just by what they've seen and heard."

Thinking of paranormal makeup, I asked, "Eliza, do you know Jon, the man who received the package at my apartment and then took Gina's spirit to the afterlife?"

She blinked at me. "That sounds like a reaper, but they generally don't accept package deliveries or allow themselves to be seen by the living, nor do I know any who would work for Rider. I don't know any at all. I've only heard stories. I've never heard of a Jon who could do that."

I sighed. "I keep coming to a dead end on Jon, but I know he is involved in all of this bad stuff I'm feeling."

"Trust your gut, Danni, and please don't let the fact that you are blood blind you to the possible danger your sister poses. A vampire who survives a bad turn is extremely dangerous, especially one controlled enough to go this long without hurting someone," Eliza said. She frowned, her brow creasing in deep thought before she looked back at me with genuine fear in her eyes. "Unless she already has."

"What do you mean?" I asked.

"Why would she lie about her husband not being there when you dropped in on her?"

"Wait," Daniel said. "Are you saying you think Shana killed her husband?"

"Impossible," I said. "Rider is her sire. He would feel if she got that bloodthirsty. Besides, she had bagged blood when we arrived, so it's not like she ran out."

"She could have killed him for other reasons than being thirsty," Daniel pointed out.

"Rider would feel her rage."

"If she felt rage," Eliza said. "She's been told her sire can feel her emotions. She knows not to feel anything strongly if she wants to stay under Rider's radar."

"Who could murder a person without feeling any strong emotions?"

"The very worst kind of monster," Eliza answered softly.

"Shana did not kill Kevin." I stood from the couch. "I'm going over there right now and I'll find him alive and breathing."

Eliza jumped up. "Danni, you need to be safe. Tell Rider."

"No," I said, moving toward the door. "He'll kill her in a heartbeat if I tell him a suspicion like this." I turned around. "I'll keep your secret that you told us what was said in a session, but you have to keep this conversation a secret from Rider, at least until I can check in on Shana first. Maybe she does want to steal Rider away from me, but that doesn't make her a killer."

"Danni, I can't let you risk your life like this."

"I'll be with her," Daniel said from behind me. "I'll make sure no matter what happens, Danni is safe."


"You're sure about this?" Daniel asked as he pulled his truck into a parking spot in my sister's lot. "The only reason we got inside the apartment without hurting anyone last time was because Rider was with us."

"He had his tech team do their stuff on the facial recognition the building uses, and I doubt he had them remove it. As far as getting in the actual apartment, it would be nice, but I just need to get close enough to sense if there's a human inside it."

"Are you good enough at that yet to know if the human is Kevin? It could be your mother."

"If my mother was in there, there'd be a dark cloud hanging over the whole building."

Daniel grinned. "True, and I'm sure the building doesn't allow rodents, so your grandmother and her ankle-biter wouldn't make it past the lobby. Seriously though, do you think they've called or dropped in? You could check with them to find out when the last time they saw or spoke to Kevin was."

I cringed. "Calling them is always a last resort in any

situation."

"Yeah, I'd rather face the possibly murderous vampire too."

I huffed out an angry breath of air as I opened the door and got out of the truck. I may have slammed the door shut before heading toward the building.

"Wait up!" Daniel jogged up to me. "I'm sorry, Danni, but I can't afford to think of her as innocent until proven murderous. I have to be on guard for anything to keep you safe because the fact is, you might not be able to protect yourself against her, given your love for her. Hell, I'm more worried about her attacking you than I am about Selander Ryan right now, and that man sent you a box of body parts."

I winced as his reminder caused a memory of the box's contents. A wave of nausea rolled over me as I saw Gina's eyes looking up at me from the mess and I imagined what she went through. I almost wished Shana was a villain, if only it ensured I wouldn't get a box with her eyes looking up at me too.

*Why are you at Shana's? What are you doing?*

Daniel and I both skipped a step as we entered the front doors of the building. We looked directly at the camera mounted on the opposite wall as we breezed past security and turned for the elevator.

"Rider in your head too?" I asked him.

"Yup," he answered, "and he doesn't sound happy."

"He's about to sound less happy."

*I'm visiting my sister*, I shot back through the link. *What else would I be doing?*

*Turn around and come back to the bar.*

*Sorry. We're breaking up. Must be interference from the elevator*, I shot back as Daniel and I stepped into the elevator and I pressed the button for the penthouse. I immediately envisioned the link in my mind and snapped it in half, disconnecting the line of communication.

"Did you just hang up on him or were you for real

about the elevator?" Daniel asked, a befuddled look on his face.

"It's telepathy, Daniel, not a cell phone. I was being a smartass with the elevator comment."

"Oh."

"We probably have like three minutes to get back outside before he sends the men he has watching the building inside to get us," I warned as the elevator dinged, stopped, and the doors opened to the same scene we'd found there the night before.

"You might as well turn right back around," Jamal told us as we stepped out of the elevator. "Mrs. White doesn't want to see you."

"What about Mr. White?" Daniel asked.

Jamal's eyes registered surprise for a second before he schooled himself. "What need would you have to see Mr. White?"

"A need to make sure he's all right," Daniel answered as I focused on opening my senses wide to scan the floor. The wall I'd thrown up to sever Rider's link crumbled, and I sensed him inside my head, hovering. Angry. Thankfully, silent.

The front door swung open and Shana stood there in a black silk robe, hands fisted at her hips. "What do you want?"

"We came to check on you. I told you before you could be in danger."

"Seriously, Danni, what part of honeymoon do you not get? Take a break from worrying about me and go satisfy your man, and let me satisfy mine in peace."

"You know, I would, but your man isn't even here. Again. You know we can tell."

Her nostrils flared as she glared at me, then slowly smiled. "Kevvie had to make a pharmacy run. I like the warming lube, and we used it all up." She turned her attention to Daniel. "Would you like to come in and sniff around to see if I'm fibbing?"

My mouth dropped open, appalled at the crude invitation.

"No thanks," Daniel said, a grin that was nowhere near friendly spreading across his face. "I can smell it from all the way out here."

I choked back a laugh as Shana's eyes burned daggers through us. She raised her middle finger, kissed the tip, and blew before slamming the door hard enough to rattle teeth.

"I believe it's time for you to go," Jamal said, walking over to the elevator. He pushed the button, and the doors opened. The other guard remained silent, eyeing us in amusement.

"I don't know if she told you, but there's a dangerous man who may be looking to hurt her or even those close to her, like your employer, but by all means, keep being an asshole to the people trying to help them," I said as Daniel and I passed him to get in.

Jamal waved goodbye as I pressed the button for the lobby and both guards laughed as the doors closed. "That went well," I muttered.

"Did your sister blow us a *fuck you?*"

"Pretty much," I answered as we descended to the lobby. "What? They didn't teach you that one in your training?"

"Nope. It did not make the curriculum."

I squeezed his arm. "I'm sorry for getting angry at you about that earlier. Thanks for bringing me here instead of fighting me about it."

"I've already forgotten your outburst," he said as the elevator doors opened and we stepped off and moved across the lobby, "and you've been through a ton of absolute shit in a very short amount of time without a moment to really catch a breath so you're allowed to snap. As for bringing you here, I know you well enough to know it's better I bring you than you figure out a way to come on your own, all alone."

"I'm never alone." I nodded toward the dark SUV with tinted windows parked across the street from the building as we stepped outside, simultaneously sending Rider a telepathic message that we were fine and on our way back. I received an angry grunt in response.

"You know what I mean," Daniel said, oblivious to the private communication as we crossed the parking lot to his truck.

"Obviously, I didn't sense Kevin there. Could you tell if she and he…"

"Your sister has definitely had sex very recently," Daniel said as he held open the passenger door for me to get in, but as he closed it behind me and rounded the front of the truck, I sensed he had more to tell me.

"You look like you have bad news," I told him as he slid inside the truck, closing the door after him. He inserted his key into the ignition, but didn't turn it.

"Jamal had the same smell," he finally said. "The same exact smell."

"Do you mean what I think you mean?"

"I'm pretty sure your sister is sleeping with Jamal."

I sat in shock for a moment. Shana knew Jamal had been sent to my apartment and attacked me. She'd been mad about it when we had the meeting at the bar with Kevin. Had her anger on my behalf been an act? "Well, that explains the surprise on Jamal's face when you asked about Kevin," I said when I could speak again. "Maybe he was afraid Shana blabbed."

"I don't think so. Did you see his face after I specifically said we were checking to see if Kevin was all right?"

I thought about it and shook my head. "I heard you say that, but I was focusing on opening my senses to scan the floor for any other humans."

"He looked petrified for a split second, way more fear than a man of his ability should have felt about his nerdy boss finding out he was banging his wife. I hate to say it, but I think Eliza could be right. Something bad ha—" He stopped talking, his unfinished statement frozen on his lips as he stared at something through the windshield that had snagged his attention.

I followed his line of sight and felt a growl rise in my throat as I saw Myra walking toward the front doors. I unfastened my seatbelt and grabbed the door handle, but Daniel grabbed me by my arm before I could open it. "No, Danni. I will fight you on this. If your sister did come through her turning screwed up, and she's sleeping with the guard who attacked you already, *and* hanging out with a shifter who doesn't like you, I'm not letting you near her. We're taking all this new information to Rider."

"Relax," Daniel said as we walked into the bar. "He loves you too much to kill you."

"I'm not worried about me. I'm worried about Shana."

Daniel gave me a sideways glance, but said nothing as we moved across the busy barroom floor. We continued on to the hallway leading to Rider's office, trepidation building with every step. I'd called Eliza on the way over and she told us she'd told Rider her suspicion that Shana had survived a bad turning and may have hurt Kevin based on what I'd told her. She didn't tell him she'd told me this or given me any information and I would go along with that, but I wished she hadn't said anything. Still, I knew how hard it was for Eliza to lie to someone, especially the man who'd saved her from a cruel sire.

I steeled myself for the inevitable scolding and opened the office door to find Ginger sitting on the couch in dark jeans, a red scoop-necked shirt, black leather boots and jacket. Rider stood behind his desk, dressed in black pants and a black T-shirt. He picked a utility belt up off his desk, gun included, and tossed it to Daniel, never taking his hard eyes off me.

"I have an important capture going down in a few that

I need to be part of. Daniel's going with me. You will stay here with Ginger until I get back, and then we'll talk about what happened tonight and why it won't happen again."

"Because you're going to keep treating me like a child or because you're going to kill my sister?" I snapped, instantly angered by his tone.

"I'm not sure yet. Both sound like a plan right now." He looked at Daniel. "We'll discuss how you ignored my order to come back here on the drive."

"You know how she is, Rider. She really wanted to see Shana, and we were already there. Even if I managed to drag her out, kicking and screaming, she'd find a way to go back on her own. At least with me, she had someone watching her back and keeping her from doing something really stupid."

"Hey! I don't do anything stupid."

They both just looked at me.

"I went to see my sister. That's not stupid. That's normal."

"I told you I don't trust your sister. The only reason I let her leave was to get her away from you. You're too blind to see it, but she doesn't have the same love for you that you have for her. She can hurt you."

"That's—"

"Stop." Daniel shook his head at me. "Just stop, Danni. After what we saw tonight, you know she can't be trusted. I know you love her, but Rider is right. You need to stay away from her."

"What happened tonight?" Rider looked between the two of us as I struggled to think of a way to tell him that wouldn't result in him running right to Shana's penthouse to kill her. "Somebody better start explaining."

"Kevin wasn't there again," Daniel told him. "Shana didn't lie about that this time, but she claimed to have sent him to the pharmacy for some lube for their honeymoon sexfest. She even invited me to smell the proof of their activities, not realizing I'd already smelled the proof that she and Jamal had recently had sex."

"Together?" Rider asked, eyebrow raised.

Daniel nodded. "Shana has been a straight bitch to Danni since leaving. Her husband appears to be missing, and she's sleeping with the same guard who attacked Danni. All that looks bad enough, but we also caught Myra going in to the building when we left. It doesn't scream sisterly love to me that Shana is giving Danni the cold shoulder while associating with people who've already shown they wouldn't mind seeing her hurt. Throw in the missing husband, and I think the woman is dangerous too."

Rider looked at me, eyes compassionate, but hard. "She's a bad turn, Danni."

I shook my head and fought to hold back the tears threatening to fall. "You told me about other bad turnings, how they wake up ravenous and go on killing sprees. Shana hasn't done that."

"Where's her husband?" He let out an angry breath. "She did wake up ravenous, Danni. I knew it then, damn it. Somehow, she managed to control her thirst and temperament enough to make sure she got out of here. That makes her incredibly dangerous," he said, repeating what Eliza had told him, not knowing she'd told Daniel and me the same thing.

"As powerful as you are, do you really think she could kill someone and you wouldn't feel it?"

"It's not about how powerful I am. It's about how evil she is."

"She's not evil. She might be a backstabbing bitch, but she's not evil, and even if she is, she's my sister."

"Danni, I know more than anyone how hard it is to put down family. This isn't a decision I'm coming to lightly."

"So that's it? No judge? No jury? No chance to defend herself? You're just going to kill my sister?"

He stared at me for a moment. "No. Your sister will not die as long as you live, but she cannot remain free."

"I've killed too. You didn't lock me up."

"The situations are different and if you'd stop trying so hard to find something good in your sister's rotten heart, you'd quit fighting me on this. She was a bad turn, Danni. Whatever goodness was once in her died with her humanity." He opened his desk drawer and removed a handful of syringes filled with hawthorn oil. "We'll talk more about this when I get back and arrange how to handle Shana. I really have to go do this capture. Ginger, you have one job and that is to keep Danni inside this building," he said as he handed her the syringes. She walked to his desk to take them. "I don't care if you have to drug her, chain her, or knock her the hell out. Do not let her leave."

My mouth dropped open as he closed the drawer and rounded the desk. "Did you really just—"

"Order Ginger to use physical violence if needed to keep you here? Yes, I did," he said, stopping in front of me. "And unlike Daniel and me, I know she won't hesitate to do it, which I'm thankful for because the alternative is you leave here, run to your sister like a fool, thinking you're saving a woman who can't be saved, and get yourself killed. I can forgive myself for letting Ginger knock you around even if you don't, as long as it keeps you safe. I could never forgive myself for failing to save your life." He kissed my forehead and gestured to Daniel that it was time for them to go.

"I mean it, Ginger." He stopped in the doorway. "Use any means necessary to keep her in this building." Then he left, closing the door behind him.

"Hey girlfriend," Ginger said as she stuffed the syringes into the pocket inside her jacket and shifted her feet uncomfortably. "Well, this is awkward."

We moved to Rider's room so Ginger could watch TV while I paced a hole in the floor, nervous energy making it impossible to relax.

"Come on, Danni. You love this show," Ginger said, setting the remote beside her where she sat at the foot of the bed, watching the TV that rose out of the bar on the side of Rider's room. "Look, Jared Padalecki has his shirt off."

I was a Dean Girl, not a Sam Girl, but even a shirtless Jensen Ackles wasn't enough to calm me down. I hadn't begged Rider to turn Shana just to lose her again a week later. And what about my mother? Shana would just disappear one day without a word. She wouldn't accept that. She'd probably blame me and Rider. Eventually, I would disappear one day as well when it became noticeable that I wasn't aging. She might not be the most nurturing mother, but it would still be hard on her to lose two daughters mysteriously.

I pulled my cell phone free from my pocket and used it to call the voicemail on the landline in my apartment. Angel hadn't been answering my phone to avoid explanations, so the voicemail had picked up all my calls. I was surprised to only find one from my mother, a call from the night before asking me if I'd heard from Shana because she hadn't been able to get her or Kevin to answer the phone and security wouldn't allow her access into their building.

"He said he's not going to kill her," Ginger said. "Try not to worry. It might not be that bad."

"He said she's a bad turn," I reminded her. "He's told me before that vampires who come through the turning bad are put down."

"Do you think Rider would lie to you?"

I clenched my teeth and kept pacing. I already thought Rider was lying to me, or at least hiding something. He'd had too many meetings with Seta for them not to have come up with enough of an idea to share something with me, anything. The addition of Jon convinced me even more that he was withholding something, so no, I couldn't completely trust his word that he wouldn't kill Shana. "Why would he mention putting down family? When you put down a dog, you kill it."

"But he said he won't kill her as long as you live, so just be patient and see what he has to say when he gets back." She took off the leather jacket and set it on the bed behind her before picking up the remote and clicking through channels. "Look. Bob Ross. Watching him paint is like yoga and meditation all in one. Give it a try and you'll be thinking of happy stuff like kitties and unicorns and severed penises in no time." She patted the space next to her.

I shook my head and managed to smile a little as I sat where indicated. "You're a nut, you know that?"

"Better to be one than to have some."

I grinned and fell back onto the bed with a sigh. I was exhausted, something that rarely happened at night since becoming a vampire, but Daniel had a point. I'd been on a nonstop rollercoaster of crap since Shana's wedding, and I'd just barely survived the Bloom right before that. I hadn't had a single worry-free day since I'd been turned. Yet, nothing I'd been through was as hard as waiting for Rider to return and tell me how he intended to take away Shana's freedom without taking away her life, and finding it in myself to trust him when I instinctually knew he was hiding something from me.

*Danni*, Shana's voice rang clearly through my head. *You have to help me. Rider tried to kill me, but I got away. All his people are after me, even that bitch, Myra. I thought she was my friend, but you were right. I know I've been awful, but you were right about everything. I'm so sorry. Please come quick.*

The exhaustion I'd just felt evaporated as alarm awakened me. I instantly forced the panic down and focused on maintaining even breathing, not wanting Rider to pick up on my emotions or Ginger to sense something was wrong. Was Shana telling the truth? I replayed everything that had happened since I woke up in my head.

Daniel and I had visited Eliza. Eliza had told Rider she thought Shana had turned badly. Myra showed up as we were leaving. Rider was ready to go on some important capture when we arrived. My stomach sank. Could Shana be the capture? Was Myra there to trick her into going somewhere else? Did Ginger know? I looked at her out the side of my eye, but she stayed focused on Bob Ross and his happy little trees. Daniel would have warned me... unless he couldn't, or didn't want to. He thought Shana was dangerous too.

*Danni?*

*Where are you?* I asked her as I discreetly slid my hand over to Ginger's jacket, quietly working my fingers toward the inner pocket.

*The industrial park near my building. There's a new building being built. I snuck in. I didn't know where else to go. I can't endanger Mom and Grandma, and I can't go near you. All Rider's people want me dead.*

*What about Kevin?* I asked, giving her a chance to come clean.

*Danni, I have to tell you something. I had an accident. Kevin was hurt. I didn't mean it. Please don't turn on me too.*

I wrapped my hand around a syringe and gently pulled it free from Ginger's jacket pocket. I knew Shana had been lying to me, but I knew Rider had been keeping something from me too. With two people I cared about keeping secrets and no idea who else I could trust, I was forced to make a decision based on my gut, and my gut said to do something crazy.

"I'm sorry, Ginger." I plunged the needle into her neck as she turned toward me. Her eyes widened in shocked betrayal as the hawthorn oil filled her bloodstream, then rolled as her eyelids lowered and she fell back on the bed. I pulled the syringe free and dropped it as I searched her for weapons, my stomach twisting with guilt. I wasn't sure Shana was telling the truth about Rider's nest being out to get her, but either way, I had to knock Ginger out. She wouldn't let me leave, and if Rider really had gone out to grab Shana, I didn't want him tipped off to where she was.

I found a switchblade in Ginger's jacket and a bigger one tucked into her boot. I put both in the pockets of my joggers and frowned at how clunky and conspicuous everything looked. Knowing I couldn't waste a lot of time, the hawthorn oil would only knock her out for so long, I quickly chucked off my shoes and joggers, switching them out with jeans and combat boots. Then I slipped the knives into my pockets and slid Ginger's jacket on, figuring those syringes could come in handy.

*I'm on my way*, I told Shana through our link, and ran down the stairs.

# TWENTY-SIX

Conscious of my emotions, I focused on deep breathing as I crossed over to the panel next to the door leading to the garage and entered the code I'd memorized from seeing Rider enter it numerous times. The door opened without any trouble and the lights automatically came on as I stepped inside to find all three of Rider's vehicles parked inside, indicating he'd gone with a group of his men in a company SUV.

Luckily, he usually kept his keys with his vehicles except when he forgot and slid them into a pocket by habit. I didn't know how to drive a motorcycle, and the Ferrari was too flashy for my covert needs. I opened the driver's side door of his personal SUV and released a breath of relief as I saw the keys right there on the dash.

I slid inside, adjusted the seat and mirrors to accommodate my shorter stature, buckled up, and started the engine. I made sure the headlights were on, used the remote clipped to the visor to open the garage door, and backed out into the alley that ran behind the bar. Then I used the remote to close the garage door and got the hell out of there before anyone realized I'd just stolen one of Rider's personal vehicles.

I didn't really know what I was doing or how long I even had before Ginger woke up and sent out the bat signal for Rider to home in on me and swoop in to snatch me up, I just knew I had to get to Shana before anyone else did if she stood a chance of redemption. It wasn't as though I'd never killed anyone. The first man I'd killed had been the result of not feeding as often as I should have, letting my bloodlust get out of hand. As thirsty as Shana had been when she'd awakened, I could easily see her accidentally killing Kevin. Even though she had bagged blood, a tiny voice in my head questioned. And where was the body? Who had hidden it? I also remembered the callous way she spoke of her husband as if he were merely the first of many rich men she would marry in her long life. The closer I got to the industrial park, the less confident I felt in her innocence, but in for a penny, in for a pound. I felt sure I was the only person willing to give her a chance. If I didn't help her, she had no hope.

The industrial park was dark, except for street lights and a few lights left on inside various buildings closed for the night. Still, between the light given off from my headlights and my vampire-enhanced eyesight, I could see well enough to find the building under construction near the back of the park. It was five stories high and fully framed, with windows and doors cut out, but that was about as far as the construction had reached. A large tarp covered the roof. I parked in front and opened my senses. After a while I picked up on a vampire I felt confident was Shana inside the structure. I didn't see or sense anyone else moving about.

*Shana, I'm coming in.*

I turned off the car, pocketed the keys, and got out, one of Ginger's switchblades in my hand. I kept my senses open, pushing them as far as I could, feeling nothing, but something odd was in that nothing. I couldn't put my finger on it, but something felt off. The air was too thick, too free of smells. I was walking toward a construction site but couldn't smell lumber. The night was still, the wind unnaturally absent. The closer I got to the doorway, the thicker the air seemed to grow, then it all shimmered as I stepped through.

Suddenly, I was in complete darkness, something over my head, and before I could react, I was lifted from my feet and tossed into a wall. I gasped in pain as I slid down it, realizing I was in an elevator as the familiar ding indicated the doors had closed. I pulled the bag off my head as I felt myself moving upward and discovered it was a pillowcase. I looked up to see Jamal standing over me.

"Payback time, bitch." He raised his leg to stomp on me. Having never loosened my grip on the switchblade, I opened it and used my other hand to catch his leg under the knee as I swung my knife hand up, plunging the blade into his crotch, pretty sure I sliced through more than balls.

"Never fuck with Danni the Teste Slayer," I growled over his screaming as I yanked the knife free and rammed it into his throat, just under his chin so the blade entered his head, cutting off the screaming as his eyes bulged and he fell to the floor gurgling blood as it spilled from the wound and his mouth.

The elevator came to a stop, and the ding was almost ominous as it opened to a completely finished marble floor. Shana stood near the back of the wide open room in front of floor to ceiling windows much like those in her penthouse, dressed in black leggings, a tight T-shirt in the same color, and matching ankle boots. I stepped out of the elevator and barely had time to register an older, white-haired woman in a loose, gray dress I didn't recognize entering from another room before I was hit from the side by a large red fox.

Acting on instinct, I grabbed the other switchblade from my pocket and swiped it at the fox as I hit the floor, cutting it across its belly. It whimpered in pain and rolled off, shifting from fox to woman, then back to fox, quickly healing itself. It was Myra.

"What the hell, Shana?" I got to my feet. "I came to help you!"

"You came to judge and meddle like you've been doing ever since I was turned. I've had enough of it." Her angry face twisted into an eerie smile. "But you are helping me. Myra has been a fountain of information since you so kindly had Rider assign her to cleaning up after me when you tricked me into getting so sick. We talked a lot, and it turns out both of us kind of hate you."

I stepped back as if physically struck by her words. Myra, back in her human form, grinned wickedly at me from my left as the white-haired woman stood a safe distance away, watching me intently. I sensed a dark, ugly magic about her and realized she'd cast some sort of spell to trick me into thinking the building was an unfinished building containing only my sister. It had all been a trap.

"You can't mean that. We're sisters."

"Not by choice," Shana said, laughing as if I'd given her the most ridiculous reason not to want to hurt me.

"They were right. The turn changed you, turned you into something truly evil. You killed Kevin, didn't you?"

"I needed the man's money, not his presence, but no, I didn't kill him. Jamal and I have been sleeping together since Kevin hired him forever ago. He even figured out what I was after witnessing you and Daniel fight and heal so quickly. He wanted that ability too, so I promised I'd turn him as soon as possible if he'd take care of Kevin for me and help with you. He killed Kevin yesterday morning and had him all disposed by the time I woke. I don't even know the details, easier for me to play innocent that way." She craned her head to see where Jamal's body had fallen, half in and half out of the elevator. "Looks like he's not even going to get the vampire goods after all. Such a shame. He really did earn it."

"Why did you have to have Kevin killed? You could have divorced him."

"His parents made sure I signed a prenuptial agreement. I thought I could suffer through the marriage for the money, but he's such a whiner. I did the world a favor."

I stared at Shana in complete shock. It was as if she had no soul. She just didn't care about anyone but herself. "Rider already suspects you killed Kevin. He's not going to let you get away with it."

"I didn't kill Kevin. I simply slept peacefully while he was murdered elsewhere by someone else. Pretty sure there's no law against that."

"It's just as bad, and he's definitely going to make you pay for this."

"Please. Myra's taught me a few things. She introduced me to Trixell," she said, gesturing toward the older woman. "She's a witch and once we're done taking care of you, she's going to make it look like we had nothing to do with it. She's a genius with magic. How else do you think I got out of my building without Rider's security guards spotting me?"

I looked at the woman again and remembered what Jon had told Rider about receiving the package. An old woman had given it to a boy to take to my apartment. She felt old and dark, and that was exactly the kind of witch Rider said his brother would work with. His brother, who heard me mention my sister to Myra while he spied through Gina. Well, now I knew why he no longer needed her. He'd just used Myra and my sister to lure me away from Rider. Damn, that evil genius worked fast.

"You idiots," I growled as I pocketed the switchblade and wrapped my hand around one of the syringes. "She works for Selander Ryan. She's going to kill all three of us."

The woman grinned, not concerned she'd been exposed, and raised her hands as her eyes grew black, full of her dark power. I screamed Rider's name in my mind and used my vampiric speed to cross the room and stab the witch in the neck with the syringe. I had no idea if hawthorn oil would do anything to her, but I knew a knife wouldn't stop her from using magic. She gasped in surprise, having been caught off guard while so focused on summoning whatever mother of a whammy she'd been summoning to hit us with, and stumbled backward, her hand over her neck. I stabbed her in the chest with another syringe for safe measure, barely managing to press in the plunger before Shana jumped me, knocking me to the floor.

"You can't stab my witch!" she screeched. "Why do you have to ruin everything? I deserve to be queen!"

"You're psychotic!" I rolled on top of her and drew my fist back to punch her in the face, but Myra shifted into her fox form and sank her sharp teeth into my elbow before I could finish.

I reached back, grabbed Myra's tail, and threw her across the room, her furry body hitting the opposite wall. Shana got in a punch, knocking me sideways.

"It's nothing personal," she said, crawling over to me, "but you have to die. Comforting Rider as we both mourn our losses is the easiest way to get what I want."

I kicked out, catching Shana in the gut to double her over. "That's your plan? Rider isn't stupid enough to not figure everything out. And he hates you." I stood and grabbed a handful of Shana's hair, yanking her head back so I could see her eyes. "He loves me. He doesn't give a shit about your big boobs or tiny hips or pretty blue eyes. He loves *me*. He'll never stop, even if you do kill me. He will never want you."

Shana let out an ungodly roar and lunged for me, wrapping her arms around my hips before knocking me back to the floor. "I'm the prettiest!" she screamed, as she started throwing punches. "I'm the best! I deserve the crown!"

I deflected her blows and waited for my opening. The second I saw a clear shot to her kidney, I took it, then rolled with her, delivering my own punches. I didn't bother with trash talk, hurt to the soul by what she'd said. She hated me. My own sister. Tears filled my eyes, nearly blinding me, but I didn't let up, continuing to land punches wherever I could connect through the watery haze.

"Why do you hate me? I've never done anything to you!"

"You've never done anything at all! You've never starved yourself, slept with guys you couldn't stand while trying to find that perfect, gullible, rich guy, or worked out until you puked. I'm the one who did everything right to be perfect, but you're the one Daddy loved more, and you're the one who landed the most powerful vampire. You don't deserve it!"

That was why she hated me? I opened my mouth to ask how any of her choices had been my fault, but claws sliced my back. Myra, in fox form again. I cried out in pain and turned to grab her.

Shana used the opportunity to wrap her hands around my neck and choke me, forcing me onto my back as she squeezed the air out of my lungs. I knew I couldn't die of suffocation, but I panicked nonetheless. Having the air squeezed out of you was scary, no matter what you were. I hit and kicked, struggling against her hold as Myra bit my arms and legs, but Shana was determined, so determined she started beating my head against the floor, making it hard for me to focus through the pain and dizziness.

I knew she'd kill me if I gave her half a chance so I summoned every bit of self-preservation I had, and forced my back off the floor with a rage-fueled growl before I sank my fangs into her throat, ready to bite out a chunk of flesh if I had to. She screamed and dug her nails into my shoulders, trying to pull me off of her. Then the damn fox jumped on my back and chomped on the back of my neck. I reached for the fox, and that was the opening Shana needed.

She shoved me onto my back, slamming my head against the marble floor, stuck her knee in my chest, and pulled a knife out of her ankle boot. I could only see her through a blur, my brain muddled from the hit I'd just taken to the head, but I was pretty sure I was about to be stabbed, and I couldn't seem to fight through the fog to do a damn thing about it.

Glass shattered, and I instinctively looked toward the sound. I saw two forms running toward us through the blurry film of my tears and near unconsciousness. Shana was snatched off of me and I was pulled to my feet. As my vision slowly cleared, Rider came into focus, shards of glass in his hair and on his clothes, blood seeping from multiple cuts on his body. Then his eyes started to glow gold and his power seeped out to fill the room.

I blinked as the room spun around me. I felt wobbly, but didn't fall, supported somehow. That was when I realized Rider held Shana and me apart from each other. His hand was inside Shana's chest. I looked down in horror to see his other hand was inside mine. Seta appeared in front of him with a fancy silver box covered in runes. She raised her eyebrows before reaching out with one hand to touch his forehead. Her power shimmered over him, healing his wounds.

"That's a freebie," she said. "It wouldn't be good for you to bleed out or not be able to hold your power during this. Are you ready?"

He nodded, his jaw clenched tight.

"Very well." She closed her eyes and Jon appeared at my side.

I tried to speak, but had no voice. Panic rose in my chest as I searched the room, but couldn't find Daniel. It was only the five of us in the glow of Rider's power, and I couldn't scream for help or ask what was happening. Shana stood frozen across from me, glaring at me with pure hatred, but didn't say a word.

"Remove their hearts," Seta said.

Rider pulled his hands out of our chests and turned them palms up, a heart in each hand. Shana's heart… and mine. I flashed back to the night he'd pulled Selander Ryan's heart out of his chest and crushed it, then blacked out.

"You're safe."

I opened my eyes and came face to face with Jon, noting we were very close, almost as if we were slow dancing. He held me tight against him, his arms wrapped around my waist. I pushed him away and noticed we were floating in a great white nothing.

I screamed and started to fall, but he pulled me back and held me tighter. "Relax. You are safe with me."

"Where are we?"

"We're hovering outside of the afterlife. It won't last long and I will protect you from any soul eaters we might encounter."

"Soul eaters?" I remembered my heart in Rider's hand. "He killed me. Rider killed me." I gasped for breath. I was hyperventilating.

"Rider is saving you, as am I. I told you I was here to help you. Relax, Danni. It will all be over soon." A dark figure in a flowing black robe flew toward us and we disappeared, reappearing in a similar-looking place of absolutely nothing. "Relax. It's almost done."

"What's almost done? What is he doing to me?"

Jon looked at me, his eyes full of sympathy. "Freeing you of a curse and protecting you from an enemy who just tried to kill you."

"My sister." My eyes burned with tears. "She hates me. She tried to kill me."

"The sister you knew died during the turning." Another dark figure in a robe suddenly appeared and flew toward us. We disappeared, reappearing in another identical expanse of pure white.

"How are you doing this?" I asked. "What are you?"

He sighed. "I don't really know, but I know the spell is almost complete. Our time here is over, but I'll see you again. Take care, Danni."

"Wait. Wha—"

I opened my eyes and stared up at Rider's ceiling as memories came rushing back. I sat up, noting I was in the same clothes I'd been wearing while fighting Shana, and patted my chest.

"It's there."

I looked over to see Rider sitting on the chaise. He'd changed into black pants and a cranberry button-down shirt, and appeared to have been awake a while watching over me. I could sense the sun had just gone down. Worry filled his eyes.

"What day is it?"

"Saturday. You've been asleep since last night. You needed the rest."

"Was it real?" I glared at him. "Did you rip my heart out of my chest?"

He looked at me for a moment, assessing. "Let me explain—"

"Did. You. Rip. My. Heart. Out. Of. My. Chest?"

"It was necessary for the spell."

"You sonofabitch!" I flew off of the bed, launching myself at Rider. He stood, trying to grab me, but I threw punches anywhere I could land one, connecting to his chest, shoulders, arms, face, and ribs. "You ripped my fucking heart out of my chest! How could you?!"

"Danni!" He grunted as I hit him square in the stomach, but managed to grab both of my upper arms and hold me away from him as I continued to struggle, now kicking, the anger inside of me uncontrollable. "Enough!"

I froze in place, standing still as a statue, and he let go

of me. I growled as I struggled against his power, but couldn't budge.

"I'm sorry," he said as he checked his lip, found a cut in the corner and slid his tongue over it to heal the damage I'd inflicted. "I know you don't like me to use my power over you, but you have to hear me out. Let me explain. I'll release you as soon as you listen to why I had to do what I did, all right?"

I quit struggling and grunted. "I don't know what story you think is going to make me just accept that you pulled my heart out of my chest like you did your brother before you killed him. I was hovering somewhere around the afterlife with Jon. I know it was a lie now that you didn't know what he was here for."

"I didn't know his role exactly, just that Seta needed his help to ensure your safety. And I wasn't for sure that we'd need him, that things would work out as they did."

"What about Shana? Where was Daniel? Did he know?"

"Just let me explain. I'll start from the beginning." Rider took a deep breath and sat on the chaise, clasping his hands together as he leaned forward, elbows on knees. "I already had Seta working on finding a way around the Bloom or at least lessening its power. When I turned Shana, I told Seta about my concerns because she's had experience with vampires who didn't come through the turn well. She immediately thought of using blood magic to help you, which is some of the most powerful magic, whether light or dark.

"Seta told me that if Shana did go bad, we could use her to help you with the Bloom while neutralizing her, solving both problems I'd come to her about in just one spell. I jumped at the chance. I allowed Seta to take blood from Shana while she slept, and I had Nannette give her a vial of yours. She also needed my blood as well as other elements to create the box you may have noticed her holding. That's why she was here so often."

"So you were moving forward with her on something and chose not to tell me?" I couldn't keep the growl out of my voice.

"When she told me I'd have to remove your hearts, I chose not to tell you because I didn't want to do it. I wanted to find another way for her to work the spell. We were looking for another way, which is why I told you to stay away from Shana, to buy us time, but you didn't. Shana was a bad turn, Danni, and once she tried to kill you, I had no choice but to neutralize her immediately. It's vampire law." He sighed. "I truly thought if I got her away from you and supplied her with enough blood, I'd have time to find another way before she hurt someone. I hacked into her building's security and placed men in the vicinity to monitor her. I didn't know about her relationship with Jamal or that Ryan had sent a witch to her after learning about her. Kevin's death is on me."

He hung his head, and I felt sorry for him, but couldn't bring myself to offer him comfort, not with the image of my heart in his hand so fresh in my mind.

"At no time was your life in danger during the spell. As your sire and a vampire of my age and power level, I have the ability to remove your heart and hold it in my hand while it still beats. I don't even have to break skin to do it. The moment I put it back, you were back to normal. I killed Ryan by crushing his heart. Not that killing him stopped him, but you get the point. I would never crush your heart, Danni, and it hurts that you would think, even for a minute, that I would."

"Did you crush Shana's?"

"No. I promised you she would live as long as you were alive. The only way I would have killed her was if she killed you, which is why I told you to stay away from her, especially after what you and Daniel told me before we headed out for our capture and I left Ginger to keep you out of trouble."

Realizing I was no longer being held still against my

will, I looked over at the bed where I'd knocked Ginger out with the hawthorn oil and felt the guilt swallow me. "Don't punish her. She never saw the hawthorn oil coming."

"I wasn't planning on it. She's been through enough punishment. She was scared to death that you snuck out to get killed and she put that on herself."

I sat on the bed and sighed. "I'll apologize. I never thought about that. Shana used telepathy to ask me for help. I realize now she probably had Myra tell her when both you and Daniel were away from me."

"Most likely. Myra was here last night. She knew there was a capture happening."

"She said you had tried to kill her but she escaped. She said the whole nest was in on it, even Myra."

"And you believed her over me when I told you I didn't intend to kill her?"

"I didn't believe either of you. I love you both and I knew both of you were keeping something from me, so how could I trust either in that moment?"

Rider looked away. "I never lied. I am guilty of not telling you everything, and I'm truly sorry if that caused you to doubt me, but by now, Danni, don't you know I wouldn't hurt you or put you in danger?"

"It's hard to believe anything when you know something's being kept from you, and you never denied that you didn't like Shana at all." I looked at him and he dropped his gaze to the floor, unable to dispute the fact. "You were right about her though. She was completely evil, and I guess she was just acting most of the time she was here after being turned, especially when she defended me to our mother. The things she said last night were beyond horrible. It was like she had no soul, no sense of right or wrong."

"It's typical behavior of someone who comes through the turn wrong, and why they are usually killed immediately before they can harm others. She just put on a good enough act to get out of here first."

"How did you get there so fast? I'd just screamed for you when you appeared not long after."

"There's a tracker on all my vehicles. The moment you left in one of them, Tony alerted me. Ginger was found immediately. Daniel and I followed the tracker and found the SUV parked outside the building before you screamed. The witch had the doors and windows sealed up tight, so Daniel shifted into his dragon form. I jumped on and he flew up, then sped down toward the floor you were on like a bullet to burst through the floor to ceiling windows lining the back wall."

"That's why you had those cuts and were covered in glass."

"Yes. It wasn't the smartest entry for a vampire, but I was desperate."

"You rode Daniel." I couldn't help but grin despite the anger still inside me.

"Yeah, and I know you're mad at me, but we'd both appreciate it if you never say that again."

"I didn't really see him. Did he come out all right? What happened to Myra and the witch? She was working for your brother. Please say she didn't get away."

"I went straight to you and Daniel took care of Myra, who was about to sink her teeth into your leg when Daniel punted her across the room. I would have liked to have asked her some questions about her involvement, if she was working with anyone else in the nest, but Daniel killed her before I could. We captured the witch. The hawthorn oil mixture in those syringes you took contains a little witch's net, which can prevent a witch from using magic. We have her locked away in a cell laced with the same magic. Hopefully she gives us enough information we can find Ryan and end his reign of terror."

"Before the next Bloom?"

He looked at me, blinking. "Haven't you been listening? The whole point of removing your hearts was to work a spell using blood magic to free you of the Bloom. It's gone."

I sat frozen in place, staring at him. I'd heard him mention Seta looking for a cure and thinking blood magic could do it, but somehow it hadn't clicked that she actually found a cure. I'd been focused on the part about neutralizing Shana. "The Bloom is gone? I'm free to go anywhere anytime I want? I don't have to stay with you in case it hits me out of nowhere?"

His face fell. "I wasn't aware that was the only reason you stay with me."

"You know what I mean. I don't have to fear being away from you and latching onto the first man in the vicinity at any given moment? Ginger and Daniel don't have to carry syringes filled with hawthorn oil to knock me out?"

"Yeah." He stood, clearly upset. "So, Seta did her thing, and it's kind of hard to explain, but she moved the Bloom into your sister. You're still half succubus with succubus needs and you're still technically Ryan's fledgling too, but you'll never have to worry about the Bloom hitting you and making you want to sex the first random guy you see to death as long as your sister carries that burden for you."

"Wait." My relief wavered. The Bloom was awful. I wouldn't wish it on anyone. "You're saying Shana is alive, but you're making her go through the Bloom?"

"Shana is in a suspended state and will remain that way as long as her heart stays separated from her body. That's what the box was for. The box's magic keeps the heart and the rest of her body alive in a way she can't hurt anyone."

"Can anyone hurt her?"

"I won't allow that."

"I want to see her."

He studied me for a moment before giving a curt nod. "Come with me."

It felt like déjà vu as we walked the hall to the same

room Shana had been brought to after she'd been turned and walked past the same guards standing outside her door.

"I'll install a lock with passcode on the door soon," Rider said as he walked me over to the bed where Shana rested in the same clothes she'd been wearing the previous night. "I'll have two men on guard at all times until then."

"She looks like she's sleeping," I said as I stared down at her.

"Just like Sleeping Beauty. There's no prince coming to wake her from this spell, though. According to vampire law, I was supposed to kill her the moment it became evident she was a bad turn. Given the circumstances, I was able to do this instead." He looked at me. "Now that you know why I pulled your heart out of your chest, can you forgive me?"

I stared down at Shana and sighed. Even after everything she'd said the night before, even knowing she'd wanted me dead, I was thankful he hadn't killed her. She looked beautiful and innocent, like a sleeping cherub, but I knew she wasn't. Rider had known all along. I'd defended her, went against him in doing so, and despite every instinct in him telling him to kill her, he'd kept her alive for me and even figured out a way to free me of a horrible curse... with a woman I'd accused him of wanting. I owed him an apology, but still, I couldn't get the image of my heart in his hand out of my head. I couldn't shake the unease of knowing he could do that.

"I think I owe you a lot. You've saved my life countless times, and you've always put my safety ahead of everything, even when I've been awful to you, jealous, or just ungrateful. I am so sorry for all of that, and I do understand why you did the spell, and knowing the outcome, I'm beyond grateful, but Rider, you pulled my heart out of my chest without giving me any hint that was coming. I was floating out in the heavens with Jon while he kept me safe from soul eaters."

"I tried to avoid all that, but once Shana attacked you, I had to act. It was either work the spell the only way we knew would work, which meant removing your hearts temporarily, or kill Shana then and there, leaving you with the Bloom."

"I know that, and I know you thought you were doing what was best for me and protecting me when you chose to just not mention the spell to me. You are always protecting me, but there are some things you have to tell me. I should have known about the spell, even if you were looking for another way to work it. Maybe then I could have prepared for it. I saw you take my heart out of my chest and it was terrifying. I couldn't scream. I couldn't move." Tears fell from my eyes. "Do you have any idea what it's like to have the person you think loves you and will always protect you do something like that and you don't know what is going on?"

The door opened and Rome stepped in, his face instantly registering his realization that he'd stepped into a personal moment. "Sorry," he said as I wiped my cheeks. "I didn't want to interrupt, but Auntie Mo has called me like five times in a row demanding I find you and tell you that you need to be at church tomorrow. Both of you, but especially you, Danni. So I told you. You can tell her I told you so she doesn't do that thing where she tries to rip my ears off my head, okay? Okay." He nodded his own agreement and walked back out, closing the door behind him.

"I guess we're going to church tomorrow," Rider said softly.

"Yeah," I said, sniffling.

"What are we doing now? What can I do to make this better?"

"I don't think you can do anything right now. I think it's just going to take some time." I dried my face and took a deep breath to gather myself. "I'm going to go to my apartment tonight."

"Okay. You should drink from Angel. Do you want me to take you? Daniel's in the bar if you'd rather he take you and bring you back when you're ready." He frowned. "You are coming back, aren't you?"

"No. I'm going to my apartment and staying the night, maybe staying a few days or more. I need some space to figure out what I'm going to do now that I have more freedom from your brother's curse. Angel wants to travel. I still need to get a job and now, without the Bloom hanging over me, I can get one. I'm not sure what exactly I'm going to do, but I know I need to do something. I need a little time to wrap my head around all this." I sniffed. "I'll still go to church tomorrow so Auntie Mo doesn't yank Rome's ears off. Tell him to send me the information. I kind of feel like maybe I could use it right now."

Rider didn't respond. I looked up to see him staring at me, fear and sorrow swimming in the depths of his blue eyes. He looked away and nodded his head. "Okay. If that's what you want. You're not my prisoner."

"Hey." I reached up to cup his cheek. "I love you. I'm not leaving you. I just need to deal with all this. It hasn't even been a full three months since I've been turned and I've been hunted and attacked nonstop, gone through two weeks of the Bloom taking over my body, been possessed, lost a friend and had her body parts sent to me. I've watched my sister nearly bleed out, then tried to save her just to lose her again, but a horrible version of her I'll have to remember now." My voice cracked. "I had the man I love literally rip my heart out of my chest. It's just all too much. I need a break."

"If that's what you need, I won't deny you," he said softly before hugging me to him and pressing a kiss against the top of my head, "but do me a favor. Daniel didn't know about the spell. Take him with you. I'll send Ginger. They're yours wherever and whatever you decide to do, for however long. Maybe I won't completely lose my mind

400

with worry if I know you have them looking out for you."

I decided not to pack. Rider seemed upset enough, and I had clothes, shoes, everything I needed at my apartment. Leaving my things in his room seemed gentler, a reminder I would be back. He walked me to the bar where Daniel sat alone in a booth, waiting for me.

"This is just a little time," I told Rider, sensing his sadness. "It isn't an ending, and hey, I'll see you at church tomorrow morning, if you want to see me there."

"I want to see you everywhere," he said softly. "I'm not the one leaving." And he turned and walked away.

It took every bit of willpower I had not to run after him..

# TWENTY-SEVEN

"You've been quiet all night," Daniel said, bringing his glass to the sink as I rinsed out the bowls we'd used for popcorn and candy during a *Saw* marathon. He'd already carried Angel to my bed once she'd started snoring. "And I should wash all this out, not the vampire who couldn't even eat any of it."

"I'm not washing, I'm rinsing, and I don't mind." I finished and loaded the dishwasher. "As for the quiet, I have a lot of thoughts all jumbled in my head."

"I can imagine. I'm sorry you went through that."

"You don't have to keep apologizing. There was nothing you could do." He'd explained earlier that Rider's power had held him back. He hadn't even seen them work the spell, unable to see through the glow of Rider's power. His eyes registered genuine surprise when I described the ordeal to him. "And it's not just that," I said, turning toward him as I folded my arms and leaned back against the counter. "It's everything. Rider told me very early on he was afraid of losing me over Shana and I think he believes he is. I hurt him and I feel awful about it, and I betrayed Ginger."

"Ginger understands."

"Then why isn't she here? Rider said he'd send her."

"And he will. Most likely tomorrow night. She's been working a solo assignment, was still technically on it while with you last night, but she was able to get away for a while. She needs to wrap that up. Besides," he said, turning to take in the apartment. "It could get cramped in here real quick. Angel has your bed. I assume you're going to get some sleep before you have to get ready to go to church. You got a sleeping bag?"

"No," I said, worrying my lip. I hadn't really thought about sleeping arrangements when I'd decided to come back to my apartment.

"I can sleep on the floor. You can have the couch when you get tired."

"You're not sleeping on the floor," I said. "We'll figure something out, but honestly, I could stay up a few more hours, maybe skip sleep altogether until after church, but I'm done with the blood and guts." I walked over to the couch and picked the remote up from the coffee table as I sat. I surfed through the channels until I landed on *The Golden Girls*. "Much better."

Daniel smiled as he settled onto the couch next to me and leaned his head back. "All right. Just roll me onto the floor if you change your mind." He closed his eyes and drifted asleep. Three *The Golden Girls* episodes later, I fell asleep too, my head somehow finding its way to Daniel's shoulder.


According to Daniel, I'd awakened after twenty hard shakes and the threat of an ice bath. I dressed in light gray slacks, a soft blue wraparound blouse, and gray ankle boots. I even took a little extra time smoothing my hair and wore light makeup and a heavy application of the special sunscreen Rider supplied me with before Daniel and I left for the church. Angel passed on attending, but Daniel, of course, would go wherever I went. I was thankful he'd made an early morning run to his apartment for black slacks and a matching polo shirt. With his unique hair, each strand a different color of the rainbow, he still stood out, but he was dressed nicely.

Rome's church was big and full of people in an assortment of dress, from Sunday best to jeans and T-shirts, and no one seemed to judge. I liked it immediately. Rider had arrived before us, dressed in black slacks and a cobalt blue dress shirt with a black silk tie. The blue brought his eyes out and I caught myself gasping a little at how incredibly beautiful he was. It amazed me how he could be so without losing any of his masculinity.

"You look lovely," he said as we met him and Rome in the seats they'd held for us in one of the back pews. Auntie Mo was up front with a group of older ladies. She craned her neck to see me and smiled, pleased we'd all made it.

"You look very nice too," I said, feeling a little awkward but not sure why as we took our seats and settled in for the sermon, which came after a selection of gospel songs soulfully sang by the choir.

I tried to focus on the sermon as it was delivered by the middle-aged, attractive minister, but was aware of Rider's contained energy as I sat between him and Daniel. As the minister went on about the power and the importance of forgiveness, I reached over and laced my fingers through Rider's. He held on tight and we remained that way until the end of church.

"Auntie Mo seemed very happy you finally took up her invitation," I told him as we exited the church and walked over to a large poplar tree, where we would wait beneath its shaded canopy for Auntie Mo. Rome and Daniel hung back a little, and I suspected Rider had requested them to. I noticed he seemed tired. "You haven't slept yet, have you?"

"No," he answered, leaning his shoulder against the tree trunk as he slipped his hands into his pockets and watched people pour out of the church. "I had a lot of things to think about, a lot of planning."

"Planning? One of the new contracts you received?" I felt a little disappointed that he could focus on business so well, but quickly shoved the selfish feeling aside. He'd looked so sad when I'd left the night before. It was a good thing he had something to keep himself occupied.

He gave a small shake of his head. "Planning how to help you without overstepping. I thought about everything you said, all that you've been through since the night my brother attacked you, and you're right. You've been through a lot with little to no time to truly deal with any of it. I want to keep you with me, to keep you safe, but you're not my pet. And you're not a child. You deserve the freedom to do whatever you wish, whenever you wish, and although I would fully support you without question, I know you want to earn your own way. MidKnight Enterprises is large enough you can work for me from a distance of your choosing, allowing you to work and travel with Angel, if you'd like."

He was giving me a job? Letting me go? "What are you saying?"

"I'm saying you can work for me. Daniel and Ginger will be assigned to guard you, but they will also be assigned to help in any assignments you receive through MidKnight. If traveling is what you want while you take time to sort through things, you can take assignments in the Pigeon Forge area and stay with Grey's pack there. I've spoken to him and he has no problem with it. You can also work out of Baltimore, where Seta's people can offer you added protection. Or…" He looked at me hopefully.

"What?"

"My brother is a little less dangerous now that we have the witch, and we will break her, learn what he's up to. Still, he's dangerous enough. You're still half succubus. You're going to need to continue caring for yourself as Nannette instructed. That means drinking an assortment of blood, including drinking from me, and it means also feeding on the controlled violence you receive from sparring, interrogation, or captures, and it means sex. If you stay here, I can make sure you get everything you need, and I promise not to push you for anything more than you want to give. It's your decision what you do and where you want to go, but I really hope you'll stay here."

"Excuse me, Rider, but may I have a moment with Danni?"

We looked over to see Auntie Mo approaching us. She moved slowly in her long multicolor dress, using a mahogany cane with an intricate design for support.

"Of course. I was about to leave anyway. Think about it and let me know," he said to me before cupping his hand around the back of my neck and leaning down to plant a kiss on my forehead, letting his lips linger a moment before pulling back. "You know where I'll always be." He released me and walked away.

I stood, a little stunned for a moment, then felt Auntie Mo's wise gaze on me. I turned my attention to her and found her staring at me, radiating warmth and compassion. "The vampire is wounded, but strong," she said. "He will be fine, and so will you. I am very proud of you, Danni Keller. You discovered your demons."

I frowned, then remembered what she'd told me the last time I'd visited her: *There are other demons seeking to destroy you, some that have been with you since you were very young, some that are a very part of you.*

"You knew my sister would try to hurt me."

She nodded. "I couldn't tell you that. Rider did, but couldn't convince you. There are some things so horrible we will not accept them until we have no other choice. And your sister didn't really want you dead. That was the darkness inside her, the darkness that was given power to control her during the turn. The turning gave you darkness too, but you are stronger than it. Your sister was weak."

She took my hand, squeezing it in her own. "You've

spent years wondering why your family has been so cold to you. I believe you are closer to understanding now that there is nothing wrong with you. You are simply the strongest. The weak, they try to make the strong weak too. They feel less powerless that way."

"I'm working on understanding. I'm working with a woman who helps me see myself in the mirror, not my fears and insecurities."

She nodded, smiling. "Yes. I have seen it and I am happy for you. You are dealing with the demon inside you that you cannot kill, but you can tame. Feed it often, but only good things. If you feed it dark things, it will destroy you, your relationships, everything you hold dear. Stay watchful."

I nodded. "I can leave now if I want. Travel. Work. I don't know what to do. I want to have the freedom to do what I want, but I don't want to hurt Rider."

She smiled. "Follow your heart, and be thankful you have options. It wasn't long ago the thought of not being with him filled you with fear. You are growing stronger in who you are, and he sees that. He respects it. You are soulmates. I told you before, there is no guarantee you and Rider will spend your lives together, but that is only because you have a choice. It's a less scary thought now that you've found your strength, isn't it?"

I thought back to our last meeting, after I'd run out and attacked Rider, desperate for him, the voices in my head taunting me with the thought of losing him, and smiled in relief. "It's much easier now. I love him beyond words, and I want him in my life, but I don't need him to survive."

"Of course you don't. As I told you, you've always had everything you will ever need. Right here." She pointed to the center of my chest. "You have much to think about, and take as much time as you need. There are no wrong answers, yet there is a right one."

Ah, Auntie Mo, I thought, grinning as she walked away.

Always with the riddles.

I crashed once we returned to my apartment, my energy drained by the sun and lack of decent sleep. Angel had crawled out of bed by then, so I changed into a T-shirt and lounge pants before burrowing under the covers and grabbing much needed sleep.

I woke at nightfall, renewed energy flowing through my veins, and brushed my teeth before joining Daniel and Angel in the living area. They were seated at the dining table, eating fresh baked brownies. The slightly burned smell permeating the air had me hiding a grin. "Who baked?"

"I did," Angel said. "They're a little crisp, but nice and gooey inside."

Daniel's face said differently, but he was being a sport and eating them. I was kind of glad to have an excuse not to partake. "You'll have to make them when I can eat that stuff again."

"Sure. By then I'll have them perfected. Do you need to feed?"

"Later," I told her as I passed them to retrieve a bag of blood from the refrigerator from the delivery made that morning, and grabbed my Dolly Parton mug from the cabinet. "We need to talk about some stuff first," I said as I poured the blood into the mug and popped it into the microwave. "When's Ginger supposed to be here?"

"Pretty soon," Daniel answered as he stood and helped Angel clear the table off. "She wrapped up her other assignment just before daybreak this morning, and Rider told her to report here after she woke."

They cleaned up while I prepared my blood and took it to the living area, setting it down on the coffee table as I took a seat and flipped through the TV for something to watch that wouldn't be too distracting once Ginger arrived and we could talk. I found a show about opossums and decided on it. Unlike most people, I think the little critters are adorable. Daniel and Angel joined me, watching along as we waited for Ginger.

I'd done a lot of thinking on the way home from church. I loved Rider dearly, but I was still having trouble not picturing my heart in his hand when I thought of him. I was both excited and scared of the choices he'd given me. I'd never seen Baltimore, but wanted to. I loved Pigeon Forge and had stayed with Grey's wolf pack when Rider had taken me there about a month ago. The thought of visiting either place was thrilling, and both locations would ensure the distance needed to truly work through the jumble of thoughts in my head. Getting away from my mother and grandmother, who had yet to notice Shana and Kevin were missing, was a huge bonus to both, but they also held the huge drawback of being so far away from Rider.

I was still half succubus with all the bad things that came with it. I could feed my need for violence from anywhere pretty easily, and I was sure I could go a while without Rider's blood without my succubus side growing stronger, making Selander Ryan's connection to me stronger.

But there was the fact that, as a succubus, I also fed on sex. It hadn't been much of an issue outside the Bloom or the fact that I couldn't drink from men without checking for venom first because I'd always had Rider to fill that need. If I went without long enough, I worried what the result might be. Would I grow as desperate for it as if I were under the Bloom's influence? As far as I was concerned, Rider and I were still very much together. I'd never forgive myself if I betrayed him. But I hadn't slept with him immediately after turning. I had time for at least a short trip, and I could always come back to take care of… my needs. If I needed to. I didn't think Rider would refuse me, although I certainly didn't like the thought of using him like that either.

A knock sounded at the door a short while later and Daniel crossed the room to open it, allowing Ginger entrance before settling back on the couch next to me. Ginger wore jeans, boots, and a red leather jacket fastened with large snaps. She set a duffel bag on the side chair and fisted her hands on her hips before narrowing her eyes on me, her bright red lips pursed. "You knocked me out and stole my jacket."

"The jacket is in my room, perfectly safe," I said, heat flushing my face. "I'm really sorry about that. I feel lousy."

"Eh, I would have done the same thing in that scenario, and no worries. I'm still your fan." She unsnapped her jacket and held it open to reveal a white T-shirt with a cartoon knife protruding from a cartoon scrotum. The scrotum had X's for eyes and a little slash of a mouth with a tongue lolling out. Danni the Teste Slayer was written around the image in a bloody red font.

"Dear Lord," I said, my voice near a whisper. "Where did you get that made so fast?"

"I know a guy." She shrugged and opened her duffel to retrieve another that she tossed to Angel. "Got you one, kid."

"Yes!" Angel clutched the shirt to her chest and ran to the bedroom. "I'm putting it on now!"

I looked at Daniel sitting next to me as he stared at Ginger, bemused. "Did you get one?"

"Nope," he answered. "I can look past the fact you stab guys in the nuts, given so far they've been really sucky guys, and punching Rome in his was just funny, but I'm not wearing anything to commemorate the events."

"What do you think?" Ginger asked me.

"Honestly, it's kind of hideous."

"It'll grow on you."

"Like syphilis," Daniel whispered.

I nudged him in the ribs with my elbow, and we all laughed. Angel returned dressed in her shirt and I did my best to ignore it as I looked at them. I loved these people.

410

Who would have thought being attacked by an incubus would lead to me finding such good friends?

"Now that we're all here, I need to tell you all some things and get your input. You know Rider has assigned you to stay with me wherever and whatever I do, and Angel, you're with me as well, since you're my blood donor. I think it only right we all have a say in where we go and what we do." I told them the three options Rider had given me, along with benefits and drawbacks of each, but skipped over the sex thing, not comfortable discussing that.

"So, what are we doing, guys?" I asked after they'd been given the information and a moment to weigh the choices. "Are we going to Baltimore, staying with Grey's wolf pack in Pigeon Forge, or are we going to stay here?"

Then I held my breath and waited to see what road my friends would put me on.

\*\*\*

*Danni and friends will appear in Blood Revelation Book Five: Vampire's Halo, then continue on to Twice Bitten Book 4: Love Potion #666*

# ABOUT THE AUTHOR

Crystal-Rain Love is a romance author specializing in paranormal, suspense, and contemporary subgenres. Her author career began by winning a contest to be one of Sapphire Blue Publishing's debut authors in 2008. She snagged a multi-book contract with Imajinn Books that same year, going on to be published by The Wild Rose Press and eventually venturing out into indie publishing. She resides in the South with her three children and enough pets to host a petting zoo. When she's not writing she can usually be found creating unique 3D cakes, hiking, reading, or spending way too much time on Facebook.

Printed in Great Britain
by Amazon